Lonnie used the mirrored wall of the elevator when she applied a hint of Plum Daiquiri lipstick. . . .

It was more psychological fortification than cosmetic. And yes, she knew how doubtlessly screwed up that was. The ride three floors down was too short for her to plan anything elaborate, which was probably just as well.

After Terry's ungracious behavior, Lonnie started thinking more seriously about her feelings for Dominick. She liked his wit and charm. She liked that he'd volunteered for a Big Brother program. She respected his intellect. And, damn it, he'd taken a bloody punch for her, which maybe shouldn't mean as much to her as it did. But it did.

She wanted the whole package, at least to try out. And if Dominick ended up dumping her, well then she'd just forward his e-mail address to Terry and Jake, and they could all start a chat room. Now it was a matter of smoothing things over after the way she'd ditched him on Saturday. When she thought about it, Dominick hadn't played any games with her so far. She was the one who'd been inconsistent with him, and she hoped it wasn't too late to start over.

PLUM GIRL

Jill Winters

AN ONYX BOOK

ONYX
Published by New American Library, a division of
Penguin Putnam Inc., 375 Hudson Street,
New York, New York 10014, U.S.A.
Penguin Books Ltd, 80 Strand,
London WC2R 0RL, England
Penguin Books Australia Ltd, Ringwood,
Victoria, Australia
Penguin Books Canada Ltd, 10 Alcorn Avenue,
Toronto, Ontario, Canada M4V 3B2
Penguin Books (N.Z.) Ltd, 182–190 Wairau Road,
Auckland 10, New Zealand

Penguin Books Ltd, Registered Offices:
Harmondsworth, Middlesex, England

First published by Onyx, an imprint of New American Library,
a division of Penguin Putnam Inc.

First Printing, September 2002
10 9 8 7 6 5 4 3 2 1

To my family—my mom, who loves me in spite of my tantrums, my dad, who has given me writer's blood, and my sisters, who remain sincere, hilarious, exquisite, & perfect.

And my editor, Audrey LaFehr, who took a chance on me, gave unfaltering, enthusiastic support, and turned Plum Girl *into something better.*

ACKNOWLEDGMENTS

I would like to thank Jennifer Jahner for seeing something worth saving and keeping my manuscript in play. Thank you again, Audrey, for all of your dynamism and insight. I am deeply indebted to my first reader (and extremely fabulous friend!), Jessica, without whose excitement, I may never have submitted *Plum Girl* for publication. Thank you Carrie for always being such a great friend, and for helping me develop a sense of humor about the opposite sex! Thanks to Lori, Kelly, Dawnie, and Jay for all of your encouragement, and thank you—with all my heart— Mom and Dad for letting me lean on you so I could write . . . and always.

Chapter One

"The punk is *begging* for it."

"What'd he say?" Peach asked.

Before Lonnie answered, she hooked the phone on her shoulder and looked around the corner, where her boss, Beauregard Twit, had just turned. When she was sure he was out of earshot, she slid the receiver back in place and said, "Sorry. I just had to make sure he was gone before I finished bitching to you."

"No problem," Peach said, chomping her gum cheerfully on the other end. "So, what did the Twit do today? Beat his top score in Minesweeper and make you take minutes?"

"Good guess, but no," Lonnie answered, pushing some of her long, dark hair behind her ear, and resting her elbow on her overly cluttered desk. "You know how I was put in charge of planning the holiday party?"

Peach replied, "Uh-huh. The one you're taking me to next week, so Mom can sit home in ecstasy thinking about all the so-called eligible lawyers I'll be meeting? Right, go on."

"Yeah, well, Twit just told me to change the menu to a, quote, Chinese theme."

"Why?"

Lonnie shrugged for nobody's benefit, and said, "I can only assume it's because he's been trying to court Lyn Tang for months and he thinks this will help win her over."

"Why, just because she's Chinese? Isn't that ploy a little obvious? Not to mention idiotic."

"I'm not clear on your point."

Peach asked, "Wait, if Lyn Tang hasn't joined the firm yet, why would she be going to the party?"

"Oh, the party's not just for the firm. There's a whole list of 'exclusive guests,' too. Twit's already invited three district court judges and two city councilmen. You know, it's all a PR thing."

"I've never understood why kissing ass is called 'PR.' What's wrong with 'KA'?"

"True," Lonnie conceded sarcastically. "Anyway, I booked the caterer over a month ago. But, of course, as soon as I tried to explain that, he just cut me off with: 'No arguments. Remember, there's no I in team.'" Lately, Beauregard Twit's use of tired corporate mantras reigned among Lonnie's top pet peeves.

"He's ridiculous," Peach consoled.

"He just waddled away without giving me a chance to say anything."

"What a fool."

"Right after he called me Lydia."

"Savage."

"Yeah," Lonnie agreed. "Well, beyond calling Lucky Noodle for takeout, I'm out of ideas."

"Which reminds me, why'd you put Lucky Noodle on our speed dial? If that doesn't prove how hurting our lives are—"

"I'm telling you, it's good. You've never even tried it."

"What can I say? I'm a vegetarian. My aversion to meat includes mystery meat." She paused before she spoke again, and Lonnie could tell she had just spit out her gum. "So, speaking of bosses, you know what Iris told me before?"

"I thought your boss's name was Cheryl."

"No, no. Cheryl's just her overly dependent, thirty-five-year-old daughter."

"Oh, yeah."

"I'm technically Iris's assistant."

"Right."

"So this morning Iris said she thinks of me as another daughter."

"That's sweet."

"Then she told me to rinse out her underwear."

Lonnie laughed. As annoying as Beauregard Twit was, Lonnie was thrilled not to have her sister Peach's job as a personal assistant to a high-maintenance society woman. Apparently, Iris Mew worked out of her home—in this case, a sprawling mansion in Chestnut Hill—organizing local charity events. Peach had gotten the job by answering an ad in the *Boston Globe* the first week she'd moved back to Boston.

Peach was twenty-two and beautiful, with light, streaky hair and glittery blue eyes. The quality of Lonnie's life had definitely been improved after her bubbly, artistic little sister moved into her studio apartment.

"So how's Dominick?"

"What do you mean?" Lonnie assumed her best act-casual tone.

Peach wasn't buying it. "Hmm, I mean: what's new with that sexy, funny computer geek who works three floors below you, e-mails you, and wants to slip his hard disk into your G drive?"

Lonnie shook her head and muttered, "I can't handle you."

Peach giggled. "What?"

"There are so many things wrong with the statement you just made," she said. "First of all, I never said he was sexy."

"It was implied," Peach said.

"In what?"

"In the way you get all awkward when he comes up in conversation. Much like you're doing right now." Lonnie opened her mouth to protest, but then shut it, realizing that yelling "I'm not awkward!" would probably only confirm said awkwardness. "Have you two met for lunch lately?"

"No. Last week he had to work through his lunches, and the week before that I spent all my lunches finalizing things for the holiday party. Or, at least, I *thought* I was finalizing things," she finished, remembering Twit's sudden request to change the entire menu.

"Okay, so I say the time for passivity has passed. Just go down to GraphNet and throw him down on his desk. Wait, he has his own office, right?"

"Would it even matter?" Lonnie asked, grinning. "And, in case you've forgotten, I do already have a practically-semi boyfriend. I know Terry is easygoing, but I don't think he'd love it if I just pounced on some poor, clueless guy. Well, some other poor, clueless guy."

Peach let out a sigh, and Lonnie told herself to ignore it. She'd had a feeling for a while that her sister didn't like Terry—or at least the idea of her *with* Terry—but she'd never felt like pressing the issue. As far as she was concerned, Terry was agreeable, entertaining, and most important, uncomplicated. But for some reason, this time she challenged Peach: "Okay, what? What's wrong with Terry?"

"Nothing, nothing."

"What?"

*"Really, nothing. It's just . . . Look, I know Terry's a real . . . *funny* guy," Peach began. Meanwhile, Lon-

nie knew that tone of voice and could just picture her sister grimacing and making quotation marks with her fingers. "But he lives in New York City." she went on, "What kind of future does this relationship have?"

"Future?" Lonnie repeated, horrified. "You sound just like Mom, and I know that can't possibly be your intention.

"By the way," Peach went on, "is Terry still coming up for Christmas?"

"Yeah. Well, no. His show's on the twenty-first. I think he's leaving the next day. But, it'll be fun—"

"Mmm-hmm," she said with perceptible lackluster.

"It *will*. You're coming with me to his show, right?"

"I don't get what the show is."

"He said it's one of those comedy contests. You know, a bunch of amateurs doing stand-up, and a talent scout in the audience. That kind of thing. Terry's just hosting it."

"Yeah, all right. I'll go."

"Thank you," Lonnie said, smiling, and then glanced at the clock. "Oh, I gotta get back to work and figure all this stuff out."

"Actually, I should get going, too. I've got a long day ahead of me; Iris's cat needs more of that specialty litter from Mansfield. See ya at home."

After Lonnie hung up, she let herself finally face the disheveled papers spread across the top of her desk. Out of habit, she glanced up at the clock on the wall again: 11:51 A.M. She momentarily debated another cup of coffee, knowing full well it was a procrastination strategy. Then she thought about Twit's Chinese whim, as well as her usual daily tasks, and the fact that all the office's kitchen had left the last time she looked were decrepit-looking packets of Sanka, and decided to stay at her desk. She plunged into the first stack to her right and thought, *Things could be worse.*

Lonnie had been temping at Twit & Bell, a very modest-size Boston law firm, for the past six months. She took the job shortly after earning her second master's degree—that one in feminist theory, and the first in sociology—with "temp" being the operative word. When she'd first taken the job, she'd been at a crossroads: she'd always loved school, but after turning twenty-seven, she felt a little old to be a professional student. Shouldn't she put all her academic training to more use? Shouldn't she, as her mother tactfully put it, "decide what you're going to do with the proverbial rest of your life"?

The question was: what? She hadn't gone to graduate school with the goal of teaching. It had just seemed like a comfortable thing to do after college. She'd had a particular affinity for sociology because she'd always been fascinated by human behavior and its infinite possibilities for analysis. In other words, she was a people watcher.

During her last semester, she'd worked at a women's shelter as part of her sociology final project. Her experience there had stirred a sincere interest in women's issues, which was why she'd enrolled in a feminist theory graduate program next, while still continuing to work at the shelter.

But she had earned her second master's six months ago, and the shelter had closed down only a month after that, so yes, she had to admit, her mother had a point about her wasting more time than she needed to temping at Twit & Bell. In her defense, though, she was paid fabulously well for wasting time. Apparently, Beauregard Twit had trouble keeping temps, and the income she made doing his tyrannical, insane bidding was helping her pay off her grad school loans.

Finally, though, Lonnie was getting more serious about her future. Over a month ago, she'd sent her résumé to several universities, in search of an instructor position. Now she was waiting to hear, and with any luck she'd have a teaching job lined up for September.

It could be worse, Lonnie thought to herself again as she logged onto the payroll database and began entering Twit's weekly hours. Six months temping as Beauregard Twit's assistant could be maddening, especially considering what a capricious twerp he was, but it had its good points. Twit & Bell was right in the middle of Boston, situated in a proud, tall building that combined old stone architecture with mirrored glass. The whole firm—which included exactly seven attorneys, four paralegals, five administrative assistants, three accountants acting as payroll, one systems analyst, and a human resource department consisting solely of elitist pain-in-the-ass Bette Linsey—fit nicely on the twenty-third floor. The firm was carpeted in plush lavender-pink, and decorated by expensive black-and-chrome office furniture and Georgia O'Keeffe prints. Lunther Bell, the firm's other founding partner, made a point of mentioning every chance he got that flowers were synonymous with female genitalia.

A message box appeared on Lonnie's computer screen. NEW MAIL. She clicked on her inbox icon and felt her heart lurch when she saw who had sent her mail. Dominick. His message was simple. *Lunch?*

I wish, she typed back. *Tomorrow?* She clicked SEND, and felt a slight pit forming in her stomach. What was her problem? She didn't understand what was going on between her and Dominick. Okay, that wasn't entirely true. She didn't understand what was going on between her and her hormones. She was involved with someone already; she had no business thinking carnal thoughts about Dominick. Thinking, dreaming, fixating . . .

"Hey, Lonnie!"

It was the gruff voice of Delia Smucker, who was

technically Matt Fetchug's and B. J. Flynn's assistant, but in reality catered a lot more to Lunther Bell. "I have something for you to do," she barked as she made her way down the hall.

She walked in hurried, ungracious strides—overswinging her hips and not really pulling it off—before she came to a full stop in front of Lonnie's desk. "Here," she grumbled, and tossed down a stack of paper. Then she dropped a stack of envelopes, which veered off into an accordion-style mess, before scattering everywhere. Lonnie looked down, then back up at Delia's face, which was unseasonably tan for December.

"Oh, so you need me to stuff the env—"

"This isn't brain surgery, Lonnie," Delia said unoriginally. "You fold the letters, put them in the envelopes, and then seal them. Okay?"

Wonderful. Except you're not my boss. And also, you're a bitch. "Yeah, okay." Lonnie turned back to her monitor and opened up one of the spreadsheets she'd been working on for Twit. "I'll do it on my lunch hour."

"No, I need it done *now,*" Delia commanded, sounding supremely put out. "Why? What does Beauregard have you working on?" She brazenly leaned over Lonnie's desk to get a look at her monitor.

"I've just got a lot to do before the holiday party," Lonnie replied, keeping an even tone, while Delia ogled her computer screen.

It was hard to take Delia's rudeness seriously, because she was equally abrasive to everyone. Not counting Twit and Bell, of course. She was even openly hostile to Matt and B. J., despite the fact that they were her direct supervisors. She was obviously smart enough to figure out that there wasn't a damn thing they could do about it, because Lunther wouldn't listen to complaints about her, and Twit

nearly drooled every time she tossed her bleached-
blond, straw-textured, semiteased hair over her
shoulders. Go figure.

"All right," Lonnie agreed, and started straight-
ening the scattered letters and envelopes. Without so
much as an insincere thanks, Delia turned on the heel
of her white, pointy-toed pump, and sashayed off.
Only instead of charging back down the hall, she
pushed through the main glass doors and headed
toward the elevators.

"I'm goin' for a smoke," she called over her shoulder, while blatantly grabbing at her wedgie. Lonnie
shook her head; some people were shameless. It was
obvious that Delia was just dumping her own work
on the already-exploited temp, rather than exercising
any real authority. Oh well.

She glanced back at her monitor and discovered
that she had a NEW MAIL message. She clicked on her
inbox. *Hey, Pretty Woman. Thought of some new material about taxi drivers. Call me tonight. Later gator!*
Okay, Terry could be corny, but it was in an en-
dearing way. And it was flattering that he trusted
her enough to try out his material on her before he
performed it live.

So, why didn't Lonnie get half as excited for his e-
mails as she did for Dominick's? After all, Terry was
her practically-semi boyfriend, while Dominick was
only her sort-of friend. Why on earth was she so
conflicted?

She stretched back in her leather chair and mulled
over that question. On the one hand, there was Terry
Pine. A twenty-five-year-old cutie with shaggy, light
brown hair and a pale dusting of freckles across his
nose. He wasn't tall, about five-eight, but he had a
six-pack that was more than drool worthy. Too bad
it just made Lonnie more aware of her own soft center and the fact that breaking two donuts into quar-
ters and quickly eating the pieces standing up still

constituted scarfing down two donuts. Most central
to Terry's appeal: he was silly, immature, and lived
four hours away. But Lonnie quickly stopped that
train of thought before it could wander too far down
the path of uncomfortable self-analysis.

Then there was Dominick Carter and the fact that
ever since she'd run into him on the elevator two
months before, she'd become strangely susceptible to
heart palpitations and sweating in southern places. She
didn't completely understand the intensity of her attraction. After all, she'd known Dominick in college.
Well, she'd known *of* him. He'd been a senior when
she was a sophomore, and friends with Eric Yagher—
the gorgeous object of Lonnie's lust, a preppy guy with
soft blond hair that felt like feathers. Back in college,
Lonnie had always been too busy looking for Eric to
take special notice of Dominick. But now her thoughts
drifted to him daily. She felt guilty about it, too, but
every time she tried to conjure up Terry's cute, freshly
scrubbed face, she'd still get images of a fuller, older
one. One darkened by a hint of five o'clock shadow . . .

A message box came up on her screen again.

She clicked on her NEW MAIL and read Dominick's
response to her lunch invitation for the following
day: *I can't—we have a business lunch tomorrow. How
about a quick drink tonight after work? Don't say no. I'll
meet you at six in the lobby?*

Lonnie typed back *okay* and started feeling more
of those sweats and palpitations coming on. *It's just
going to be a quick drink,* she thought to herself, and
rested her elbows on the desk to support the weight
of her forehead in her hands. So what if this would
be the first time they'd been out together when one
of them didn't have to rush back to the office? So
what if it included alcohol? So what if it didn't take
even one drop of any mind-altering substance to
make Dominick look damn good?

Then again, for all she knew, Dominick might have

someone in his life already. Although she had a strong feeling that he didn't considering what he'd told her last month about spending his thirtieth birthday playing poker with his brothers. Surely if he had a girlfriend, he'd have had better plans than that.

For probably the millionth time that month, she mentally replayed the day she'd run into Dominick. She had just narrowly escaped Beauregard Twit, grabbing her long, furry ice-blue coat and heading to lunch before he could thrust another task on her. Once safely inside the elevator, she'd pressed *L* and contemplated what to get. Should she go across the street to the new salad place and waste a perfectly good Wendy's that was six blocks out of her way? When the elevator jerked to a stop on twenty, the heavy brown doors opened, and a tall, dark-haired man entered.

He gave her a small smile as soon as his eyes met hers, and she offered the requisite phony smile in return, inwardly cursing the affected standards of elevator etiquette. She stared straight ahead, as if there really were something fascinating about those heavy brown doors, until his voice broke her forced gaze. "Lonnie?" She turned to him, her green-honey eyes searching. "Lonnie Kelley."

That time it was more of a statement than a question. She searched his face for about three seconds before it clicked. "Dominick!"

He smiled widely and nodded. "Yeah, how are you?"

Once Lonnie brightened and kicked herself out of zombie mode, she said, "Good, good. What about you? I haven't seen you since college!"

"Yeah, back in college when you"—he hesitated before picking the most tactful verb—"dated my friend, Eric." *Dated?* Lonnie thought incredulously. *More like made a raving fool out of myself on a daily basis for him. Sure, I remember Eric.*

"Eric?" Lonnie repeated, deliberately vacant. Then she waved her hand and threw in casually, "Oh right, *now* I remember." The elevator *dinged* and the doors opened to the airy, pink-marbled lobby. Dominick held out his hand, waiting for her to step out first. She did, and asked, "So how is Eric?"

Dominick just shrugged. "Actually, we sort of lost touch after college." They walked toward the front doors of the building and then paused for an awkward moment, both not knowing how to end a conversation with someone they hadn't seen in eight years when the reunion had barely progressed to banal small talk. Just then Lonnie's stomach growled audibly, prompting Dominick to ask her to lunch.

And he'd certainly been charming. He'd told her about his experience working as director of Web site development at GraphNet, an Internet company three floors down from Twit & Bell—the whole time punctuating his stories with self-deprecating humor. He'd described his plan of starting his own company that would design corporate software, and told her all about his brownnosing protégé, Harold. And the whole time Dominick had been talking—despite her best intentions—Lonnie had been checking him out. It wasn't like her to feel a sexual attraction for a man so quickly, but that day with Dominick it hit her suddenly and profoundly.

Probably six feet tall, dark eyes, hair almost as black as her own. Not handsome exactly, but the sexiest grin she'd seen since . . .

Then she'd caught herself, feeling embarrassed, afraid that Dominick had somehow read her mind and knew what she'd been thinking. And, speaking of that, what the *hell* had she been thinking to check Dominick out when she already had a perfectly adorable practically-semi boyfriend named . . . Terry? Terry, that was it.

Chapter Two

"**W**orking hard?"

Lonnie looked up and smiled. Her favorite attorney, Macey Green, was taking the time to make conversation with her when she virtually never offered that opportunity to anyone else in the firm. It wasn't that Macey was rude. She was simply all business. Crisp and articulate, she was a shark of an attorney who, for some reason, had taken a special liking to Lonnie—who, in return, respected her tremendously.

"Hi!" she said cheerfully, and then noticed the black leather coat and briefcase in Macey's hand. "Are you heading out?" she asked.

"Yes. I have a few errands to take care of before my court appearance tomorrow." With her free hand, she combed some pale blond hair neatly behind her ear. "What are you working on?" she asked.

"Macey!"

Lonnie glanced over and saw Lunther Bell barreling down the hall toward her desk. In truth, she never knew quite what to make of Lunther. His I'm-just-a-humble-good-ol'-boy demeanor always seemed more like a well-honed shtick than a genuine personality. There was something else, too. Lonnie couldn't quite put her finger on it, but there was something odd about Lunther Bell that she just didn't trust.

"Macey, hold up!" he called as he jogged the last few steps to get beside her. He had a big smile on his face, not that it enhanced his physical appearance all that much. On a good day, he resembled a less stylish version of The Penguin. "I wanted to talk to you before you left tonight."

Lonnie couldn't help noticing Macey's expression change. The changes were subtle—a slight tightening of her full mouth, a barely perceptible squinting of her blue eyes—but her reluctance to speak with Lunther was clear.

"I'm afraid I don't have the time," she replied in a clipped tone without even looking at him. Instead, she shifted her briefcase to her other hand and smiled at Lonnie. "Have a nice night, Lonnie," she said, and walked briskly through the main doors. Lonnie assumed that Lunther would follow her out so he could catch her before the elevator came. But instead he stayed planted where he was, surveying the papers in his hands.

Abruptly, he glanced at Lonnie and gave her a forced smile. "Well, I guess I'll go fax this." He walked past her and set his papers on the large white machine. He punched in a number and hit SEND before turning around to attempt chitchat again. "Modern technology," he announced. She could only assume he was referring to the fax machine. "Gizmos, gadgets, you name it, they've invented it. It all gets a little confusing to me." He inserted an artificial-sounding chuckle, and Lonnie just smiled amiably.

The fax machine started beeping, indicating a confirmation sheet was coming out. But when Lunther turned back to grab it, it slipped out of his chubby hand and floated out of reach. He clapped his hands together in an effort to catch it midair, but the fly-away sheet continued to elude him, until it landed on the floor not far from Lonnie's chair.

"Here, I'll get it," she offered, and wheeled her chair a little closer to the piece of paper.

Lunther came up alongside her just as she was reaching for it, and shooed her hand away. "No, no," he insisted. "Now don't pay me any never mind. I've got it." Despite his words, he was gritting his teeth as if he were just barely containing his rage. He bent down to pick up the sheet, and ended up shoving his behind in Lonnie's face. She almost gasped.

She didn't mean to stare. Honestly, she didn't, but . . . *Good Lord.* Okay, yes, Lunther weighed around two-eighty, so that, in and of itself, suggested a large rear end. But still . . . the bulbous monstrosity in her face seemed disproportionate even to his body. She'd never noticed it before; his suit jackets obviously worked wonders. Only now his jacket had ridden up and flapped over across his back, allowing a completely unobstructed view. Hell, he looked like a beaver, and Lonnie couldn't tear her eyes away.

Lunther stood up and spun around, and she averted her gaze so he couldn't tell what she'd been thinking. "Well, 'night," he said quickly, and plodded heavily back to his office.

Less than a minute passed before Lonnie checked the clock again: 5:48 P.M. Twit hadn't emerged from his office in the past half hour, so she hoped she could just slip away to freshen up in the rest room before meeting Dominick downstairs. Of course, at that moment, she heard a door swing open, and within seconds caught a glimpse of her boss waddling around the corner and toward her desk.

"Leslie? Oh, good, you're still here. I know you secretaries like to cut out early whenever possible," Twit said. Well, there went the freshening-up plan. She knew that she should correct her boss when he called her by the wrong name, but she really didn't care enough. Anyway, she figured it was only a matter of time before he went through every other L name until he accidentally stumbled upon Lonnie. She was waiting for that day, and delayed gratification was perfectly fine with her.

"Did you need something?" Lonnie asked with as much eagerness as she could muster, considering her panty-inflaming-but-utterly-platonic friend was waiting downstairs, and she had yet to apply some Plum Daiquiri lipstick.

"Yes. I just want to let you know that within the next couple days I'm going to be expecting some confidential materials—faxes, actually—and I want you to keep an eye out." He altered his inflection, making his words deliberately slow, so she'd be sure to comprehend. "We really need to be discreet—that is to say, *careful*—with confidential faxes, okay?"

Her expression remained even, and she replied, "Sure, Beauregard, no problem. When any faxes come in, I'll bring them right to you."

Twit held up his hand as if to say *sloooow down now,* and interjected, "Now, wait, Leslie. I never said 'any' faxes. I mean, I don't want you to bring in materials from the Atrium." The Atrium was a café on the second floor that faxed a list of daily specials to every company in the building. Lonnie hardly classified that as confidential, but apparently Twit wasn't as optimistic about her reasoning skills.

Looking at him, bemused, she just answered, "I understand, really. Don't worry."

With a curt nod, Twit turned and duckwalked back around that damn corner. *Okay, five more minutes,* she thought as she scurried to the rest room. She looked at herself in the mirror and sighed. Curvy was one thing—and a description she'd heard since adolescence—but she was starting to think that if she didn't locate a treadmill and/or a craving for lentils and hummus soon, her curves might push right through her size nines. She shelved these insecurities for the moment, though, and quickly applied just enough lipstick to give her mouth a hint of wine color, before heading out the door.

She found Dominick leaning against a marble column in the lobby. Her stomach dropped, but then, she had skipped lunch (not counting the nutrient-deficient-but-immensely-satisfying two Kit Kats and diet Coke she'd had at her desk earlier). She held her ice-blue coat at her side and moved purposefully toward him. Her heart fluttered when Dominick's face broke into a wide grin, and his eyes gave a superquick scan of her body in her wine-and-black paisley dress. She loved the dress; it came right below the knee, with black lace trim at the hem of the skirt and long sleeves. It hugged her body without being tight, which—she hated to admit—made her feel sexy.

Damn, why did she have to wear this dress when she was already feeling sexy just being near Dominick? Now, all she'd need was a spicy Bloody Mary to warm her blood, and she'd probably crawl right into Dominick's lap. Then again, who was she kidding? She'd never been the instant gratification type. And definitely not the uncontrollable-passion type. Not for a long time, anyway.

"Hey, you," he said, smiling.

"Hey," Lonnie said, returning his smile. She was only five-four, so even with high heels she was a good five inches shorter than he was; for a fleeting moment she had an image of herself jumping up and wrapping her legs around his waist. *Oh, God,* she thought to herself, *I need help. Of course, if I tried to jump on Terry, he'd probably just fall backward. Stop it, already.* Dominick's lovely voice broke her winding train of thought.

"So, what d'ya think? Rattlesnake?" he asked, his dark eyes flickering.

"Hmm . . ." She angled her head slightly to the side and smiled up at him. "Sure, okay. Let's go to Rattlesnake."

The booth was secluded, and the bar itself was lit only by small table candles and muted pink rays from streetlamps outside. Lonnie and Dominick were on their second drink, and he was telling her about his family in Connecticut. She already knew that he was the youngest of three boys in a close-knit, middle-class family. Now he was telling her about a big brother program in east Boston he'd volunteered for a year ago because he'd never experienced being an older brother. Apparently, he'd wanted to do the job better than his own older brothers, who still derisively called him "Dotcominick" because of his affinity for computers.

Lonnie told him about her work in east Boston at a battered women's shelter that had started as part of a sociology project but continued until the shelter had closed down five months ago.

They had been seated at the table and talking for about an hour already, and neither was making a move to go anywhere. Now he was telling her an amusing story about his family, and she was trying to stay focused on what he was saying rather than the way his mouth formed the words. It was hard, though, because his mouth was beautiful. His lips were wide and subtly full, his teeth were white, and his tongue was . . . well, she'd like to find out.

While he spoke, he absently ran his hand over his chin and occasionally shrugged his shoulders, which she couldn't help noticing were broad and strong. He looked hard and solid . . . but so *huggable* that Lonnie had some difficulty focusing on the conversation. Instead, her mind wandered through a lascivious maze of graphic images. The most innocent—by far—involved wrapping herself around Dominick's naked, muscled body, feeling him everywhere with her hands, her mouth, her breasts, and seeing what he would do about it.

She felt a warm flutter between her legs, but instead of that being a signal she was fantasizing too much, it was a foreshadowing. Pretty soon, the warmth turned to heat, the flutter turned to pulsing. Not to mention, she was experiencing a fierce need for him to take her right on the little square table. What had come over her lately?

"So, enough about my family. What's yours like?" he asked, and she had to restrain herself from reaching out to touch him.

"What do you want to know?" She went for an even, casual tone, and took more than a sip of her spicy Bloody Mary. The intention was to calm her nerves a little, but she forgot the other effect the drink would have on her body. More heat.

He moved the small candle over and extended his arms so that his hands were only an inch away from hers. She wondered if he was battling the same urge to make physical contact. He lightly rapped his knuckles on the table and said, "Well, let's see. So I know you live downtown with your younger sister the artist, and that your parents have a condo in Brookline. And that you all have dinner together there—what, every week?"

"Well, it depends if I have other plans." She paused and then added, "Yeah, every week."

His grin widened. "So, when you're not hanging out with your family and temping at Twit and Bell, what do you do?"

"Hmm, you mean besides sleep and eat?"

"What do you like to do for fun?"

"Um . . . campaign for a feminist utopia."

Now she grinned. Their eyes locked, and her pupils were so dilated with infatuation, they appeared coal dark, rather than green–honey-brown.

Dominick cocked his head and said, "No, smartie, what do you *really* like to do for *fun?*"

Lonnie's heart felt like it was going to jump out of her chest. Suddenly, Dominick's index finger was grazing the back of her hand, and it hadn't escaped her attention that his question had come out dripping with sexual suggestion. Another finger joined the first, and the two began trailing slow, sensuous circles on the back of her hand. His hands were warm and strong and gentle, just as she had thought they would be. She imagined his heated fingers circling on a much more sensitive spot and immediately flushed at the thought—which was ironic considering all the Spice channel–esque notions she'd been having a minute ago. But then they were just notions and in no danger of becoming reality.

Fluidly, his thumb slid into her hand, against her palm, and followed the same rhythm as his other fingers. They moved slowly, hypnotically, applying deliberate pressure and making her breath catch. Something so simple shouldn't be so arousing, but considering that she'd started out hot and aching for him to touch her, it was inevitable that anything could send her over the edge.

Sudden anxiety clutched her chest.

And just like that, she withdrew her hand. Awkwardly, she brought it up to her hair, and moved black, silky strands behind her ear. She looked around, then said, "What time is it anyway?"

He looked at his wristwatch efficiently, but Lonnie could tell he was a little unnerved by her abrupt withdrawal. "Uh, seven twenty-five," he said.

"Oh."

"Yeah."

She thought she should say something before one of them started whistling. "I don't usually go out after work. What about you?" She toyed with the wedge of lime on the edge of her glass.

"Uh, no. Not that often. My staff goes out for happy hour a lot, but I'm not really into that scene." He shrugged with an irresistible mix of confidence and self-deprecation. God, he was sexy. She had to keep reminding herself that that was not enough of a reason to bust up her relationship with Terry.

She and Terry weren't officially exclusive. In truth, they weren't officially anything, and she liked it that way. The superficial, simple connection they shared was about all she could emotionally handle right now. And she definitely couldn't be involved with two men at once. It would be too confusing—too *un*her. She was Catholic, after all. (Well, most days.)

Oh, God. Why did Dominick have such a maddening effect on her?

"I should probably go soon," Lonnie said. "There are some things I've got to do at home." Damn it, why was she lying? But she couldn't stop herself. And Dominick didn't protest at all.

"Oh, okay, yeah. I should probably head home, too. I'm supposed to test some software tonight, anyway." He left a twenty on the table and waited for Lonnie to go out ahead of him. Her gut was knotted the whole walk to the subway station. When they parted, she got on the T, flushed with lust and sick to her stomach.

Chapter Three

"So I want to hear more about this little rendez-vous," Peach called from the bathroom. She'd just taken a shower, after a long day of personally assisting Iris Mew and her overly dependent, thirty-five-year-old daughter, Cheryl. Fifteen minutes earlier, Lonnie had arrived home and started describing her evening, when Peach abruptly stopped her: "Hold that thought. Do you mind if I jump in the shower real quick? Smelling like cat shit is breaking my concentration."

Now she emerged from the bathroom, snuggly wrapped in her appropriately peach-colored terry-cloth robe, with her gold and bronze hair swept into a wet bun and her glittery eyes sparkling. She chimed, "So how was it? Wait, how come you're home so early?" Lonnie glanced at the clock that hung on the wall opposite Peach's mural: 8:05 P.M. So it wasn't the longest evening she'd ever spent with a man . . . certainly not as long as she'd wanted to spend . . . What was her sister's point?

"Well, we were just going for a quick drink."

Peach's eyebrows angled toward each other skeptically, demanding elaboration. For a moment, Lonnie considered lying about how abruptly the evening had ended, but she knew it would be a futile effort. "And, anyway, I told him I had some important things to take care of at home." She avoided her sister's eyes, and moved past her into the bathroom.

"Important things to take care of at home," Peach echoed flatly. "What's at home? Just me. Let me guess: you were anxious to find out how it went with the claw mutilator today, right? Well, just so you know, I think I was even more traumatized than Mr. Whiskers."

"Oh, Iris's cat was declawed?" Lonnie said sympathetically, in between splashes of water, as she washed her face. "But doesn't a vet do that?"

"I refuse to call him that after what I witnessed today. Vets are supposed to love animals," Peach said forcefully.

Lonnie patted her face dry and came back out, meeting Peach's disapproving gaze. "Okay, so what did you have to do here that was so important?" There was sarcasm in her tone, but it was diluted by what Lonnie knew was genuine caring.

"Who knows? Who knows why the hell I do half the things I do? Let's drop it."

"Did you fool around with him?"

"No."

"Did you kiss at all?"

"*No.* Hello, does anyone here remember that I'm involved with someone already? Someone who's coming to visit me in less than a week?"

Peach rolled her pale blue eyes. "Please, you guys aren't exclusive. Wait, you're *not*, are you?" Lonnie could swear she heard panic in her sister's voice. Was Terry really that bad? He couldn't be; he was just a harmless, preppy class-clown type, who was content with their monthly visits that consisted of making out and sharing a few laughs. At least, he was content for the moment.

"Admit it, you just don't like Terry because you

still blame him for breaking up you and What's-His-Name."

"Hey," Peach protested, "What's-His-Name was possibly the best relationship I've ever been in."

"You had four dates. How could that be your best relationship?"

"Only four dates, that's how," she answered glibly. "And, contrary to what you may think, I don't blame Terry for that little incident; I blame *you*. Is that better?" Lonnie knew perfectly well what her sister was referring to—the night they first met Terry.

Several months ago, Lonnie had gone to New York for Peach's graduation from NYU. One night, they'd gone to a comedy club downtown with Peach's latest love interest—a fellow art student named Something-or-Other. Just as the show was starting, Peach went to the rest room, leaving her date and Lonnie at the table, which was right in front of the stage.

Terry, the club's emcee, was in the middle of his opening jokes when he focused his attention on Lonnie. In front of the crowd, he asked her: "So what are you doing with *this guy*?" Then he launched into a series of one-liners at What's-His-Name's expense. Of course Lonnie had waited to make sure Peach's date wasn't taking offense before she gave in and laughed—along with the rest of the audience.

By the time Peach returned to the table, the first comic had started performing, and her date had settled into an uncomfortable silence. After ten minutes of ignoring his sullen posture, Peach, confused, tried to break the ice. "This place is great, isn't it?" she'd said.

What's-His-Name whipped his head around to face her, and snapped, "Yeah, this place is great if your sister's guffaws are any indication."

"My wha—?" Lonnie started.

"Look," he went on waspishly, "I've got a headache. I'll call you tomorrow or something." And with that, he got up, pushed his way through the clusters of chairs, and left the club. Never to be heard from—at least not by the Kelley sisters—again. After the show, Terry approached Lonnie, and they'd been dating ever since.

"And, may I remind you," Peach said, breaking Lonnie's reverie, "that thanks to Terry making fun of him, and you laughing, Derek was so mortified, he never called me again. I got blown off because of you two. Well, especially you."

"Why especially me?"

"Your laugh can be a little much."

"I didn't know his name was Derek."

"Derek Something-with-an-S."

Peach had to be one of the only people on the planet who almost never got blown off. It figured that the one time she did, it'd had very little to do with her.

"Well, we never specified that we'd be exclusive, per se, but that's not the point," Lonnie said now. "The point is . . ." Peach narrowed her eyes speculatively, putting her hands on her slim hips, and Lonnie plopped onto the yellow-and-blue-striped sofa. "Look, the point is that Terry and I have this set routine and . . . it works fine for both of us. So why am I going to start something with Dominick that inevitably is going to get all confusing, and I'll just end up getting hurt in the end?"

Peach sighed. "Right, I forgot the 'every man's out to dump me' obsession," she said, making quotation marks with her fingers.

"Hey, point out one time when it hasn't happened." She started to respond, but Lonnie cut her off. "You know, it doesn't even matter. I can't do two guys at once." Peach's eyebrows shot up. "You know what I mean," Lonnie amended. "I can't see two guys at the same time."

"See? You see Terry, like, once a month."

"What's your point?"

"Lon, it just seems . . . Look, ever since Jake, it seems—"

"Jake has nothing to do with anything. All I'm saying is that I'm involved with Terry right now. That's just how it is."

"You act like it's a prison sentence. You do have free will."

"I know that, jeez," Lonnie said, frustrated. "I *like* Terry."

"Yeah, but you like Dominick more. I can tell."

"Can we please drop this?"

Peach sighed one more time before relenting. "Okay. I give up for now."

Lonnie leaned back on the soft, striped pillows and closed her eyes. Why did dating have to be so damn difficult?

Dominick tossed his tie, which had become significantly loosened over the course of the evening, and his coat onto the kitchen table, grabbed a pizza box out of the refrigerator, and headed into the living room.

He thought about Lonnie. She'd become prettier since college. Of course, he'd always thought she was cute, but he'd thought that about half the girls he met in school. Lonnie's look was always different, though. Back then she'd had carelessly wavy hair, mismatched clothes, and a sort of sweetness about her. She was definitely the last person he expected to see eight years later. The girl in the elevator was heavier than he remembered, with tamer hair, but still, he recognized her almost immediately. There was something about her now . . . something intoxicating.

It had to be intoxicating, or why else did he turn into an asshole wherever she was concerned these days? He remembered the first time they had lunch, when he'd known how much he was rambling on about his job but couldn't seem to stop himself. There he was, sitting across from this smart, sweet girl—with sexy eyes and a luscious mouth and great breasts—and he'd wanted to impress her. And she'd just looked at him with those pretty eyes, and smiled like she was actually interested.

Then tonight he'd gotten unequivocally shot down.

Dominick shook his head as he stared at the TV, not registering the program in front of him. Everything had been going well. They'd been sitting at a private table, and things were just starting to get interesting when he scared her off. Even though the bar was dark, he could see some color drift to her cheeks after he touched her, and then the conversation went to hell. She'd come up with an excuse to leave, which he brilliantly topped off with the admission that lately his nights consisted of testing software.

He didn't know why he was so irritated by what had happened that night. It wasn't as if they knew each other *that* well. They just emailed occasionally (okay, nearly every day), had a few lunches (with no awkward silences), and now they'd gone out for exactly one after-work excursion (throughout which, he'd pictured her lying naked on their tabletop). Fine, so she was just an acquaintance. No big deal.

So why did he still feel so frustrated? True, there was *that* kind of frustrated playing a part—he hadn't been involved with anyone for a while. But mostly what he felt was disappointed. By the way Lonnie reacted tonight, it was pretty clear that the idea of a more-than-platonic relationship with him left her cold. *That's that*, he thought, because now he had his answer.

Lonnie lay awake staring at the ceiling, listening to Peach's even breathing across the studio apartment. Peach's bed was shielded by an oak-and-canvas partition screen, and there were tiny, iridescent moons hanging from the ceiling above her. Lonnie rolled over to her side and let the thickness of her mattress and the softness of her puffy cream comforter relax her. She sighed, thought about what happened, and suddenly felt *un*relaxed all over again.

Damn it! Why had she acted like such an ass? She knew her behavior at Rattlesnake hadn't seemed logical. How could she explain to Dominick that her luck with men was never great, and her last serious relationship had left her utterly crushed and disillusioned? Her *only* serious relationship, if one wanted to be technical. And how could she tell him that now she was involved with someone already . . . someone who invoked far less confusing feelings in her?

Lifting up, she made a futile attempt to fluff her feather pillow before setting her head back down. She closed her eyes and thought about her track record with the antithetical—that is to say, *opposite*—sex.

Her only real date in high school was her senior prom. She'd gone with a boy from her calculus class who had seemed perfectly nice in a dull, harmless sort of a way. That is, until he'd gotten drunk at the pre-party, passed out, and missed the whole dance entirely. Then in college she'd barely dated, finding most of her male classmates crass, obnoxious, and obsessed with baseball hats. When she'd met Eric Yagher during her sophomore year, she couldn't help but like him. Here was a guy who actually said "please" and "thank you" (albeit, it was usually when he was asking to copy her Spanish homework). And here was a guy who actually asked "busy day?" (granted, it was inevitably followed up by: "feel like dog sitting?"). And he was gorgeous, not that it was any excuse. Whatever the reasons, Lonnie had invested all her romantic energy in him because she couldn't see him for the self-centered, pretty boy that he was.

Until the winter formal. She'd planned to ask Eric,

acting on a tip that he didn't already have a date. She'd practiced the phone call a million times in front of the bathroom mirror, so there was really no excuse for what happened. On the first phone call, she choked and told him she was just calling to ask what day their Spanish exam was scheduled. On the second call, she paused, then told him she'd accidentally called his number, and hung up. On the third call, she started, "Would you happen to have"—then quickly added—"the weather forecast for tomorrow? I didn't know if I should plan on rain." *Plan on rain?* She wanted to die. Finally, on the fourth call, determined and a little delirious at that point, she blurted: "Eric, do you have a date for the formal?"

"Yes, I do," he'd said bluntly and unapologetically. "I'm taking a girl from Syracuse I've been seeing."

She hadn't even known he'd been seeing anyone. But then again, why would she? They were hardly tight, despite her lust-based delusions. Immediately, she started scrapping to save face. "Oh, great!" she yelped a couple pitches too high to be believable. "That's terrific! Well, I was just curious, but that's great!"

Before she could finish her congratulatory squealing over the fact that he had a date, Eric demanded, "Is this what you've been trying to ask me for the past two days?" It was one of the more embarrassing moments of her life.

It was also one of the more infuriating, and ultimately, *defining* moments. Okay, so Eric didn't want to take her to the formal, but did he have to be so thoroughly *un*charming about it? After that, Lonnie had absolutely no use for Eric Yagher, or his blond hair that felt like feathers. And she'd entered into what some people might call a "dating slump," but what she considered life as usual.

Slump life went on hiatus when she was twenty-two. She'd sat down next to a brilliant Ph.D. student named Jake on the first day of her Religion and Society graduate seminar, and they'd immediately clicked. *Unfortunately*, she thought now as she rolled onto her other side.

Throughout their yearlong relationship Lonnie was completely in love with Jake. It had to be love, she figured, otherwise why wouldn't she have noticed the way he constantly used hackneyed BS to keep her pacified? With all his sweet talk, she had honestly never seen the "reconciliation" with his ex-girlfriend coming. That was the euphemism he'd used for screwing around with her behind Lonnie's back. Up until that point, things had seemed perfect between them. But what did she know? Lonnie had never been one of those girls with a boyfriend since age twelve. Her experience with relationships was limited, to say the least. Not to mention, Jake was the only man she'd ever slept with. In *the biblical sense*, anyway. And that was four long years ago.

Terry was the first person she'd gotten involved with since she and Jake broke up. They'd spent many warm nights kissing and cuddling in his New York apartment, but they'd never made love. He never pushed her. Not yet, anyway. Terry had told her more than once that she was different from the groupielike women he met at the comedy club. He'd told her she was "pure" and "perfect"—the "marrying kind."

She could never tell if he was serious or not when he made comments like that. With Terry, everything came off as a joke. Nothing was serious; nothing was heavy: nothing was painful. It was such a relief. And she hardly had the presence of mind to get offended by his sexist thinking when it seemed to be getting her off the hook so well. The truth was, she'd had little desire to make love since Jake had broken up with her. As weird as she knew it was, the mere idea left her cold.

Lonnie didn't want to believe any of her issues had to do with old-fashioned ideas about love and sex. She didn't want to be wired that way, but it was hard not to see some connection. And as much as she liked Terry, she had a strong feeling that she'd never be in love with him. There was just something missing. That special something that had made Jake's leaving her for his ex-girlfriend more gut twisting than she ever would've thought possible. That special something that forced her to indulge in so many revenge fantasies, she began to wonder if she was a normal, sane person after all.

For a long time, she'd mentally replayed things Jake had said to her: stale promises he'd made about their non-existent future, and all his cheesy words of love (*gag*). Okay, so obviously rage had skewed her memory of things a bit. But his betrayal hadn't made any logical sense to her, and in the end she'd decided that she didn't believe in love after all. That's why meeting Terry was so fortuitous. What she had with him was perfect: convenient, uncomplicated, fun.

Then Dominick Carter dropped into her life out of nowhere, and for the first time in so long, she started having carnal fantasies that didn't stop short. They didn't stop *period*. She pictured him naked. Naked *and* aroused. She imagined what his erection would feel like against her bare flesh. Between her legs. Pressing inside her, deeper, deeper . . .

She didn't know him well enough to love him, but she desperately *wanted* him, and it scared her to death. What if she got in over her head (again)? What if she fell for Dominick, let herself feel secure with him, and then it all got thrown back in her face (*again*—not that she was bitter, or anything)?

Still, four hours later, she regretted her behavior at Rattlesnake. She'd alienated Dominick when in her heart what she'd really wanted was to pull him closer to her, in every possible way.

Chapter Four

The next morning Lonnie tried to stifle a yawn and looked at the antique clock that hung on the wall: 9:34 A.M. Twit had given her bookbinding-cleaner duty, and she was trying to make the best of it.

The apple of Twit's beady eye was collections, a small book room that held valuable history and law books, including several first editions. Three times a year, the books needed to be cleaned in order to preserve them against any dust-mite or paper-worm damage. A special cleaning service came in, spent an hour going through each book, thoroughly dusting it and wiping its binding with special solution. And this time, Lonnie got to watch them to make sure they didn't steal anything valuable.

Looking around the room, she accidentally caught the eye of one of the cleaners. He had dark gray hair, and appeared to be in his late forties. He held her gaze for a minute, and gave her a knowing smile. Knowing what, she had no idea. She gave a quick closed-mouth smile in return, and averted her eyes. Pretty soon, she heard soft footsteps on the carpet approaching her. "Hi, you bored?" he asked, wiping his hands on an already-dirty rag.

"Uh, no . . . No, it's not too bad. I'm just supposed

to stay here to make sure you guys don't need anything," she fibbed.

"Well, you're an improvement from the last one they had watching us," he went on, his eyes scanning her navy tights, down to her navy heels, and back again. Then he winked, and she tried not to toss the Cheerios and jellybeans she'd had for breakfast. For some reason, winking was a significant pet peeve, right up there with Twit's corporate mantras and decrepit packets of Sanka.

"So, are you guys about done?" Lonnie asked, looking around.

"I didn't mean to make you nervous," he said, and winked again. Then he paused and added, "Actually, the little red head was a lot friendlier." He walked back to the bookshelf, and the significance of his words hit her. Little redhead. She thought for a moment. He had to be talking about Ann Lee, Lunther Bell's assistant. At four-eleven, Ann definitely qualified as little, and her frizzy, shoulder-length coif was the only red head of hair in the firm.

Now she was thinking about Ann's bizarre disappearance. Maybe disappearance was too strong a word, but no one from Twit & Bell had seen or heard from her in over two weeks. At least that was the official story. One day Ann hadn't shown up for work, which led to another, and then another, and nobody was saying much about it. That alone was Lonnie's first indication that someone had to know something.

She figured Lunther had to have some clue where Ann was—if for no other reason than he seemed completely unfazed by her absence. When people asked about Ann, Lunther would just smile and say, "A good secretary's hard to find."

Hmm . . .

"Okay, come on, Leeza! Staff meeting. Look alive!"

Beauregard Twit whizzed past Lonnie's desk, making only millisecond-long eye contact before waddling on to the large conference room. Lonnie jerked to attention. She had been typing up some of Twit's notes while simultaneously having an erotic fantasy, and she'd just unzipped Dominick's fly when Twit's voice broke in.

She had totally forgotten the Tuesday ten o'clock staff meeting.

Qualitatively speaking, however, it wasn't that implausible that Lonnie would forget, because the Tuesday meeting rarely amounted to more than an hourlong ego war. There would always be awkward attempts at chitchat first. Human resource specialist Bette Linsey would brag about her rich husband, Reginald, and their perfect little blond-haired daughters, Burberry and Skylar-Blaise. B. J. Flynn would tell a self-aggrandizing story about his life, while Matt Fetchug would snort in disbelief.

Then Twit would take over, which primarily entailed standing on his soapbox and trying to manifest his disingenuous image as the aloof embodiment of legal brilliance. And while he would try his best to grandstand, demoralize, and inspire awe all at the same time, Lunther would inevitably barge in late, loud, and blustery. He'd talk over everyone with some obnoxious blabbering, and audibly plop all two hundred eighty pounds of himself into a chair. Twit would act nonchalant, of course, but still get that tic under his eye that betrayed his anxiety.

In other words, just business as usual at Twit & Bell.

Lonnie shuffled into the conference room, behind B. J. and his so-called assistant, Delia Smucker. She could've sworn she noticed Delia slipping B. J. a dirty look behind his back as the young, pint-size associate swaggered over to the conference table.

Unintentionally, Lonnie took the seat directly

across from Bette Linsey. *Shoot*. It was too late; she'd
already made eye contact. "That's an interesting
dress you've got on," Bette said in her nasal, super-
cilious, own special way. Lonnie knew it couldn't be
a genuine compliment, since that would be very *un*-
Bette, and glanced quickly down at her olive green
dress with navy swirls defining its pattern. Like most
of Lonnie's dresses, it was long-sleeved and went just
past the knee, so Bette couldn't have been implying
it was indecent in any way. Probably it just wasn't
conventional enough for her. Bette Linsey's wardrobe, on the other hand, made two basic statements:
there are three colors in the rainbow—white, black,
and khaki—and Ann Taylor is God.

"Oh, thanks," Lonnie said.

"Yes, how unique," Bette said, touching a French-
manicured hand to her cropped cut. She fingered a
few of the sleek, pointed locks that framed her con-
servatively made-up, middle-aged face. "I swear, I
have no patience when it comes to selecting clothes.
That's why I have Juliet do all of my shopping for
me. It's just not worth the trouble!"

Juliet Duveaux was Bette's au pair, and anybody
who worked at Twit & Bell for more than ten minutes would know it. Nearly every day Bette talked
on her cell phone to Juliet, and at top volume the
conversations were hard to miss. She would go from
her office to the kitchen, refill her "I [heart] Saks"
mug, circle the long way around, and go back to her
office, the whole time loudly crooning things like:
"Oh, Juliet, did Burberry really get the highest scores
in class again?" Or: "Now, Juliet, I don't know how
they do things in *Pahrlhee*, but you just tell Skylar-
Blaise no crème brûlée until she finishes her
dejeuner."

Lonnie wouldn't have believed it herself if she
hadn't witnessed it so many times. Bette pulled in a
nice salary at the firm, but certainly nothing that

would explain her lavish lifestyle. The only thing that did explain it was her marriage to "fabulously successful" Reginald Linsey, who sold mutual funds.

"I mean, I feel just terrible about it," Bette was saying, and Lonnie broke out of her distracted trance, feeling almost embarrassed that she had missed whatever led up to it. *Almost.* "But what can I do? Reggie just insists on taking the girls to Cabo this coming week, and I simply have too much work to get through. But I told him he can make it up to me with a cruise of my choosing." Lonnie forced herself to nod with feigned interest as her head bobbed up and down and her teeth felt cemented in a Cheshire grin.

"Okay, everyone, let's get started," Beauregard said as he gave his papers one final shuffle. "We're going to have to make this meeting fairly quick because Lunther and I have to be in Chicago for a business litigation conference by late this afternoon."

"Where is Lunther anyway?" Bette asked, glancing around the airy conference room.

Beauregard looked uncomfortable, and his words betrayed a certain defensiveness when he replied, "Uh, Lunther had certain vital matters to attend to this morning, as did I, of course. However, I think it's important to touch base at these weekly meetings and—"

"'Scuse me, 'scuse me, folks!" Lunther's voice boomed as his beefy body surged through the doorway. "Don't mind me, everyone, just let Beau keep inspiring the troops, and I'll just plop myself down here in a nice chair, and I won't say another word. Go on, Beau. Don't pay me no never mind." Then he chuckled in his own consciously folksy way, and pounced down on a comfy, leather-backed chair.

Beauregard's eye started twitching. "Ahem, yes, now as I was saying—"

"Where's Macey?" Bette asked.

"Macey?" Beauregard repeated. "Yes, well, I believe she had some briefs to tend to . . . and, as I said, this is going to be a quick meeting." Undoubtedly, Lonnie was the only one palpably disappointed by Macey's absence. In general, the staff didn't seem to like Macey very much. It wasn't that they disliked her, either, but they always appeared uncomfortably intimidated around her. But for some reason, Lonnie had a particularly good rapport with her. And even though she was temping as Beauregard Twit's assistant, she offered Macey help whenever she could.

Now Lonnie's attention drifted back to the meeting in progress, realizing that Beauregard was addressing the conference table, and doing his best impression of a leader. "Now, as I mentioned, Lunther and I will be in Chicago until Thursday—"

"Go, Bears!" Lunther blurted, and then chuckled.

"Uh, yes, *any*way," Beauregard said, struggling to keep his tone even, while his eye tic danced wildly, "Clara and Mel aren't here right now, but I'm assuming their cases are progressing nicely and their caseload is being managed according to the normal, uh, administrative procedures." Lonnie sighed to herself. This meeting was getting more pointless with each absentee.

Beauregard turned his attention to Clara and Mel's assistant, June, and asked, "Do you have any updates or points of interest we should be made aware of at this juncture?" *Huh?*

June must have wondered the same thing: she was visibly taken off guard by Twit's question. "Oh, uh, no," June said. "Everything's on schedule with Clara and Mel. In terms of their caseloads, that is."

Beauregard nodded dramatically. "Yes, very good. Now—"

"Bette, wasn't your assistant supposed to get bagels for this meeting?" Lunther interrupted.

"Yeah, that's what I thought, too," B. J. added immediately. "I skipped breakfast thinking we were getting fed this morning. What's up with that?" Delia rolled her eyes.

"Where *is* your assistant?" Lunther asked.

"People—" Beauregard began.

"I had him courier some items over to the post office," Bette explained. "Although, I expected him back by now."

"Did he drive or take the T?" Matt asked, a glimmer of mischief in his eyes. Lonnie wondered if anyone else noticed it. She knew Matt didn't care about Bette's assistant or his errands, or anything else at Twit & Bell except his own casework. If she had to guess, then, she'd say that Matt just liked prolonging Beauregard's tortured displacement as leader of the meeting.

"Ahem!" Twit nearly yelped. "Now, a final point of query: the status of the new stationary supplies we ordered from Paper Depot last week. Lisa?" His eyes went to Lonnie.

She pulled herself upright and answered, "Uh, they're scheduled to arrive by the end of the week." *I told you that three times already.*

"Ah, well"—Beauregard paused, as if considering this— "that sounds acceptable." *As if you had a choice.* "Were you able to get the specifications that I wanted for my letterhead?"

"Well, they said at the standard price, they could only increase the size of your name to eighteen-point font. Any larger than that, you'd have to pay for graphics."

"Hmph." Twit was visibly disappointed. "Very well, I'll take the eighteen." He finished, "And, Linda, don't forget to water the plant on my desk while I'm in Chicago."

It's a cactus. "Sure, no problem."

"And I just want to give everyone a reminder," B. J. announced. "Happy hour at Whiskey's this Friday

night. I expect to see more people this week, especially
my fellow twenty-somethings over here," he said, looking right at Lonnie and Matt. B. J. and Matt were both
her age, but she didn't have the heart to tell them that
she all but lived like a sixty-year-old anyway.

"Hey!" Delia squealed in mock-annoyance-that-
was-really-real-annoyance. "Many of us are young *at
heart*, you know." Lonnie noticed her slip a sly glance
at Lunther. What was that about? Lunther and Twit
had met in law school, and now were both in their
late forties. Delia, on the other hand, just recently
celebrated her thirty-fourth birthday. Lonnie knew
that because Twit had put her in charge of getting
Delia a cake with her favorite flavors. Of course, per
Twit's instructions, the cake had to be a surprise, so
she couldn't *ask* Delia what her favorite flavors were
in the first place. In the end, all of Lonnie's sleuthing
had landed her back at chocolate, and no one had
saved her a piece.

B. J. went on, "I want to know why Lonnie never
goes to happy hour. Lonnie, do you have a husband
and five kids stashed somewhere we should know
about?" He cracked up at his own suggestion.

Great, now everyone was looking at her for some
kind of reaction. She knew B. J. didn't mean any
harm, but still, she didn't love being put on the spot.
He was beaming at her with his quintessential trying-
too-hard smile, and her heart turned over. She wasn't
made of stone, after all. So she just smiled and said,
"I'm going to get there one of these days, I'm telling you."

"I don't know, Lonnie," Matt drawled. "You've
said that before." His eyes were gleaming again, and
his mouth quirked into a mischievous grin. He was
just a troublemaker, that's all there was to it, but she
couldn't help finding him entertaining sometimes.

She returned Matt's smirk and announced to the
room, "I'll go to happy hour this week, okay?"

"I'm going to hold you to it this time," B. J. pronounced, and shifted his short, skinny leg to cross perpendicularly over the other.

"I'd go, too," Bette offered with what Lonnie assessed as pseudoregret. "But Reggie and I like to spend Friday nights having 'family time' with Skylar-Blaise and Burberry. It's just so utterly special, I couldn't miss a second of it."

"Well, in conclusion, then—" Beauregard started.

"Meeting adjourned!" Lunther exclaimed. Beauregard's mouth dropped into an awkward O . . . as if the words had literally been stolen right from him.

Lonnie quickened her pace back to her desk when she heard her phone ring. She sprawled over the expanse of the desk, with her stomach settling against the layers of scattered papers, and grabbed it on the third ring. "Twit and Bell; Beauregard Twit's office," she squeaked out, her voice strained by her position.

"Hey." It was Peach.

"Hey! What's up? How's your day going?" She was careful not to pull the phone off the desk while she walked around and sat down in her chair.

"Pretty good," Peach replied. "Iris is gone all day so it's just me and Cheryl. I had a few errands to run earlier, but now I'm just sort of killing time."

"Cheryl doesn't work?" Lonnie asked, listening to Peach pop two bubbles before she answered.

"Well, she's sort of into phone sales. She works out of her home. Out of her room, to be more precise."

"What does she sell?" Lonnie asked. "Wait, is she agoraphobic or something?" she added, while simultaneously reading the message on her computer screen.

NEW MAIL.

"I don't think so. She just has no confidence. Iris hasn't been around much this week, so I've ended up spending more time with her, and she's actually not as lame as I originally thought." Lonnie mmm-hmmed and clicked on her inbox to get her new mail.

"Actually," Peach continued, "she's really into cooking. That's what she sells—her recipes. But it's all mail order, so she doesn't have to deal with people much."

Lonnie's stomach sank in disappointment. Two e-mails from Terry and one from Macey Green. None from Dominick. The two from Terry had the subject heading "FWD" so Lonnie knew to disregard them immediately. What she didn't know was why he kept sending her forwards when she'd told him how annoying they were. Nine times out of ten they were stupid chain letters that promised you eternal misery if you didn't pass them on to twenty of your closest friends.

She clicked on Macey's message. It was brief and cordial, but she still felt a rush of hero worship: *Hi. Can you come see me about a research project if/when you get a free moment? Thanks so much, MG.*

"So she's not agoraphobic, she just avoids people and the outside world?" Lonnie asked. Against her better judgment, she scanned the forwarded messages from Terry. One was a chain letter, and the other a list of jokes about rabbits. She was about to delete them when she got another mail message. It was from Terry, too, but it was a sweet message telling her that he couldn't wait to see her on Saturday. She appeased her guilt about Dominick by not deleting the forwards.

"I don't know," Peach said. "I think she's just shy. But don't worry, I'm gonna work on her."

"Uh-huh, you want to hear a joke? Wait, you're gonna what?"

"I'm going to work on her."

Lonnie let out a small sigh. "Peach, maybe you should just let things be."

"Why? It's not like Cheryl's happy this way, hiding in the house all the time. You know, I wouldn't be surprised if she's never even been on a date. I'm gonna find out."

"Wait a minute. You're not going *ask* her?"

"Please, Lonnie, I think I know how to be subtle," she scoffed mildly.

"Look, just don't try to be some kind of miracle worker with this woman. She's obviously been living this life for thirty-five years already, and . . ." Lonnie grappled for an overall point. "Just don't fix it if it's not broke, as they say."

"Oh, good. One of your ever-inspiring trite platitudes."

"Hey, I just don't want this to blow up in your face. I know you. You'll say you just want to help her with her shyness, and suddenly she's performing at a karaoke bar wearing a shirt that says 'Coed Naked Limbo.' "

Peach laughed. "Do you have *any* idea what you're talking about? Now, what's the joke?"

Lonnie said, "Wait, seriously, do you understand what I'm trying to say? This woman could have deep psychological problems you know nothing about. Don't unleash Norman Bates and then get fired; that's all I'm saying."

"Lon, let me worry about Cheryl Mew. Please. You're forgetting I was a psych major for almost six months. Now, what's the joke?"

Lonnie gave up, deciding it was easier just to run with her sister's latest enterprise. She read the first joke on her screen, "Okay, what kind of jewelry do rabbits like?"

"Oh, God. *What?*" Peach asked, her voice weary with dread for the impending punchline.

"Fourteen-carrot-gold jewelry," Lonnie read, confused. Then she got it. "Oh. *Carrot.*"

"Good-bye."

"Wait—"

"From Terry?"

"Yeah, but it was a forwa—"

"Uh-huh. No comment."

Lonnie giggled. "It's not like he wrote it!" she protested. "He doesn't use this in his act or anything, *jeez.*"

Peach laughed. "Okay, okay. Look, I gotta go anyway. But before I forget, Mom said she wants us to come over for dinner tomorrow night since she and Dad are going to be in New Hampshire this weekend."

Lonnie had forgotten that her parents were visiting some longtime friends for the weekend. "Oh, I forgot! All right, I'll go if you're going."

" 'Kay. Later."

"Bye." After Lonnie hung up, she got another alert: NEW MAIL. She clicked on the icon, and felt more than a little disappointed to see a message from Twit asking if any faxes had come for him. Since Lonnie's e-mail address was preset in the system as TEMPID@ TWITBELL.COM it didn't help Twit when it came to addressing her correctly. His message read: *Libby— any faxes? If there are, I've already asked you to bring them to me ASAP.* She rolled her eyes; her boss knew how to make an employee feel like excremental waste. Lonnie felt like typing back *Don't call me, I'll call you, Twit-head, halitosis-breath!* But it hardly seemed professional, so *Nothing yet; I'll let you know* ended up on the screen instead. She pressed SEND and leaned back in her chair to contemplate her next course of action with Dominick.

He hadn't e-mailed yet today. It was only 11:15, but they usually exchanged at least a line or two first thing in the morning. But then, what could she expect? The night before, he'd made a move on her and she'd recoiled like his hands were made of banana slugs. Admittedly, not her finest moment, but surely Dominick had to know how attracted she was to him. To her, it seemed painfully obvious that the man's mere presence sent her into a manic state. Even if he couldn't feel her heart beating like she'd just run five miles, or the abnormally humid condition of her body.

Well, at the very least, she wanted to keep Dominick as a friend. That much she was sure of.

Chapter Five

Lonnie walked quickly to Macey's office. She'd just sent Dominick an e-mail asking him if he wanted to go to happy hour at Whiskey's on Friday night. It was three days ahead of time, but she didn't want him to make other plans. Plus, she figured the sooner she did Rattlesnake damage control, the better.

Lonnie knocked on Macey's door. Although Macey was supported by a paralegal, she hadn't had her own administrative assistant since her last one abruptly left the firm a year ago. "Come in." Macey's voice had a sultry, throaty quality that Lonnie wondered if men in the office had noticed.

"Hi, Macey. You wanted to see me?" Lonnie crossed the plush, lavender-pink threshold into Macey's immaculate office. Macey sat behind an ornately carved teak-wood desk, her blue eyes glowing with the reflection of light off her thin silver laptop.

"Yes, hi. You can close the door. Please sit down." She motioned toward the royal blue, high-backed chair facing her desk. The first time Lonnie sat in it, she noticed that it was surprisingly soft, despite its rigid appearance. Sort of like Macey herself, maybe. Lonnie wasn't sure yet.

Macey closed her laptop, folded her hands on her

desk, and smiled at her. "First of all, how have you been? I realize I haven't been in the office much in the past two weeks." Lonnie lit up, and knew it was borderline ridiculous. But Macey always projected a kind of invincibility that was awe inspiring. And being beautiful only added to her radiant presence. Lonnie replied humbly, "I've been okay. I'm just trying to solve the catering problem for the party next week."

Macey furrowed her dark blonde eyebrows and, with businesslike concern, she asked, "What catering problem?"

Lonnie waved her hand casually—not wanting to appear overly martyred—and said, "Oh, well it's not the end of the world or anything, but the Twit—uh, I mean, Beauregard—just told me yesterday that now he wants Chinese food for the party. I know I have to cancel the caterer we already booked, but yesterday I left messages at four different catering companies, and no one's gotten back to me yet. Sorry, I don't mean to complain—"

"I see. This has to do with Lyn Tang, I presume?" Lonnie thought she saw the beginning of an eye roll, but then Macey seemed to catch herself, and her face returned to inscrutable. "Let me give you a number," she said, and pushed some of her shoulder-length hair behind her ear. Normally Lonnie would loathe being pitied, but somehow it felt fine at the moment, as Macey rooted through her desk drawer looking for the number. Finally, she pulled out a gold business card.

"Here," Macey said, handing the card to Lonnie, who rose off the chair to take it. "Make sure you speak with Meijing personally." Lonnie looked down and saw that the card was for Bunker Properties. Before she could question it, Macey explained, "Meijing is a Realtor but she's also an unbelievable cook, and she will make the time to do this for you. Make sure to mention my name, and tell her I'll take care of any and all expenses promptly."

Lonnie nodded. "Okay. Thanks so much. Is she a friend of yours or . . . ?"

"Yes, Meijing and I are friends, in a manner of speaking. I'd call her myself, but I think you should do this. You'll make a connection that way."

Lonnie nodded again, probably too eagerly, but what else was new? "But you shouldn't cover her expenses."

Macey smiled. "Oh, don't worry, Twit and Bell will be paying in the end, but in the short run, we can't have Meijing worrying about money." She rolled her desk chair over to the minifridge near the plate-glass window. She grabbed a Snapple for herself, and one for Lonnie, and rolled back to her desk. "Now, the next issue is: do you think you would have time for an extra project? And please, be candid about your time constraints and previous obligations."

"I'd love a project!" Lonnie offered, too quickly to appear candid about her constraints and obligations.

"Oh, terrific," Macey said, and sighed with relief, which was uncharacteristic of her usual fortresslike demeanor. Could it be that she was the only person at Twit & Bell who Macey Green considered a *friend*? Warm self-approval flooded Lonnie's chest, as she waited to hear about the latest project.

"Okay, now this would have to be done very discreetly, and kept between the two of us." She held up a small spiral notebook and lowered her voice. "In this notebook, I have outlined several hypothetical case scenarios." She flipped open to the first page. "You will see that I've listed a group of citations next to each scenario." Lonnie nodded. "Each citation correlates with a real, precedent-setting case that is documented in *The Black Book*. Are you familiar with *The Black Book*?" Lonnie nodded again, recalling the fat legal encyclopedia in question. "Wonderful," Macey said. "What I need is for you to look up each citation and write down the name of the case it references. Does that make sense?"

Lonnie processed her assignment. "Yes, I understand."

"I realize it's not glamorous, and believe me, I would do it myself if I didn't have too much on my plate as it is." She set down the notebook and refolded her hands. "Let me know your thoughts, Lonnie."

Well now that she mentioned it . . . Lonnie thought the assignment was a little strange. It wasn't that it would be difficult, but it just seemed odd. After all, if Macey had written down the citations in the first place, wouldn't she know what cases they referred to?

"It's not just that I'm too busy," Macey amended. "I trust you; you are obviously very intelligent." Lonnie felt her cheeks glow with a proud, rosy pink. *She trusts me. She thinks I'm intelligent.*

"I'd love to help. If I can. I mean, I'll see what I can find."

"Great." She sighed again, sounding relieved and grateful.

Lonnie stood to go, with her Snapple in one hand and the spiral notebook in the other. Macey asked, "By the way, how much longer are you going to be with us?"

"Well, I was hoping to line up a teaching position for next fall," Lonnie replied. "But so far there's been no word. Don't worry, I'm not going anywhere yet."

She'd meant the last part lightheartedly, and was surprised when Macey muttered, "I doubt I'll be here that long." Then she motioned to the notebook. "Let me know what you turn up."

"Yeah, sure, of course. By the way, when do you need it done?"

Macey thought for a second, and said, "How does the end of next week sound? And, Lonnie, remember what I said. We have to keep this confidential, so it would probably be a good idea not to have that notebook lying around." Macey's tone was back to cool and businesslike, but when her blue eyes locked with Lonnie's, they betrayed a certain urgency.

"Okay. I'll just go put this in my bag right now."

"Now don't leave on my account." It was Lunther Bell. And he was slowly pushing the door all the way open. Except Lonnie remembered shutting it. Did she leave it ajar by mistake?

The door finished opening and revealed Lunther's full-size form. "Pardon me, ladies," he continued in the same I'm-just-a-Southern-bumpkin style. Lunther often seemed to forget that he was from New Jersey. His eyes, Lonnie noticed, immediately zeroed in on the spiral notebook in her hand.

How much had he heard?

Lunther said, "I just wondered if I could have a word or two with you, Macey. About a legal matter, a'course." Translation: beat it, ignorant temp. Lonnie could take a hint. She politely excused herself and left Macey's office.

The good news Thursday morning was that she got a seat on the 8:15 T. The bad news was that it was the first seat by the door, which meant if anyone boarded who looked more "in need" than her, it would be Lonnie's civic duty to give up the seat. *Please don't let anyone handicapped or elderly get on. Please no crutches or canes or pregnant ladies.* She had a splitting headache—the only cure for which she figured was Starbucks—and Beauregard was scheduled to be back in the office today. She decided she could use a little fortification.

Lonnie leaned her head back against the wall of the T, right under a poster for adult education that read: *Are you tired of your life?* She closed her eyes and thought back to the night before. She and Peach had gone to dinner at their parents' town house in Brookline.

On the T heading there, Lonnie had issued a warning to Peach that if their mother annoyed them—excessively more than usual, that is—it was going to get ugly. Of course Lonnie adored Margot, who was actually a near-perfect mother. She was superaffectionate, and had the self-sacrificing thing down pat. Unfortunately, she was a little bit of an overachiever when it came to that nagging-about-things-you-already-know-but-are-trying-to-forget part. And Lonnie could always count on her to hit the basic talking points. Point one: career update. Point two: husband-prospect update. Point three: you-have-such-a-pretty-face-and-if-only-you'd-just-lose-fifteen-pounds pep talk. Oh, goodie.

Occasionally, Margot tried to be subtle. For instance, instead of making a direct comment about Lonnie's weight, she'd just serve her smaller portions than everyone else, and slice her a superthin piece of pie for dessert. Then she'd conversationally say things like, "So, I hear Delta Burke's lost some weight." But Lonnie was no fool, and she knew the way her mother's mind worked. Margot figured that if her daughter slimmed down a bit, she'd gain the kind of confidence needed to secure a prosperous career—not to mention, a successful man. Her mother meant well, but Lonnie just didn't share her oversimplified, reductive reasoning.

The night pretty much went the way she had expected. As soon as she and Peach walked through the door, Margot captured each in a loving bear hug and called to their father who was in the other room. "Jack, the girls are here."

"Nazi storm-trooping pigs!"

Okay, so he was watching the news.

"Jack!"

"They're stealing your freedoms! Does anyone even care? They're stealing your *freedoms*!"

Margot waved her hand and shrugged in dismissal. "He's watching his news shows. Jack, I'm putting dinner out in five minutes!"

"Yes, *fine*, " he answered in a very put-out voice, as if she'd been telling him that most of his adult life.

Four minutes later, Margot put out dinner: baked rigatoni with garlic bread and broccoli on the side. Lonnie skipped the broccoli, although she did accept her puny portion without question . . . or furtive augmentation. The truth was, despite her regular slips, she *was* trying to watch her weight. But not for any other reason than lifting her own mood. She could deal with curvy, and had accepted that she would never be skinny, but chubby just wasn't comfortable to lug around every day. She wasn't there yet, but she didn't feel all that far from it.

There had only been one point when Margot was more direct than usual. Point two. Over dessert, she'd flat-out asked: "So, Lonnie honey, where's this relationship with Terry *going*?" Of course, Lonnie didn't have much of an answer. Somehow, saying "nowhere, that's the point" isn't the best way to pacify your Catholic mother. So Lonnie just circumvented the issue, which she'd had a lot of practice doing in her own head anyway. Sure, Terry was a great kid, but—wait, did she just think of him as a *kid*? This was worse than she thought. Terry was only twenty-five and a silly comedian, and now she thought of him as a *great kid*?

The T came to a jerking stop, and Lonnie hopped off the train, bustled past the panhandler who was hitting an overturned bucket again and again with no variation, and walked quickly down the street to Starbucks.

"Venti, double soy, decaf cappuccino, no foam," the man directly in front of Lonnie ordered brusquely. "A grande, caramel macchiato, with skim milk. Light on the whipped cream. And a tall Americano. Don't leave room for milk."

The cashier nodded curtly, and hollered to the

drink maker: "Venti, double soy, decaf cappuccino, no foam! Grande, nonfat caramel macchiato, easy whip! Tall, no-room Americano!"

The drink maker echoed fiercely: "Venti, double soy, decaf cappuccino, no foam! Grande, nonfat caramel macchiato, easy whip! Tall, no-room Americano!"

The man moved to the side to wait for his drinks, and Lonnie went up to the cashier, who appeared so expectant and poised to shout, it threw her. "Uh, a grande coffee," she ordered, and watched the cashier's crestfallen expression as he quietly filled her cup. She paid and took her coffee, but just as she was turning to leave, the first man was whipping around with his drinks, and bumped into her. *Of course.* Luckily, she was able to jump out of the way quickly, and her ice-blue coat was spared, as a big splash of soy cappuccino landed on the floor next to her feet. Her wooden heels weren't as fortunate as her coat, but she could deal with that later. She gave the man her best "you idiot" scowl, and left.

As she walked the one block to her office, she started to feel great about how she'd just avoided a disastrous incident. It was a mini–adrenaline rush; she was practically whistling by the time she got to the twenty-third floor. Heading toward her desk briskly, she glanced at the clock on the wall: 8:43. She was early, too? Fabulous.

Just as she was thinking her day wasn't off to a bad start, her soy-stained wooden heel caught on the now-*annoyingly* plush lavender-pink carpet, and Lonnie stumbled. Instinctively, she reached forward to grab her desk for support, and half of her coffee spilled onto the newly cleaned desktop.

"Fuck!" she exclaimed louder than she would've intended if she'd thought about it before it flew out of her mouth. Luckily, she was early and the office was quiet. The one thing she had noticed since she'd

started working at Twit & Bell was that while lawyers did stay very late, they often didn't come into
work till after nine thirty or ten in the morning. Lonnie tossed her precious, nearly martyred coat onto
her leather chair, and went to the kitchen to get some
paper towels.

The kitchen was pathetic. Delia usually took care
of everything—stocking the drawers with napkins,
coffee filters, tea bags, and Sweet'N Low, not to mention making the coffee every day. For the past week
or so, though, Delia seemed to have abandoned the
task. Now, Lonnie noticed, there were no paper towels in the rack, or napkins in the drawers.

She headed down the hall to the supply room,
where all the paper goods were kept, and as she
approached, she heard faint voices. One of them was
definitely Lunther's, whose office was next door.
Lonnie ignored what she was sure was pointless
blather—i.e., Lunther's specialty—and let herself into
the walk-in supply closet. Once inside, her balance
wobbled slightly as she tried to reach the fourth shelf
for the rolls of paper towels. The other voice in
Lunther's office got louder, and suddenly became
clear. It was Macey Green's.

"Don't you dare threaten me," Macey said. *What?*
Lonnie instantly panicked, because she shouldn't be
overhearing this conversation, but there was nowhere
for her to go without bringing more attention to herself. Obviously, Lunther and Macey hadn't noticed
that someone was in the supply room right next
door. She tiptoed her soy heels over to the door and
started closing it, because the last thing she wanted
was for Macey to walk out of Lunther's office and
see her standing right there.

Just as she was nudging the door closed, she heard
Macey's voice more clearly, as if she were suddenly
closer. She had to be at Lunther's doorway, on her

way out. Lonnie froze. Impulsively, she decided to stay hidden behind the half-open door and wait till Macey left.

"I've made it very clear—" Lunther began.

"So have I, and at this point, you should be the one who feels threatened."

"Look, Macey—" he growled in an angry voice that Lonnie had never heard him use.

Macey cut him off, in a more impassioned voice than Lonnie had ever heard *her* use, "Don't fuck with me, Lunther. Or your diapered balls will end up in a sling!"

Diapered balls? It was times like this that Lonnie wished she were more sexually experienced so she would be familiar with all the terms.

Then Macey's voice changed back to cool and even. "Figuratively speaking, of course, since I wouldn't touch them with a ten-foot pole covered in latex."

"You bitch," Lunther snarled.

"Just you remember: you've been warned." And with that, Macey walked down the hall, in the opposite direction from the supply room, thank God.

Lonnie released a barely audible sigh of relief, and crept back to the shelf for paper towels. She could only reach high enough to grab one roll, but that was fine as far as she was concerned; she just wanted to slip back down the hall unnoticed. Just as she was stepping out and silently shutting the door, an abrupt noise shattered the silence. It sounded like an off-key horn blast. Another one sounded. Then another—*oh, no*. Her jaw dropped in horror. *It couldn't be!* But, it was. Lunther was passing gas—and with abandon.

She contorted her upper body to steal a peek into Lunther's office. From where she stood, she could see a beefy hand grabbing a can of Lysol off the desk. *Spritz, spritz. Horn blast. Spritz.* She shut her eyes and shook her head in disbelief.

Chapter Six

"Hey, are you taking lunch today?" Matt Fetchug stopped at Lonnie's desk wearing his characteristic cocky grin. He was actually very cute, with medium brown hair and a nice build . . . not that she was really looking. He had the kind of generic-handsome look that many women liked. Lonnie glanced up from her computer screen and smiled at him.

"I don't think so," she answered. "I have to finish doing this PowerPoint presentation for Twit. I've got four more slides to go, I think." Earlier that day, she'd made arrangements with Meijing, who'd agreed to cater the holiday party. It had been fabulously easy; she'd simply described the function, gave an estimated number of guests, and Meijing promised to take care of the rest. Lonnie had thanked her profusely and groveled unabashedly, even though it hadn't seemed necessary.

"What, you design his presentations?" Matt asked in a voice that would've been appalled if he cared more.

"Yeah, sort of. Well, how it works is, he gives me a huge stack of incoherent notes on a particular subject, and then I somehow turn it into a PowerPoint slide show by a ludicrous and unrealistic deadline. It's a nice little system we've got worked out." She topped off her statement with her favorite exploited-and-loving-it smirk.

Matt smirked back. "Ah, I see. So what's the dead-line for this? You can't break for lunch?" Lonnie figured she technically could, but she'd feel too guilty to really enjoy herself. Plus, she secretly hoped that Dominick would send her an e-mail asking her to lunch. She hadn't heard from him since that night at Rattlesnake, which was three days ago, and almost definitely indicated the blow off. But still, she hoped maybe . . .

"I'd better not," she said, only mildly apologetic, because she knew that it was probably of little consequence to Matt whether or not she went to lunch. He was a quintessential schmoozer. When he wanted to, he could charm everybody, but he didn't seem to like *anybody*. In fact, the few times she had gone to lunch with him, she'd spent the whole time listening to him make fun of people. Granted, he was usually amusing, but she wasn't going to get behind on her work to catch his act. Now if it were Dominick, that would be another story.

Oh, why hadn't Dominick responded to her e-mail? Okay, so she'd acted sort of weird at Rattlesnake. Was he going to hold a grudge forever? She'd asked him to go to happy hour with her on Friday night. Wasn't that compensation enough?

Fine, maybe not.

Probably not.

Slim-to-none chances, and when it came to men, her luck generally leaned toward bad.

"All right," Matt said. "Well, good luck with your work. Actually, is Twit even in? I haven't seen him today."

"Yeah, he's been holed up in his office all morning,

but I fully expect him to come out and verbally abuse me anytime now."

"And call you 'Lola,' " Matt snorted. He glanced over his shoulder and muttered, "Oh, man, look who's coming this way." Lonnie looked past Matt's mocking sneer, and saw B. J. swaggering toward them. It was really a shame that B. J. had the kind of over-compensating personality that lent itself to ridicule, because in some ways, he reminded her of an overeager little kid.

"Hey, you two," B. J. called. "What's this little tête-à-tête about?" He stopped in front of Lonnie's desk, next to Matt, and flashed her a 100-watt smile. Now she felt really bad.

"Hi, B. J. How are you?" she asked.

"Just ahead in all my work, bored stiff, the uzh," he answered proudly.

Lonnie saw a slight jerk at the corner of Matt's lips, and she feared whatever he was about to say. Since she'd started temping at Twit & Bell, she'd noticed that Matt and B. J. had an odd—and distinctly inequitable—relationship. B. J. seemed to be under the impression that Matt was his friend. At the same time, he looked up to him so much it bordered on pitiable, and Matt completely exploited it. Sometimes he'd act as if he and B. J. were close buddies, offering him advice about legal matters or women, and B. J. would desperately lap up the whole big-brother bit. Then, without hesitation, Matt would mock him right to his face, and B. J. would crack up like it was a shared joke.

Now Lonnie nervously anticipated Matt's response. But all he said was: "Man, how do you get your work done so fast?" Good, he was in schmoozer mode.

B. J. shrugged and said, "This stuff's wicked easy." He turned to Lonnie. "By the way, Miss I-Don't-Ever-

Go-to-Happy-Hour, don't think I've forgotten about tomorrow night. Don't even think about not showing up."

She smiled feebly and forced a nod. Please, she didn't feel like going now! The reason she'd never gone to happy hour before was that she'd never wanted to spend her Friday night with the bizarre Twit & Bell crowd. TV movies and takeout Thai held a lot more appeal. Sure, she'd been coerced into agreeing during the staff meeting on Tuesday, but who takes anything that goes on in those meetings seriously? Or remembers it?

"By the way," Matt said, "you're coming to the holiday party on Monday night, right?" Undoubtedly he was making sure he'd have someone to be cynically miserable with that night, if that mood happened to strike him.

"Uh-huh," she replied, and focused some of her attention back on PowerPoint. "Are you kidding? You think I'm going to put the whole thing together and not go?"

"How many people are coming?" he asked. She gave him what she thought was a pretty accurate number, because she'd managed to confirm most of the guests coming Monday night. Except for Lyn Tang, who was reportedly "out of the office" every time she called. How typical that Lyn Tang was the one guest Twit cared the most about confirming. In fact, lately he appeared all but obsessed with getting Tang on staff.

Clicking her mouse, Lonnie added absently, "I'm dragging my little sister, too."

"Whoa!" B. J. exclaimed, leaning his arms on top of her PC. "There's *another* one of you? I should've been told this sooner!"

"How old's your sister?" Matt probed, obviously just as intrigued by the idea.

"She's twenty-two."

"Boyfriend?" Matt asked.

"No comment. I don't pimp for blood relatives."

"Well, a boyfriend's no impediment, anyway," Matt said, cockiness on full blast. Lonnie just laughed and rolled her eyes.

"Does she look like you?" B. J. asked.

"No, and no more questions. Guys, seriously, I have to finish this thing," she said, and motioned to her computer screen.

Matt said, "All right, all right. But bring her to happy hour tomorrow night."

B. J. gave his predictable agreement, and the two of them headed for the elevators. Lonnie shook her head in half amusement, half exasperation, until she realized they had given her a good idea. If she guilted Peach into meeting her at Whiskey's, maybe the night wouldn't be a total loss.

When she got home that evening, she found Peach working on her mural, which took up one full wall. Peach had titled the mural *BosYork* because it was an urban scene that combined features of her two favorite cities. She'd started it soon after she'd moved in with Lonnie, but with her hectic schedule as Iris Mew's personal assistant, she was only able to work on it sporadically.

Lonnie looked at her sweet little sister, with her slim body covered by white overalls, her streaky gold hair in long pigtails, her pretty face smudged with periwinkle paint, and figured she was too angelic looking to turn her down. So she asked her if she'd meet her at happy hour the following night. At first, she mentioned something about remulching Iris's indoor plants, but then she agreed. Lonnie figured that Peach felt sorry for her because Dominick had blown her off. Luckily, this was one of those times when Lonnie had no problem with pity.

Whiskey's was a spacious, stylish bar, with dark wood, upholstered booths, and cozy lighting. Tonight it was also a jam-packed madhouse of suits. Lonnie'd been there about twenty minutes, just talking to B. J. and waiting for Peach.

"So, I told you about my ex-girlfriend who just got engaged, right?" B. J. asked. Lonnie mentally reviewed the stories he'd already told her that night: graduating first in his class at Penn Law, breaking his gym's all-time bench-pressing record, getting on stage at a Blues Traveler concert and jamming with the band on his slide guitar. Nope, he hadn't told her about the ex-girlfriend getting engaged yet.

"No, I don't think so," she said amiably, and took a sip of her extra-spicy Bloody Mary. She slipped sly glances at the door behind B. J., while he launched into a story about an ex-girlfriend who got engaged to a neurosurgeon, only to confess to B. J. that she'd never gotten over *him*.

". . . And at that point she told me point-blank that I was the greatest lover she's ever had." *Sure she did.* "And her fiancé was only three or four feet away!" Then he stopped abruptly, and his expression turned more serious. "Oh, wait. You don't mind me telling you this, do you? I mean, I don't want you to yell 'sexual harassment' because I was telling you about being great in bed."

"Oh, no, it's okay." *It's also a load of crap.*

"Hey, check that out," B. J. said, and motioned with his chin for Lonnie to turn around. She glanced over her shoulder and saw Lunther at the other end of the bar talking to Delia. He had two cigarettes hanging out of his mouth; when he exhaled, he took them both out at once, as if they were joined. Delia had her hand firmly planted on his upper arm, and she appeared to be in giddy hysterics over whatever he was saying. Then she leaned in to whisper something in his ear. Granted, the bar was loud that night, and it was difficult to hear over the din of the crowd, but whispering directly into your boss's ear? That seemed a little too intimate for Lonnie. And whispering into *Lunther*'s ear seemed a little too icky. But it was typical of Delia to be clueless about behavior that was not appropriate.

She turned back to face B. J. and he had a smug grin on his face. "Something's up," he said. Then he raised his eyebrows expectantly. It took her a few seconds to realize that he'd meant it as a double entendre. And in light of the subject matter—double ick.

To avoid commenting, she glanced around the bar casually. Okay, so she also stole another peek at the door.

All of a sudden, her stomach dropped, her heart raced, and her pantyhose burned on her skin. *Dominick!* What was he doing there? Could it be a coincidence? Obviously this was a popular happy hour spot, and his company was just as geographically close to it as hers. He couldn't possibly have come to meet *her* or he would've answered her e-mail. Wouldn't he?

Before she could gather herself together, she felt an arm around her shoulder, and instantly, she was pulled against a man's chest. It happened so quickly that she didn't even have a chance to be disoriented. She lifted her face up to see who had grabbed her. It was Matt. "Hey, it's our raven-haired temp," he said loudly to B. J. and then smiled down at Lonnie, who was in the comfort equivalent of a half nelson at the moment.

"Uh, hi," she said, lacking some of her usual friendliness as she tried to push away from him. He slowly let her go, sensing her resistance.

B. J. commented, "Yeah, I know, I've been telling her about Jennifer's engagement."

"Here's our raven-haired temp," Matt said again, and Lonnie realized he was a little drunk. "The girl's probably smarter than half the people in the office and she's the friggin' temp." His remark came with a sneer, and Lonnie wasn't sure how she was supposed to take it. Was it intended as a compliment or a put down? Whatever it was, Matt was acting like an asshole, and she didn't feel like indulging in small talk. She wished Peach were there. Plus, she'd lost sight of Dominick and now had no idea where he'd gone.

Lonnie extricated herself from Matt and B. J. with the old "going to the bathroom" line, and made her way around the bar to try to find Dominick. Finally she spotted him—sitting in a booth, talking to an attractive redhead. From what Lonnie could see, there were two other girls in the booth, too, who were talking to each other. They all appeared to be in their early twenties.

Great, so not only had Dominick lost interest in her altogether, he'd moved on to someone else, and decided to meet her at the exact place Lonnie would be. Talk about *tactless*. Not that they were an item or anything, but still . . .

She clutched her drink tighter and sighed. Could this have been more of a disaster?

Dominick was laughing agreeably as Mo, a graphic artist with a cubicle adjacent to his office, told him a story about her latest designs being rejected by upper management. She didn't seem to mind that *he* was upper management himself while she told him the story. Maybe it was because their departments had nothing to do with each other. Although, he also figured out that she was interested in more than just business talk. It may have been a while for him, but he wasn't completely clueless. Mo was looking up at him from under her lashes, edging her drink closer to his and laughing at nearly everything he was saying. She was cute, and from what he could tell, smart and entertaining. Too bad the entire time she was talking to him he couldn't stop thinking about Lonnie.

He'd gotten back from his business trip only a few hours ago, and stopped in the office to check his messages, because the network had been down for the last couple days. He'd never expected the e-mail from Lonnie asking him to meet her at Whiskey's. His trip had been completely spur-of-the-moment. He'd scheduled a business lunch with the reps from E-Bizz Inc. on Tuesday at GraphNet, but at the last minute, they'd insisted on meeting at their home base—in New York City. Lately they had been hedging about their account, and Dominick wasn't about to argue with one of GraphNet's biggest sponsors. So he'd spent the past three days in tedious meeting after meeting with the E-Bizz people—the only bright spot being his complimentary room at the Plaza.

Lonnie's e-mail shocked him. He was sure after Monday night's debacle, she'd want to establish some distance between them. She had to be one of the sweetest girls he'd met in a while, so he knew she wouldn't just dismiss him entirely. But still, he figured she'd wait a while to get in touch with him, now that she realized he was interested in more than a platonic relationship. He'd only come tonight because she had no idea he'd been out of town, and he didn't want her to think he'd purposely blown off her e-mail.

Okay, and he'd come to see her . . . and feel the situation out. After all, she *had* asked him to meet her at a bar on a Friday night. Maybe that meant she *was* interested. After the way she acted at Rattlesnake, he knew it was a long shot, but he was hoping like hell it would come in because despite everything, he still woke up hard every morning with thoughts of her curvy body and wet, wine-colored lips.

Then, just like that, those thoughts went down the drain. He'd come in and seen her with another guy's

arm around her. It looked like he knew Lonnie pretty
well by the close way that he was leaning in to her
and holding on to her almost possessively. Dominick
had looked away quickly, inwardly denying he was
that jealous, as his blood boiled and gut churned so
fiercely he thought he might lose it. Normally he
didn't even have a temper, but when it came to Lonnie, he couldn't seem to control the intensity of his
feelings. Why the hell had she asked him to meet her
if she was with someone already? The guy could've
been just a coworker, but that wasn't how it had
looked.

Damn it all! Here he had this cute graphic artist
interested, and he couldn't stop thinking about Lonnie, who was obviously playing games. He didn't
need this. Christ, he was thirty years old! He wasn't
some college kid anymore, and he sure as hell
wouldn't play games.

He didn't care how much he liked being with her,
or how mystified he was by her collection of degrees,
or how much he lusted after her gorgeous mouth
and full, round breasts. He was tired of trying to
read her. Period.

Then again . . .

Maybe I'm overreacting, Dominick thought, as he
nodded to whatever Mo was saying and hoped affirmation was the appropriate response. Lonnie
hadn't heard from him since Monday. She probably
took that as a sign he wasn't interested anymore,
which was far from the case. Obviously, he'd need
to clarify that. Stat.

Well, that settled it. He'd found the rationalization
he'd been looking for, and now he could go try to
find her. Mo asked, "So, what's the deal with the
guy in your group who wears power suits when the
whole office is business-casual?" Harold, his overeager protégé.

"Mo, I'm sorry, but will you excuse me? You just

reminded me of a phone call I needed to make. For work." It was a lie, but what was the alternative? Have her think something was wrong with her when there was absolutely nothing wrong with her? That wasn't how he operated.

"Oh, yeah, okay," Mo replied, and Dominick could tell she was disappointed. But he figured she was young, smart, and good-looking, so she'd get over it soon enough. He said good-bye to her two friends across from him, and left the booth in search of Lonnie.

It didn't take long to spot her. She was the pretty girl with the black hair and the lost-puppy look in her green–honey-brown eyes. She was standing at the bar, not talking to anyone. God, she looked sweet. Okay, he had to get his infatuation in check. He still didn't know what the situation was with the guy who'd had his arm around her.

With his Guinness in his hand, he started to walk toward her.

Chapter Seven

Lonnie was not exactly in the best mood of her life. The night had actually been sort of fun before she'd seen Dominick with another woman. Now she just wanted to go home, knowing this "thing" with Dominick Carter should not be bothering her as much as it was. But she couldn't leave because Peach hadn't arrived yet. Lonnie just hoped that Peach got there soon, and in the meantime, that nobody from Twit & Bell came over to make conversation. It was bad enough that she'd just had to deal with a slimy guy who'd tried to hit on her by sauntering up and saying, "I may not be the best-looking guy here, but I'm the only one talking to you."

She felt a hand tap her shoulder. *Oh, please, what now?* She spun around and found herself face-to-face with Dominick. Actually, her face was more aligned with his neck, and if she leaned over just a little more, she could kiss it. Lick it. All of a sudden, her mind went blank of everything except how happy she was that he was there. She knew there was some reason why she'd been feeling hopeless about him a minute ago, but for the life of her she couldn't remember what it was.

"Hey, you," he said. His jet-dark eyes were molten, and his face verged on five o'clock shadow. In other words, he looked like he always looked, and it was driving her crazy.

Lonnie smiled sociably and tried not to rip open his shirt and run her tongue down his stomach. Speaking of his naked flesh—*who, me?*—she wondered if he had hair on his chest, or if he was china doll–bare like Jake. Or worse, if he shaved it, like a guy Peach had dated. No, no, surely Dominick wouldn't do anything that cheesy. The guy Peach dated also shaved his butt, now that she thought about it, which made her wonder about the state of Dominick's *extremely* fine ass. All she'd been able to learn so far was that his butt was rounded and firm and cute as all hell. That information was hardly enough to satisfy one's curiosity.

Now he was standing in front of her, after she'd resigned herself to the fact that she'd blown it, and her heart was pounding so hard she wondered if he could hear it. She had to be very careful about her enthusiasm, though, because she still had no idea if he'd come to Whiskey's in response to her e-mail, or if he was there for something else . . . someone else. So she kept her tone even, and said, "Hey, Dominick. I didn't know you'd be here tonight."

"I got your e-mail"—*Yes*—"and I didn't get a chance to tell you, but I had to go to New York on Tuesday. I just got back tonight."

Oh, to hell with pretense . . . at least, for the moment. "I'm so glad you came," she said honestly.

They both relaxed and started talking, and pretty soon they were unconsciously inching their bodies closer together. She was touching his arm when he said something funny, and he was lightly placing his hand on her waist when he'd lean in to hear what she was saying. After about twenty minutes of talking by the bar, they moved to sit in a booth. Peach still hadn't arrived, but Lonnie knew the commute

from Chestnut Hill could be a time-consuming has-
sle. Another reason why Peach was her best friend.

"So, how much longer do you think you'll be at
Twit & Bell?" Dominick asked, and leaned back
against the booth.

"Hmm, I guess if I were really ambitious I'd say
until I make partner, but realistically? Probably until
the summer." He was giving her that sexy grin again,
and she needed to take another sip of her Bloody
Mary to calm her nerves.

"What happens then?" he asked. A little too casually, she thought, but she wasn't sure.

"Well, you know how I was thinking about teaching at a university?"

He nodded and leaned forward. "Right, well, it
was either that or a master's in marine biology. Or,
I'm sorry, marine biology *theory*."

She squinted her eyes teasingly at him—*ha ha,
smartie*—and finished, "So, I actually sent résumés
out a few weeks ago, and I'm hoping I'll hear soon.
Most likely I wouldn't be contracted, but I could get
a one- or two-year-long position as an instructor."

"Well, would you stay in Boston?" He stretched
back against the booth—a little too casually—again.

"Um, I don't know." Before she'd said it aloud,
Lonnie hadn't actually acknowledged it to herself.
She loved Boston, she'd grown up there, and she
knew the city inside and out. What would it be like
to move away from her parents and her sister and
her homey studio apartment? She'd gone away to
college for four years, but somehow that was different. In fact, only after Lonnie had graduated and
moved back did she realize that college was surreal
and in no way resembled *life*.

"What would you teach?" He leaned forward
again. "Because, I mean, if it sounds interesting,
maybe I could just hire you as my private tutor. Then
you wouldn't have to leave."

His thumb was sliding up and down on his glass, moving on the moist condensation, and she found herself looking at it far too long, getting entranced by its slow, seductive rhythm. For all she knew, the rhythm could have been entirely in her head, but the more her eyes darted back to Dominick's thumb—as it lightly stroked the glass—the more erotic she found it. And distracting. Finally, she forced herself to look back up at his face. She curved her mouth into a skeptical grin and asked, "Why would you need a tutor?"

Dominick held his hands up in mock self-defense. "Hey, I'm a big fan of continued education." It was the first time she'd really noticed his hands. Strong looking with blunt-tipped fingers. She wondered how they would taste. How they would feel probing inside her and making her shudder. Immediately, an image flashed through her mind of his mouth replacing his fingers and her body coming alive against his tongue.

She shook off the thought. And she mentally chastised herself for being the most ridiculously horny woman on the planet! When on earth had she become so sexually charged? Well, she knew the answer to that, but still, her preoccupation with sex lately just didn't seem normal.

"Okay, then," she said, determined to keep the light, easy flow of the conversation. "I could tutor you in feminist social theory, feminist literary theory, and women's studies. Take your pick."

He paused, then smiled teasingly and said, "Let me get back to you."

Lonnie took another sip of her drink and pushed it aside. The ice cubes had melted, and all that remained were a few swallows of diluted tomato juice and an errant lime wedge floating near the bottom of the glass.

"So, you're really a feminist, huh?" Here it came. The part where the guy tried to learn more about her views, but the way he phrased the question made it obvious that the answer "yes" would come loaded with all of *his* generalizations and preconceptions. Lonnie didn't feel like lecturing him, or silencing herself. But this moment was inevitable if she wanted to get close to someone . . . to be completely honest about who she was . . . to find out if he was an ignorant, insensitive clod so she could cut her losses now.

Wait! What was she thinking? Hadn't she decided she was just going to be friends with Dominick? That was right. Although, now that she thought about it, she didn't particularly want an ignorant, insensitive clod for a friend, either.

"Hello?" he asked mildly.

"Oh, hello." With deliberate diplomacy, she answered his question. "Well, I believe that while most people today claim they favor equality of the sexes, they have no idea what that really means because, on the whole, people haven't really revised conventional characterizations of males and females."

"How can you say that?" Dominick asked, his tone curious, not angry. "More and more, girls are entering science and math fields, there are almost as many female doctors as male, and it's becoming almost the norm for companies to offer comprehensive day-care packages to their female employees."

She nodded respectfully, but she wasn't surprised by his argument. "True, but have you ever researched how many women in said companies ever rise higher than middle management?"

"Oh, 'the glass ceiling' thing?" he asked, not sounding wholly believing.

"Yes, exactly. Look, the term might be passé, but the reality isn't. Do you think mothers who work in companies with day-care packages are going to complain? Do you think they're going to rock the boat?" Before he could answer, she continued, "But it's more than that, Dominick. Life doesn't begin and end in corporate America. I think there's still sexism everywhere, despite how desensitized people are today. Look at the way women are represented in films and television. Look at the difference between men's and women's magazines. All I'm saying is that if you really look, you'll see that there are still very negative stereotypes about women everywhere."

"So, what, you don't watch movies or TV? You don't read magazines?" He sounded borderline testy, but it didn't surprise her because despite her best attempt not to lecture him, she sort of was.

"I function in the society we have, but that doesn't mean I'm not aware of some inequities. Economic *and* social." Lonnie tilted her head and looked right into his eyes, trying to see if he'd lost the openness she was sure he had prior to this conversation. Hell, she might as well know now if he was going to respect her opinions, or just dismiss them immediately.

After a moment, he nodded, and his tone was relaxed again when he asked, "So, where does that leave you in terms of the opposite sex? I mean, do you, like, hate men?"

Textbook blockhead assumption, Lonnie thought. But he was such a sexy blockhead, and Lonnie really thought he had promise with these issues. She'd just have to work on him. . . . Great, now she sounded like Peach.

"No, why would I? I'm talking about social structure here, not individual people." She paused and added, "Although, I'm not going to lie to you. There are definitely some men I like more than others. *A lot* more."

Then a slow smile started to creep over Dominick's face, and Lonnie smiled back. "Okay, enough about me for the moment," she said. "What about you? What's GraphNet doing to try to keep you?"

He shook his head and replied, "Oh, they don't even know that I'm planning to leave. I think they assume I'm just waiting to become a vice president, but—"

"What do you mean? You're close to becoming a vice president?" she asked, impressed despite her general apathy toward corporate America and its myriad stratification.

He shrugged as if it were no big deal. "Well, yeah, but it just doesn't interest me. I want to start my own company so I don't have to 'play the game' anymore. I can just call the shots, and be sort of the elusive, enigmatic puppet master of the whole operation."

"Ah. Sort of like a *Wizard of Oz* thing?" Lonnie asked. "Interesting."

Then a small silence fell. It was only a few moments long, but it was enough for a perceptible current of tension to run between them. Suddenly the air was thick and stifling. And smothering, in a foggy way that seemed to call for getting naked. What were Lonnie's intentions toward Dominick again? Her mind was a little fuzzy on that at the moment. She was too busy imagining herself in the movie *Flashdance*, kicking off her heel and running her stockinged foot between his legs. He shifted in his seat, almost as if he knew what she was thinking. Of course he couldn't, but she fantasized for a second that he did.

Dominick moved his empty glass to the side of the table for the waitress to take. "Do you want another drink?"

Lonnie shook her head. "No. I'm all set, thanks."

He nodded, and the silence fell again.

After a few moments, Lonnie asked him if he'd done any interesting touristy things while he was in New York. As soon as the question came out of her mouth, she felt a pang of guilt. New York reminded her of Terry . . . which reminded her that she was falling for another man. And fast.

Omigod! She just remembered Terry's impending visit. He was coming to Boston the very next day and she'd completely forgotten! She needed serious help.

Luckily, Dominick didn't seem to notice her momentary unease. He told her about being forced to go on a carriage ride through Central Park to appease an E-Bizz partner whose brother was in town from North Dakota and had always dreamed of it.

"I mean, who dreams of that?" Dominick asked, and winced, trying to shake off the memory of the god-awful smell that people never told you about when they were insisting you simply *must* take a carriage ride through Central Park.

Lonnie giggled to herself because the way Dominick said things was so funny and he was just so cute. She asked, "So, I take it you're not in agreement with the ninety-nine percent of the human race that's been socially programmed to define all carriage rides as 'romantic'?"

Dominick shrugged, and said, "I guess it's just not my thing."

Boldness overtook her. Well, boldness and longing and vodka. She leaned forward, resting her hands in the middle of the table, and asked, "So, smartie, what *is* your thing?"

It didn't go unnoticed by Dominick that her voice was heavy with sexual suggestion. And then it happened: he felt Lonnie's fingers grazing the back of his hand. *Oh, Christ!* She was doing the exact same thing to him that he had done to her at Rattlesnake. Was she messing with him? Trying to make up for what happened? Had she just had too much to drink? Before he could respond to her slow, erotic touch, a girl rushed over to their table.

"Omigod, Lonnie, I'm so sorry I'm late!" Peach was slightly out of breath, and Lonnie immediately felt guilty. She'd made Peach come to Whiskey's just to mitigate her inevitable terrible time, and then she hadn't even ended up having a terrible time.

"Hi!" Lonnie pulled her sister's hand so that she

fell into the booth next to her. She could tell the exact second when Peach realized the man across the table was Dominick.

"Dominick, this is my sister, Peach."

"Right, the artist," he said affably, and reached across the table to shake her hand. "How are you doing? It's nice to meet you." Peach shook his hand and said polite hellos, but Lonnie could tell she was looking for a way to extricate herself from the booth, and give them time alone. Her sister was incredibly sweet like that. Not to mention a hopeless matchmaker. But there was no way Lonnie was going to blow off Peach after she'd come all this way just for her.

The three of them made small talk for a little while, and Peach explained why she was so late. Something about making tinfoil wings at the last minute for the Women's Auxiliary Christmas Pageant, and sewing Iris's Wise Man costume.

"So, is this the famous younger sister I've heard so little about?"

Matt again. He'd come up to their table, and appeared to be sober now. Peach smiled up at him and introduced herself. Then Lonnie introduced Matt to Dominick, who said a pleasant hello but held a dark glare in his eyes.

"Did you see Lunther and Delia?" Matt asked, grinning. He expanded, "Delia must be wasted or something. Last time I looked, she was trying to shove a third cigarette into Lunther's mouth, and she kept cackling and grabbing his knee."

"What?" Lonnie said, surprised, and looked around for Lunther and Delia. She spotted them sitting in a booth with B. J. The display looked about as shameless as Matt had made it sound. "Are they always like that at happy hour?"

Matt shrugged. "This is the first one I've seen Lunther at since I started working here." That was less than a year before. "But Delia usually just comes on to the skankiest guy in the place."

Lonnie reserved comment about Delia's obvious aversion to change.

"People are so weird," Peach said, smiling. Matt smiled back and asked her if he could buy her a drink. The two of them went over to the bar together, and Lonnie and Dominick were alone again. But they didn't pick up as intimately as they left off. She was thinking a little more clearly now, and it wasn't as if she were going to go home with him that night, or bring him home with her. It was too soon.

She wanted to wait for the right setting. She wanted to wait for a night when they'd gone on a *real* date together. She wanted to wait till she'd stopped at a drugstore and picked up some condoms. And she wanted to wait until she wasn't so damn scared.

Lonnie had just finished changing into her white cotton tank top and green hearts-and-stars pajama pants. She climbed into her high, full bed, and slid under the puffy cream comforter in ecstasy. She knew Peach wasn't asleep yet because only minutes before, she'd tossed her pink kimono over the partition-screen and went to bed in only underwear. Lonnie spoke into the darkness. "Sorry I made you come tonight. But did you have a good time at all?"

"Yeah, I had a great time, and you didn't make me do anything. Why didn't you mention how cute Matt was?" Peach asked.

"I don't know. It never occurred to me that he'd be your type—"

"Is there something wrong with him?" she interrupted. "Tell me now."

"No, no," Lonnie said. "I don't know him that well, but he's pretty funny. Definitely smart. It's . . . it's just that he's sort of . . . I've just never felt like

I could trust him. I guess he's too much of a charmer for me."

Peach remained silent for a moment and then said, "I'll work on him."

"I'm sure you will," Lonnie replied dryly. "Good, now you'll be more excited about the party I'm forcing you to go to Monday night."

"You're not forcing me. Although, now that you mention it, it probably wouldn't hurt for you to make some other friends. No offense."

"Suave, as always."

Peach just laughed. "So, how did you leave things with Dominick?"

"We're meeting at Borders tomorrow." Terry had said he would be getting into Boston sometime in the evening, so she figured she had the whole day open to spend with Dominick.

She heard Peach sit up in bed. "My God, you actually found someone who shares your deviant obsession with bookstores? This is too much."

"What's deviant about it? You've got books and coffee. That's heaven, baby." As Peach settled back in her bed, Lonnie added wistfully, "I really wanted to kiss him tonight."

"Kith him? You're twenty-seven. I think you can skip the retainer at night."

Lonnie giggled and bluffed, "I will when you skip the lumberjack snoring."

"Liar."

"Lumberjack."

"Academic."

"Starving artist."

"*Hussy.*"

"Yeah, right."

" 'Night. Love you."

"Love you, too."

Chapter Eight

Dominick and Lonnie had been sitting in the Borders café for nearly three hours on Saturday, for the most part ignoring the books they'd grabbed from the stacks. She'd told him all about her functioning phobias of trains, elevators, and white sauce in restaurants. He'd told her all about his brief stint working for the IRS help desk six years before, and how his brother David had recently been "born again." Time was both slipping away and standing still.

Dominick had gotten there first, taken three books from the software/computer shelf, and snagged a table in the café. When Lonnie arrived, a thrilling kind of anxiousness invaded his body. Her hair was windblown and wild. Her face was pink from the cold, and her furry blue coat was wrapped tightly around her as she rubbed her hands up and down her arms to warm herself up. She'd spotted him right away, and after selecting a few of the paperbacks on display, she sat down across from him.

Now, they'd both gone through two cappuccinos and a lot of conversation, but had yet to make a dent in any of the books. Not that Dominick had any interest in looking at his computer books. One of them was about Power Builder, a computer language he'd already learned three years ago. The other two promised to be unbearably dry dissertations on manipulating code. The only reason he'd even selected them was to show Lonnie that he was on a comparable intelligence level. Sure, he had a nice title at GraphNet, but a lot of people could work their way up in any company if they learned the industry and put forth a strong effort. He wanted Lonnie to think he was *intelligent*, not just hardworking.

"So, how long have you lived alone?" she asked him now, leaning her elbows on the table and resting her chin in her hands.

"Three years," Dominick replied. "I've had bad luck with roommates."

"Me, too," Lonnie said. "The last roommate I had—way before Peach—kept a poster of Antonio Banderas on the bathroom door, and insisted I refer to him as 'her boyfriend, Rudolfo.'"

He laughed. "Well, my last roommate neglected to tell me he was in a Ska band, and that they needed a place to practice their sets." Her eyes widened, and he went on, "Most of the time I could deal with it. But there was this one time—when I had a presentation the next day—that I had to be a dick and ask them to leave. See, the thing was, they were all twenty-one, and they thought I was 'the man.' So when I asked them to leave, suddenly they looked at me like I was some kind of narc. After that, I never said anything again. The guy only lived with me for a year, anyway."

"You didn't complain about their music again because you wanted them to look up to you?"

"That's dumb, I know. I think it was a vanity thing; I just wasn't ready to be an 'old man' yet. Now, of course, I couldn't care less," he finished, smiling.

"How come the neighbors never complained?"

"Oh, of course that year the apartment below us

was vacant." He paused and added, "Actually, once I called the police myself because my head hurt like hell. And when they showed up, they told my room- mate's band there'd been an anonymous complaint, and to stop playing. I just shook my head and said 'Oh, I'm sorry, man. That sucks.'"

Dominick quirked his mouth into a self- deprecating half smile. "I can't believe I just told you that. I've never told anyone that before."

"Why?"

Her greenish eyes were doing that glimmering pupil-dilating thing again, and he lost his focus for a second. Then he said, "I wasn't exactly proud of it. It was a prick move, and it's not something I'd do today." She just smiled. Straight white teeth below shiny, full lips. *God, help me.*

She asked, "What time is it?"

"It's"—Dominick looked at his watch—"ten of four. Do you have to be anywhere soon?"

"No, no," Lonnie said, biting her lip, unsure why she'd even asked in the first place.

Before any kind of perceptible silence could fall, though, Dominick spoke. "Hey, I know we're proba- bly both sort of sick from the cappuccinos, but do you want to go somewhere and get something to eat?"

"Oh, are you hungry?"

"I'm always hungry."

And I'm always eating. "Yeah, that sounds good. Let me just make sure I have enough money on me." She reached down to get her small black bag off the floor.

Dominick gently put his hand on her arm to stop her. "It's okay. I got it."

"No." Lonnie shook her head. "I want to pay. Really." She emptied out a couple of items from her bag as she rooted for her wallet.

"What's that?" Dominick asked, motioning to a small square container.

"Oh, that's just my lip balm," Lonnie said, and then added impulsively, "Kiwi-flavored." *Oh, Lord, what made her say that? Why didn't she just ask him to kiss her flat-out?*

"Ah . . ." He smiled a little wolfishly. "Interesting."

They'd just left Borders and were standing on the patio outside deciding where to go next when a clean-cut–looking man came out of nowhere and started pulling on Lonnie's bag. He tried to grab it quickly, but it was slung across her body, and there was no way to take it without pulling it over her head.

Lonnie screamed out of surprise and instinctively started fighting him, pulling the purse closer to her and trying to fend him off with her other hand. It all happened too fast for her to think about what she was doing. Or for her to register that Dominick had shoved the guy off hard. And then she heard a loud *whop* and the guy bolted. He'd run off without getting her bag, but he'd managed to punch Dominick.

"Christ!" Dominick yelled, and brought his hand to his forehead, which now had a bleeding gash on it. The guy must've been wearing a ring, to boot. "Are you okay?" he asked Lonnie.

"Me? Yeah, I'm fine," she answered, a little out of breath. "Oh, Dominick, your head." She brought a hand up to his face, and then looked around to make sure the psycho purse snatcher was nowhere in sight. "Come on, let's go back inside, and . . : blot this with napkins or something." She was a novice when it came to post-mugging etiquette, but she was winging it.

"No, don't worry about it," he said.

"Dominick—"

"It doesn't even hurt," he lied.

"You're not walking around with a bleeding head

wound. Now don't be ridiculous. Come on." She took his hand and pulled him with her back into Borders. He tightened his fingers around hers and didn't protest anymore. They rode the escalator to the second floor with their hands still locked, and made their way to the one-stall bathroom. *Please don't smell. Please don't smell*, Lonnie thought, inwardly preparing for the worst. They pushed the door open, and thank God, it smelled like pine needles and Glade.

The door shut and locked behind them, and Lonnie dropped her bag on the floor. She faced Dominick, with her back toward the sink. "Here, let me see," she said, and brought her hand up to touch his face.

Instinctively, though, he pulled back before she could make contact. "It's okay," he said, and swiped his forehead with the back of his hand carelessly. "You're making too much out of it."

"Don't touch it like that. You might infect it. Here, just turn your face." Her tone was caring but insistent, and this time when she brought up her hand, Dominick didn't resist, but let the natural warmth of her palm seep into his cheek. She kept her soft hand on his face, cupping it gently, soothing his cheek and jaw in an almost motionless caress.

Their eyes locked, and a shock ran through him, sending hot blood to his groin. He'd already felt a jolt from her hand in his and the closeness of their bodies as they rode up the escalator. Now—in this tiny, confined space—sexual awareness dulled his senses and sharpened his breath. His heart hammered even harder when he raked his eyes down Lonnie's generously curved body, and back up to her flushed, pretty face. She was just plain *hot*. Like before, the wind had blown her hair into untamed waves, and her cheeks and mouth were left rosy from the coldness outside. Pink and tousled, she looked like she'd just had hot sex, not a platonic stroll in the freezing cold. But then, maybe he was standing too close to her to be objective.

"Um, let me just wet a paper towel," she began quietly, "and I'll clean you up a little." Gingerly, she slid her hand off his face and grabbed one of the paper towels that were neatly stacked on top of the sink. With her other hand she turned on the faucet and then moistened the towel with ice-cold water. She turned back to face him, this time moving even closer, while she gently pressed the wet towel to the gash on his forehead.

He winced.

"I'm sorry! I'm sorry this hurts a little. But let me just clean off the blood," she said, and alternated between applying pressure on the wound and featherlight swabbing near his brow.

The gash hurt like hell, but he didn't see any reason why she should know that. He went for a joking tone. "I used to work for the IRS, remember? I've taken worse hits than this."

She leaned in closer. "I know. I know. Real men don't need peroxide," she said, while Dominick tried not to notice how close she was standing, and how much heat was fusing the space between their bodies. All this heat couldn't be coming from him alone. He glanced down. Lonnie's breasts were jutting out of her open coat, almost touching his chest. She was full and round and looked pillow soft to touch. At that moment, he felt desperate to run his hands over her, to feel her, to make her nipples hard. On top of that temptation, her mouth was two inches from his, and her lips were invitingly parted. Pouty and wet and ready.

Then Lonnie pressed her body even closer, and Dominick's control was almost shot. Their stomachs were nearly grazing each other, and there was no way she could be missing his erection. He sucked in a breath and waited for a change in her expression.

But her face betrayed nothing. She was calmly patting his forehead, her eyes focused on his wound.

Was she really oblivious to what she was doing to him? He wanted to grab her ass and haul her up against him, against his throbbing cock. He wanted to rub her breasts and shove his tongue in her mouth. Granted, these weren't some of his more refined moves, but right now, he was too turned on to care. He'd been nursing a potent attraction to Lonnie since he'd run into her two months ago, and he'd finally reached the breaking point. Jesus, he was fully aroused and they hadn't even kissed.

To hell with it. He made his move. Lightly, he ran a hand around her waist and nudged her closer. And she responded. Automatically, her hand fell from his forehead to his shoulder, while the other one slid around the back of his neck. She wasn't looking at his wound anymore, but she wasn't looking into his eyes either. Her long black lashes were lowered, and the paper towel was lost somewhere.

Wordlessly, she leaned in, took his mouth with her own, and gave him a slow, drugging kiss. He groaned. Tightening his arm around her, he left not a hint of space between them. Her arms looped around his neck, and with their bodies firmly entwined, their mouths clung to each other.

Her lips were soft and sweet, as she gave him gentle, suctioning kisses. Then she pulled back to let their hot breaths intermingle for a minute before she kissed him again. This time, her mouth only brushed his. At first, he followed her lead, but it took all his self-control not to run a hand behind her neck and tug her down into a harder, more unrestrained kiss. She'd told him her lip balm was kiwi flavored, but that wasn't how she tasted. Not that he ate kiwi often, but he didn't need to for him to know. She tasted like plums.

Yes. She started rubbing against him. Her breasts

strained against his chest; her lower stomach stroked his erection, and he got painfully harder. Just when he knew he needed all of her mouth, she ran her tongue along the inner seam of his lower lip, urging him to open up. He opened for her, and her tongue swept inside. *Wet. Hot.* He groaned again, licked deep into her mouth, and finally took control of the kiss.

Their hands were everywhere. She tangled her fingers in his hair, gripping him to her while he rubbed up and down her back almost roughly. She stood on tiptoe, trying to align their bodies; Dominick helped her by taking her bottom in his hands, lifting her up, bending his own knees, and pressing his groin into the crotch of her jeans.

She let out a startled gasp. Within seconds, she was grinding against him, barely choking out her encouragement. "Ah . . . ah." She couldn't get out any more words. Instead, their mouths devoured each other. Fists of cotton filled Lonnie's hands as she clutched the front of Dominick's shirt, trying to balance herself.

How had this gotten out of control so fast? he wondered. Then he thought, *More.* Blindly aroused by her thick moans, he backed them against the counter and ground into her even harder. They moved to the same pulsing rhythm, feverishly rocking their bodies against each other, pressed to the tiny counter and desperately exchanging full, wet kisses.

Eventually, though, they stopped kissing and, breathing fast, focused solely on the heat of their bodies moving hard into each other. "Ah . . . God . . . *God,*" he muttered hoarsely, because her body was so warm and round and pliant, and the sight of her head thrown back and her eyes half closed was sending him dangerously close to the edge.

Then her head fell forward again, and she gasped

into his mouth over and over—each breathy uttering making his lust more raw. He wanted her so much, he felt in pain with it, and his heart was pounding loudly in his ears. Pounding. Pounding . . .

Suddenly, he realized it was the door. Someone was pounding on the bathroom door. Lonnie must've realized at the same time as he did, because they both froze.

It took a few seconds for either of them to formulate an effective sentence. Lonnie spoke first. "Omigod, someone needs to get in here." That probably shouldn't have taken as much thought as it apparently did. Both of them straightened and moved several inches apart.

"Just a minute!" Lonnie called to the faceless door pounder. She gathered up her bag, moved past Dominick to open the door, and braced herself for the inevitable embarrassment. Apparently the lead-fisted door pounder was a little old lady with tightly set white curls and a tightly set disapproving frown to match.

"Hmph!" she groused irritably when she saw that the two of them were in the one-stall bathroom together. It probably didn't help that Lonnie's face was even more flushed than before, and her lips were puffy and glistening from kissing. Not to mention Dominick's rumpled hair and the still-present bulge in his pants. Although he was hoping that without bifocals the little old lady was none the wiser about his state of arousal.

"Pardon me," Lonnie said sweetly but briskly, and she pulled Dominick by the hand out of the tiny bathroom.

The escalator ride and walk through the store to the main exit was wordless. Dominick could only assume that Lonnie felt awkward, even a little embarrassed, by what had happened. He couldn't believe it himself. He'd known he was attracted to her, but he'd had no idea it would be that passionate. All it had taken was one of her soft, gentle kisses.

He wanted more. What he'd felt of her body so far left him wanting. Lusting. Aching . . .

Lonnie trailed behind him through the revolving door, still shocked by what had happened. It was as if all the sexual impulses she'd kept buried for so long had come pouring out. She could feel the embarrassed heat on her cheeks.

They were outside again in cold wind that whipped their hair about ferociously. A big part of her wanted to stay, diffuse the momentary tension, and spend the rest of the evening with him. But she couldn't. Terry would be in town anytime now. He hadn't given her an exact time, and knowing him, whenever he got to Boston, he'd go right to her apartment without calling first. She really had to be getting home.

And maybe a small part of her was relieved. She didn't know what to say to Dominick; it was all such sensory overload. She felt infatuated and alarmed all at the same time. She didn't want to get hurt again, and realistically, just because he'd taken what she was so clearly offering a few moments ago, didn't mean he was looking for a lasting relationship. Sure, in theory she wasn't either. But she knew it wasn't that simple. Knowing Terry might be waiting for her only confirmed her decision. She had to leave.

"Dominick," she began, and he noticed that she'd lost the easy, light tone she'd had before. Now she seemed anxious and uncomfortable. "I, uh, I've got to get home, actually."

"But—" he started, then paused. *What the hell is she talking about?* he wondered, as he waited for her to explain.

"I can't explain right now," she said loudly so she

could be heard over the wind. Unfortunately, her volume only made her sound more abrupt.

Dominick just stood there, looking confused. Then his face turned blank. Finally, he nodded, his expression unreadable. "Things to do?" he asked pointedly.

Lonnie blushed in spite of herself. What was her problem? Why couldn't she just tell him that a friend was in town visiting?

Because Terry was more than a friend, and she wasn't ready to get into that with Dominick.

"I . . . yeah, things . . . I'll talk to you later, okay?"

She turned and hurried up School Street, leaving Dominick standing there, watching her frantic departure. Abruptly, she turned around midscurry and called out, "Uh, I'll e-mail you. Um, bye!" With that, she bustled toward the subway. She tried not to think about the expression she'd seen on Dominick's face right before he'd disappeared out of sight. His mouth had been closed stoically, his dark eyes bored into her, and she could swear they were hooded in anger.

Lonnie walked into her apartment and threw her keys onto the wooden table that Peach had painted sunshine yellow. She did this every day, but today was the only day that the keys belted so hard against the table that they coasted savagely across it and knocked over the skinny vase in the center. In other words, she was mad as hell. At herself. Now there was a new emotion.

"Hey!" Peach called from the bathroom. "How did it go?" she asked cheerily.

Lonnie grumbled something unintelligible and threw herself facedown on her bed. Apparently, Peach wasn't taking the hint because she came out of the bathroom and repeated her question. "How did it go?"

"Go away," Lonnie mumbled plaintively, but with

her face buried in her pillow, it was just immaterial muttering as far as Peach was concerned. She sat down on the bed next to Lonnie.

"What happened?" she asked, her tone neutral.

That got Lonnie's attention. So much for her attempt at high drama. She rolled over onto her side and looked at Peach. "Why don't you sound more alarmed?"

Peach said, "Because how bad can it be? After last night, it's obvious he wants you. He kept looking at you like you were made of chocolate. What could you possibly have done between then and now?"

Lonnie rolled onto her back and stared up at the ceiling. "Oh, I don't know. I don't know." She rolled back over to her side and propped herself up with her elbow. "I don't know what happened. One minute we're having this great day together, the next minute I'm getting mugged—"

"Whoa—*mugged*?"

"And the next minute we're sort of, well, grinding against the sink—"

Peach blinked her eyes hard. "Wha—?"

"And then I ran off because I thought Terry might be here, and also, I felt weird, and now I don't know how I'm going to face him again."

Peach said, "Okay, I think you'd better back up and tell me exactly what happened. And don't leave anything out. Particularly the dirty parts; they could be important." Lonnie took a breath and started over, this time giving her the full story about the psycho purse snatcher and the erotic bathroom incident, as well as her awkward, abrupt fleeing. When she was done, Peach just sighed and went back to the bathroom, which Lonnie didn't take as a great sign.

"Peach, what? Tell me."

She stuck her head out of the bathroom door. "Lon, can I be honest?" Lonnie sat up eagerly, which signaled it was okay for Peach to proceed. "You're sabotaging yourself."

Her face fell.

"I'm sorry, but it's true," Peach said firmly. "Every time things start progressing with this guy, you act like . . . well, you act like . . ."

"Say it."

"An asshole."

"Great."

"Well, what do you want? First you say you don't want to get involved because of Terry."

"Right. That's why—"

"But then you obviously forgot all about Terry when you were kissing Dominick. I'm sorry, but I don't get it."

Lonnie sighed, feeling nauseous. "Me, either. Wait. What?"

"I don't get why you're clinging to this relationship with Terry when there's a new guy on the scene. And he's *local*. What's the problem?"

"I . . . It's complicated."

"Okay, well, I suggest you simplify it soon, because at the rate you're going, Dominick's gonna lose interest in you altogether. Is that what you want?"

No! "I don't know what I want." Just then the phone rang. Peach grabbed the receiver off the wall. "Hello. Sure, hold on." She passed the phone to Lonnie.

"Hello?" Lonnie said.

"Hey." It was Terry. "Listen, I'm almost at South Station. Then I'll take the train to your place. Where did you say I had to switch subways?"

"Park Street. Change from the Red Line to the Green Line. But, Terry, are you sure you don't want me to just meet you at South Station?" She'd offered a few days ago, too, but he'd said no because he didn't want to commit to a time when he would arrive.

"No time. We'll be there in—" He raised his voice, obviously asking the other train passengers. "How long to South Station?"

Lonnie heard voices in the background yell, "Five minutes!"

"Thanks, you're beautiful," Terry replied to the crowd. "So, Lon, I'm really excited to see you. It feels like it's been longer than a month."

"Yeah," she agreed feebly. Terry being sweet was the last thing her conscience needed right now.

"Annnnd," he went on, dragging his voice, "I got you a little something, too."

"You did?"

Peach, who had started dabbing some paint on her mural, glanced over.

"Yep. I bought it last week. It reminded me of you."

"Oh . . . that's so . . . sweet." *Damn it.*

"I gotta go. We're going through a tunnel soon, and I'm not just saying that," he joked.

"Okay. I'll see you in a little while," Lonnie said. "Bye."

She hung up the phone and Peach asked, "How did it go?" Lonnie flung herself backward on the bed again. Immediately, she bolted up again, ashamed of her melodramatic behavior. "I'm sorry. I don't know why I'm acting like this."

Peach sat down on her sister's bed and put her arm around her. "Don't worry," she said, smiling. "I'll help you through it."

Fuck! Dominick walked angrily down the sidewalk, not even noticing the savage cold whipping against his face and undoubtedly giving him windburn. *That's it, I've had it. I'm done—adamantly, immutably, and irrevocably done with Lonnie Kelley.* He stopped in a convenience store and bought a pack of Camels. He ripped through the clear plastic and foil, and tapped the box on the side of his hand. A cigarette popped up. He snatched it out and brought it to his mouth.

Shit, what was he doing? He'd quit smoking eight months ago. Before he could change his mind, he tossed the cigarette onto the ground and chucked the pack in the nearest trash can. Lonnie might've messed with his mind—yet again—but he'd be damned if she was going to reverse eight months of progress. His forehead started throbbing, as the icy-cold wind blew harshly on the open gash. He kept walking. His apartment wasn't far from Borders, so he'd left his car parked at his building.

Maybe Dominick had no right to be so annoyed, but he couldn't help it. He and Lonnie had just spent a great day together, and then yet again, with no warning, she'd acted aloof and fled from him as fast as she could. Why did she blow hot and cold like that? And, more to the point, why did he let her? The truth was, Dominick was really angry with him-self. He'd broken up with his last girlfriend over a year ago, and since then he'd only had some sporadic dates that didn't lead anywhere significant. It was always because of him. He worked too much to have the time to meet many eligible women, and he never seemed to get that excited about the ones he did meet.

And then came Lonnie. Why did she have this weird hold on him? So what if she was smart? So what if she was funny? So what if she was beautiful? And so what if he'd just found out she was also a great kisser? Did that mean he had to keep jumping through hoops every time she tossed him a crumb? Great, now she had him mixing metaphors. Enough was enough. He was done. This time he meant it. Maybe he'd give Mo a call, after all.

Terry's little gift—the one that "reminded" him of Lonnie—was an eight ball, which just happened to be her most known pet peeve. The guy thought he was a freaking comedian.

Now Lonnie, Peach, and Terry were stuffed in a cab, heading back home after a three-and-a-half-hour comedy show downtown. The show itself was fine; Terry hosted it wonderfully. So wonderfully, in fact, that a very skinny and very blond coed came up to him afterward and complimented his ear off. He practically drooled on her bare shoulder, and stood several inches closer than necessary. Not to mention, he couldn't seem to resist touching her arm more than once during their interminable conversation. Lonnie was steamed.

Okay, okay. It wasn't that she had deep, everlasting feelings for Terry. It wasn't that she expected him to have them for her, either. And it wasn't that they even had a commitment. But still. She couldn't help but remember the way they had met—the way he'd schmoozed her after the show, bulldozed her with jokes and flattering remarks, and called her promptly the next night to ask her out. Now she wondered if he still did that on a regular basis. If she hadn't been standing nearby tonight, would he have gotten that girl's number, too?

For some reason, the idea really put her off. Here she'd been stressing over her growing feelings for Dominick, and for all she knew, Terry picked up a girl at every show. Of course, he was clueless about her current ire. Well, why wouldn't he be? He really barely knew her. The thing was, she knew how ridiculous she was to feel this sense of annoyance after the way she'd acted like an overheated hussy in Borders that afternoon. Yet, she couldn't help it.

Finally—as the cab turned the corner onto her street—she accepted the fact that her anger was really irritation, and she wasn't so much irritated as she was . . . well . . . *turned off*. She glanced over Peach's head at Terry, and her suspicions were confirmed. From the moment he'd showed up on her doorstep with the dumb eight ball, she just hadn't felt sparks.

No attraction, no zing. She normally did—at least she had until certain recent developments had forced her to realize that a spark was a far cry from a raging inferno of scalding, searing lust. To put it mildly.

The cabdriver let them off in front of Lonnie's building, and Terry allowed Lonnie to pay the fare without sparing a backward glance. After the taxi pulled away, Terry put his arm around Lonnie, and said, "Man, I'm tired. Good show, huh?"

"Uh-huh," she replied tonelessly. The elevator ride was quiet; Peach, for once, failed to fill in the silence. Inside the apartment, Peach went to the bathroom to brush her teeth and get ready for bed, and Lonnie decided it would be a good time to try out the flannel, checkered, long-sleeved pajamas that Aunt Kim had given her for Christmas two years ago. Speaking of that, where was that long underwear she'd gotten for her birthday? .

"Hey," Terry whispered, while he stripped to his briefs. "Is your sister staying here tonight?"

Obviously, genius. "Yeah, I think so. Why?" She was playing dumb, although she knew perfectly well what he was getting at—Peach normally stayed at their parents' town house when Terry visited.

Luckily, their parents were away, and since Peach hated staying in the house alone, she'd be spending the night at their apartment.

"Why?" he echoed on a whisper. "Because . . ." He came closer and quirked his mouth into a mischief maker's grin. "What about the booty?"

I can't believe I used to find this cute. "Oh . . . well, it wouldn't be right. I mean, with Peach here." She finished tearing the plastic wrapper, and the checkered pj's spilled out. Terry caught one look of them and grimaced painfully.

"What is *that*?" he asked.

"My new pajamas," she replied briskly, unwilling to acknowledge that they were about as alluring as a beekeeper suit. Peach emerged from the bathroom, patting her face dry.

Once Peach was in her bed, behind the partition screen, and everything was dark, Terry made his move. He slid his hand over Lonnie's side, to her stomach, and then slithered up inside her flannel pajama top. Her eyes flew open. Obviously turning away from him hadn't relayed her desired message: she didn't want "the booty" tonight. Fooling around with Terry was always fun—and always relatively innocent—but now, the thought of kissing and caressing him filled her with dread. Part of it was because of the way he'd been flirting with that comedy club groupie, and part of it had little to do with him . . . and a lot to do with somebody else.

Terry's hand applied pressure, coaxing Lonnie to roll over and face him. Fine, she guessed she owed him that much.

She rolled over, which he instantly mistook as an invitation. He swooped his head down to kiss her, but she pulled hers back before his lips could make contact. Even in the dark, she could see hurt cross his features. "I just don't feel comfortable," she whispered soothingly. "With my sister here and everything."

He sighed heavily. Now he was angry, but at least he wasn't hurt. "Well, why is she here? Usually, we have the place to ourselves."

"My parents didn't want her to," she lied. And not very convincingly, she might add. But Terry didn't seem to think she was fabricating anything. He was too busy sulking, which, in all honesty, Lonnie could understand. But it still wasn't going to change anything at the moment. "Do you mind if we just go to sleep?" she asked, her voice barely audible.

"Whatever," he growled, and flopped over onto his stomach with an audible thump. She rolled over so their backs were to each other.

Oh, Dominick. She thought about the fun she had with him, how easy it always seemed to be with him. That is, until she inevitably did something stupid.

Okay, that was *it*! She was twenty-seven years old already. It was time to stop wasting her life with a guy she couldn't love, just because the one and only man she had ever loved broke her heart four years ago. It was time to stop closing herself off to real relationships because of what Jake had done. It was time to let this thing she had with Terry go, and it was time to *grow up*.

Chapter Nine

12:38 P.M. Lonnie's eyes darted off the clock and back to her coffee cup, which she'd accidentally filled to the rim, and now she was tremblingly close to spilling the scalding liquid on the hallway carpet. She was heading to the library at the far end of the office to get some extra work done. Since the holiday party was later that night, the office had a half day of work. Lonnie was one of the only people left, and she figured this would be a good time to work on Macey's project.

Only minutes before, Beauregard had left. Of course he'd stopped at her desk first and asked if any confidential faxes had come for him yet. When she'd told him that she didn't think so but she'd double-check, he'd told her not to bother since he'd already gone through her desk earlier.

On the way to the library, she stopped at Bette's office to drop off some résumés that had come in on Twit's fax machine. The door was open, but Bette wasn't around. She probably went home for the day, too, so Lonnie walked in far enough to toss the résumés into Bette's inbox. As she was turning back to the door, her coffee teetering, something struck her.

Something was different about Bette's office. . . .
What was it?

What was it?

Wait! The pictures that were usually on her desk
were gone. Silver-framed photos of Bette's husband,
Reginald, and their children, Skylar-Blaise and Burberry, were missing. Knowing Bette, Lonnie thought,
she'd sent the picture frames somewhere to get them
professionally cleaned—for an exorbitant price—and
they'd be back on her desk in a few days.

Lonnie carefully pressed her hip against the glass
door to the legal library, pushing it open while trying
not to spill her coffee. She had her bag, which held
Macey's little spiral notebook, slung around her, and
she was ready to work . . . even if she didn't fully
understand the purpose of the assignment. She
looked around the deserted room. Its decor had a
wonderfully homey quality—long, thick oak tables,
mocha brown suede sofas, and soft-lighting lamps
with emerald green glass shades. The stacks themselves were high and dense with multicolored
leather-bound books, and the aisles that separated
them were narrow strips of Oriental rug. She decided
to sit at one of the tables so she'd be more productive; the last time she'd sunk into one of the suede
sofas, she'd sort of fallen asleep.

She set down her cup, took the spiral notebook out
of her bag, and opened to the first dog-eared page.
For an instant, she got a seventh-grade urge to doo-
dle smiley faces for Macey to find later. Luckily the
urge wasn't uncontrollable. She walked down the
second aisle to retrieve the black legal encyclopedia
that Macey had told her to use.

As soon as she saw it on the fifth shelf, she reached
up to grab it, and suddenly, heard voices coming
from the next aisle over. Unlike Lunther's and Macey's conversation the other day, these voices weren't

muffled. She could hear every word that Bette Linsey was saying. She just didn't know whom Bette was saying things *to*, because the man talking with her was whispering harshly, making his voice impossible to distinguish.

"I don't like being cornered like this," Bette said.

"Now you know how *I* feel," the man whispered savagely. "Look, if you just tell me what I want to know—"

"You don't have any right to *ask*!" Bette snapped.

"Shh! All right; just calm down!" he ordered. Lonnie had a dumbstruck déjà vu of the other morning in the supply room, and she knew she shouldn't just stand here eavesdropping, but she found herself in the same dilemma that she'd been in then. What was her alternative? They were obviously right in the next aisle, and she had no idea when they were planning to leave. She didn't want them to catch her tiptoeing out of her aisle, but she also didn't think she should noisily make her presence known since whatever she'd overheard so far was obviously not intended for her ears. She'd rather not make her intraoffice work relations any more awkward than necessary. It seemed like the best thing to do was to wait it out.

Bette lowered her voice back down and commanded, "Get out of my way." Her tone was steely and unyielding. Obviously the whispering man was holding her there against her will—or at least physically blocking her—yet she didn't sound afraid. Just annoyed.

In a strained tone that sounded as if words were being ground out, he protested, "Don't hold out on me, Bette! I'm *desperate*. I don't—I just don't know what I'll do if it's true!"

"Get out of my way!" Bette ordered, and Lonnie heard her stomp down the aisle and toward the library entrance. But she didn't hear the glass door creak open. Where was Bette? Why wasn't she leaving? *Oh, no.* This wasn't the best plan after all. Now if Bette walked over and saw Lonnie just standing here, it would look eight million times worse!

Then she heard her voice. "By the way!" Bette called out, and Lonnie figured that she must've just paused at the door for a few moments. "You're *pathetic!*" The door creaked open and creaked closed.

Good, Bette was gone.

Too bad she left Lonnie alone with a strange man who admitted to being "desperate," but not before she'd taunted him with some insulting words. Lonnie's heart was not only racing, but it seemed to be beating in her throat, as she tried to move stealthily down the Oriental rug. She got to the end of her aisle and froze in fear. Suddenly, she felt totally vulnerable—both surrounded and isolated. She decided the best thing to do would be to just calmly walk back to her table with a book in hand and act completely clueless. Until the pepper spray in her bag was within grabbing distance, that is. Just in case.

When she reached her table, she set down the book, and felt a twinge of uncertainty about leaving. What about Macey's project? But then, the library would always be there tomorrow after work, and even though it would be Christmas Eve, the attorneys were sure to stay late. The near emptiness of the office this afternoon was a once-a-year aberration. That settled it. With notebook still in hand, Lonnie picked up her bag, ignored her untouched coffee, and turned to go.

Aah! B. J. startled her by being right behind her.

"Omigod! B. J. you scared me!" She let out a breath. "What are you doing just standing behind me like that?"

He smiled, but it was so forced it looked painful. "I was about to say hi when you turned around. What are you doing here? Everyone went home for the day."

Lonnie didn't want to jump to conclusions. B. J. might have been the whisperer from a minute ago, but it was possible he'd just come in. Then again, if he'd just come in, she would've heard the door creak. "Oh," she said and motioned to the encyclopedia, "Just getting some work done."

He nodded, and after an almost imperceptible pause, his forced smile turned positively plastered. "So, you psyched for the party tonight?" He balled his little hands into enthusiastic, bony fists when he said the word "party." Something definitely wasn't right with B. J.

Lonnie smiled in a way that she hoped looked normal, and answered, "Yeah. Well, probably more stressed. If anything goes wrong, Beauregard will be looking to me." She shrugged. "But what the hell, right? Listen, I should get going—"

"Yeah, I'm pumped about tonight. The only question is, which girl I'm taking. Three different girls I know have been trying to get me to ask them, but I still haven't decided. See, they're all equally hot."

And equally fictional. "Well, make sure you introduce me to whomever tonight. See ya later." She left the library, praying she wouldn't hear the door creak open behind her, because B.J had really given her the creeps. He had to be the whispering man from the stacks. Seeing her in the library had obviously caught him off guard; he'd tried to act congenial, but it was a blatantly uncomfortable front. Lonnie wondered what he was so worried about, and what Bette Linsey had to do with it. But it was none of her business anyway, so she headed back to her desk to shut down her PC.

And to fortify herself for a little confrontation with Dominick.

Lonnie used the mirrored wall of the elevator when she applied a hint of Plum Daiquiri lipstick. It was more psychological fortification than cosmetic. And yes, she knew how doubtlessly fucked up that was. The ride three floors down was too short to plan anything elaborate, which was probably just as well.

After Terry had left on Sunday afternoon, Lonnie asked Peach if she'd noticed the way he flirted with that skinny blonde after his show. From the melodramatic gagging gestures her little sister made, Lonnie took that as a yes. And Lonnie started thinking more seriously about her feelings for Dominick. It wasn't just the way that Terry had flirted (shamelessly) with that groupie. It was more. It was their overall lack of chemistry. It was the superficiality of their relationship. It was the freaking eight ball.

And then there was Dominick. She loved his wit and charm. She loved that he'd volunteered for a big brother program. She respected his intellect. And, damn it, he'd taken a bloody punch for her, which maybe shouldn't mean as much to her as it did. But it did.

Now it was a matter of smoothing things over after the way she'd ditched him on Saturday. When she thought about it, he hadn't played any games with her so far. She was the one who'd been inconsistent with him, and she hoped it wasn't too late to start over. She'd just have to remember to take it slow, though, and not to get in over her head the way she had with Jake.

When the elevator let Lonnie off on twenty, her palms started to sweat. Suddenly, she had a memory of Dominick's face when he'd been aroused and grinding against her. His eyes had been heavy lidded and his lips parted, and his body had felt so powerful when it'd moved against hers. *Yum.* There was no one at the receptionist desk, so Lonnie circled the floor until she found a door with Dominick's name on it. DOMINICK CARTER, DIRECTOR OF WEB SITE DEVELOPMENT .

The door was slightly ajar, and she knocked. "Come in." *He's there!* Why hadn't she planned more, again? She gently pushed open the door and stepped into his office. The room was fairly big, but overcluttered with computer equipment and stacks of papers everywhere. He looked up, his face revealing definite surprise, and she noticed he was wearing glasses. She'd never seen him wearing glasses before, and they looked sexy as hell on him, but they didn't quite fit with the gash on his forehead, which had scabbed over and was now surrounded with purple and pink bruising.

"Hi there," she said a little cautiously. She didn't want to act overconfident and bubbly like nothing had happened, but she wasn't going to act like she was Satan, either.

"Hi," he said crisply. Okay, he was still mad. She closed the door and walked closer to his desk.

Dominick glanced over to the door she'd just shut, and then back to her. His expression was impassive and his tone flat. "Is there something you need? I'm sort of busy at the moment." Make that very mad. Words lodged in her throat, and she was doubting the logic of coming downstairs after all. Finally she spoke.

"A lot of work?" *Great question.* Not only was it a lame attempt at filling the silence, but it practically guaranteed a one-word answer.

"Yeah." Uh-huh. He didn't look up for another moment or two, but just kept writing. Then he eyed her again, waiting for her to say her piece. His eyes were dark as night, and piercing, making her so nervous that she blurted: "Dominick, what's going on between us?"

He narrowed those potent eyes, leaned back in his chair, and tossed his pen down on the desk. "You're asking *me* that?" He shook his head and sat forward again. "Look, Lonnie, I don't have time for this—"

"Then make time." *Did I actually say that?* Now his eyes widened behind his glasses, and impassivity gave way to frustration.

"What?" He stood up, and now he was the one looking down on her, rather than the other way around. "Lonnie, I'm *working*. I've got a *staff* out there. I'm backed up against a wall with four different deadlines, and you—" He shook his head again. "What is it with you, anyway?" He held out his hands in an angry gimme gimme gesture.

"Is it some sort of feminist torture thing?" he went on. "Mess with a guy's head, then, what, go laugh with your friends?" He knew he was making no sense, but he couldn't stop himself from trying to spew the knotted emotions she'd been stirring in him for a while now. He finished, "You know what? Don't even answer that; I don't have the time."

Lonnie looked at him dead-on, and said simply, "I'll leave you alone, then." She'd be damned if she was going to grovel!

She turned to go, and Dominick moved fast. He bolted out from behind his desk and caught her arm just as she was turning the doorknob. "Oh, wait!" he shouted.

When she turned to face him, her expression was unreadable. He looked into those beautiful green-honey eyes and wanted to forget everything else. "I—I'm sorry. I didn't mean to bite your head off like that. I just—ah hell." He released her arm, plowed his hand through his hair, and sighed. "Lonnie, let's just forget everything and start over, okay?" *Yes, yes, yes!* "Friends?" *No, no, no, NO!* He was trying to be nice, to wipe the slate clean of all the misfired signals and awkwardness. She should be glad. She should be basking in how wonderfully progressive he was.

Screw it. In one motion, Lonnie leaned her body closer to his and brought both her hands up into his hair. She pulled his head down, and vaguely heard him say in a low voice, "Lonnie?" Ignoring him, she lifted her mouth to his. Before she could kiss him, though, he yanked his head back an inch and said huskily, "Probably a bad idea."

She tightened her fists in his hair and just whispered, "Please," before she gently bit his lower lip. She felt some of the tense resistance in his body ease, and he didn't move his head away. Instead, he let her kiss him softly, and he kissed her back in spite of his desire to remain stubborn. He sighed as she moved her mouth across his cheek, and over to his ear.

"Lonnie," he whispered gruffly, "what are you doing to me?"

She licked up the outer shell of his ear and then back down again. He shuddered and gripped her butt, hauled her against him, and moved them both back against the closed door. She was sucking on his earlobe when he whispered, "Don't mess with me."

"I'm not," she whispered back, and rested her forehead in the crook of his neck. She hadn't planned this, and she had no idea what would happen next.

"Lonnie?" Dominick pulled back from her, his eyes heavy lidded just as she'd remembered earlier. "What's going on here?" he asked, and his voice was both soft and gravelly at the same time. He put his hands at her waist tentatively and waited for her response.

Placing one hand affectionately on his cheek, she looked straight into his coal-black eyes. "I'm sorry about the other day," she said quietly. "And I'm sorry if I've given you mixed signals. For some reason, I'm always screwing up where you're concerned. But, I . . ." She tried to think of how to say she was crazy about him and desperate to find out firsthand if he snored. "Well, I'd like us to spend more time together. I mean, if . . . you know . . . that sounds good to you, too."

Say something, please.

Dominick's face creased into his sexy-as-sin grin, and Lonnie suddenly knew that she couldn't bear whatever his response was going to be. She moved her hand from his cheek to his mouth. "Don't say anything. Just blink twice if you agree." He blinked three times, and she cocked her head to the side, moved her hand away from his mouth, and said, "Okay, smartie, what's three blinks supposed to mean?"

He wrapped his arms tightly around her waist, hauled her up against his chest, and whispered into her ear hotly, "It means I want us to spend more time together. Naked."

She let out a laugh before pulling back a few inches and turning more serious. "Let's take it slow, though, okay?"

"Slow," he repeated, and sucked in a deep breath. "Fine time to tell me," he teased, and pressed his hips against hers. She almost collapsed against him in surrender. Then he kissed her on the cheek. "No problem. Slow," he murmured, and kissed her again.

Well, this had gone better than she'd expected. She should probably leave now before she mucked it up somehow. Anyway, Dominick obviously had a lot of work to do, and Lonnie had promised to meet Peach at home in a little while to get ready for the party.

The party. "Hey, what are you doing later?" Lonnie asked.

"Just working. Why?" He trailed hot, suctioning kisses down her throat while she told him about Twit & Bell's holiday party. He started rubbing her breasts, and when he felt hard, swollen nipples through her dress, he lost a little of his concentration and had to ask her to back up and repeat some of what she'd said. She repeated it a little breathlessly, and he agreed to work straight through the early evening so he could meet her in the lobby of the Easton Hotel, where the party was being held, at eight o'clock.

When Lonnie finally opened the door to go, she looked over her shoulder at Dominick. He looked tousled and dazed and delicious. "By the way," she said, smiling coyly, "when I'm done with you, I think you'll have a whole new appreciation for 'feminist torture.'" She slicked her tongue over her plum lips, and Dominick had to remind himself to breathe.

Chapter Ten

Lonnie might as well have floated through the door to her apartment. This time she tossed her keys so carelessly they missed the sunshine-yellow table altogether, but she didn't even notice. Letting out a contented sigh, she slipped off her ice-blue coat, dropping it onto the shaggy cream rug, not sparing it a backward glance. She wasn't sure if she could really still taste Dominick on her or if it was a false memory, but either way, she couldn't help running her tongue over her bottom lip and remembering what had happened in his office earlier. She was vaguely aware of a stupid grin on her face, but she couldn't care less.

Then she noticed Peach's ornate red-gold-and-black patchwork coat hanging on the partition screen. "Peach? You home?"

"In here!" her sister called from the bathroom. "Hold on a second."

The bathroom door opened and Peach emerged, wearing her terry-cloth robe. She was followed by a slightly roly-poly woman with short dark blond hair, a bashful expression, and a plum silk robe on that looked oddly familiar.

"Hey," Peach said, smiling brightly. "Lon, this is

Cheryl, Iris's daughter. Oh, hope you don't mind. I let her borrow your robe while we did mud facial treatments."

"Oh, no, no," Lonnie said, trying not to notice the brown splatters all along the robe's collar. "How come you're home?" she asked Peach. "I didn't think you'd get home from work for another hour or so."

"Iris left for Vermont this morning, and I only had a few things to take care of anyway," Peach said. "Cheryl's gonna help me pick out what I'm wearing to the party tonight." Cheryl quirked her mouth into a self-deprecating grimace, as if to say that her input was going to be worthless.

"So, you and Iris aren't spending Christmas together?" Lonnie asked.

"Lonnie," Peach scolded. She rolled her eyes and exchanged horrified looks with the ceiling. Lonnie immediately backpedaled.

"Oh, I'm sorry! I didn't mean to pry—"

"It's okay," Cheryl said. Her voice sounded soft and unused, and her face was as round, guileless, and cushy as a Kewpie doll. "Mom went skiing with some women from the Horticultural Society. I could've gone but . . . I didn't feel like dealing!" She sighed the last part—as if to say *phew!*—and Lonnie found her charming in an unintentional sort of way. "I really like your apartment," she added politely.

"Oh, thanks, but I think Peach's mural takes most of the credit," Lonnie said.

Peach snickered, "Yeah, right. *That* thing?" She motioned to *BosYork* with her thumb. "It's horrible! I hate it; it's my worst painting yet." This reaction was typical for Peach, who, like most artists, was supercritical of her own work, even though it looked masterfully like something no one else could hope to create.

"No, it's gorgeous!" Cheryl exclaimed. Her eyes surveyed the wall adoringly.

"Okay, enough about that subpar mess over there," Peach said, drawing their attention away from the mural. "I want to pick something out for tonight that'll get Matt's attention."

"I think you've already got it," Lonnie commented, and flopped onto the sofa.

"True, but still . . ." Peach kidded. "Cheryl, what did you think about the pale blue dress I showed you before? Do you think I should wear that with the silver heels? Or should I wear the fuchsia cat suit with the floor-length black cardigan?"

"Um . . ." She hesitated, appearing eager to help, but at the same time reluctant to give fashion advice. Or possibly, just reluctant to offer her opinion, period.

"Hey, Cheryl," Lonnie interjected because she thought it was a little rude to talk about a social event with someone who wasn't included, "did you want to come to the party tonight? I'm sure I can sneak in another guest." She wasn't sure, but what the hell?

It was irrelevant anyway, because Cheryl didn't appear interested in going. At the mere suggestion, her eyebrows shot up and her face contorted painfully, revealing utter terror. She swallowed hard, started trembling, and Lonnie couldn't help noticing that this was a less than normal reaction. The bashful, Kewpie-doll thing had a certain charm, but Lonnie could see that this shyness was too severe for a thirty-five-year-old woman. She just hoped her sister knew what she was doing.

"No, no," Cheryl said finally. *Very* finally.

Peach said, "Fine, you don't have to come tonight, but don't forget after the holidays we're going out for a night on the town. We're gonna get dressed up and go out somewhere fun—I know! How 'bout the Cactus Club?"

Cheryl suddenly looked queasy, and did an abrupt

about-face to stare at *BosYork*. Nope, this was definitely not normal.

"Cheryl," Peach said coaxingly, "now, don't get all weird." She walked over and put her hand on her friend's silky mud-splattered shoulder. "Face it, you have Social Anxiety Disorder. We've talked about this. It's nothing to be ashamed of."

Lonnie rolled her eyes and hit her forehead with her palm. *Is this what six months of psych training had wrought?*

Cheryl only stared more intently at the mural, and her body quivered. Never one for awkward tension or silence, Peach spoke again. Her tone was breezy, but affectionate. "Like I've said before, there's absolutely nothing to be embarrassed about. We all have issues. I mean, take Lonnie—"

"Hey—"

"We're talking *classic* fear of intimacy."

That got Cheryl to turn away from the mural . . . and to look curiously at Lonnie. Great, now she thought they were equally maladjusted and shared some sort of soul connection. Peach went on casually. "Well, in my sister's case, the fear of intimacy provides an excuse to indulge in her other, bigger issue: fear of abandonment."

Oh, please. What did her sister know? While she was audaciously diagnosing Cheryl Mew, Lonnie was tackling both her fears in Dominick's office, as well as tackling him.

"Do you mind?" Lonnie injected testily.

Peach held up both hands in a surrendering gesture. "Relax. I'm not perfect, either. For instance, I obviously have a debilitating fear of rejection, or I'd submit my portfolio to an advertising agency."

Lonnie was about to tease her sister and point out that fear of abandonment was fundamentally a fear of rejection, when she realized she was serious. Peach

hadn't just been trying to make Cheryl feel better;
she was genuinely insecure about her talent as an
artist. Lonnie wanted to talk to her more about it,
but there was no way she was breaking into a sister
heart-to-heart in front of Cheryl Mew. Maybe Cheryl
was an okay person, but she was still a stranger, and
Lonnie honestly didn't know what to make of her
mute, disciplelike reverence for Peach.

"Well, Professor, you'll be very happy to know
that I'm cured." Lonnie allowed herself to indulge
in a dramatic pause, and then finished, "Dominick's
coming to the party tonight." With that, she stood
up and headed toward the bathroom. "I'm taking a
shower now, so—"

"Freeze!" Peach commanded. She pounced on the
sofa enthusiastically and drew her knees up to her
chin. "I want details."

She gave her the abridged version—again, the
Cheryl factor—and when she was done, Peach
heaved a big sigh, like she'd never been so
relieved . . . or surprised. Really, had Lonnie been
that hopeless of a case?

Okay, okay . . .

"If you ask me 'what time is it' one more time—"
"*Peach.*"

"All right, all right." Peach opened her silver purse
to take out her watch. "Hmm, it's eight-o-nine, which
makes sense since it was two minutes ago when you
asked what time it was, and I believe my answer was
eight-o-seven."

"Okay, okay," Lonnie said hastily and looked out
the subway window. Of course she only saw black
since they were underground, but she was waiting
to see the green sign for their stop. She'd told Dominick she'd meet him in the lobby of the Easton Hotel
at eight o'clock. Now it was already ten minutes past

that time, and they were still on the T. By the time they got to the hotel, it would probably be eight-thirty, and it was all her fault.

While Peach had gotten dressed early, Lonnie had waited, figuring she'd grab one of her tea-length dresses, put on some lipstick, and be out the door. Who was she kidding? She hated the way half her dresses looked, the way her hair looked, the way her ears looked. In other words, she was having one of those self-critical I'm-Medusa mental breakdowns that later made her feel sick with shame. Of course, Peach felt the need to point out that she'd never stressed over her appearance for Terry.

Ultimately, Lonnie chose a form-fitting, red satin dress that was covered in elegant black lace netting. It was long sleeve and came just below the knee, and she finished off the outfit with glittery black heels. Fine, she'd admit it: she was trying to look sexy for Dominick on their first official night together as more than friends.

As they hurried to the entrance to the Easton, Lonnie was about to ask what time it was again, but stopped as soon as she saw Dominick through the glass. He was sitting on a marble bench in the lobby of the hotel, looking gorgeous in a dark suit and deep red silk tie. "There he is," Peach said. "Oh, Lord. You two are already a lookalike couple. This is too much."

Lonnie was vaguely aware of her sister saying something, but was significantly more preoccupied with the pit burning a whole through her stomach. She couldn't believe the effect Dominick had on her; she prayed it was remotely mutual. They walked through the revolving door, and her eyes locked with his. He stood quickly and smiled. "Hey, you. Hi, Peach."

"Dominick," Lonnie blurted, "we're so sorry we're late! Have you been waiting long?"

He looked at his watch. "Uh . . . about twenty minutes," he said, grinning as if it were just so cute that she'd been late. Maybe this hopeless, starry-eyed infatuation wasn't just her.

"It was my fault," Peach offered. "Sorry."

But Dominick didn't seem the least bit concerned about laying blame. "This is for you," he said, and handed Lonnie one purple tulip.

"Thank you. It's so pretty!" It really was, and she'd always found red roses clichéd.

"I hope you like tulips. I just think roses are sort of clichéd."

Kiss me. "It's perfect." *Want me.* Lonnie ignored her quickening pulse, looked over at her sister, and said, "Let's go. The sooner I get in there, the sooner I can get blamed for anything that doesn't go right. Well, 'right' according to Twit's master plan that I'm expected to mind read."

"Gee, when you put it like that . . ." Peach said, and the three of them headed for the ballroom.

As soon as they walked into the party, Matt made a beeline for Peach. Lonnie reintroduced him to Dominick, and the four of them made small talk for about ten minutes before B. J. came over. She was a little surprised that Matt was there already. She figured he'd show up later since he made it clear he had better things to do than socialize with Twit & Bell people. But, then again, the party was probably a great place to make outside connections, especially if you were a networker. Matt was.

"Well, kids," B. J. began jovially, "looks like Lonnie's shindig is a success so far. Then again, the night's young, and you never know who's gonna get drunk and shake things up a little." He balled his fists enthusiastically—this time on the word "shake." Lonnie wasn't sure if it was her imagination or if something was different about B. J. Usually, he came off as trying too hard but still relatively pleased with life. Tonight he seemed edgy, though, and his normally easy smile was almost manic. On the other hand, she could've been reading too much into his manner because of what'd happened in the library earlier.

"B. J., this is Dominick. He works downstairs at GraphNet," Lonnie said, introducing them. "Dominick, B. J." After they shook hands amicably, Dominick's hand settled on the small of Lonnie's back. She could feel the heat from his hand through her satin dress, and when he started lightly grazing his fingertips back and forth, it made concentrating on B. J.'s latest tale of magnificence more difficult than usual.

". . . Of course, now I feel like a total shit," B. J. was saying, "because I promised to be at three different parties on New Year's Eve. Two are on the Cape and one's in the North End." Lonnie nodded with as much empathy as she could muster, but New Year's Eve had never been a holiday she celebrated. In fact, the few years that she'd gone to New Year's parties she'd gotten depressed halfway through the night. It always seemed like people were forcing it, and as far as she was concerned, noisemakers and streamers didn't make up for the fact that another year had slipped by.

"What about you? What are you two up to for New Year's?"

You two? Lonnie felt like wringing B. J.'s pencil-thin neck. What if Dominick already had plans that didn't include her? By B. J. speaking about them as if they were a couple, he'd just steered the conversation in an awkward direction. Lonnie couldn't say "I don't know yet" because that implied she thought they were a couple, too. It was definitely too soon for that, and she didn't want to scare Dominick off. But she didn't want to say "nothing" in case he *was* free, and willing to make it a not-awful New Year's, after all.

"Actually, I'm not a big New Year's person," Dominick said conversationally. "Maybe I can persuade Lonnie to hang out with me. Just stay home and order a pizza that night, or something." He smiled down at her, and his good-natured grin nearly stole her breath. *Perfect answer.*

She decided to take control of the conversation before B. J. unwittingly stuck his foot in it again. "So, has anyone tried the food yet?" she asked, curious about how Meijing had managed with the catering on such short notice. Matt looked away from Peach for a minute to answer.

"Yeah, it's really good," he said. "I didn't know we were having Chinese. Of course, I had to explain to B. J. that fried rice isn't finger food."

"I told you, I was just looking for a fork," B. J. protested, embarrassed but only mildly defiant.

"Right," Matt smirked. "Ever hear of *chopsticks*?" he asked rhetorically. "They were sitting right there." He snickered, and turned back to Peach. "By the way, are you hungry? Do you want me to get you something to eat?"

Lonnie watched her sister hesitate; then she smiled and said, "Yeah, let's both go over." Peach and Matt headed toward the buffet table, leaving Lonnie with B. J. and Dominick. Three words came to mind: beat it, B. J.

Luckily, he didn't feel like staying anyway. "I should probably go mingle with the bigwigs for a while. Nice meeting you, Dom. See ya later, Lonnie." He turned and left—some buoyancy missing from his usual swagger.

Good, now it was just her and Dominick. Shit, now it was just her and Dominick! Maybe it was ridiculous, but she still found herself on edge around him. She had a feeling it was equal parts sexual tension and uncertainty. She turned to face him, and his hand slid off her back and dropped to his side.

"So . . . I hope you're having fun so far," she said, smiling brightly. "But if you thought B. J. was odd, wait till you meet my boss."

He laughed. "Oh, yeah. I'm actually going to meet the famous Twit. Do you want me to have a talk with him about lightening up on you?" he kidded.

She squinted her eyes. "Oh, please! Talk about disempowering. No thanks."

He grinned. "Okay, okay, but don't say I didn't offer."

"To be macho? Believe me, I *never* will." She grinned back and leaned closer.

His eyes changed from teasing to intense. Penetrating. Hot. He took her hand with his, and rubbed his thumb in a circle on her palm a few times before he asked in a low voice, "So what time does this party get out, again?"

"Oh, no. You *are* having a bad time," she said, and her green–honey-brown eyes looked up at him apologetically.

"No, no, it's not that. It's just . . . you. You're standing there driving me crazy in that dress." His eyes moved down her body, and he shook his head as if amazed. Lonnie knew he must be exaggerating, but still . . . a few more endorphins started swimming in her brain.

"You like it?" she asked innocently, and folded her hand over his. Of course, his hand was strong and warm and wonderful. Before he could answer, Beauregard Twit shuffled over and interrupted them.

"Lexie, glad you could make it," Twit began hurriedly, and Lonnie almost felt appreciated. "I may need someone to make sure water glasses get refilled." She avoided glancing up at Dominick because she knew if she did, they'd probably both crack up. "Also—think *carefully*," Twit said. "Did any confidential faxes come before you left the office today?"

She shook her head. "No. Sorry, Beauregard. Still nothing." Jeez, she knew Twit was waiting for a fax, but this bordered on obsession! Couldn't he just call the sender and remind him to fax it as soon as possible? What was so pressing, and so confidential, to make Twit this anxious?

"Beauregard, this is Dom—" she began, but he'd already strutted away like a fast-forwarded peacock.

"So . . . that was your boss?" Dominick asked, nodding slowly.

"Uh-huh."

"Friendly guy."

"He'd be lost without me, can't you tell?" she drawled sarcastically.

He laughed. "So would I, Lexie. So would I."

Lonnie laughed into his shoulder, which was partly an excuse to lean into him. As she turned her head, she noticed Delia swaying to the seasonal music in the far corner of the room. She was fairly easy to spot in her white, crushed velveteen minidress. She was talking to Lunther, and, *Jesus*, she was leaning in close. In fact, from where Lonnie stood, she could see Delia's arm draped over one of Lunther's shoulders, her body half pressed against his side and her mouth dangerously close to his ear. Lonnie pulled back so she could get a better view; she honestly couldn't believe how obviously Delia was coming on to Lunther. And at the company party!

Just then Lunther turned his head and looked directly at Lonnie. *Shoot!* She was caught gawking with abandon at him and Delia. Before Lonnie could break her eye contact with Lunther, she noticed something in his expression. Something contemplative . . . or agitated, she couldn't tell which. He looked as if seeing Lonnie had made him remember something.

Abruptly, he disentangled himself from Delia and started making his way over. . . . *What?* He was walking straight toward them with an intense look on his face. What on earth could he want with *her*? At work, they barely exchanged two words weekly.

"See that man coming toward us?" she muttered, turning back to Dominick. He angled his head to the side. "Don't look."

"No, then I don't see him."

"It's Twit's partner." Only Lunther didn't approach them, after all. Not right away. Lonnie turned her head to see that he'd been intercepted by Macey, and they were having what appeared to be a rather heated conversation. Unfortunately, she couldn't hear what they were saying.

It was only a matter of seconds before Macey stalked off. Lonnie reflexively whipped her head around to follow Macey's trail out of the ballroom. What was she upset about? *What did that creep say to her?* Then Lonnie glanced at Lunther, who was frozen in place, paused—as if considering whether or not he should approach her.

Her luck ran out, and he moved forward again.

"Hello there, Lonnie," he said.

"Hi," she replied brightly. She was surprised that he knew her first name since Twit was constantly changing it. "Oh, this is my friend, Dominick."

Dominick shook his hand. "Hi. How're you doing?"

"Hi. Well," Lunther said, hitching up his pants a little, "I trust you're having a good time tonight."

She nodded. "Yeah, a great time. What about you?" When in doubt, strain the limits of small talk.

She braced herself for a response instructing her not to pay him any never mind, but instead, he just nodded back and agreed. "It's a real great party." He appeared antsy, despite his light conversation— as if he wanted to say something but didn't know how to spit it out. But she did barely know the man;

maybe he always acted this way in public. "Soooo—" he started clumsily.

"There you are!" Macey exclaimed, approaching Lonnie quickly. She swept up beside them in a heartbeat, blocking Lunther's access to the group. *Where did she come from?*

"Hi, Macey," Lonnie said, with a *genuine* smile. "Are you having a good time?"

She smiled. "Everything is wonderful so far. You have obviously done an incredible job."

Her face flushed with pride. "Oh . . . thank you. Meijing's cooking takes a lot of the credit, I think. Oh, Macey, I want you to meet my friend Dominick." She felt strange calling Dominick her "friend," when he was more than that, but what could she say? *A friend whose cock I'd like to sample?* No, that would hardly be a viable alternative.

While Dominick and Macey exchanged pleasantries, Lunther fidgeted about where he stood. He shifted his leg weight several times, and wiped sweat from his pudgy upper lip. Macey didn't even glance in his direction. Finally, he did an about-face, and abruptly left.

"Will you excuse me?" Macey said suddenly. "I want to go thank Meijing for the terrific job she's done with the catering. Pardon me." She skirted away.

"Isn't Macey cool?" Lonnie said, turning back to her extremely fetching *friend*. "Don't you think she's beautiful?"

Dominick shrugged. "I don't know. I didn't really notice."

"Oh." She felt a pang of foolishness as she realized that she'd just made a point of directing her date's attention to another woman's desirability. Boy, she really was rusty.

He put his hand on his stomach. "Wanna get something to eat?"

"Sure," she agreed. They approached the buffet table, and Lonnie smiled hello to Bette Linsey who was explaining to another woman why au pairs were truly "divine inventions."

Lonnie had just begun surveying the long expanse of delicious-looking Chinese dishes when, all of a sudden, Delia—literally—*got in her face.*

Shoving her body right in front of Lonnie's, she blocked her access to the dim sum. Her dangling earrings were unencumbered by her hair, which was efficiently plastered into a half-teased upsweep. A gust of hard alcohol breath hit Lonnie's nose, and she tried to back away, but Delia just leaned in closer. Their faces were mere inches apart when Delia sneered with disgust.

"You know something?" she said seethingly. "You don't know a damn thing about nothing." *Seems reasonable.* "You don't have a *fucking* clue." Then she stomped off.

Lonnie's face scrunched in confusion. "What the hell—?"

Dominick shook his head, equally confused, and put his hand on the back of her neck. He massaged it lightly, grinned, and said, "I thought the people I worked with were weird."

She was about to agree and make a joke about it, but his fingers were working the back of her neck unbelievably. Was it possible to climax from a neck massage? She felt heat pulsing between her legs. She turned to look up at him.

Unconsciously, her lips parted more and her pupils dilated. He noticed.

For a moment, he had the same intensity in his own face. His fingers strummed beneath her hair, and an irrational part of her wished he would tighten them, pull her to him, and kiss her passionately right there. Instead, his hand kneaded her skin even more deeply, and she thought she'd start moaning if she didn't put a stop to this.

Luckily—sort of—he got himself in check. If they were going to take it slow, then they'd better not tear off their clothes and do it on the buffet table, no matter how logical that option seemed. His hand dropped, and they averted their gazes just long enough to get back to reality.

"So . . .," she said a little breathlessly, "hungry?" She meant the food.

He didn't. "God, yeah."

The rest of the night moved along briskly, but it still seemed too long to Lonnie. Her glittery heels were starting to hurt and her stockings were starting to chafe. She was glad Peach finally met the Twit & Bell staff she'd been hearing about for the past six months. Matt had turned on the charm most of the night, making his interest in Peach clear.

Lyn Tang had showed up at 9:30, and Beauregard had done nothing to conceal his joy. The minute she walked in, his mouth dropped into an awed O and he rudely abandoned the conversation he'd been having with Bette and Lonnie about Bette's new yacht. Without even excusing himself, Twit abruptly walked away, sidled up to Lyn Tang, and began what would become a long night of obsequious fawning. From what Lonnie could see, Lyn had been more than gracious, but hadn't given any indications about joining the firm.

Now Lonnie looked at the clock. 11:44 P.M. She was sitting alone at a table because Dominick had just excused himself to go to the bathroom. As she sat there, she watched people mingling and saying good-bye, and she couldn't help thinking that while the party was a success, the whole night had seemed *off*. More than once, Lonnie had spotted B. J. trying to talk to Bette. She always either coldly dismissed him, or just dodged him altogether. Earlier, Lonnie had tried to introduce Peach to Macey, but Macey had acted perceptibly distant and distracted. Suffice it to say, Peach hadn't been all that impressed.

Suddenly Lonnie felt a hot, enticing breath on her ear. "You want to get out of here any time soon?" *Hell, yes.* Dominick's voice was low and sexy, and practically impossible for her to resist at the moment. He was standing behind her chair, crouched down, and she leaned into him a little. She could smell Dominick's cologne; it was subtle, but it was still having an arousing effect on her.

"Mmm . . . that sounds great. But Peach looks like she's having fun. Let's wait a little longer." It looked like her little sister was charming Judge Stephens, his wife, and Matt across the room.

"Okay," he murmured, and lightly nuzzled her hair with his forehead.

Lonnie sighed dreamily and leaned in to him a little more. He groaned softly. "Lonnie, you're making me crazy. I know we're taking it slow, but how about one kiss? C'mon, one kiss. *Now.*" She opened her mouth to protest, but she couldn't. She was desperate to kiss him. Peach was still immersed in conversation so she figured it would be okay.

He took her hand and they hurried out of the ballroom and down the hall. "Where are we going?" she called after him, but he didn't answer. He just steered her around the corner to a room with an open archway. A gold-plated sign that read COATS was screwed to the adjacent wall. The second they entered the room, Dominick grabbed Lonnie's waist and pulled her to him. Their kiss started breathy and passionate, but within seconds, became white-hot and wet. Lonnie clung to Dominick's shoulders, as he backed them both into a rack of coats and against the wall for support. Except it didn't feel like the wall. . . .

It felt like a person.

Aah! Lonnie jumped forward, startled, her heart suddenly racing. Was someone there? Before she

could say anything, she heard a sweeping noise, and
then a loud thud. She and Dominick looked down
and saw Lunther Bell's head and torso sticking out
from under the coats. There was a smeared crimson
line running down his neck and over his Adam's
apple.

"Aah!" Lonnie screamed, and buried her face in
Dominick's shoulder, willing away the image of
Lunther lying on the floor with his eyes wide open.
"Omigod, Omigod . . .," she was muttering to no
one, and shaking. Dominick put both his arms
around her and held tightly.

"Holy shit," he muttered soberly.

"Is there any way he's not dead?" Lonnie mumbled into his shoulder. "You know . . . maybe he's
just . . . catatonic?" She was grasping at straws and
she knew it. She had no experience with corpses, and
even she could tell that Lunther was dead. His face
was stark pale, his eyes were wide and blank, and
his mouth hung open lifelessly. He couldn't have
been dead long since Lonnie had just seen him in the
ballroom . . . *Wait.* When was the last time she'd seen
him at the party? She couldn't remember.

"He's dead, baby," Dominick said softly. "We've
got to get someone. Come on." They started back
down the hall, but hotel security stopped them in
their tracks.

"Ma'am, what happened?" a security guard asked.
He was dressed in a dark blue suit, with a prominent
yellow badge on the lapel, and a mother-of-a-walkie-
talkie hanging on the front of his pants. "We heard
screams," he added, and motioned his head to the
other security guard, who was a foot behind him.

Lonnie was near frantic. None of it seemed real,
yet she'd never felt a more visceral fear or revulsion.
She thought she was going to throw up. She felt like
crying. She didn't even like Lunther, but it wasn't
that kind of crying. It was a shook-up, horrified, for-

whom-the-bell-tolls kind of crying. Tears burned the corners of her eyes, and vomit stayed clogged at the top of her throat.

"There's a man in the coatroom. He's . . . he's dead." The security men pushed past her and Dominick, and headed to the coatroom. Thank goodness she'd worn a black wool coat that night and not her beloved ice-blue one, because she was absolutely never going in that coatroom again, and planned *never* to retrieve what she'd left there.

Lonnie squeezed her eyes shut and tears started to fall. Silently, they streamed down her face, taking some of her black mascara with them, and sliding into the corners of her mouth. She swallowed, pressing the salty taste to the roof of her mouth, and shook her head. She couldn't believe it. Lunther Bell was dead.

Chapter Eleven

"Let's start from the beginning."

Lonnie managed a nod, and Detective Joe Montgomery flipped another page in his pad. She'd already told him twice exactly how she'd found Lunther's body. How, when, and why. The why was what she'd been dreading most. *What was I doing in the coatroom? Making out with my date. Hi, I'm twenty-seven.* She'd briefly toyed with a more explanatory approach. *Wink, wink. Nudge, nudge. Suffice it to say, Detective, I haven't been "getting any" for quite some time.* But ultimately, there had been no need. She'd flushed when she'd told him that she and Dominick had sneaked off, and he hadn't seemed too interested in that anyway. He was far more concerned with the details of Lunther's evening prior to discovering his body. And, unfortunately, she came up three-quarters empty on that subject.

After the security guards alerted the police, it had been a matter of minutes before the whirring blasts of sirens intruded upon the party. Everyone had bolted out of the ballroom to see what was going on. Lonnie had heard some talk in the lobby about a heart attack, but she remembered seeing blood on his neck, and with the way the police were questioning people, she wasn't so sure. It had taken almost an hour for the commotion to settle. Now, it appeared that most everyone had left. Lonnie and Dominick remained, each reiterating what happened to a separate cop, while Peach waited for them on a lobby sofa.

Lonnie couldn't help wondering exactly how the police had divvied up the interviews. The cop questioning Dominick was a small-framed rookie in uniform, with an oversize police hat that kept slipping down the side of his head and over his ears. Meanwhile, Lonnie was answering to a big, hulking plainclothes detective who was gruff, abrupt, and one helluva close talker. Her nerves were already frayed, so Joe Montgomery's guilty-until-proven-even-guiltier demeanor did nothing to help her state of mind.

"You've worked at Twit & Bell for what, six months?" he asked without looking up.

"Yeah, a little over six months, I guess."

"So you knew Mr. Bell pretty well, then?"

"No!"

Montgomery's head shot up at her strong reaction. Now he stared hard. She labored to gulp before qualifying, "Uh, what I mean is just . . . I mean, I barely even knew him. That's all."

His eyes continued to bore through her. Great, once the guy started looking, he overdid *that*, too.

"Twit and Bell's a pretty small firm, isn't it?"

Lonnie didn't need two master's degrees to figure out where this was going. "Yes, but . . . well, of course I *knew* Lunther. Technically. But I just meant that I . . . We hardly ever interacted, that's all."

"Uh-huh," he said, and wrote something else down on his pad. She tried to release a sigh without sounding guilty. This was ridiculous! Why was she getting so worked up? She hadn't done anything wrong, and certainly she had an alibi since she'd spent the whole night with Dominick. It wasn't as if Detective Montgomery had said anything accusatory, anyway. It was Lonnie. Her conscience was inherently guilty by default.

While Montgomery flipped back a few pages and scrunched his eyebrows, pondering something he undoubtedly didn't care to confide, Lonnie surveyed him. If she had to guess, she'd say he was in his early forties. His bulky stature indicated that he was one of those very developed guys who stayed intimidatingly strong no matter how old they got. Hard lines were etched along his mouth and around his eyes to give him a look that was somewhere between craggy and sexy. His hair couldn't decide if it was brown or gray, but his eyes were very clearly green.

"So let's see here. You didn't really know Bell, but you exchanged a little small talk earlier in the evening," he read from his pad. "Only for a few minutes."

"Right. Lunther left after Macey came over."

"Macey Green," Montgomery said.

"Mmm-hmm."

"Did Bell say where he was going when he left?"

"No. He didn't say anything, really. He just stood there for a second sort of awkwardly, and then he walked off." Montgomery nodded and jotted something down.

"And you and your boyfriend stayed there talking to Macey?"

"Yeah, well, no. I mean, she left, too. She went to talk to the caterer. They're friends."

"You saw her talking to the caterer?"

"Well, no, but I wasn't really looking—"

"Before Macey left, did she say anything to you about Bell? Were any words exchanged about him at all?"

"No, no. Nothing like that."

"Think back. Who did you see interacting with Bell over the course of the evening?"

She sighed. "Detective, it was a party. He could've interacted with most of the people there. I don't know."

"Let's try this again." His tone became stern, and she became a compliant eight-year-old. "What did you *see*?"

"Right, sorry," Lonnie said, nodding. "Well, I saw him with Delia Smucker early on."

"Secretary, right?" he asked without flipping back to check his notes.

"Administrative assistant, yes." Nothing like political correctness when you're talking to an impatient, overdeveloped grouch with handcuffs.

"Who else?"

"Um . . ." She searched her memory. "I saw him talk to Macey very briefly—"

"When was this?"

"Right before he came over to Dominick and me. Why? I mean, what does this have to do with what happened?"

He ignored the question. "What did Macey and Bell talk about?"

"I have no idea. They were fifteen feet away from me."

"Did they appear amicable?" he asked, grilling her with his eyes.

She pondered the question for a second. No. In truth, they'd appeared to be anything but amicable. They'd looked like they were arguing, but still . . . how much was she supposed to tell Montgomery? Was he fishing for something against Macey? She didn't want to go along with that.

But she didn't want to withhold information, either. Honestly, she doubted she even could with Montgomery imposing on her personal space and demanding concise, accurate answers. Talk about pressure. "No, I guess I wouldn't say they looked amicable," she managed. "But like I said, I couldn't hear anything, so—"

"Were they fighting? Is that what you're saying?"

Surveying the room helplessly, Lonnie just shrugged. "Detective, I really don't know. You should ask Macey. I'm sure she can explain it much better."

"Yeah, it's just too bad she was nowhere to be found when I showed up on the scene," he said mildly. But his nonchalance was unconvincing.

Oh, no, what have I done? She'd certainly never meant to say anything against Macey! Yet, somehow, she'd managed to implicate her.

"Detective, how did Lunther die exactly?" Lonnie probed.

He ignored her question again. Instead, he asked, "So you didn't see Bell in the ballroom the rest of the night?"

"Well, I didn't *not* see him there. I mean, I just didn't notice him one way or the other. I couldn't tell you *for sure* that he wasn't there." She folded her arms across her breasts to hug herself and ward off some of the chill. Now that she had no coat, she was shivering. Apparently Montgomery wasn't the chivalrous type; he looked quite content in his thick, warm coat, and made no move to offer it to her. Not that she would've taken it, or anything. Unless he absolutely *insisted*, of course, as any decent man would.

"What do you think about the people you work with? Or, for . . . whatever." Was this a trick question? She thought they were all head cases. Was she supposed to tell *him* that?

"Well . . . I like them, I guess. But I'm not close with anyone there, or anything." He arched a brow. She started backpedaling. "I don't have anything against them! Or, *anyone*. What I mean is, everyone at work seems really, *really* nice."

"Okay, okay, kid." Surprisingly, she thought she detected a hint of amusement in his voice.

"Detective?"

"Yeah."

"I heard people saying something about a heart attack before, when they were taking Lunther. . . ." Her voice momentarily trailed off, before she cleared her throat and continued. "I just mean . . . Well, there was blood. I remember. On Lunther's neck. Was he . . . stabbed?"

"Oh. No, no. Apparently he cut open the back of his neck on a nail that was jutting out of the closet wall," he replied, and closed the pad.

"So then, he did have a heart attack?"

"Apparent sudden cardiac failure. Yeah."

Now she was really confused. If Lunther suffered cardiac arrest, why were the police still here asking questions?

Montgomery kept his cop's eyes on Lonnie, and maintained his frustratingly inscrutable expression. "Is there anything else?" she asked, not wanting to appear uncooperative, even though she hoped like hell there was nothing else.

He paused and then said, "Yeah. Think back. Have you noticed anything out of the ordinary around the office over the last couple weeks? Anything at all?"

Lonnie searched her brain and, quite predictably, it went blank.

"Has anything happened?" he prodded. "Anything strange?"

She shook her head because she couldn't think of anything to tell him. Not about the office, anyway. "Well, this past weekend I got mugged. Almost got mugged, I should say. But that didn't have anything to do with work."

"Where were you?" he probed with interest.

"Borders, downtown. Like I said, it wasn't related."

"Did you report it?"

"No," she admitted, feeling appropriately foolish.

"Why the hell not?" he demanded in pissed-cop fashion. *Stupid, stupid.* Why did she even bring up the mugging? It wasn't relevant, and it would only make Montgomery think she was some clueless, lazy citizen who couldn't be bothered with pesky tasks like filing a report. But his imposing presence had made her ramble. Jeez, did he have to be such a close talker? She'd felt like she had no breathing room already; now he was leaning in even closer in annoyance.

"Well . . . I was going to, of course. . . ." Not exactly the truth. She'd pretty much forgotten all about it the moment Dominick's mouth covered hers. And when his tongue nearly grazed her tonsils, the mugger could've been a giant bug-human hybrid for all she cared. "I just . . ."

"Were you hurt?"

"No."

"Next time, you report it," he ordered gruffly. "You understand?"

"Yes, Detective. I will." She gave him a trying-too-hard smile, and the corner of his mouth twitched up, spoiling his tough-guy image. Lonnie was getting the strange feeling that he *enjoyed* rattling her.

"All right. Now let me just ask your sister a few questions, and you can be on your way."

"Okay," she said warily.

While Detective Montgomery talked to Peach, Lonnie made her way across the lobby. Dominick and the rookie were standing, and obviously not talking official business anymore. The cop's pad was closed and he was nodding profusely while Dominick explained something to him using hand gestures.

She came up beside them, and Dominick smiled

warmly, slipping his hand into hers. "Hey," he said, and leaned down to kiss her on the cheek. "Are you okay?" She nodded and felt him squeeze her hand comfortingly anyway. "I was just explaining to Chris here how to replace his motherboard." She knew computer-nerd talk when she heard it. Before she met Dominick, she never realized how adorable it could be.

"Chis Stopperton," the officer said, extending his hand to Lonnie.

"Hi," she replied, friendly in spite of the fact it was the middle of the night and she wanted nothing more than to shed her stockings and dumb heels. She'd caught a glimpse of her reflection earlier, and noticed that her black hair was combining nicely with her paled face and raccooned mascara, making her into a veritable goth chick. Coincidentally, that had been around the same time her mind had gone on autopilot. Now, she just wanted to slip under the covers and thank God for her life, over and over, until she fell asleep.

Then she had a thought. "Hey, Chris . . .," she began, and appreciated the open friendliness that awaited her question. Unlike Montgomery, this guy might actually give her some information. "What exactly happened tonight?" she asked. "I mean, at first I thought Lunther might have been stabbed or something, because of the blood . . . and then the police were questioning people. But, now . . . I mean, if it was a heart attack, then—"

"Stopperton!" Detective Montgomery shouted. "You ready to go?"

"Oh . . . yeah, okay," Chris replied.

"Kid, come on," Montgomery called to Lonnie. "I'll take you and your sister home." He turned to Officer Stopperton. "Chris, drop Mr. Carter off—"

"That's all right," Dominick said. "I'd rather take a cab. It's no problem."

Montgomery nodded and motioned to Officer Stopperton, who turned and bid his good-byes to Lonnie and Dominick.

"What time is it?" Lonnie asked.

"Uh . . . one forty-six," Dominick replied, and gently brushed a lock of hair away from her face. "Tired?" She just nodded. There was a faraway quality about her right now that he didn't exactly know how to reach. He hadn't realized how sensitive Lonnie was until they'd found her boss's body and he'd held her for a long time while she cried. Now she was collected—as if she'd come to terms with the shock of what happened—but he could tell she was still affected. He just wished there was something he could do to make her feel better. "Do you want company tonight?" he asked softly, his hand still lingering over her face and down her neck.

"No, it's okay. I just want to go home with Peach and try to forget what happened."

"Okay," he agreed, a little disappointed.

After they said good-bye, Lonnie hooked her arm in her little sister's. "Let's get outta here." Peach sighed, sounding as exhausted and drained as she looked. They headed outside and into the police cruiser that was driving them home.

As tired as she was, Lonnie had almost unbearable trouble sleeping that night. She tossed restlessly, her body in anxious, tense knots. And when she finally did drift to sleep, she had haunting dreams about pain and blackness and death. Thank God she and Peach were spending the next two nights at their parents' town house. Christmas would be the perfect excuse for Lonnie to hide away from the world . . . and to forget the way Lunther Bell's corpse had looked lying at her feet.

Chapter Twelve

Peach and Lonnie finished Christmas Eve dinner and sprawled themselves out in their parents' cozy family room. There were two thick, cushy sofas, and each had claimed one. Margot crocheted peacefully in a suede recliner, and Jack read E. L. Doctorow in his Barcalounger. Peach had promised not to tell their mom about Dominick. Even if it was a ridiculous superstition, Lonnie didn't want to jinx the relationship by talking about it too confidently, too soon. The last thing she needed was to go on effusively about the new guy in her life, and then get blown off and have to explain to her mother—who'd undoubtedly use the incident to springboard one of her "this is why you need to join MENSA and find a nice engineer" pep talks. No thanks.

"Peach, I circled some Sunday want ads for you, honey," Margot said. "I left them on the kitchen counter, so don't forget to look at them."

"How come? My job's okay," she said serenely, while she strung turquoise beads on twine.

"I know it's 'okay,' but I think you should start looking for something that uses more of your special skills. You don't want to be someone's personal assistant forever."

"Forever? It's only been a few months. Anyway, I'm not ready to try something else yet. Not when I'm making such progress with Cheryl." Peach tossed her beaded twine to the side and brought both hands behind her head to prop herself up.

Margot nodded approvingly. "I know, honey, you're trying to help your new friend, but still, I think—"

"What progress have you made?" Lonnie asked curiously.

Peach answered, "Oh, little things, like now Cheryl can go to crowded restaurants without freaking out. And I got her to be assertive with a saleslady at Filene's yesterday."

"Well that's nice," Margot said. "How about becoming a consultant?"

"But I don't know anything about consulting," Peach protested.

"They'd train you."

"What would I consult about?"

"They'd teach you that."

"Then, how is that using my special skills?"

"What about your art?" Lonnie asked. "Not to sound like Mom or anything, but you should really do something with it. You're so talented."

"Oh, didn't I tell you? Last night, Judge Stephens's wife told me about an art contest her company's sponsoring. The first prize is five thousand dollars." Margot shot forward, and Peach finished with, "I'm entering it."

"What do you have to do?" Lonnie asked.

"Apparently they're looking for a new logo. Something really cutting edge for the company to reinvent itself, and minimalist is out. I have to come up with a design and submit it. Whoever's design gets chosen wins five thousand dollars."

"Omigod," Lonnie said excitedly. "That sounds great!"

"Mmm-hmm, that sounds good, honey, but you'd better get started," Margot advised. "Have you come up with any ideas yet?"

"Mom, the party was just last night!"

"Okay, okay." Margot held up her hands defensively. "Don't kill the messenger." Peach and Lonnie rolled their eyes at the same time.

"Why is the prize so big?" Jack asked suspiciously. "Five thousand for a *design*? Peach, how much do you really know about these people?"

"Dad . . .," she whined.

"Now, wait a second. This could be important," he warned sternly, pointing his finger at no one in particular. "Whatever you do, just do not give them personal information about yourself. Don't tell them your bank account number—"

"*Dad*," Lonnie broke in, "please, she's not an idiot."

"Jack, read your book. I'll deal with this," Margot chided, and Jack snorted in discontent.

"Just so you know," Peach explained, "the prize is big because whatever logo the firm chooses, they're gonna get all rights to it and trademark it for all their products. The five thousand is their way to give an artist a big enough chunk that she can't later claim she's owed anything."

"Mmm-hmm, the contest sounds great," Margot encouraged. "Still, it's only a one-shot thing so it won't hurt to look through those want ads I circled." Peach put a throw pillow over her face to keep from screaming. Margot didn't notice and crocheted merrily.

"Well, I just have to tell you, Lonnie, honey," Margot said as she wielded her hook, "I'm a little surprised that Terry didn't make plans to be with you on Christmas." *My turn*, Lonnie thought. It was hardly a secret that Margot didn't envision Terry as her son-in-law—especially with the bevy of oh-so-slick comments she made to drive that point home daily. What she failed to realize, of course, was that Lonnie was now 100 percent sure that a future with Terry was the last thing she'd want. She didn't need any convincing; she wanted Dominick.

"Don't get me wrong," Margot continued. "Terry's a nice boy and everything, but . . ." She stopped crocheting, looked from Lonnie, who was curled on her side, to Peach, who was lying flat on her back. "I just never want my girls to settle. You are my jewels. My *jewels*. And you deserve someone worthy of you."

Like Dominick, Lonnie thought, but held her tongue.

"Someone kind and smart and dependable."

Like Dominick? Lonnie thought so, but only time would tell. The last time they'd spoken was right before he left the hotel the night before. He was going to Connecticut to see his family for Christmas, and he wasn't coming back to Boston until Monday. Lonnie had given him her cell phone number and hoped he would use it at some point.

"In fact," Margot was saying, "now, Lonnie, don't say no"—*Uh-oh*—"but, I want you to meet someone."

"Mom, *please.*" Lonnie pressed her face to the couch cushion. "How come you're never trying to set Peach up?" Unfortunately, her indignation was diluted by giggling when she heard Peach exclaim, "Hey!"

"Because Peach is only twenty-two, and apparently she just met a nice young man at your law firm. You're the one I'm worried about, Lonnie. You're too picky; you close everyone off without giving them a chance." The "you're-too-picky" speech. Lonnie knew it pretty much by heart so she didn't feel that guilty about barely listening. "You think I would've gone for your father if I'd been as picky as you?"

Jack just grunted and turned a page in his book.

Margot went on as if Jack weren't there. "Maybe he wasn't exactly Big Man on Campus, but he was reliable. When he said he'd call, *he called*. And he's always been there for me. That's what's important."

Lonnie never disputed that, but her mother seemed to think there was a fleet of nice, reliable men at her feet—whom she was mercilessly crushing with stiletto heels. *Please*. She almost never met anyone, much less had a selection to choose from. Okay, so she never particularly tried to meet anyone, but Margot didn't know that.

"Mom, who could you possibly know who I would have any prayer of finding appealing?" Lonnie asked.

"Now, what's that supposed to mean?"

"No, I just mean—"

"Let me tell you, I could set you up with a very nice young man who'd treat you well. But you never have an open mind about anyone—"

"Uh-oh," Peach injected, "that doesn't sound good."

"Who, Mom?"

"Well . . . ," Margot began carefully, "what about . . . Thomas Ellabee?"

"What?" Peach shot up into a sitting position, while Lonnie rolled onto her stomach and groaned in disgust.

Margot's eyebrows rose. "What's wrong with Thomas Ellabee? He's an engineer. Not to mention, *he* still goes to church every Sunday, which is more than I can say for you two."

"Yeah, too bad he also has a frosted, feathered bouffant," Peach countered, and Lonnie laughed into the cushion.

"Oh, Peach, what—? A bouffant? What on earth are you talking about?" Margot asked, annoyed. "Thomas has a nice, thick head of blond hair. Many men would kill for that head of hair. Why do you have to always butt in when I'm trying to help her?"

"Mom, I'm sorry," Peach persisted. "But I refuse to let my sister go out with a guy who looks like he has his hair 'set' at the beauty parlor." She made quotation marks with her fingers, and Jack audibly cleared his throat in irritation with the whole conversation.

Margot huffily shoved her crocheting aside. "This is exactly what I'm talking about! Your sister's too picky—"

"Hey, I didn't say anything!" Lonnie cried.

"—and you're not helping matters, Peach. There's nothing wrong with Thomas Ellabee. In fact, he's one of the most courteous and *successful* young men in our parish."

"I know, I know. And he says 'horse pucky' instead of 'bullshit.' He's still not in her league. Besides, I have an automatic distrust for anyone whose default expression is a contented smile. It's *weird*."

Lonnie rolled back onto her side to face them. "Would you two mind not talking about me like I'm not here? I know that works with Dad, but—" Jack heaved a great, martyred sigh, and turned the next page with all his might. "Look," Lonnie went on, half giggling, "I'm not interested in Thomas Ellabee. And, no, it is not because I'm too picky. And it's *not* because of Terry. If you want to know the truth, Mom, I'm glad Terry isn't spending Christmas with me. I really don't like him all that much anymore."

"Really?" Margot's eyes lit up, and Lonnie silenced her before she could push the issue.

"Leave my love life to me, okay?"

"But—"

"I'm with Lonnie," Peach piped in.

"Oh, mind your own business," Margot chided.

"My sister *is* my business."

"Enough," Lonnie said. "Now, please, Mom. I love you, but back off."

Margot shook her head helplessly, and picked up her half-crocheted scarf to resume stitching. "All right, I'll butt out. I just love my girls too much, that's the problem. But that's it; I'm not going to say another word." *Yeah, right.*

Peach closed her eyes dreamily, Lonnie rolled to her other side, and Margot pushed her recliner a little farther back, as a peaceful silence fell on the room. Until Jack's voice surprised everyone. "Finally! I thought that conversation would never end!"

Lonnie and Peach both started to laugh. Soon Margot was laughing, too, and Jack was trying not to . . . and for that moment, in their little family room, everything was okay.

On Christmas Day, Margot and Jack Kelley's Brookline town house was filled with relatives. They wove in and out of rooms, mingling, taking pictures, and promising to stay in better touch from this point forward. Lonnie tried not to spend an excessive amount of time in the dining room, where Margot and Jack had laid out an elaborate display of food, but it was difficult. Jack had cooked prime rib and vegetables, while Margot had made penne alfredo, her famous stuffed mushrooms, and chocolate cream pie. Plus, half of the relatives brought pastries. Was this some kind of test of Lonnie's willpower? Because if it was, she might have to live with a little failure.

"Lonnie!" Aunt Christy's voice sang through the archway to the dining room, where Lonnie had just been eyeing the food covetously.

"Hi, Aunt Christy!" Lonnie greeted her sixty-year-old, favorite aunt with a tight hug. Christy was Margot's oldest sister, and the most cheerful person Lonnie had ever met. She was also soft, round, and she usually wore cashmere, which made her the cuddliest, too. "Merry Christmas. How have you been?"

"Just perfect, baby doll," Christy answered brightly. "How about you?" She pulled back and scanned Lonnie's face with concern. "Your mother told me about that man from your office who died the other night. How are you holding up? Is it true he just had a heart attack right there at the party?"

Lonnie sighed inwardly, feeling like an asshole. Here she'd been contemplating a prime-rib–and-cannoli sandwich, and she hadn't given one thought to Lunther. To the fact that his life had been snuffed out. Irrevocably. She knew it wasn't completely incomprehensible. He was an overweight, middle-aged man, and—from her memory of happy hour—a heavy smoker. A heart attack actually made sense. But that still didn't make it feel any less bizarre to think that this had happened to someone she used to pass in the hall at work every day.

She sucked in a breath and told Christy what happened at the party—how no one had actually witnessed Lunther's heart attack, and how she'd found the body.

"But what on earth was he doing in the coat closet?" Christy asked, her light green eyes wide with feeling.

"I don't know," Lonnie replied, shaking her head. "That's the one part I don't get, because he was *behind* all the coats. . . . I still can't figure it out. The police were asking all sorts of questions, but then they confirmed that he'd had a heart attack. So, basically, I'm confused."

Just then, Margot bustled into the dining room carrying a plate of cranberry bread. "Hi, you two," she said cheerily. "Do you need anything while I'm getting stuff from the kitchen?"

"Margot, you didn't tell me how beautiful Lonnie's

gotten! She looks terrific," Christy exclaimed, and
Lonnie blushed at the over-the-top compliment.

Margot set down the bread, absently wiped her
hands on a dish towel, and said, "Yes, I know. Lonnie has a very pretty face." *Implication: everything but
her face sucks. Thanks, Mom,* Lonnie thought, annoyed.
Within minutes, six more relatives had come into the
dining room, and they were all talking about what'd
happened to Lunther. They couldn't believe Lonnie
and Peach had to make official statements to the
police.

"Were you arrested?" challenged annoying, prepu-
bescent cousin Joey. "Did you have to spend the
night in jail?"

Peach curved her mouth into a what-the-fuck? expression, while Lonnie answered in a consciously
even tone. "No, Joey, my boss had a heart attack. No
one was—"

"Did they take your fingerprints?"

"No, it wasn't—"

"Mug shots?"

"No, no—"

"Then what's your *point*?" The thirteen-year-old
rode out of the dining room on his scooter, even
though Margot had asked him earlier not to ride it
in the house, and Lonnie mentally noted the pitfalls
of the rhythm method.

"Peach, you should eat more. You're too skinny!"
Aunt Kim squealed.

Margot nodded. "Yeah, have more to eat, honey."
And she cut Peach a large piece of chocolate cream
pie. This was only minutes after she'd interrupted
the discussion about Lunther to try to force a plate of
boiled turnips on Lonnie, claiming it had "negative
calories." Lonnie's fists clenched uncontrollably. *I've
had enough! Even if it is petty!*

She pondered how she could most efficiently escape the dining room, go into the bathroom, lock

the door, and repeat "Serenity now; serenity now."
Believe it or not, that really worked . . . most of the
time. But before she could escape, Aunt Kim spoke
again. "And, Lonnie, your hair is"—she reached her
hand out to touch a few strands—"gorgeous." She
sighed. "Glossy black hair. You get that from our
mom." Lonnie's heart clutched a little at the thought;
Grandma Deborah had died two years ago, but she
was still very much with the family.

"Really?" Margot said to Kim. "I've been trying to
get Lonnie to lighten it. Just a little, you know, go
for a more all-American look." *A little!* Margot had
flat-out suggested on more than one occasion that
she dye her hair ash blond. Although, as soon as
Lonnie had threatened to go traffic-cone orange, the
subject had been mysteriously dropped. *Damn it all!
Why can't my mother just accept me the way I am? Why
is it never good enough?*

Luckily, at that moment Uncle Nicholas barreled
in and announced he was taking pictures of the family in front of the Christmas tree and he needed them
to come into the living room for a dorky, embarrassing group shot. Well, those weren't his *exact*
words. As everyone shuffled out of the dining room,
Lonnie used the exodus as the distraction she needed
to sneak upstairs and hide. She turned on her heel
and went the long way around through the kitchen.
Peach followed her.

"Hey, where are you going? Don't you want to
be immortalized by yet another traumatizing family
photo session?" She jogged up to Lonnie until she
was next to her. Lonnie turned her head to look at
her, and there was no mistaking the glare in her
green-honey eyes. "What's wrong?" Peach asked.

"Mom. That's what's wrong!" She was beyond irritated, even though she truly didn't want to be. "Did
you hear that crack about my hair?"

"Sure, but it's just her usual. She gets on me about

my hair because it's not one uniform color," Peach said. She shrugged. "It's not like she knows what looks good."

Lonnie's sigh came out more like a growl, and she brought her hands up to her forehead. "It's not just that. It's everything . . . It's . . . it's that 'Lonnie's got a pretty *face*' crap—"

"You do have a pretty face," Peach said calmly.

"Whatever—that's not what she's getting at. Don't you hear the way she emphasizes *face*? She's just trying to make me feel bad about my weight. For like the millionth time."

"You're reading too much into it."

Lonnie felt like she was going to explode. She wasn't sure where all this rage had come from, but Peach's comment just increased her blood-boiling frustration tenfold. She stopped on the top step and looked squarely at her little sister. "Fine, I'm reading too much into it. That's why your stocking was filled with Twizzlers and chocolate jingle bells and mine was filled with single-serving packets of sugar-free oatmeal. Now, if you'll excuse me, I want to be alone!" She stormed into the bathroom and shut the door—careful not to slam it, though, because of the guests downstairs. (She wasn't exactly an expert on this rage thing.)

She waited until she heard Peach go back down to the party before she started chanting into the mirror: "Serenity now; serenity now . . ."

Lonnie's mood picked up after the hordes of relatives had cleared out and she was comfortable in her hearts-and-stars pajama pants and NYU sweatshirt, sitting in front of the flickering Christmas tree, and her cell phone had just rung. It was Dominick.

"So, how's it going with your family?" she asked him, moving a little closer to the fireplace to feel heat off the still-burning embers.

"Uh . . . pretty good. Unless you consider five masses in two days excessive." He started telling her about how his born-again brother David added myriad religious twists to the Carters' Christmas—which had always leaned more toward an all-American agnostics-giving-gifts kind of tradition. Lonnie laughed, amused and giddy with liking him. Then she gave him the abridged version of her Christmas. Leaving out the part where her mother had made her feel like Elvira the Heifer. And the part where she'd started crying a little thinking about Grandma Deborah, but it was probably because she'd had too much wine.

"It's snowing here," she said, unconsciously hugging her legs to her chest and resting her cheek against her knees.

"Yeah? You should go outside and make a snowman," he teased. "Or, snow*person*."

"Snow*diva*, " Lonnie corrected, smiling to herself. God, she wished he were there to hug.

Dominick's tone turned more serious when he asked, "So, how are you doin'?"

Lonnie sighed. "Okay. I'm still having trouble believing it all really happened." They talked about Lunther's death only for another minute or two because there didn't seem to be much to say that wouldn't be obvious and pointless.

"Oh, shit! I just realized," he said. I'm using up all your long distance minutes."

"Don't worry about it." She wasn't. She was having too good a time talking to him, hearing his low, sexy voice, picturing him on the other end. . . .

"I'll let you go anyway," he said.

"Okay."

"I'll see you Monday. Merry Christmas."

"You, too. Bye, Dominick."

"Bye . . . Miss you." *Click.*

What? He missed her? Well, hell, she missed him,

too, but . . . wasn't it too soon to be saying it? Was this a bad sign? Who was it who'd told her that when guys fall *in* fast, they also fall *out* fast? Oh, wait, it was B. J.; he'd been hovering at her desk one morning, offering unsolicited observations on the sexes. Well, considering the source, at least she could disregard that warning immediately. Still . . .

She had to be careful. She wasn't going to pull away from Dominick like she'd done before, since he didn't seem to be a big fan of that approach. And more importantly, it wasn't any fun for her. But she'd have to keep her guard up. In her own mind. He'd never have to know how skeptical she was about the relationship. He'd never have to know that she was mentally preparing herself for it not to last. And with any luck, she'd never get her heart broken again.

Chapter Thirteen

Lunther's wake was on Thursday, the day after Christmas, and in the proverbial spirit of the season, Lonnie was trying not to show just how desperate she was to leave. There had been a brief, closed-casket service that morning, followed by a lunch at Lunther's home. Honestly? It was depressing, awkward, and morbid.

His older brother, as his only next of kin, had organized everything, since Lunther had lived alone since his divorce several years ago. His house was a large, six-bedroom colonial in Cambridge. Lonnie had borrowed her father's car to make the drive through the snow, and now, after having been at the wake for nearly an hour, desperately wanted to go home and not see anyone from Twit & Bell again until the office reopened on Monday.

She thought she'd make the rounds and be sure to say good-bye to all her coworkers. First, she approached Delia, who was sitting alone on the window seat in the far corner of the room. Lonnie figured she should get her over with first since she promised to be the most unpleasant. Because of the thick carpet, Lonnie's boot heels were soundless as they traipsed over to the window, and she wasn't sure if the element of surprise would be good or bad with Delia.

"Delia?" Lonnie said softly, and watched a matted broom of white-blond hair whip around as Delia turned to face her. Her expression conveyed something less than elation.

"Yeah," she demanded. Well, so far she wasn't *as* hostile as she'd been the last time she'd seen her—which had been at the holiday party.

"I'm going to get going," Lonnie explained, knowing Delia didn't give a rat's ass. "So I just want to tell you again that I'm really sorry. I know you worked with Lunther for a long time—"

" 'Kay." With that, Delia turned back around and resumed her staring out the window. It took a second or two for it to sink in that the conversation had really been so awkwardly terminated. Well, awkwardly for Lonnie. In general, Delia seemed oblivious to awkwardness. Otherwise she wouldn't act the way she did half the time. Regardless, she definitely seemed far too bitter right now to be concerned with the temp's condolences.

Mentally shrugging, Lonnie turned and walked away. Oh well, she tried.

Next, she made her way over to Matt and B. J., who were hovering around the hors d'oeuvres. They both looked stoic and unemotional. Lonnie knew, however, that a lot of men handled shock that way. And grief. And love. And life, in general.

"Hey, guys," she said.

"Hey," Matt said coolly. Schmoozer mode was on standby.

"Hi," B. J. said with a toned-down version of his usual friendliness, and he piled a few more Southwestern egg rolls onto his plate. "Jesus, I can't even believe I'm here right now, you know? I can't even believe this happened to Lunther." He shook his head, as if disgusted with fate.

"Yeah," Matt said. "Bell was a great guy." *Since when?* Matt had never expressed a positive opinion about anyone at Twit & Bell. But Lonnie figured that's what death could do. After exchanging a few more trite words, she said good-bye to them and looked for Bette.

She found her by the fire, carefully pressing a monogrammed handkerchief to the corners of her eyes. Lonnie expressed quick condolences to Bette, who was polite and gracious—much appreciated. If Macey were there, Lonnie would've said good-bye to her, too. But Macey wasn't there, and Lonnie couldn't help feeling she was rather conspicuous in her absence. After all, Twit & Bell was not a very large firm.

Now where was Twit-head?

Lonnie circled the living room and foyer, but still couldn't find Beauregard. Then she heard—"*Beauregard.*" It was Lunther's brother, Henry. Lonnie turned around and found Twit, appearing uncharacteristically sheepish. "Don't play games with me," Henry demanded fiercely. "I want to know what you were doing in Lunther's study."

After a nervous chuckle, Beauregard darted his eyes around and said, "Henry, please, lower your voice." He *heh heh hehed* again. "I told you, I got lost on my way to the bathroom." Then he slapped Henry Bell lightly on the shoulder. "My deepest apologies about that, Henry. It was an honest mistake." He turned to go and saw Lonnie standing there watching.

"Beauregard," she started, "I just wanted to say good-bye—"

"Oh, Leah. Glad to see you. It was good of you to come." The kind words put her off guard. "So sad . . . ," he went on, then dropped his head dramatically and covered his eyes with his palm. His shoulders heaved lightly in what Lonnie could only assume were restrained sobs. Yet when he looked up at her again, his eyes looked dry and clear to her. But what did she know? Maybe his tears were all cried out. It was time to leave.

Lonnie grabbed her ice-blue coat from the front-hall closet and slid it on. She was hastily pulling her hair out of the collar when she spotted a familiar face. It was one of those sudden jolts of familiarity; she had no idea how she knew the man she was looking at, but she *had* seen him before. That much she knew.

Why was he so familiar? She was looking at a clean-cut man standing by the foot of the stairs, talking to an older woman Lonnie didn't recognize. Damn her selective memory! How did she know him? How . . . how . . . *holy shit* !

It was the mugger!

That couldn't be, but she knew it was. Once she placed his face, there was no doubt in her mind. He was the man who tried to snatch her purse outside of Borders the week before—the one who punched Dominick and fled. But what was he doing at Lunther Bell's wake? Could it possibly be a coincidence? She had trouble believing that.

Looking back, the mugging *had* been strange. The man had zeroed in on her bag, even though she was hardly an easy mark with the bag slung across her body and held closely at her side. Yet, he'd been so relentless, so determined to get the bag. And now, if he also knew Lunther . . . Let's just say, Lonnie didn't believe in coincidence very much. Still, she couldn't imagine how it all fit together.

Her curiosity should've mobilized her into action, but she was too shocked to do anything but stand there, frozen, staring at the mugger. He was leaning casually against the railing while he spoke to the older woman. His thin build gave him a deceptive air of harmlessness. He must have just arrived because

Lonnie'd been at the wake for an hour already, and hadn't seen him.

She swallowed hard and felt more than a flutter of fear in her chest. She momentarily considered turning and leaving before the mugger saw her—just in case he was a psycho with a ruthless vendetta against her. But even she knew that wasn't the most reasonable scenario. There had to be a logical explanation for what happened at Borders, and the fact that the mugger knew Lunther. Now if she could just stop deliberating, with her mouth going dry from nervousness, and her heart racing from fear, and confront him.

When Lonnie saw him go up the stairs, she finally pushed her anxiety aside and followed him. She crossed the foyer and climbed the carpeted steps. She felt comforted in the knowledge that there was a house full of guests downstairs.

She was about fifteen feet behind him when she glimpsed him turning the corner at the end of the hall. Treading faster so she wouldn't lose him, she spotted him going into the bathroom as a woman came out.

Lonnie decided to do whatever she was going to do before she lost her nerve. She marched over to the bathroom door and knocked hard. When he responded, "Yeah, just a minute," his voice was mild and even—emboldening her more than a surly one would have—so she knocked again. Much harder. Hurting her knuckles, but she didn't mind.

"Yeah, okay, okay!" he called, his impatience blatant but not deterrent. To be honest, she sort of liked pounding on the door; in a totally inappropriate way, it was a stress releaser. So she kept knocking until he swung the door open, exclaiming, "*Jesus Christ, what the hell*—"

He stopped as soon as he saw her face, and she said, "Hi, remember me?" She hadn't planned that corny opener, but so be it. Right now she had to get to the bottom of this. It was all too weird; she had to know if that mugging was a deliberate, calculated attack.

He sighed and dropped his chin to his chest. "Ah, crap." He shook his head, as if he couldn't believe his rotten luck. What about her rotten luck that day at Borders? She'd been in the middle of a perfectly lovely day with Dominick when he had burst in and tried to steal her bag. *And he is going to answer for it right now.*

This wasn't like her; she really wasn't the confrontational type. But, she'd never been mugged before, either.

"Look," he said, and held his hands up to keep her calm, "I'm sorry about that, okay? It was just . . . It was a misunderstanding."

She narrowed her eyes, half confused, half suspicious. "What do you mean? You assaulted me!"

"Uh . . ." He looked around, as if the answers he needed could be found in the sink or on the towel rack.

"You deliberately tried to grab my bag, right?"

"I know. Look—"

"No, I mean, it wasn't a random mugging, was it?" Lonnie demanded. "It was deliberate?"

"Yeah, like I said, I'm sorry about that."

"Well, did you have me confused with somebody else?"

"No."

"But," she persisted, less angry now but more confused, "If you meant to grab *my* bag, how could that be a misunderstanding?"

"Uh."

Does he think that qualifies as a complete thought?

He looked antsy and agitated, but Lonnie didn't feel the least bit afraid. It seemed the more tenacious she was with him, the more he retracted. Peach had once told her that confrontations almost always came down to who blinks first, and now Lonnie could see what she meant. Peach claimed that all that mattered was attitude, because ultimately everyone was profoundly insecure inside, and "hostile projections of ego" were little more than bluffs.

"Well, maybe misunderstanding was the wrong word," he finally conceded.

Lonnie shut her eyes in annoyance and spoke sternly. "Let's go about this a different way. I'll ask you a couple questions, and you'll answer them. Otherwise, I'll make a scene downstairs. Trust me; you don't want that." He sighed and dropped his head back, looking to the ceiling for sympathy. "And, I can be *very* dramatic," she lied.

"I said I was sorry!" The mugger was definitely testy by this point. "It's not like I even got the damn bag! What's the big deal?"

Lonnie ignored his tirade, unwilling to let him turn the tables; she didn't want to lose control of the confrontation now. "First of all, what are you doing here? How did you know Lunther?"

Apparently he figured out it would be easier just to pacify her and answer her questions. "He's my stepuncle," he said. "His brother Henry is married to my mother." Perhaps that was the older woman he'd been talking to at the foot of the stairs.

"Did he have anything to do with what happened at Borders?" Lonnie asked.

"Yeah . . . Listen, I'm sorry if I scared you that day." His voice softened a little, but Lonnie wouldn't let herself get sucked in by kind words. "And I'm sorry I punched your boyfriend, or whoever." He put his hands in his pant pockets and went on. "It was stupid—I mean, I shouldn't have agreed to do it. But Uncle Lunth offered me two hundred bucks and—"

"He paid you two hundred dollars to mug me?" She couldn't imagine why Lunther would have wanted to attack her; she thought he'd barely noticed her around the office.

"I was just supposed to grab your bag," he said defensively, as if that was worlds apart from mugging. "All he wanted was the bag."

"But why? Why me?"

He shrugged. "All I know was that he was pretty hot to get whatever you had in that bag. He said it wouldn't be a big deal—just follow you, wait for an opportunity, and then snatch it. He told me he'd make sure you got it back somehow, and with all your money and credit cards, too." He sighed and added, "I shouldn't have agreed, but I needed that two hundred, and I figured it would be easy. How the hell did I know you'd clutch that thing to your side all the time? And then stay in Borders for *hours*?" The mugger's softened tone was now put out, and Lonnie mentally congratulated herself for not buying the remorse he'd offered a minute ago.

"Believe me," he continued, "when I came back and told him I didn't get it, he was pissed. He said I'd messed up something critical to the security of his company. And then he called me a fuckup." Lonnie resisted the urge to comment. "So that's our warm little family, and that's the whole story. It's all I know. *Really.* " He'd given her more information than he had to; Lonnie figured she better quit while she was ahead.

"Fine," she said, and moved aside so she was no longer blocking the door. The mugger sighed with relief, and brushed past her. He only got a few steps down the corridor, before he turned around. "Listen," he called to her, "you're not going to make that scene now, are you? This is, like, over. Right?"

She nodded . . . in spite of the nagging feeling that it was far from over.

Sunday night, Lonnie lay in bed mentally preparing for work the following day. She'd just gotten off the phone with Dominick, who was still in Connecticut but planned to return the next morning. She could barely wait that long to see him. And talk to him face-to-face. And kiss him senseless, if possible. The idea alone sent shivers through her body.

Her smile faded only when she started thinking about Twit & Bell. She wondered if her coworkers would act differently after Lunther's death. Would they just carry on as usual? Or, would there be a distinct somberness throughout the office?

Over the weekend, Lonnie had thought about what Lunther's stepnephew told her. It was still hard to believe that she had been the target of some nefarious corporate plot. She'd talked it over with Peach, and they'd come to the consensus that Lunther could have been after only one thing. Only one thing made sense.

Macey's spiral notebook.

The day he'd been looming in Macey's doorway, he must have heard Lonnie say she would put the notebook in her bag. The rest of that week, Lonnie kept the bag locked in her desk, so Lunther wouldn't have had access to it. Of course, he also would have had no reason to think she'd keep the notebook in her bag over the weekend—or even use that bag when his stepnephew followed her on Saturday. Perhaps that proved just how desperate he'd been.

But, *why*?

She'd flipped through the notebook to see what she was missing, but all that Macey had written in it were some hypothetical case scenarios, and the citations listed next to them that she'd asked Lonnie to look up. Was Lunther after those citations, too? Or did the hypothetical case scenarios somehow tie into him? For all she knew, maybe he'd just been paranoid, and envisioned something far more damaging in Macey's little notebook.

It probably didn't even matter anymore since

Lunther was dead. But still, she couldn't help wondering about the notebook, and remembering the heated conversation she'd overheard between Lunther and Macey more than a week ago. They'd both threatened each other. Lonnie tried to remember exactly what they'd said that morning, but without knowing the source of their animosity, it didn't help her make sense of anything.

Instead, more questions flooded her mind. Before Lunther'd had a heart attack, did Macey have any idea how desperately he wanted that notebook? Did Macey even realize that Lonnie had unwittingly become mixed up in a feud that should've had nothing to do with her? *Dear God*, Lonnie thought as she finally drifted off to sleep long after midnight, *what has Macey gotten me into?*

Chapter Fourteen

"What are you *doing*?" Delia's raspy Boston accent broke Lonnie's concentration and granules of Sanka flew everywhere.

"Oh . . ." Lonnie looked down at the lime green tile, now covered in decaffeinated brown soot, and glanced back up at Delia's disapproving scowl. What was she going to say? Technically, she'd been trying to fill the large coffeepot with hot water and a dozen Sanka packets, because there was nothing else in the kitchen, including filters. But Lonnie didn't want to tell Delia that she'd only been doing it out of utter boredom.

Over three hours ago, she'd finished most of her daily tasks, and Twit hadn't given her any other work. In fact, he hadn't come out of his office all morning. He hadn't even left for lunch . . . or, at the very least, popped his head out to bark a food order at her and then slam the door without giving her money to pay for it.

"Well, I was just going to make a pot of coffee in case anyone wanted—"

"Haven't you ever made coffee before?" she condescended. Rolling her eyes obviously, she muttered, "*Jesus,*" and pushed past Lonnie—who rolled her

eyes in return, but with a lot more subtlety, and
looked around for a broom.

"I hope you don't expect me to clean up your
mess," Delia scoffed.

"I'm just looking for a broom, but I guess it's in
the supply closet," Lonnie said, struggling to keep
her voice toneless instead of asking the bitchy assistant why she was truly outdoing herself this
afternoon.

"Good, because my kitchen-duty days are over,"
she snapped, and grabbed a can of diet black cherry
soda out of the refrigerator. Then she grumbled
under her breath, "Fucking *over.*" She slammed the
refrigerator door so hard, some fliers flew away from
the magnets that had been securing them in place.
Then in one motion, she shook the can and yanked
the soda tab up, and burgundy liquid spurted out,
foaming over the top and trickling onto the floor.
Delia looked down, then back up, and smirked.
"Aw . . . looks like you'd better grab some paper
towels, too, while you're in there."

Lonnie's mouth dropped open incredulously. What
the hell was this woman's problem? In fact, Lonnie
was beginning to wonder why Delia had become
positively unbearable over the last couple of weeks.
When she'd started temping at Twit & Bell six
months ago, Delia was never friendly to her, but she
mostly just ignored her. Lately she'd been more and
more hostile, and now it was all somehow targeted
at *her.*

"What's with you?" Lonnie demanded.

Delia just scoffed. "Oh, grow up, Lonnie. I can't
think of one damn reason why I need to be nice to
you. If I'm in a bad mood, you can just suck it up."

"Wha—?"

"And, by the way, I'm forwarding Lunther's phone
to you. You can deal with all the fucking dolts still
calling for him." She gave her hair one more *screw-*

you toss, and strode out of the kitchen. Lonnie stood there dumbfounded for another second or two before heading to the supply room.

As she cleaned up, Lonnie realized that Delia had donned the same miserably hateful expression she'd had at the holiday party when Lunther'd walked away from her, and when she'd started a rumble at the buffet table. She shuddered to think what Delia's temper would be like if someone *really* crossed her. And Lonnie couldn't help wondering if she was volatile enough to be violent. After two seconds of deliberation, she made a mental note to steer clear of Delia and not hang around the office after hours.

Lonnie abandoned her whole Sanka-pot idea, then killed another half hour at her desk going through new e-mail—which included two from Terry. Groaning inwardly, she closed her inbox. She felt guilty that she hadn't replied to him yet, but in her defense, the only e-mails he'd sent her so far had been forwards.

She glanced at her PC clock in the bottom corner of her monitor: 2:25. Hmm, it seemed like over five hours ago it said 2:21. Suffice it to say, this day was dragging. She still couldn't believe Twit hadn't emerged from his office all day. The only reason she knew he was in there at all was because she'd caught a glimpse of his duckwalk when she'd first entered the office that morning . . . just before he'd disappeared around the corner and shut his door audibly.

Having her boss out of her face should've been a liberating feeling, but Lonnie found it unsettling, at best. The last time she'd seen him had been at Lunther's wake, when his body had been racked by dry sobs, and she'd gotten sidetracked with the mugger, anyway. It just seemed odd that Twit's longtime partner had died, and Twit wasn't bustling around the office, working double time to make sure Bell's accounts were covered and the firm was on schedule.

What could he be doing in that office? It was more than odd. . . . It seemed, well, suspicious.

I'm being paranoid. What *could* Twit be doing in there, if not assembling some outrageous stack of work for her? The mother of all PowerPoint presentations, or something equally tedious? That sounded like Twit. Yes, undoubtedly, he'd unload a project big enough to make up for all the task-free hours she'd had that morning. And, if she wasn't at her desk the second that he needed her . . . Well, she knew Twit. He'd get that infuriated eye tic no matter how unreasonable it was.

This whole day was just plain weird! Was it that Beauregard hadn't asked her if any confidential faxes had come that day? It had gotten to the point that Twit's daily, obsessive requests for some mythical fax were a staple in Lonnie's routine. No, it was more than that. The first day back at the office since the day of the holiday party—since Lunther's death— and half the staff hadn't even shown up. Among the no-shows were B. J., Macey, and Bette.

Maybe she should call Dominick again. He'd called her first thing that morning, but she was ten minutes late getting in, and just missed his call. In his message he said that he had several meetings on his schedule, but he'd call her later. Then he'd left another message when Lonnie was busy wiping black cherry soda off the lime green kitchen floor Now she picked up her receiver, dialed his work number, and felt disappointed to hear his voice mail pick up.

Just then she saw Macey walk through the main glass doors. Before Lonnie could say anything, Macey hastened past her, waving a quick hello as if not to bother her while she was on the phone, and smiled behind dark sunglasses. She moved briskly down the hall toward her office, and Lonnie started deliberating her options.

Should she tell her about the mugging? That

Lunther had orchestrated the whole thing because he was worried about the "security of the firm"? Hell, what did that even mean? She didn't want to imply that Macey was doing something wrong, but she had given Lonnie the notebook and wanted her to keep it a secret. That seemed rather suspicious now, but Lonnie was sure Macey had an easy, innocent explanation. That settled it. She rose from her comfy leather chair and headed down the hall.

She knocked gently on Macey's door. "Yes, come in," Macey summoned. Lonnie walked into the familiar office, remembering the many times she'd come in to discuss a project and ended up talking about other, more interesting subjects. She remembered all the times that Macey had pleasantly offered her a Snapple and let down a bit of her icy facade. (Lonnie assumed it was at least partly a facade.)

"Hi, Macey. Do you have a minute?" Lonnie asked, slightly reserved.

"Hi!" She welcomed her with a sweet, open smile crossing her lovely features. "Come in. Come in," she added brightly, and motioned toward the blue armchair.

"Hi," Lonnie repeated, relieved by Macey's good mood. "I don't want to disturb you, but—"

"Nonsense," Macey interrupted, and waved her hand in complete dismissal of the idea. "Lonnie," she started, "I just want to first say that I'm sorry I didn't have more of a chance to talk to your sister last week. Unfortunately, I was somewhat preoccupied at the party, and, well, the point is, she seemed like an independent, interesting woman, and I regret not getting to know her."

"Oh . . . thank you," Lonnie replied, a little lacking for words. "Well, she enjoyed meeting you, even if it was brief. Macey," she continued, eager to bring them onto the topic of Lunther and the notebook, "I just wanted to apologize for not getting your research project finished in time. I know it was supposed to be done by Friday, but with everything that happened, I—"

Macey held up her hand to stop Lonnie from explaining. "Don't give it a second thought. In fact, if I could have that notebook back as soon as possible, that would be great."

"Oh, okay . . . But, don't you want me to finish the project?" What, was the project no longer important?

Macey shrugged, smiling amiably and looking more relaxed than Lonnie had ever seen her. "Nope." *Nope?* Macey did not use words like "nope." "It's just not relevant anymore." She wheeled her chair over to the minifridge. "Snapple?" she asked, beaming, and handed Lonnie a raspberry iced tea.

"Macey, actually, I was sort of wondering—"

BRRRINNG!

" 'Scuse me a sec," Macey said, and picked up her ringing phone. *'Scuse? A sec?* Macey was abbreviating words; now this was disconcerting. "Macey Green . . . Oh, hi! How are you? Me? Bloody hell, do you even have to ask?" she enthused into the phone, and laughed.

Lonnie stood up and moved toward the door, hoping that Macey would stop her. But Macey didn't stop her. She just smiled . . . and waved good-bye with one finger. *Huh?*

As she was shutting the door behind her, Lonnie heard Macey say "natch" two times, in succession. Okay, it was time to panic.

Lonnie couldn't help but wonder if heart palpitations and intense panting were the norm for everyone who lived on her floor, as she opted for the stairs over the elevator. Climbing the five flights to her apartment definitely seemed better in theory than in practice, a distinction she vowed to remember next time she came home. So much for regular exercise.

Once she got her key in the door, she feebly turned the lock as she mildly huffed and puffed—fully aware of how ridiculously out of shape she must be, but choosing to blame most of the discomfort on her platform Mary Janes. She walked into her studio apartment, and noticed mid–key toss the broad silhouette sitting on her sofa. It looked uncomfortably familiar.

"Hey," Peach called. "Lonnie, you remember—"

"Detective Montgomery," she finished. "Hi. Is everything okay?" She looked warily at Peach, and then back at Montgomery. To be fair, it wasn't just Montgomery that made Lonnie nervous. It was police, in general. Besides a default guilty conscience, she'd seen way too many movies in which innocent women were framed, arrested, and demonized with absolutely no warning. In other words, she occasionally watched Lifetime. Yes, she'd been planning to tell Montgomery about Lunther's stepnephew, but she'd figured a brief phone call would suffice.

"Everything's fine," he said bruskly. "But I was hoping I could talk to you a little about what happened last week at the Easton."

"Um . . . okay." Why her? She felt like screaming at him: *I don't know anything else! Leave me alone!* But then it hit her: Lunther *was* murdered, after all. He had to have been. And since she was the one to find him, Montgomery was here to confront her about it . . . and . . . *Omigod, I'm going to be the patsy. Me. The temp!* Come to think of it, hadn't she seen that movie, too?

Lonnie slowly shook off her ice-blue coat and placed it on the armchair nearby. Then without thinking, she sank into the same chair, on top of her coat, crushing it mercilessly. All right, she had to calm down. She was just getting paranoid.

"Why don't you just tell us what's going on?" Peach suggested, generally braver than her older sister.

Detective Montgomery glanced at Peach—not dismissively, but quickly—and then down at his notepad. "Maybe you wouldn't mind giving me and your sister a moment or two alone."

"It's a studio apartment. Am I supposed to wait in the shower?"

"Detective," Lonnie broke in, "have I done something wrong?" Her heart thudded in her chest, even though she hadn't done anything illegal since she was thirteen and—under heavy peer pressure—shoplifted exactly one pack of gum. She swallowed hard, wondering if Detective Montgomery were out to get her for some reason. Could he know about the gum? "I don't understand what's going on . . . Plus, whatever you tell me, I'm just going to tell my sister word-for-word, anyway, so . . ." Her eyes darted to Peach's reassuring face, silently telling her they were in this together. Whatever *this* was.

Montgomery sighed, as if exhausted by her ramblings. "Okay, kid, it's like this." He dropped his notepad to his side and leaned forward, resting his elbows loosely on his legs. "I've checked you out, and—"

"What? Checked me out? Why?" Green-honey eyes shot wide with alarm.

"Okay, relax," Detective Montgomery said, putting out his hands, and patting them down in a hushing motion. Lonnie swallowed hard again and felt like an idiot.

"But, Detective, I don't understand—"

"Calm *down*. Jeez, I've never seen someone so nervous. You got something you want to confess while I'm here?" Lonnie just shook her head overeagerly. "Then relax." She nodded overeagerly. He sighed again. "Look, based on what I've checked out, you seem to be a trustworthy, law-abiding citizen. Am I right?" Another manic nod. "I wondered if you could just keep an eye out around your office." He softened his tone. "It's only natural that after Bell's death at your company's party, people are bound to act a little different. What I want you to do, is make a note of anything you notice. In particular, behavior that seems out of the ordinary for particular people, or comments made about Bell that catch your attention. Even if they seem off-the-cuff."

Lonnie let out a breath she didn't realize she'd been holding. "O-okay . . . except I don't understand why you want me to do this. I thought you said Lunther had a heart attack, didn't you?"

"Yes and no. Bell did have of a heart attack, but we believe that heart attack was induced."

"But how—"

"Textbook poisoning job. You off someone with potassium chloride and make it look like a heart attack. We've seen it dozens of times."

This time her swallow was an almost painful *gulp*. "You're absolutely sure?" she asked.

He shrugged. "Nothing's absolute, I guess. But the autopsy showed more potassium in Bell's system than his body would've reasonably produced on its own. And also . . ." He paused and stroked where his beard would have been if he had one.

It appeared that he wanted to tell her something, undoubtedly something that he was not supposed to share with a possible suspect he'd just met. Lonnie figured he'd tamp down whatever it was, but instead, he spoke again. "Look, there's no way I should be telling you this, but . . ." She and Peach waited expectantly. "There had been threats."

"What, you mean *death threats*?" Lonnie asked, incredulous.

He nodded.

"But when, who—?"

He held up his hand to stop her from pushing the issue. "I'm not at liberty to say anything else. I just want you to understand why your help could be very important."

She exhaled a deep, wavering breath, and her stomach was knotted even more than when she'd first seen Montgomery sitting on her sofa. Could someone she worked with at Twit & Bell actually have *killed* Lunther? It seemed too far-fetched for words. Still, she couldn't deny the very real presence of Detective Montgomery in her apartment telling her just that. She recalled how different the office dynamic had been that day. Beauregard and Macey had acted peculiarly, B. J. and Bette hadn't even shown up, and Delia had noticeably upped her bitch factor. Even Matt had behaved oddly; he'd said a quick hello in the morning when he passed her desk, but he didn't stop back even once to chat. Still, that wasn't enough to convince her she worked with a *killer*.

Finally she said, "So, basically, you want me to be . . . an informant?"

"Let's call it an unofficial informant. I should tell you, you're under no obligation to help me, but I would really appreciate it if you would. Just pay attention at work; keep an eye out for anything strange.

"Of course, you understand"—His voice hardened into a stern warning—"you'd have to keep this all to yourself. You absolutely couldn't say a word to any of your coworkers about me talking to you."

Lonnie thought for a minute. Should she agree? Oh, hell, how could she not? He was only asking her to pay closer attention to her coworkers, who probably weren't guilty anyway. Also, she was still in obsequious-with-law-enforcement mode, which left her considerably pliable. But still, she needed to get something straight. "How can you be sure that I'll be safe?" she asked.

"Safe?" he repeated.

"Yeah. I mean . . . what if we're dealing with a psychopathic maniac here?"

He shook his head. "Oh, no. I have no doubt that whoever killed Lunther was after him, and only him." Montgomery leaned back against the sofa cushions. "I've been doing this a long time, kid. I've learned to trust my gut. At least, most of the time." He drew himself upright again, and pointed his finger at her. "*But* you cannot snoop around or do anything obvious, like asking people a million questions. Remember, I just want you to keep your ears and eyes *open*. Nothing more. Got it?"

She nodded. "Okay. Got it, Detective. I'll help in any way I can."

"Great." he said.

"So, then, you definitely think it was someone at Twit & Bell who killed Lunther?"

He shrugged. "Don't get me wrong. We're looking into several possibilities. But having a set of eyes and ears at Bell's firm would really be a help."

"Okay."

He smiled. "Thank you. I mean it. We really appreciate it."

"Who's 'we'?" Peach piped in. "Where is your partner, anyway? Don't cops go everywhere in pairs?"

That seemed to throw him a little. He just cleared his throat, and said, "Well, I thought I could handle this myself. Good night." He picked up his notepad, slipped it in his front pocket, and headed to the front door. "I'll be in touch."

"Oh, Detective, wait!" Lonnie said, rushing to the door herself. "I almost forgot . . ." She told him about Lunther's connection to her mugging, and how he'd been after her bag.

"Stepnephew, huh?" Montgomery repeated. "Interesting."

"W-why's that?" she asked, trying to learn his thought process.

He shrugged. "It's just that poisoning is usually a female crime. So what was in the bag?" Oh, no, it was happening again. If she mentioned the notebook, she'd be implicating Macey, whom he hadn't seemed too fond of the night of the murder. Infinite seconds passed while Lonnie considered her best course. She didn't want to unintentionally confirm any misperception that Montgomery had about Macey, but she wasn't going to withhold information during an official police investigation. Ultimately, she decided to come clean with the detective.

So she told him. "Well, I can't be sure," she said. "But I think Lunther might have been after a notebook I had in there."

"A notebook?" he said.

"Yeah. It had some different cases outlined in it. And some citations." He waited, and she knew that wasn't going to be enough. "It was Macey's," she finished. He gave her a look that was a cross between *why am I not surprised?* and *aha!* Lonnie didn't try to defend Macey, though, because she knew with no reasonable argument, Montgomery wouldn't listen anyway. So she'd just have to find out what was going on herself—then she could clear Macey of any suspicion, and convince Montgomery that her friend and mentor was innocent.

Lonnie opened the front door like an auditioning butler, and Montgomery stepped through. Impulsively, she asked, "Detective? Why *me*? I'm just a temp."

He half smiled. "That's why. Like I said, I checked you out, and on top of that, I've got fifteen years of character judgment under my belt. I trust you to do what's right." Interestingly, she didn't mind his civic-duty guilt trip. "But like I said, you can't mention to anyone at Twit & Bell that I've spoken to you about this. Just in case." She nodded yet again. Then he winked, and she chose to ignore it. It was hardly a time to dwell on her pet peeves.

Lonnie smiled good-bye and started to shut the door, but before it closed all the way, she heard Montgomery's voice. "Hey, kid," he called to her from down the hall.

She opened the door wide again, and he said, "To tell you the truth, the only thing that seemed fishy about you was that you haven't had a boyfriend in four years." He smiled broadly now and continued down the hall, chuckling. Once again, she got the distinct feeling that Detective Montgomery got a kick out of intimidating her.

Lonnie locked her door and went to join Peach on the sofa. Peach spoke first. "That was so weird." She grabbed one of the yellow-and-blue-striped throw pillows, clutched it to her stomach, and turned to Lonnie. "Don't you think?"

"Yeah . . . It doesn't seem real. Then again, life is getting stranger by the minute."

Chapter Fifteen

"**B**eauregard Twit's line."

"Hey." A curt male voice. Lonnie hadn't done anything to make Dominick dislike her lately, so she could only assume—

"It's Terry." *Damn.* She hadn't recognized his voice right away because Terry was never curt, his tone was never clipped, and his demeanor rarely deviated from hyper.

More to the point: she didn't feel like talking to him at the moment. In fact, she hadn't *technically* spoken to him since his visit over a week ago. It wasn't all one-sided; he hadn't called her either. True, he'd sent her some e-mails, and she hadn't gotten around to replying, but it wasn't as if she was "avoiding" him.

"What, are you avoiding me?" he demanded. Lonnie shrunk lower in her chair. So he *had* noticed.

"N-no, of course not," she lied. "I've just been . . . really busy." She borrowed that line from the Every Lying Asshole's Handbook. "I was actually going to write you an e-mail after I finished this thing I've got to do for Twit."

"I haven't heard from you since before Christmas,"

he said. Apparently he wasn't going to let her off the hook that easily.

"Well . . . I . . . it's not like *you* called *me*, either, Terry." Not that she'd minded. In truth, she'd just assumed that things were naturally cooling off between them—especially after seeing the apparent way he flirted with other women.

"Me?" he said. "Oh, is that why you're being all distant?" Now he'd misunderstood and thought she was all broken up about the fact he hadn't called. "You're right, I should've called." *No, you shouldn't have, really!* "I've just been really busy at the club, working double sets." Lonnie rolled her eyes. So, Mr. Sensitive had pretty much forgotten she existed, too. Could there be any more proof of how hollow their relationship was? Of how fast it was going *nowhere*?

"But I want to see you and make it up to you." *No!* Couldn't Terry just let things taper off? "How about tonight?"

"Tonight?" she repeated incredulously. "What are you talking about?" Oh, no, he wasn't in town again, was he? She knew Terry wasn't a horrible human being or anything, but she just didn't want to see him now. She didn't want to hurt his feelings though, or ruin the chance for them to stay friends. "Are you in Boston?" she asked, keeping the dread out of her voice.

"No, no. I mean, I want you to come to New York tonight," he said. "Come on, Lonnie, it's only a four-hour drive. If you leave by five, you can get here in plenty of time for New Year's."

"New Year's?" she repeated absently.

"Duh!" (She *detested* that.) "Tonight's New Year's Eve! What'd you forget?" Obviously she'd tried to. Not only did she hate New Year's on principle, but also, she was hoping she and Dominick could spend the night together, like he had hinted at the holiday party. She hadn't spoken to him yet about it, though, so at this point, she *was* free. That still didn't mean she'd go to New York.

"Terry, I can't do that," she said, with more unyielding resolve than she'd meant to reveal. There was a pause.

"Why not?" he finally asked, his voice bordering on curt again. Peeved was a side to Terry she'd never really seen. Even when he'd gotten grouchy on the night he'd visited, he'd had the jokes rolling again by the next morning. "Why not?" he repeated.

"Because . . ." *I don't like you enough. I'd rather watch TV in my underwear than pay a few tolls. I'm falling for another man.* "I just can't."

"So what are you going to do for New Year's, then?"

"Nothing," she said honestly.

"You'd rather do nothing than come to NYC?" (She wasn't crazy about the singsongy way Terry always drawled "NYC," but at least it was better than "duh.")

"Terry, it's nothing personal. I just . . . I don't want to go to New York tonight." There was another pause.

Then: "Fine."

"Terry, are you mad?"

"No, no. Of course not."

"Oh, good," she said sincerely. Another pause. "Well . . . have fun!" she added in an overly enthused voice. "Whatever you end up doing."

"I will."

"Okay . . . well . . ."

"I gotta go," he said quickly. "I'll talk to you later."

"Okay, no problem! Bye!" Lonnie heard his click before she'd finished her over-the-top closer. She wondered if he'd noticed she was trying too hard. She slid the receiver in its cradle, let out a sigh, and tried to remember what she'd been working on before he called.

Her phone rang again.

"Beauregard Twit's line." She knew she was omitting the "Twit & Bell" part, but it seemed too morbid to say Lunther's name like that, now that he was dead.

"Look, Lonnie, this isn't easy for me to say." It was Terry again.

"Ter—?"

"I've been doing some thinking and . . . the truth is . . ." He sucked in a deep, audible breath.

And then he blew.

"Lately you have begun to flare a temper in me"—his voice rose angrily—"that I can barely CONTAIN!"

What is this? New material? "Terry, what are you talk—"

"Look, I've been thinking a lot about this, and I've decided that we just don't have boyfriend-and-girlfriend potential. Do you realize that I could have *lots* of women! And I plan to!" Apparently, he *was* serious, and he meant every hostile word. "Okaaay?" he taunted bitterly. "Do you *get* it?"

"But—" She got everything except the part where *he* was the one giving this speech. She'd known all along that they didn't have long-term potential, but what was he so angry about? Was this because she didn't want to go to New York for New Year's?

"And if you think this is about New Year's, it's not!" he shouted. "I just don't see you in my future, and the truth is, I NEVER HAVE!" Her eyes widened to match her shock. She never knew that Terry realized their incompatibility in the long run. But by his tone, it sounded like he'd done one better: he'd not only noticed, but managed to nurse an intense loathing for her, as well.

"Terry, please, calm down," she said evenly. She

wanted to stop his tirade before he said something that made it impossible for them to stay friends. Well, friendly. It didn't work anyway.

"You don't know two shits about me, Lonnie!" he went on at the top of his lungs, while she remained agape. "You think I'm just this happy comedian, twenty-four seven. Well, I'm NOT! I have a darker, more complex side that you don't even get! That you don't even stimulate! And lately, the *mere thought* of you makes me so angry—"

"Just *wait*! Tell me why you're so mad all of a sud—"

"Look, I don't want to get into all this now, all right? The point is: you flare a temper in me. That's it. Just get it through your head once and for all: I do not want to see you anymore! Do you *get* it? Do you—"

She hung up on him. Exactly how much of the insane, belligerent diatribe was she expected to listen to? The guy obviously had issues. She should've known that being a comedian, he had the potential to be too eccentric—i.e., *nuts*—for her.

Still, part of her wondered if she should start panicking; this was the second guy who had dumped her cold. First Jake, now Terry.

But as Lonnie slumped back in her leather chair and tried to take in what just happened, she experienced an odd sense of liberation. Of relief. Even though Terry's demented decree should have been terribly insulting, she couldn't take his rejection that personally since she'd never really opened herself up to him. And now that he was no longer dangling in the background, she had zero baggage impeding her relationship with Dominick. No guilt, whatsoever.

Still reeling with surprise, wonder, amazement, and exhilaration, she shook her head and thought to herself, *Big changes ahead*.

*　　*　　*

"Butt break?"

Dominick looked up from his monitor to see Mo standing in his doorway. Her hands were braced on the doorjamb, as she leaned her upper body over the threshold to his office. She had a cigarette already in the corner of her mouth, which could've looked semitrashy, but she carried it off well, and just looked very cute.

"Hey, Mo," he said, smiling. "Uh . . . I'll have to pass. I don't smoke"—after a two-second pause he added—"anymore. I quit."

"You quit? Congratulations," Mo replied sweetly. "Some of the girls and I are going outside now, so I just thought I'd ask." Dominick couldn't help but be impressed that she was able to keep the cigarette firmly in her mouth the whole time.

Mo lingered a few more moments, and then smiled sheepishly and said, "Well . . . good luck with your work. I'll see ya later." And she left. Dominick was flattered by her interest, but to him, she was still a kid. Well, she wasn't a kid in some very obvious ways, but still . . . she was too young for him. He didn't want a girl fresh out of college. He wanted someone more mature. A full-grown woman. A luscious, brainy, adorable, full-grown woman. Three months ago, he didn't have a clue what he was looking for, but now it seemed so clear. So urgent.

Dominick pushed back from his desk, and rose out of his chair, determined for the moment to forget all the work he was supposed to catch up on. He was going upstairs to see Lonnie, because he hadn't seen her since the night of the party, and that was way too long ago. He missed her voice. He missed the expressions she made when she was teasing him. And the expressions she made when she was being serious. He missed her. Phone conversations weren't cutting it, not for one more second.

Dominick headed to the elevator and passed his

protégé, Harold, on the way. "Where you headed, D?" Harold asked expectantly. In truth, Dominick felt sorry for the poor bastard. He was always bored, because he frenetically zipped through his projects way ahead of the deadline and then had nothing to do. If only he weren't so damn irritating!

Dominick immediately felt guilty at the thought, because he knew Harold didn't mean any harm. He was a smart kid, ambitious, too, but he wasn't Dominick's first choice for the position. He was Dominick's *mother's* first choice. Harold's aunt's neighbor played bridge with Mrs. Carter's former accountant. Of course he didn't have to bow to his mother's pressure, but she would've been an unbearable martyr if he didn't, and Harold was clearly qualified.

Sure, Harold was qualified when it came to computer languages (and overqualified when it came to his wardrobe), but the kid was less than swift in other ways. For instance, during a critical meeting with E-Bizz's CEO, Mitch Jay, Harold unabashedly corrected the pompous old guy's pronunciation of the word "banal." In turn, Mitch Jay had responded with a brittle smile and a voice laced with contempt: "Pardon me." Harold had replied: "No problem. Don't worry about it, M." There were countless other episodes like that. (Although, if Dominick didn't have to make it his business to keep high-powered sponsors like Mitch Jay happy, he probably would've found it all somewhat funny.)

"I'm just heading out for a few minutes," he said to Harold. His protégé's face dropped, and Dominick took pity on the guy. "Uh . . . would you do something for me while I'm gone?" Harold straightened up eagerly and shifted his Hermes tie. Dominick said, "Check the preliminary commands I've written for that new link. The file's open on my screen."

With ecstatic affirmation, Harold turned on his heel and headed to Dominick's office. Dominick just laughed to himself. He was certain that Harold wouldn't find any errors in his work, but hey, at least it gave him something to do for about half an hour.

The elevator doors opened on twenty-three, and Dominick felt anticipation pool in his chest. He'd been to her office once before to get her for lunch, so he knew where her desk was. Not that he would've missed it anyway; it was the one you passed as soon as you entered Twit & Bell, with the six-inch-thick layer of papers covering it.

She wasn't there. He noticed that her computer's screen saver was on, so she must have left at least several minutes before. *Now what?* He looked at his watch: 10:43 A.M. He decided to wait five more minutes, and leaned against her desk, feeling slightly like an idiot with each passing second. Not that there was anyone to feel like an idiot in front of, since the office seemed deserted. Finally, he gave up. He spotted the end of a red pen peeking out from under a stack of papers, so he snatched it up, scrawled a note to her on the first blank Post-it he spotted, and headed back to the elevators.

He'd been hoping like hell she'd be there! He wanted to persuade her to take a little break with him. They could go to a coffee shop. Or to an empty conference room. He'd leave that choice up to her. He knew he couldn't have lunch with her because he already had a lunch meeting scheduled with GraphNet's copresidents, and he was being very careful to maintain his good standing despite his intention to leave the firm. It was absolutely critical to maintain a high-quality job performance right up until the end if he wanted to lend credence to his own business.

Shoving hard on the glass doors to GraphNet, he headed back to his office. As soon as he entered, he had to hold back a frustrated sigh. He'd forgotten that he'd just given Harold a project, which involved the overanxious putz sitting at *his* desk. "Bad news, D," Harold stated grimly . . . but, oddly, with some perceptible glee in his eyes. "So far, I've come across quite a few errors. Four to be exact, and I'm only halfway through this file." *What?* That couldn't be; Dominick never made mistakes, and certainly not with basic programming code!

He went to look over Harold's shoulder. Harold had printed out the file and marked it up with a red pen. *My protégé marked up my work with a fucking red pen!* Dominick looked at it. . . . *I'll be damned.* Harold was right.

But how? How had Dominick made such careless mistakes? Where had his concentration gone lately? True, he'd been thinking about Lonnie more, but . . .

Just then an image of her dark, wet mouth came into his mind, and his dick started to harden.

He just answered his own question.

Chapter Sixteen

Everyone sat uncomfortably around the conference table. Twit was ten minutes late, and that was positively unheard of, because Tuesday-morning staff meetings were his top priority. Lonnie tried to use the time constructively, though, by looking around, trying to read her coworkers' faces, and noticing anything that seemed—as Detective Montgomery had put it—"off." Everyone appeared somewhat fidgety, but then, that wasn't much to report since *she* felt the same way. Where was Beauregard already?

Speak of the devil. Twit bustled through the glass door, gripping his legal pad with one hand and holding the other hand up to the staff. "My apologies," he said, and took a seat at the head of the table. "This is going to be a very quick meeting," he added, and shuffled his papers. So far, Lonnie had yet to see Twit actually refer to any of the papers he shuffled during staff meetings.

The conference room was filled, and everyone seemed curious about Twit's purpose. Lonnie was curious, too, but in a less invested way, which was the great thing about being a temp. Of course, Twit loved the attention he was getting, as the Twit & Bell staff looked quizzically and expectantly at him, and he gave his papers a final, twentieth shuffle.

"Okay, people, I called this meeting to make an announcement." He paused for dramatic effect. Unfortunately, he waited way too long to resume, and it backfired. A couple people started talking among themselves. Bette picked lint off her silk lapel, B. J. pulled at a hangnail, and Matt took out his PalmPilot. "Ahem!" Twit cleared his throat, and people looked at him again.

"I know everybody has probably been wondering what is going to happen now that Lunther is not with us anymore," he began. He must have realized that his mouth had curled into a merry smile, because suddenly he forced his lips into a tightly pressed line. Then he looked down at his lap and brought one hand up to his forehead. "Oh, my old school chum, Lunther!" he exclaimed in a sober voice, wincing and shaking his head. He hit his hand on the table a few times in succession. "Oh, why, why, WHY?" he bellowed. Everyone glanced at each other questioningly, and then looked to Lonnie, as if she would understand the psychological state of her completely weird boss. She just shrugged.

Then Twit composed himself. He straightened his shoulders and addressed the group again. "Now, it won't be easy, but we have to try to pick up and go on after the terrible loss we've suffered." Dramatic pause. "The announcement I want to make isn't an easy one." Another dramatic pause. "But it's one that I think will be for the best." A dramatic eon passed by. "What I'm about to announce is for the good of the company, and for the good of each and every individual at this table." The earth rotated around the sun about a million times. "And here it is. I've decided not to take another partner."

The room was silent. Lonnie tried to be discreet, sneaking glances at each attorney's face to compare expressions. Matt and B. J. appeared neutral to the idea, but then, they were relatively new to the firm, and the youngest associates, so neither could qualify for partner yet anyway. Clara and Mel were impassive. Macey wasn't even present.

Twit went on. "Now, this is not final, but for the time being, it's the way I think it has to be. I will pick up where Lunther left off, and sometime—in the very indefinite future—I'll start considering the idea of taking a partner again." He leaned back and gripped the arms of his throne. "Are there any questions about what this means?"

Is this guy a jerk or what? Here he makes them wait ten minutes to hear a condescending, power trip of a decree, and then asks if everyone comprehended what just happened. Not that Lonnie cared who advanced to partner, but still, she found Twit's superior behavior ludicrous. Bette spoke first.

"Fine by me," her nasal voice declared. "Saves me paperwork." She gave a let-them-eat-cake, close-mouthed smile.

"Yes . . ." Twit began officiously. "Uh, thank you, Bette, for sharing those thoughts. Are there any other questions about my plans for the firm? Or my intended philosophy of leadership?" *What the hell is he talking about?* Whatever his "philosophy" of leadership was, the staff would certainly know it by now. He'd been their boss, and exercised his leadership, for years.

Unless . . .

Was it possible that Twit had less say in the running of Twit & Bell than Lonnie had thought? She knew he and Lunther had started the firm together, so she'd always assumed they were equal partners in every way. But if that were true, why was her boss suddenly acting like he'd been elected king for a day? She scrutinized his face, and saw traces of that almost insuppressible merry smile. Then she glimpsed a few of her coworkers. From what she could tell, they were somewhere between surprised and puzzled.

She would've like to have seen Macey's reaction, but she was, yet again, absent from the Tuesday-morning staff meeting.

"I'm just glad you're the one in charge now," B. J. said to Twit. Lonnie turned her head and looked at him strangely, because it seemed like an odd thing to say. Quickly, B. J. qualified, "Hey, you gotta respect a boss who's a die-hard Celtics fan." He pointed at the boss amiably.

"Yes. Well, thank you, B. J.," Twit said, nodding heavily.

"Of course, that's no offense to Lunther or anything," B. J. added, defensively holding his hands up to the room. "He was from New Jersey, so I can understand why he liked the Jets."

"Nets," Matt corrected loudly enough for everyone to hear. B. J. blushed.

"Well, I just want to say," Delia broke in, making her abrasive voice as soft and sweet as she could, "that I realize you have a *temp* helping you out, Beauregard"—*the name's Lonnie, you witch*—"but I'd be happy to give you any extra assistance you need, as you make the transition to . . . you know . . . not working with Lunther." Then she flipped her deader-than-normal hair over the shoulder pad of her eighties-looking sweater.

Now Twit blushed. "Well, thank you, Delia. That is certainly considerate of you. I'll have Luna confer with you after the meeting." *Like hell.* He cleared his throat and shifted in his chair, and Lonnie tried desperately to think of anything other than Twit having a hormonal reaction to Delia. Or Twit having hormones at all, if possible.

"So if there's nothing else," Twit announced, and leaned his head back on his chair. "I'll cease my offi-

ciating here, and proceed this meeting to its conclusion." Then he shut his eyes, as if in deep reflection.
Everyone just sat there, confused.

After a few seconds, Twit crept one eye open and
glanced around the room. Then he opened both eyes,
and clarified, "Oh . . . that is to say, *meeting adjourned*." With that, the room cleared out. While Twit
sank back into his affected Zen Buddhist posture,
Lonnie hustled back to her desk in disbelief.

Immediately, she spotted the pink Post-it stuck to
her monitor. She snatched it off, and her pulse quickened a little when she read it.

> *Lonnie—I must've missed you. Call me, D.*

Dominick had stopped by to surprise her and
she'd missed it because of that joke of a meeting.
How typical. She fell into her chair and grabbed the
phone receiver. She dialed Dominick's office number
and waited. *Please not the voice mail—*

"Dominick Carter." Her heart jolted. She wondered when just the sound of his voice would stop
having that effect on her. She could just picture him
on the other end, cerebral looking in his glasses, and
sexy as hell.

"Hi, it's me," she said simply, but her voice defied
her attempt to act casual, and dropped a lusty oc-
tave lower.

"Hey," he replied, sounding very pleased that
she'd called. "Where were you before?"

"Oh, pressing meeting. Twit wanted to let us know
that from now on the firm will be under his own
despotic rule, and then he asked if we understood
English."

"What?" Dominick laughed.

"Well, that's the condensed version," she said
brightly. "So what's new with you?" *When can I see
you? When can I lick you?* Unconsciously, her body

language mimicked her thoughts, as she clutched the phone tighter to her ear and leaned her mouth as close to the receiver as she could.

"Not too much," he said. "I wanted to ask you to lunch today, but I have a meeting. And since I took those two personal days last week, I've got to catch up on a lot. I'm going to be working late, I have a feeling."

Her heart sank. "Okay."

"I'm sorry I won't be able to see you tonight, for New Year's Eve."

"No problem." She tried to sound cheery, even though she really felt somewhat deflated. It wasn't New Year's Eve, which always sucked and was obviously continuing in that tradition. It was just . . . she knew this thing with Dominick was too good to be true. Here they hadn't seen each other in almost two weeks, and obviously, he was losing interest. Why else would he give her the beginnings of an I'm-going-to-be-busy-for-a-while, don't-call-me, I'll-call-you, blow-off spiel?

"How about tomorrow night?" he asked.

"Huh?" Now she was confused. "W-what about tomorrow night?"

"Want to go out tomorrow night? Well, stay in, actually."

Her heart immediately rose back to the surface. She smiled into the phone and said, "Hmm . . . What did you have in mind?"

He laughed. "I've got a lot of things in mind, but they don't all have to happen tomorrow night." She clutched the phone even closer and smiled into it. Had any man ever had this strong of an effect on her? She honestly didn't think so. Suddenly, it was all becoming clear. Terry had been her transitional man, and Dominick was the real thing. The *one*.

He said, "I was thinking I'd make you dinner at my apartment." *And get laid after.* Okay, so Dominick was a nice guy; that might not be part of his plan. But even if it was, Lonnie had no problem with that. In fact, the thought of his naked, sweaty body on hers seemed like the best idea she'd had in a while.

Yet she wanted to see him on her own turf. She was still a little gun-shy (so to speak), and the comfort of her apartment would help put her at ease. So she offered, "How about I cook you dinner this time? Peach says I have to get over my disdain for our miniappliances."

"Oh . . . okay," he agreed. "What time should I come over?"

"How's seven thirty?"

"Great. I'll bring wine."

"Okay." She felt her pulse between her legs, and gave him her address.

"What are you going to do for New Year's?" he asked. She knew she should probably make up some great-sounding plans to keep him guessing, but it wasn't her style.

"I don't know, maybe rent a movie," she said. He then suggested that she rent *Mobsters*, claiming it was really good. Her heart turned over in her chest; how *cute* was he? Of course *Mobsters* looked like ten-year-old crap, but still, for some reason, she found his suggestion unbelievably adorable.

"So, I'll see you tomorrow night," she said.

"Absolutely."

"Okay. Bye."

"Wait—red or white?"

"Red."

"My kind of woman."

"You have no idea," she teased.

"Christ, I can't wait till tomorrow night."

"Bye," she said again, and they both hung up at the same time.

Lonnie leaned back in her chair and felt like fanning herself off. She knew this blood-boiling reaction was over-the-top, but what could she do? The attraction seemed to get stronger every time they talked. It wasn't Dominick's looks, although she definitely liked those. It was everything. . . . It was him. It was them. They clicked. She sighed happily.

"Lucy!" *Well, that didn't last long.* Beauregard Twit's booming beckon was unmistakable. "Lucy, come in here A-SAP!" he called from his office. Lonnie went to Twit's office, knocked lightly on the ajar door, and pushed it open. Beauregard was at his desk, writing.

"Did you need something?" she asked him.

"Yes," he answered matter-of-factly. "What time is it? My clock's broken."

"Oh." That threw her off. "I'm not wearing a watch; I'll go check." Inwardly rolling her eyes, she went back around the corner and looked at the clock on the wall. Then she bustled back to Twit's office to give him the vital data. "It's eleven o'clock."

He clasped his hands together under his chin and looked upward, contemplating the information. Then he said, "Let me know when it's eleven fifteen, will you? Best." He went back to writing. "Best"—which Lonnie assumed was supposed to be an abridged version of "best wishes"—was Twit's favorite closer. Basically, it was his very suave way of saying "This conversation is terminated, now beat it."

Lonnie went back to her desk and started entering Twit's hours in the payroll database. Within moments, her phone rang. "Twit & Bell," she answered. She'd stopped saying "Beauregard Twit's line" after Delia had forwarded Lunther's phones to her, too.

"Hey," Peach said.

"Hi!" Lonnie was glad it was her sister and not Twit wasting more of her time.

"What's going on?" Peach asked, and Lonnie filled her in on her morning so far. Then Peach told her about Iris Mew and the Chestnut Hill charity circuit.

"Oh, I forgot! I asked Dominick over tomorrow night. Is that okay?"

"Yeah, sure. It's about time you guys got your groove on," Peach noted.

"He's just coming over for dinner. I'm not planning anything beyond that," Lonnie explained, as she made a mental note to shave her legs all the way up and pick up more strawberry body lotion.

"Mmm-hmm. Well, whatever. I think that sounds great. And, don't worry about me being in the way—"

"I wasn't."

"—because tomorrow night I made plans with Matt," Peach finished.

That was news. "When did this happen?" she asked.

"Well, I'd given him my e-mail address at the party, but then I hadn't heard anything, so I sorta forgot about it. But today he sent me a message asking me if I wanted to go to the Bruins game tomorrow night." There was a pause, and Lonnie could hear a muffled voice in the background. Then Peach said, "No, you're wearing that one. Hold on, Lonnie." Her voice was farther away when she said, "Cheryl, you have a great figure. People would kill for your heaving bosom, so stop hiding it. You're wearing *that* one."

"Peach?"

"Yeah, sorry. Cheryl's just having cold feet about tonight."

"Why, what's tonight?" Lonnie asked curiously.

"Remember that catering thing we were going to try to set up?"

"No."

"Oh, I thought I told you. At Iris's tea social, I overheard a woman mention her housewarming party next month. So I got the idea for Cheryl to cater the party. Well, first we have to convince the woman to have the party catered. You see?" Peach finished, obviously cheery at the prospect of Cheryl's culinary debut.

"So Cheryl's interested in professional catering now, or . . . ?" Lonnie asked.

"Weelll . . . ," Peach said, and Lonnie understood the subtext perfectly: *No, but I'm pushing her toward it, for what I deem is her own good.* In some ways, Peach was like their mother, and Lonnie knew that ultimately, they both meant well. That still didn't make it okay. "She loves to cook, and I told you that she freelances her recipes to make a living. So, I asked her: 'Why not freelance your talent?' Anyway, we got in touch with Iris's friend, and she's meeting Cheryl for dinner to discuss the possibilities."

"So, how does Cheryl's 'heaving bosom' factor in?" Lonnie inquired.

"What? Oh, no, that's something separate. This dress looks adorable on her and"—her voice rose higher—"she's just gonna have to trust me!"

"By the way," Lonnie interjected, remembering Twit, "what time is it?"

"Quarter after eleven. Well, a little past."

"Oh! I gotta go," she said hastily.

"No problem. I'll call you later or see you at home."

Lonnie carelessly chucked the receiver back into its cradle and hustled to Twit's office. She pushed open the door, but Twit wasn't there anymore. Could he actually have realized the time on his own? It seemed too much to hope for, but Lonnie just shrugged and headed back to her desk.

Halfway there, she heard a persistent beeping noise. It was strident and relentless, and it didn't take her long to realize it was the fax machine run amok. She darted over to it, and tried to figure out why it was beeping. There was no incoming fax. Then she noticed the tiny green PAPER OUT light flashing.

Quickly, she grabbed a hunk of plain white paper
that was stacked next to the machine, and slid it into
the appropriate compartment.

And she saw something. Under the chunk of paper
she'd just grabbed, was a sheet with writing on it.
She picked it up and skimmed it. *Oh, no!* It was Twit's
confidential fax! It read:

The Office of John Pally, Private Investigator
<u>CONFIDENTIAL</u>

BT: I received your payment. I'll be out of
state for a while, but we should be set. JP
<u>Here are the names:</u>
Ann Lee
Sandra Neemas
Courtney Adams
Mabel Wills

Lonnie immediately panicked. It was a gut reaction, but a fairly logical one, considering how many
times Beauregard had asked her about the fax. Each
time she'd said it hadn't arrived, and it had been
sitting there the whole time. The date on top got cut
off, so she wasn't sure the exact day it'd come in,
but somehow it had gotten lost under the stack of
white paper next to the fax machine. Now that she
thought about it, it made sense how it could happen.
Twit's fax line was always flooded with menus and
fliers, so staff members often swung by to sift
through the items that came in. That was why Lonnie
had to straighten the table regularly. Somehow, this
fax must have gotten lost in the shuffle. *Great, now
what?* Twit was going to kill her!

Then again . . .

He hadn't asked her about the fax this week. In
fact, the last time he'd mentioned it was at the holiday party. He didn't even bring it up at Lunther's

wake—which would be grossly inappropriate for the average person, but remarkably slick and discreet for Twit. Maybe he'd gotten the information he'd needed another way. Or maybe the fax was no longer relevant.

Really, was there honestly any need to call Twit's attention to the fact that the fax had been misplaced if he didn't even care about the damn thing anymore? Okay, that settled it; she wouldn't tell Twit about the fax unless he asked her again. She looked down and reread it. And then the other shoe dropped.

Ann Lee.

What did it mean? Lonnie didn't recognize the other three names on the list, but her curiosity was definitely piqued. If only the fax had given a clue as to what happened to Ann Lee. Why did she leave Twit & Bell? Where did she go?

Impulsively, Lonnie decided to make a copy of the fax for Montgomery. She didn't know what the list of names meant, but she figured he'd want to take a look. He'd told her to keep an eye out for anything "off," and this mysterious list of women's names seemed to qualify. She had to make a copy quick, before Twit accosted her. Since he wasn't at his desk when she'd last checked, that meant he was lurking around somewhere. And he'd demonstrated several times in the past that he was not averse to snatching things directly out of her hand.

Checking over her shoulder, Lonnie hastened past the water cooler and darted around the corner. Furtively, she slid the fax onto the photocopier and pressed PRINT. Of course, nothing happened. Then several loud beeps and buzzers sounded. Desperately, she laid her arms on top of the machine, in a half-baked attempt to muffle the noise. She looked around for Twit again. Good, still no sign of him. She focused her attention back on the copier. WARMING UP flashed incessantly on the touch pad, and the whole machine convulsed into an industrial, metal-slamming-on-metal symphony.

"Be quiet!" she whispered urgently to the machine, and checked over her shoulder three more times before her copy finally slid out. She grabbed it, along with the original, and rushed back to her desk. She folded both copies up and put them in her bag, figuring, at this point, Twit would be none the wiser.

Lonnie had no idea what any of it meant, or if it meant anything at all. But she was starting to suffer from that gut thing Montgomery had mentioned, and she just knew something strange was going on. Why had Twit hired a PI? What did Lunther's former assistant, Ann Lee, have to do with it? How was she connected to the other women on that list?

And why had Twit stopped asking about the fax after the holiday party?

Chapter Seventeen

"I'll be right back." Lonnie left Dominick on her sofa while she went into the bathroom, shut the door, and leaned all her weight against it. She took a deep breath and tried to calm her nerves. Tonight was the night. She could feel it. And she was terrified . . . in an exhilarating kind of way.

She crossed to the mirror and looked at her reflection. Before Dominick had arrived, she curled her hair just enough so it would hang down in loose waves. She'd tried not to overdo it with the mascara and Plum Daiquiri lipstick; she hadn't put on blush because her cheeks were already flushed with anticipation.

Now, over two hours later, everything she'd felt before Dominick arrived had only intensified. And it showed. Her wavy hair was untamed, her cheeks were rosy pink, and her mouth was wine stained and ready.

So far the night had been perfect. They'd had linguini with red clam sauce, Parmesan biscuits, and a bottle of cabernet sauvignon, while they'd shared random personal stories and Lonnie struggled to stay focused on the conversation. Honestly, she tried, but her mind just wouldn't cooperate. When Dominick told her about his family, she imagined running her tongue down his body. When he talked about religion, she pictured him sweaty and thrusting. (She really felt guilty about that one.) And when he asked her whom she considered a strong role model for women, she forgot the question because she was busy picturing herself biting his perfectly rounded butt. Well, *not hard*

Hey, it wasn't her fault that everything he did was so arousing. Then again, maybe she was just sex starved. Okay, make that more than likely. Now, as she looked in the bathroom mirror, she hoped tonight was the night. Knowing that everything was officially over with Terry only made her feel more liberated and uninhibited than ever. Or maybe that would just be her convenient excuse to tear open Dominick's clothes with her teeth.

Earlier, she'd gone to the drugstore to buy a box of condoms (just in case) and the saleswoman's eyes lit up approvingly. Apparently, Lonnie had shopped there for four years and had never bought anything more interesting than the *Star*. Hell, the CVS cashier was rooting for her—that should count for something.

All right, enough stalling. She took a few more deep breaths, stepped out of the bathroom, and walked toward Dominick. She smiled as innocently as she could and hoped it would help mask her dirty mind. He smiled back casually, but his eyes—black and scorching—bore through her with an intensity that wasn't difficult to read. He was sitting in a relaxed posture, with one arm spread along the back of the sofa.

She sank down next to him, but jerked forward just as her back hit the cushion. "Oh, I forgot!" He raised an eyebrow questioningly. "Dessert," she said, and rose to her feet again. She went into the kitchen—which was more of a minialcove with a ministove and a minifridge—and retrieved the pastries she'd bought in the North End yesterday afternoon.

"What's this?" he asked eagerly, courteously. Throughout the night, he'd complimented her on her cooking, her apartment, her taste in books, and her sense of humor. He acted enthused by her; he made her feel appreciated. The only thing he hadn't complimented was her appearance. Lonnie hated herself for caring about something that superficial, but she'd wanted so much to look good for him. *Hot.*

"Do you like pastry?" she asked, and sat down next to him again.

"I like everything," he replied, and peered curiously into the box. He took out a chocolate cannoli and bit into it. After he swallowed, he said, "Aren't you going to have any?"

Lonnie ignored his question, and zeroed in on the powdered sugar that dusted his lower lip. For a new twist, dessert was the last thing on her mind. Before she could chicken out, she made her move. She leaned in to him, and slowly, methodically, brushed her thumb across his lip. He stared directly into her eyes while she touched him. His breath came up shorter and her heart beat faster. Both fell silent as she moved her thumb on his mouth rhythmically, and an electrifying sexual awareness scorched the air between them. Suddenly, Lonnie felt something hot and wet on the tip of her finger. Dominick was lightly flicking his tongue on her as she traced his lip.

The wet heat of his tongue immediately stirred a matching reaction between her legs, and without thinking, she pushed her thumb farther into his mouth. He sucked it, and she held back a moan. She moved her body until it hovered over his, and straddled him. Instantly, his arms coiled around her, and his eyes closed as her finger slid in and out of his mouth, plunging deep while he licked and sucked it.

Then Lonnie took her hand away and licked up the bare trace of powdered sugar on his mouth. That's when his composure broke. Within two seconds, they were all over each other, breathing hard, kissing, licking, and sucking. Lonnie spread her legs wider, sinking as far into his erection as she possibly could, and let out short, breathy moans when he rocked himself against her. It wasn't enough. She shoved her long skirt all the way up, so he could grind right into the damp crotch of her panties.

Then they were on the shaggy cream rug, gripping each other and saying things that might embarrass them later. He reached under her sweater and bra to feel her breasts, and the minute he ran his hands over her nipples, he groaned loudly. Lonnie started to pull her sweater over her head, but stopped midway when she felt Dominick's hand slide inside her panties. Her body jolted, her eyes shut tight, and her moan sounded more like a sharp scream, as he moved his hand on her, whispering about how wet she was right before he slipped a finger inside her.

"*Christ*, Lonnie," he breathed in her ear, as he pushed deeper and harder with his finger, "you're so hot. . . . You . . . you look so hot tonight. . . . God, I . . . I've wanted this all night." It took all her energy to respond.

"Me, too," she whispered breathlessly, and jerked her body against his finger because it felt so good. "I thought . . . when you . . . when you didn't say anything about how I looked—" She stopped herself from continuing because her insecurities sounded ridiculous, and also, she was too turned on to speak anymore. His hands were even more adept than she'd fantasized they would be; they were gentle but powerful, expert but intimate, all at the same time.

He let out a short, strained laugh, and murmured, "I didn't want to say anything because I didn't want you to think I was only after your body." She tried to laugh herself, but she couldn't because she was panting, as his finger propelled her closer and closer to orgasm. Oh, Lord, she was so close. So close . . . So close . . .

Suddenly, keys clanked and jangled outside the front door.

Oh, no, Peach was home! Immediately, Lonnie pushed him off her. They scrambled to their feet, and started to adjust themselves. Although, with the exception of Dominick's hard-on, he was fine. It was Lonnie who looked like she just had a wild few hours in bed. She incoherently mumbled "act natural" to him, before she'd rushed into the bathroom to straighten herself up.

Peach entered the apartment laughing. "What do you mean, you don't believe in knock-knock jokes? Oh, hi, Dominick!" He stood there, feeling awkward, while Peach and Matt strolled over.

"Hi, Peach, how're you doing? Hey—Matt, right?"

"Yeah. How's it going?" Matt replied.

The bathroom door opened and Lonnie came out. Dominick gave her a once-over. She'd combed her hair and put her sweater and bra back in place, but she still couldn't do anything about her rosy, used lips, and her just-fucked, flushed face. More than anything, he wanted to touch her, hug her. But instead, he and Lonnie took seats in separate armchairs and made conversation with Matt and Peach.

"I'm telling you," Peach was saying, "you should've been there." She'd just finished describing the Bruins game, and the fight that had broken out only two rows behind them. She and Matt had raced home to see if they'd be on the ten o'clock news.

"So, Lonnie, what did you think of Twit's announcement yesterday?" Matt asked, with a lop-sided, mocking grin.

"Oh. The word ridiculous comes to mind," she said. "Didn't you find it strange that—" Then she stopped herself. She didn't know what to isolate; she wanted to ask Matt if he'd found every single thing about Twit & Bell strange these days. But she remembered what Detective Montgomery had told her about total discretion, so she proceeded lightly. "I don't know. It just seemed strange that Twit would make a blanket statement like that about not taking another partner. Well, you're an attorney. . . . How'd *you* feel about it?"

Matt shrugged. "Honestly, I couldn't care less. I'm putting in another year there; then I'm moving on to a bigger firm, anyway."

Lonnie nodded. "But didn't Twit think his announcement would alienate the others?"

"The guy is totally blinded by ego. What does he care?" Matt leaned back against the couch and rested his hands behind his head.

"I see your point," she agreed, and added off the cuff, "I guess B. J. feels the same as you."

He snorted, "B. J. is just lucky he even has a job at this point." That made him snicker.

"Which one was B. J. again?" Peach asked. While Matt launched into an unflattering description, Lonnie glanced over at Dominick. He made penetrating eye contact, as if to say: *I don't know when we're going to finish what we started, but when we do, neither of us will be able to walk for a week.* At least, that was how she chose to interpret it.

"So, why's he lucky to have a job?" Peach asked, and Lonnie snapped out of her lustful trance. That was a good question, and she was also interested in the answer.

"Simple," Matt said, smirking. "As an attorney, B. J. sucks." His smile grew wider. "He's screwed up with three different clients already. The guy's a complete asshole." His face was positively beaming now, as if nothing gave him greater pleasure than illuminating B. J.'s defects. No one said anything, so he continued. "That's why he was so obsessed with the idea that he was getting fired."

"*B. J. was?*" Lonnie was shocked because B. J. always acted confident, especially when it came to his casework. Of course she figured a lot of it was pretense, but she never dreamed that it was *all* pretense.

"Hell, yeah. B. J. was completely, psychotically obsessed," Matt sneered, his voice thick with ridicule. When no one responded to that, he switched gears and made his tone milder. "See, he'd worked with Lunther on a couple of cases, and he'd made blunders—we're talking *big-time blunders*. And Lunther told him if he screwed up one more time, he was out. Then, a few weeks ago, he lost a client."

"How?" Lonnie asked, wide-eyed and keenly interested.

"It was some dinky finance firm. The account was relatively small potatoes, so Lunther gave it to B. J. But they thought he was incompetent, and instead of switching to another attorney they changed firms." He paused, grinned devilishly, and said, "I've gotta tell you, Lunther was angrier than I'd ever seen him."

"But, I thought you said the client was 'small potatoes,'" Peach said, quoting with her fingers.

"*Relatively*," Matt repeated.

Lonnie couldn't believe what she was hearing! All this had been going on while B. J. was proudly sauntering around the office, bragging about how he breezed through his work. Life was so strange. Still, she failed to see why Matt was so utterly, shamelessly, smug about the whole thing.

Suddenly she remembered what B. J. had said at the staff meeting the day before—that he was glad Twit was the one in charge now—which she'd thought was very odd at the time. Now it made more sense.

"Why didn't he get fired?" Dominick asked, although Lonnie sensed that he was only politely curious about B. J. She, on the other hand, was fascinated.

"I don't know. Lunther was probably going to, but—"

Matt didn't need to finish the sentence; everyone was thinking the same thing. Lunther died before he had the chance.

"Sorry about interrupting you and Dominick tonight." The apartment was pitch-black, and Peach and Lonnie were lying in their beds, wide-awake.

"Oh, it's okay."

"No, really," Peach went on, "Matt asked me if I wanted to watch the news coverage of the game at his place, but I didn't know if I wanted to go to his apartment yet."

"I'm glad you came back here." Lonnie was grateful that Peach, for all her free-spiritedness, was still cautious. They were both like their father that way. Lonnie asked, "So, do you like him a lot?" She couldn't help but wonder what her sister thought of Matt after tonight. Had she noticed the profound enjoyment that Matt seemed to get out of his so-called friend's misfortunes?

"Umm . . . he's okay. I don't know." She paused. "He bought a chili dog."

"Huh?"

She sighed and repeated, "He bought a chili dog. At the game." Lonnie rolled to face the partition screen, and Peach finished with, "I just don't know if I can be with someone who eats that. A hot dog's bad enough, but then cow flesh on top of it? I just don't know if I can make a relationship like that work."

"Oh. Yeah," she agreed gently, because she admired Peach's vegetarian principles, even if she couldn't relate. Not only were cheeseburgers a weakness, but no matter how hard she tried, she just couldn't get her conscience to engage the red-meat issue beyond the calorie count.

"Did you have fun with Dominick tonight? I mean, before Matt and I busted in on you?"

"Yeah." Especially the half-naked writhing part. Not that she had tons of experience with fully naked writhing, but inexperience seemed easy enough to fix. She said good night to Peach, and soon they both drifted off to sleep.

Early the next morning, Lonnie met Detective Montgomery at Espresso Royale to discuss what she'd observed around the office since they'd talked on Monday. She'd written down a few notes, but was still unsure if there was much purpose in it. On top of that, now he was getting on her case about her large café mocha.

"How can you drink that *crap*?"

"It's good; I like it."

"You got so much sugar and chocolate in that, it's not even coffee anymore." He winced as if her drink was the foulest concoction he'd ever seen.

"Sorry, we can't all be 'manly' and order black coffee, pretending it's the best thing we've ever tasted," Lonnie replied. Normally, she was more polite, but Montgomery had been teasing her for the past five minutes. The man seemed to get a big kick out of rattling her, but now that she wasn't afraid of him anymore, he was getting a reaction another way. Namely, by acting like an obnoxious punk. And here she was doing him a favor!

He chuckled and said, "What happened to the nervous little girl from the other night? The one who thought I could cart her off to jail without a moment's notice? I think I like her better."

You would, she thought. "I'm twenty-seven. I think that qualifies me as a woman."

He sighed. "Ah, God. So you're one of those?"

Those? By now she knew he wasn't out to get her. But he was still a royal pain.

"I only mind being called a 'girl' when it's meant to reduce me. Now, can we get back to the case?" She kept her tone even, because something told her that if she encouraged Montgomery's badgering, he'd be merciless.

"Okay, okay. What d'ya got?" He took out his notepad and waited for her report.

"Let's see . . .," she began. "Well, I'll just give you the list." She handed a sheet of paper across the table to Montgomery and explained, "See, I've numbered things in terms of abnormality, with 'one' being 'very odd' and 'eight' being—"

"I get it, I get it," he cut her off, and scanned the list. "What *is* this?"

"What?" She straightened up in her seat, a little indignantly.

"What's this—'Bette's bragging reduced'? 'Twit stayed in office a lot'?" Well, sure, with *that* inflection, of course it sounded dumb. " 'Hang-up calls'?"

"Yes. I've been getting hang-up calls ever since Delia forwarded Lunther's phones to me."

"Uh-huh." His expression was bland. "Solicitors and anyone else who would have no reason to know Bell died. Next"—Lonnie's blood was boiling— " 'Delia spills soda'?"

"Wait, I didn't get to finish writing that! What happened was—"

He held up his hand to silence her. "Really, that's okay." He shook his head and waved the paper, as if demanding an explanation. "You call this helpful?"

"Hey, what's your problem?" Lonnie asked, annoyed. "Those are perfectly valid observations."

She went on to explain why, and finally he nodded, half convinced.

"Okay, okay," he said. "What's this one? 'Mail delivered late on Thursday.' " He cracked up laughing.

Lonnie gritted her teeth. "That's why it's number *eight*. If you were listening before—"

"Okay, I'm sorry," Montgomery said, still chuckling. "This is . . . this is good, really. But I think from now on, look for things that are a little more tied into *motive*."

Lonnie scoffed, "What makes you think there'll be a next time?" She snatched her list out of his hand. "Is this my tax dollars at work?"

Montgomery laughed, and leaned in closer across the table. He softened his tone. "Look, I'm sorry, all right?" Yet he was still beaming with amusement at her expense. She just scowled. "Really, this is helpful. I'm giving you a hard time this morning, I know."

"Why are you?" Lonnie asked, relaxing her posture a little.

"I don't know. You're like the little sister I never had." He squinted his eyes, and appraised her with blatant cockiness. "Actually," he corrected, "you're not *exactly* like a sister." Either he was trying to annoy her or come on to her, but either way, it gave him far too much pleasure.

"Please, you're old enough to be my butler. Can we get back to the case now?"

"I'm forty-three," he said, mildly indignant. "But you can relax. You're not my type, anyway." He leaned back and flashed the confident smile of a middle-aged hunk who knew he still held appeal. "I like my women compliant."

"Yeah, that sounds about right."

"You're a little high maintenance for my taste."

"Fascinating. I'm crushed, by the way. Now, about my notes—"

"And you're high strung, but you just don't know it."

"Well, you're overbearing and overdeveloped," she said without thinking. Then a giggle burst from her throat. "Hey, now you've got me doing it!"

He just grimaced. "Yeah. All right, so what else d'ya got?" She gave him a saccharine smile and took the folded-up copy she'd made of Twit's fax from her bag.

"Here," she said, passing it to him.

"What's this?" he asked, as he took it.

She shrugged. "I don't know what it means, but I just know Beauregard asked me every day if this fax had come in, and then since Lunther died, he hasn't mentioned one word about it. He hasn't seen it yet." He scanned the contents, and she added, "Ann Lee was Lunther's assistant. One day she just stopped showing up for work."

Detective Montgomery folded up the paper and slipped it into his front pocket. "I'll look into it. Thanks. I mean it." He seemed completely sincere. . . . What was the catch?

"No problem," Lonnie said, and decided to take advantage of his gratitude, which promised to be ephemeral, at best. "Detective, I just have to know," she probed. "What did you mean the other night when you said there had been threats against Lunther?"

"Kid, I can't get into all that with you."

"Why not? You can trust me! Anyway, how do you expect me to keep an eye out when I don't even know what's going on?"

He pondered that for a moment, and then yielded. "It was nothing specific," he explained. "But we had it on file. Bell's brother—"

"Henry."

"Right. A couple weeks ago, Henry comes into the station and wants to file a report, saying his brother had gotten some death threats. But the problem is, the guy doesn't have any real information. All he knows is what Bell told him—that someone he knew had threatened to kill him more than once."

"Oh, God," she muttered to herself.

Montgomery continued. "But Bell wouldn't tell him who it was—claimed they were empty threats. Apparently, he'd told Henry in passing, never realizing he'd take it any further."

"But why was Henry worried?" Lonnie asked. "I mean, if Lunther didn't think the threats were serious . . .?"

He shrugged. "I can only assume that Bell was a real asshole, because, I gotta tell you, Henry believed it. He was absolutely positive that if someone had the chance, they wouldn't hesitate to kill his brother. And as it turns out, he was right."

Lonnie had always thought there was something underlying Lunther's disingenuous good-ol'-boy bit, but was it even more than she thought?

"Then when we got the call about his death," Montgomery continued. "Well, the way he was found . . . let's just say, it didn't feel right." She thought about the way Lunther had been backed up against the coatroom wall, and undeniably, it *was* strange.

Montgomery gave her notes a once-over. "There's nothing here about Macey Green." He looked up at her. "So you didn't notice anything off about her? Nothing at all?"

"N-no."

"Think, Lonnie. Anything at all?"

"*No*, Detective. I can't think of anything." Why was he so suspicious of Macey? Was he still zeroing in on her just because she'd left the holiday party before the police had arrived? Lonnie realized that she'd have to snoop around a little more if she wanted to get information that would get Montgomery to give up his Macey theory. If she could just find evidence against the real killer . . . Hopefully the fax would turn up something important.

"Okay," Montgomery said. "Now, before I go, is there anything else? Anything at all?"

Lonnie considered telling him what she'd learned the night before about B. J. But she couldn't do it. B. J. was too harmless to commit murder, and the last thing she wanted was to mar his career any more than *he* already had. She couldn't implicate him with a clear conscience when she didn't believe for a minute he could be a murderer. So she just shook her head.

Montgomery got up to go. "I'll be in touch. Thanks again."

Lonnie knew she'd have to look a lot harder if she wanted to find out who the real killer was, and keep Montgomery from coming down hard on the most convenient scapegoats. But how would she do that without attracting attention and making herself a target?

She half smiled good-bye to the detective, took a final swig of her mocha, and told herself it was just the sugar making her shake.

Chapter Eighteen

"Are we gonna kiss, or are we gonna eat?" Lonnie was sitting on Dominick's lap, with his office door firmly shut. She snuggled closer. She knew she should get back to work, but since it was Friday, she was feeling lazy.

"You choose," Dominick murmured, and kissed her jaw softly. He tightened his hold on her, and she squirmed just enough to feel him hard underneath her. She sighed languorously, and kissed his mouth. Slowly and deeply.

"That's not fair," she whispered into his mouth after they broke the kiss. "You know what I'll choose every time." He smiled against her lips, and ignored his ringing phone. "Aren't you going to get that?" she asked, running her fingers through his hair and over his ears. He just made a low, husky sound, and nuzzled her hair.

She'd told him last weekend that Lunther had been murdered, and he'd suggested that she get a new job, just to be on the safe side. When she told him she couldn't yet, because she'd said she'd help with the investigation, Dominick had made her promise to meet him for lunch every day so he could keep an eye on her and make sure she was okay. That annoyed her a little at first, because the last thing she wanted was for her dating companion/potential lover to *coddle* her. However, it didn't take long to see that what Dominick was really trying to do was manipulate her into coming downstairs to make out with him every day. She could live with that.

"So, how's it going upstairs?" he asked, strumming her spine with his fingers. "Have you found out anything incriminating about anyone?"

Lonnie had debriefed him on her coworkers more than once, and—unlike a certain ungrateful detective—Dominick found her observations interesting *and* valid. Now she shrugged. "Not really. You know that fax I told you about?" He nodded. "I gave a copy of it to Montgomery yesterday, but I haven't heard from him yet about what he's turned up."

"I know I've said it before, but that guy has nerve asking you to get involved in all this. He should do his own damn job," Dominick said.

"Well, *technically*, I'm not supposed to investigate—just to pay closer attention to what goes on around the office."

"I know, but still," Dominick said, and brushed some silky hair away from Lonnie's face.

"I should probably get up before I break your kneecaps," she said apologetically.

"I think this guy has the hots for you," he said, either ignoring what she'd just said, or not registering it at all.

"Who, Montgomery?"

"Yeah."

"Get outta here. He loves to annoy me, but that's about it."

"I'm serious," Dominick said. "I think this whole informant thing is just his excuse to put the moves on you."

She laughed. "Where are you getting this?"

One hand slid up through her hair, and another

tightened around her waist. "Because . . . who
wouldn't have the hots for you?" he asked huskily,
and her heart liquefied. Somehow, Dominick's sweet
talk always struck her as far more sincere than Jake's.
And as far as another man being interested in her,
well, he had absolutely nothing to worry about.

"You weren't interested in me in college," she argued mildly.

"How would you know?" he teased. "You were
always following Eric around with your eyes bug-
ging out of their sockets." Grinning, he added, "It
was pretty embarrassing."

She flattened her palms on his chest and shoved.
"Hey." He laughed. "Is this what I come down here
for?" He was still laughing. "You're hysterically
funny," she said sarcastically, and he pulled her to
him.

"Sorry," he said, not sounding sorry at all, and
she just grinned. "Forgive me?" he mumbled against
her neck.

"Um . . ." He placed gentle openmouthed kisses
on her skin. "I . . . hmm . . . okay," she breathed.
Then she said into his hair, "I should really get
back." He groaned his disappointment, as she disentangled herself and slid off his lap.

"Okay. I guess I should start doing something that
resembles work one of these days, anyway," he said,
and his sexy grin almost changed her mind about
going back upstairs.

"What are you implying?" she asked innocently.
"That I keep you from getting your work done?"
Standing over him, she spread her legs and locked
his in between. She bent down to whisper in his ear,
"I don't do anything."

His voice was strained. "Oh, yeah . . . you don't
do anything . . ." He ran his hands up and down on
her butt, and then tightened them to grasp her.

Her heart fluttered wildly in her breast—which,

at the moment, was rising and falling to match her excitement. Dominick must have noticed, because suddenly his head was nearly buried in her sweater and his eyes were glazed as he monitored each heaving breath she took. She couldn't help it; his gently possessive touch never failed to arouse her.

A knock at the door broke their concentration. "Damn," he whispered, and she pulled back, feeling overheated. When she was on the other side of Dominick's desk, he called, "Yes."

It was Harold. He poked his head in. "D? Oh! Excuse me. I didn't know you had company. I was just calling you, but let me know when—"

"It's okay," Lonnie assured him, and headed for the door. "I'm just leaving. I'll talk to you later, Dominick."

"Okay—oh, wait!" Dominick called to her. He turned back to Harold. "I'll be right back." Then he walked with Lonnie to the elevator. "Listen, give me the names of those women listed on that fax. I'll look them up on the Internet, see if I find out anything."

"Oh, no. I don't want you getting involved in this," she said.

"If you're involved, I'm already involved," he said simply. "Come on, you can't do it, or people in your office will know you're up to something."

"No. I don't want you to take the chance," she said. "Besides, I left the fax in my bag, which is locked in my desk."

"But—"

"Really," she insisted. Then she leaned up to give him a firm, sweet kiss on the cheek. "Thanks for offering, but for now, I'm going to deal with it myself. Okay?"

After a pause, he just shrugged. "Okay, if you're sure."

"I'm sure."

*   *   *

An hour later, Lonnie was walking from the bathroom back to her desk when she overheard a familiar voice. It was a savage, hoarse whisper that could only belong to the man who'd accosted Bette in the library a few weeks back. And, what a coincidence, it was coming from B. J.'s office.

She hadn't planned to eavesdrop, but she caught B. J. saying something about being "desperate," so she'd lingered in the hall to hear more. "Look, I said I'd owe you, all right?" he was saying. "I'll owe you *big*. Whatever you want, just *please*—

"Look, I need this favor," he whispered urgently, although Lonnie wondered if B. J. had any idea how loud his whispering actually was. "Yes, yes . . . Whatever you want . . . Okay, okay, I'll do it. So, anyway—hello? Hello?"

As soon as she heard him slam down the phone, she darted away before he could catch her. When she got to her desk, she found Twit waiting for her, looking disgruntled and put out. He must've been waiting there for all of two minutes. "Hi, Beauregard," she said amiably. "Did you need something?"

"Uh, yes, I did. But I've been standing here waiting so long, I've forgotten what it is." He looked up at the clock. "I'm running behind now. I'll call you in when I remember what it was." He turned to go, but B. J.'s voice stopped him.

"Beauregard!" B. J. called, and hurried down the hall, jogging his skinny little legs toward Lonnie's desk. "Great news. I just got off the phone with that buddy of mine I told you about. He scored us tickets, third row, half-court."

What? He was on the phone with a *buddy* of his? The guy he'd begged and bribed? The guy who'd hung up on him? B. J. needed new friends.

"That's terrific!" Twit declared, and patted B. J. on the back.

He shrugged. "Please, like I'd said before, the guy

was thrilled to do it for me. He owed me some favors." *Maybe B. J. was dropped on his head as a baby.*
"Anyway, anything for a pal."

He patted Twit on the back and started to turn
around, when Twit said, "Wait, B. J. Actually, since
your friend owes you anyway, would you mind terribly getting one more ticket?" B. J.'s face fell in horror.
Clearing his throat, Twit added, "I was hoping to
take a lady friend, too." Now Lonnie's face fell in
horror.

Okay, that was enough. Watching B. J. squirm. Picturing Twit having a lady friend. Picturing Twit having a friend, period. A girl could only take so much.
She was about to interrupt and put a halt to everyone's discomfort when Twit looked at her quizzically
for a second, and then shuffled away from her desk.
She caught a glimpse of B. J.'s plastic joker smile
before he turned on his heel and trailed after Twit.
She couldn't believe how much she'd underestimated
B. J.'s issues. She'd known he was insecure, but this
was ridiculous. There was only one word she could
think of to describe him . . .

Desperate.

Just then a message appeared on her computer
screen. NEW MAIL. When she opened her inbox, she
couldn't have been more surprised. It was a forward
from Terry—who she hadn't heard from since he'd
annihilated her on the phone a few days ago.

What a weirdo. So apparently she "flares a temper"
in him, but not enough to get banished from his forward distribution list. Just her luck. She hit DELETE
without opening it, and went back to work.

Later that day, Lonnie found herself thinking about
B. J. again. She wondered if she'd done the right
thing by omitting information about him when she'd
talked to Detective Montgomery. Could B. J. really
be a *killer*? The idea seemed too hard to swallow . . .
yet she couldn't say anything for sure anymore. It

was becoming painfully clear that the Twit & Bell staff had more going on beneath the surface than Lonnie had thought.

Still engrossed in thought about the murder investigation, she absently clicked on her latest NEW MAIL message. Dear Lord, it was another e-mail from Terry. This one wasn't a forward, but an actual message. It read: *Hey, Lonnie Anderson, what's new in Beantown?*

What on *earth*—was this guy *insane*? He'd told her in no uncertain terms—and a winding, maniacal monologue—that he couldn't stand her. He'd *dropped* her, for pete's sake. Did she actually need to explain to Terry the rules of etiquette that applied to dumping someone on their ass, cold? Generally speaking, congenial little e-mails weren't welcome.

Whatever. She pressed DELETE, and went back to mulling over her B. J. dilemma.

Okay, that was it. She had to clear her conscience about B. J. She'd tell Montgomery all the information she'd initially omitted . . . right after she tried to get some answers herself. After all, it was only right that she first corroborate Matt's account of B. J.'s professional disgrace. How much of it was true, and how legitimate was B. J.'s fear that Lunther would fire him?

Lonnie pushed away from her desk, and made her way down to Bette's office. Who better to ask about the status of B. J.'s employment than the human resource specialist? Although Lonnie had a feeling that pesky "confidentiality" bit was going to be a problem. She knocked on Bette's open door and poked her head in. "Bette? Could I talk to you?"

"Lonnie." She looked up from her paperwork and creased her waxy face into a bogus smile. "How nice to see you," she crooned, and motioned with a French-manicured finger. "Come in."

Before she could come up with a suave opener, Lonnie noticed that something was different about Bette's office. Oh. Her pictures were back. Yep, there they were, all lined up. Reginald, Burberry, and Skylar-Blaise. Not to mention the obligatory family shot with their dog, Ellis, and their cat, Josephine. It wasn't fair that someone as snobby and shallow as Bette had such a picture-perfect life, but it seemed in keeping with the basic cruel irony that governed the universe.

"Dear?" Bette's nasally, patronizing voice broke the spell, and Lonnie jerked to attention.

"Um . . . Bette, I was wondering . . ." *Time to improvise.* "Should I put together some sort of goodbye party for B. J.?"

Bette's pencil-sculpted eyebrows shot up. "B. J.'s *leaving*?" Lonnie thought she heard a trace of excitement in her voice. Poor B. J. Then Bette regarded her skeptically and said, "This is news to me." *Interesting.* If Lunther was in the process of firing B. J. when he died, would Bette be this surprised?

"Oh," Lonnie started backpedaling, "maybe I got my information wrong, but—"

"Where *did* you get your information?" Bette was using that patronizing voice again—as if she fully expected her to admit she'd made it up.

"Uh . . ." Lonnie stumbled, "it must've been a rumor around the water cooler. . . . I can't remember the *exact* source. . . ." Glancing up at Bette's squinted eyes, Lonnie decided to bluff. Well, to bluff *better*. She needed to look at Bette dead-on, completely confident in her assertions, and see what she revealed. It was worth a try, anyway.

"Forgive me, Bette." Lonnie spoke more firmly now, and made unfaltering eye contact. "I was under the impression that B. J. was leaving because of Lunther—uh, that is to say, because of what the situ-

ation was before Lunther passed away . . . *tragically*."
She threw in the last part for good measure, and
waited to see if Bette would take the bait.

"I wasn't aware that anyone knew about B. J.'s
problems with Lunther."

"Actually, it was hardly kept a secret." When it
came to inventing false claims, passive voice was key.
And, thank goodness, Bette played right into it.

She snorted and shook her head in disgust. "Of
course not. Why am I even surprised? That puny
little reject just can't keep his big mouth shut, can
he?" Lonnie assumed she was referring to B. J., in
which case *reject* was only fair, but *puny* seemed like
a pretty low blow. She didn't interrupt, though; she
just let Bette talk.

"B. J. is lucky that Lunther never got around to
firing him. But, then, I'm sure he had other things
on his mind that were far more important than B. J."
She chortled and added, "Which isn't exactly a
stretch." Obviously, once Bette got going, she didn't
need much encouragement.

"Lonnie, *dear*, do yourself a favor and don't waste
even a brain cell recognizing B. J.'s existence on this
planet." And she thought Matt was harsh. "He just
doesn't get it, you know? You can't try to be somebody by lying about who you are. You're either born
somebody or not; you either have status or you don't.
He's so desperate to con every possible kind of ac-
ceptance out of people that they see right through
him. People see through desperation. It's that
simple."

Was it that simple? Lonnie didn't know. When it
came to Twit & Bell, she didn't know very much
anymore. She left Bette's office, headed for her desk,
and retrieved the emergency Mounds bar she'd
stored in the third drawer a month ago. She knew
unequivocally . . . it was time.

*   *   *

"Laurel, I need this faxed A-SAP." Twit tossed two paper-clipped sheets onto Lonnie's desk and kept going, like the Energizer duck.

"Sure, no problem," she said to dead air.

Lonnie saved the Word document she'd been working on, pushed away from her desk, and headed over to the fax machine. After she'd loaded it and pressed SEND, she started refilling the paper tray. She thought of the fax she'd given to Montgomery. Even though she'd only given it to him the morning before, and technically he was under no obligation to give her the play-by-play of his investigation, she still hoped he would called her as soon as he found out anything.

The fax machine sounded, and the confirmation sheet inched its way out. Absently, Lonnie grabbed it, tossed it in her inbox, and continued thinking about that list of women. What did Ann Lee have to do with the others? And what was Twit planning to do with the names? She bit her lip, trying to figure it out, but she couldn't. Montgomery said he'd look into it, so why was she worrying about it? Why was she suddenly so fixated?

She couldn't discount what Montgomery had told her about poisoning being a more female crime. It seemed logical, therefore, that he would want to check out those women as soon as possible. The only thing was: Montgomery seemed to think he had a highly viable suspect already, right under everyone's nose. Macey. Which was ludicrous. Just because Macey was a strong, aloof woman, didn't mean she was a murderer.

Lonnie shook her head in frustration. She just wished she knew where the investigation stood. There was only one way to find out.

She took out Montgomery's card, as well as her cell phone, and headed to the elevator. On the ride down to the lobby, she remembered that she hadn't told Montgomery everything the day before. She'd omitted any information about B. J. because she hadn't wanted to implicate him. Sweet, clueless, hopeless B. J.

Now she wasn't so sure about her decision. After talking to Bette, she knew that Matt had been right: B. J. was on the verge of being fired. And he knew it. Matt had described B. J. as *obsessed*, which would explain why he accosted Bette in the library. Undoubtedly, he was grilling her for information about his job status. It also explained why Bette avoided him at the holiday party, and why B. J. returned to his gregarious old self after Lunther died.

That settled it. First she'd ask what Montgomery had learned about the women on the list. Then she'd tell him about B. J.

The elevator doors opened, and she stepped out into the pink-marbled lobby. Once she was safely hidden behind a wide, cylindrical column, she dialed. After two rings, he picked up. "Detective Montgomery."

"Hi, Detective. This is Lonnie Kelley."

"Hi there. How are you doin'? Got any information for me?" She could hear a lot of muffled voices and phones ringing in the background.

"Uh, sort of." For all she knew, Montgomery had checked out B. J. and found out about his job troubles. "What do you know about B. J. Flynn?"

"You on a secure line?"

"Um . . . yeah," she answered, hoping it was true.

"Okay . . . let's see here . . ." She could hear him rustling papers, and then he said, "Twenty-six, white male . . . middle-class background . . . law degree from Dinkle College. He's an associate . . . been with the firm almost a year." When Montgomery finished, Lonnie was speechless. *Dinkle College?*

"That's it? What I mean is, you haven't . . . I don't

know . . . investigated him more thoroughly than that?"

Montgomery casually replied, "Not really. He's not high on our list of suspects. Not that I should be telling you that. Or any of this, for that matter."

She ignored the last part and pressed on. "But I thought everyone was a suspect. Well, except me, of course."

"B. J.'s got no visible motive. That's not to say he couldn't have done it, but first we look at people who are more obvious suspects. The ones with something immediate—usually money—to gain from murder. Or the ones with an emotional connection to or history with the victim." She couldn't help thinking that Twit fit into both those categories.

Montgomery added, "From where I sit, I doubt B. J.'s gonna profit from Bell's death. Especially since the firm's net worth is gonna drop."

Lonnie thought about that for a minute.

"Lonnie?"

"Oh, yeah, I'm here," she said vacantly. "I don't get it—why haven't you interrogated anyone here yet? Why does everyone still think Lunther's death was just a heart attack?"

Montgomery sighed heavily. "Look, I gotta be honest with you. This case is a little lacking in the evidence department. If the potassium chloride was slipped into Lunther's glass, we'll never know, because the tables were cleared at ten-thirty and the dishwashers were loaded by eleven. At this point, our best hope is to wait for someone to trip up. That usually happens when they don't know anyone's watching." He paused and added, "What did you want to tell me about B. J.?"

"Wait. First tell me what you found out about the fax I gave you. Have you checked out the women who were listed on it?"

He sighed, which she'd learned wasn't a great sign, but by no means indicated defeat. "Kid, I can't tell you every detail of the case," he said.

"Why not? You've told me everything so far!" she said without thinking, and then her hand flew over her mouth. "I mean—"

"Yeah, you're right. Jesus, I confide less in my damn shrink."

"You don't strike me as the type to see a shrink," she remarked.

"I don't. I just said that," he replied, chuckling.

She rolled her eyes and grinned in spite of herself. "Detective, *please*. I want to know what you found out about the fax I gave you. I *need* to find out."

"Boy, have you gotten an attitude since I first met you. Now, listen—" There was a pause and some muffled talking before Montgomery said, "Shit, I gotta go—"

"Wait, please! Just tell me about the fax, and then I'll fill you in on B. J. whenever it's convenient, okay?" Her voice was calm but forceful. And he relented.

"Ah, Christ." He sighed for the millionth time and continued. "I can tell you that we ran all those women's names through the computer, and only one came up." *Ann Lee?* "Sandra Neemas. She'd pressed charges against Bell for sexual harassment. Actually, she started to press charges, but then she dropped them. To tell you the truth, it's a total fluke that her name is even still on record here. It should have been deleted a long time ago."

"How long ago?"

"Uh . . . I guess a year ago. Right after she dropped the charges." Lonnie felt nauseated. She always knew Lunther was a slob and a buffoon. But a sexual harasser, too? What a creep. "But we already checked her out," he went on. "She's been in living in London for the past five months. The other three women had

similar stories, but they've all got alibis, so I've ruled
them out."

"What do you mean 'similar stories'?"

"No, that's it."

"But—"

"I gotta go."

Finally, she yielded to the nonnegotiable tone in
his voice. "Okay."

"Hey, do me a favor?" Montgomery added before
getting off the phone. "Forget everything I just told
you. And stop snooping before I arrest you."

"Bye, Detective," she said, ignoring his silly threat.
In some ways, Montgomery was as absurd as every
other person in her daily life. Well, except Dominick.
And Peach. And Margot. Okay, not Margot.

Lonnie switched off her cell phone and emerged
from the far-off corner of the lobby to go back to
work. On the elevator, she thought about what Montgomery had told her. He'd said the women had *similar stories*. So that meant they all worked for Lunther?
He'd sexually harassed *all* of them? How could she
find out for sure?

Macey! She was the only person Lonnie could ask
about this. Did she know what'd happened to these
women? Maybe this was why she hated Lunther so
much. She'd have to ask her. Not only did Lonnie
want to find out who killed Lunther for justice's sake;
she also wanted to clear Macey . . . who didn't even
know she was a suspect.

Then she remembered that Macey was out of the
office that day, making a court appearance. That
meant Lonnie would have to wait all the way till
Monday to talk to her.

Damn it all!

Lonnie pushed hard on the glass doors to Twit &
Bell and charged over to her desk. She plopped into
her chair and tried to calm her nerves with some
semideep breaths. It didn't work. Her heart was beat-

ing fast and her stomach was working on burning a hole through itself. She felt wired. She needed to *do* something. And she didn't even know what.

"Luanne, it's about time!" Twit barged stormily toward her. "I could've been to the moon and back by now." There couldn't have been a worse time for Twit's antics. He pointed his finger at her. "I need punctuality and reliability from my assistant, Lorna. Is that perfectly clear?"

Lonnie inhaled a deep breath, gritted her teeth so hard they hurt, and shot icy eyes at him. "Oh, *stuff it!*"

She vaulted off her chair, pushed past him, and stalked to the bathroom. And she'd be damned if she'd tell him later that she was just moody with "female problems." Enough was enough! She had more important things to think about than hand-holding Twit through another day of megalomania. Like protecting her friend and mentor. Like finding Lunther's killer. Like justice for all women, which somehow fit in.

First thing Monday, she'd talk to Macey.

Chapter Nineteen

"I still don't get it," Peach said, penciling an image on her large sketch pad. "How come Mom didn't invite me to dinner?"

"What are you talking about?" Lonnie called from the closet. "She asked us both; you said you had other plans. Have you seen my blue Nikes?"

"I think you got the order wrong there. First I mentioned I had plans on Saturday night. *Then* she asked us to dinner. Don't you get it?"

Lonnie emerged from the closet disheveled—her ponytail was lopsided from crawling around looking for her sneakers, and the knees of her nylon running pants were torn open from a roller-blading "incident" at the Public Gardens last spring. "Get what?" she asked absently, and brushed a stray clump of hair away from her forehead. "I can only find one."

"Why are you gonna wear your blue ones? They're ugly. No offense."

"I like them."

"Now, back to Mom . . ." Peach paused just long enough to grab a different pencil and change the angle of her pad. "It seems painfully obvious that Mom wants to get you alone tonight so she can talk about me."

"What?" Lonnie scoffed because the suggestion was ludicrous, and her sister was hardly the paranoid type. "What are you talking about? Why would Mom do that?" She bent on her knees, lifted the comforter up, and looked under her bed for the other sneaker. "Yes!" She strained to reach for it, and shoved it on forcefully.

"I'm serious," Peach said calmly while sketching. "She's obsessed with the idea of me getting a 'real job.' She thinks that taking an entry-level position with 'growth potential' at some company I don't care about is what my life needs. She figures I just need to be convinced, and that's where you come in." She looked up. "Don't you see? This dinner tonight—it's a sneak attack to bring you over to *her* side."

"That's crazy. I'm the last person she'd try that with. She knows I'll defend your side no matter what." Lonnie stood and looked down at her just-laced feet. Maybe the sneakers were a little ugly . . . but in a fun way. What was the difference anyway? She was just having dinner at her parents' town house—it wasn't like she had to dress up for the occasion. Her mother had mentioned something about "looking presentable," but it was just one in a long string of nagging commands, so Lonnie hadn't given it too much consideration.

Just then there was a knock at the door.

"Oh, that's Cheryl." Peach set aside her pad and went to open the door. "Hey," she said.

"Hi!" Cheryl enthused sweetly, and followed Peach inside. "Hi, Lonnie," she said, and sat down on the rug.

"Okay, did you bring the dress we agreed on?" Peach asked, sounding a little like a teacher on the cusp of admonishing a student.

Cheryl nodded sheepishly, and pointed to the shopping bag she'd rested against the sofa. "Are you sure . . . ?"

"Yes," Peach commanded, leaving no room for negotiation.

"So, are you guys excited for tonight?" Lonnie asked, as she put on her puffy white parka. The coat, she could admit, was definitely ugly. But it had been raining the last time she checked and, if nothing else, the suffocating white monstrosity was waterproof.

"Sort of," Cheryl answered shyly, with flushed cheeks and a tremulous smile, and pushed a short dark blond lock behind her ear. That night she and Peach were double-dating with Matt and his uncle, Jean-Paul. Peach had set up the whole thing—although, Matt had warned her that his uncle was not the stuff of dream dates. Apparently, Uncle Jean-Paul was a forty-nine-year-old widower who'd moved from France to America more than fifteen years ago but still insisted on speaking French in mixed company—and the less people understood, the better he seemed to like it. Granted, not what Lonnie would consider a *ten*, but Peach said they had to start somewhere.

"Do you guys know where you're going yet?"

"Matt's uncle picked a place," Peach replied. "A new restaurant in Newton. Chez Noir, I think it's called." Lonnie nodded and reserved comment. "Actually, I'm spending the night at Iris's house afterward, okay? It's just easier. Oh! I forgot," Peach exclaimed, turning her attention to Cheryl. "I have to teach you to French kiss before we go."

What?

Okay, her sister was a force that needed to be stopped. "Peach!" Lonnie cried scoldingly.

"What?" Peach asked innocently. "She asked me to."

Cheryl's cheeks went from pink to scarlet in .5 seconds, but she nodded. Lonnie gave up. All they needed was for Cheryl to start calling Peach "sir," and the Peppermint Patty–Marcy metamorphosis would be complete. . . . But, hey, it wasn't any of her business. Anyway, she had to admit that Cheryl appeared a lot happier than the first time she'd come to the apartment, so maybe Peach's intrusive brand of therapy was actually helping, after all.

"Which reminds me," Peach proceeded, "do we have any really soft plums?"

Lonnie squinted her eyes, bewildered by her sister's thought process. "Uh . . . no, I don't think so." Not only didn't they have any "really soft plums," but spicy-hot V8 and lime JELL-O were the closest things they ever had to fruit. "Why?"

"To practice kissing. How else do you think I'm gonna teach her?" Then Peach's tone changed to teasing. "Look, Cheryl, I *like* you and all, but—"

"Okay, okay," Lonnie said, shaking her head. "Have a great time tonight, you guys."

She zipped up her bulky parka, grabbed her keys off the table by the door, and left before Peach could ask her if they had any really hard bananas.

On the T, Lonnie used her cell phone to call Dominick.

"So, what's the deal? How long do you think dinner's going to run?"

"Hmm . . . I should probably be home before nine."

"Let's do something after then." *Yes!* Although she figured it would take a good hour to clean up her act since she looked particularly rumpled and slovenly at the moment.

"Okay. I'll call you when I get home. What are you doing now?"

His voice was breezy and husky and blood-rushing all at the same time when he said, "Oh, I'm just here hanging out with my other girlfriend."

"Well, don't let me keep you."

"No, it's okay. I like you better, anyway. So, you're gonna call me when you get home?"

"Mmm-hmm. I want to"—*attack you*—"see you."

He lowered his voice and said, "Me, too."

After they said good-bye, Lonnie switched off her phone absently, and let warm anticipation swirl through her. Dominick had jokingly said his "other girlfriend." Well, that settled it, then; he considered her his girlfriend. It just seemed too good to be true. He was too wonderful, and she liked being with him too much for all this to work out.

She stopped herself, though, because she was feeling too giddy to indulge in her default relationship-pessimism. Plus, she had another Dominick-centered matter that was commanding more of her interest at the moment. Namely, her barely containable desire to ravage his body.

So she wasn't exactly a well-practiced diva in bed. She could improvise, couldn't she? In the deep recesses of her mind, she seemed to recall liking sex with Jake. A lot. She had a vague recollection of being pretty passionate and uninhibited, too. Although, four years may have warped the memory. Nevertheless, wasn't sex supposed to be one of those riding-a-bike things? Wasn't it all supposed to come back to her? Hmm . . . She had a feeling she'd find out soon enough.

Margot's face fell the minute she opened the front door. "Oh, *Lonnie*, " she whined disapprovingly, and scanned her daughter standing before her.

"What?" Lonnie asked, as she walked into the foyer, glancing down at herself and then back up. Margot grabbed her arm before she could move farther into the house.

"I asked you to look presentable!" Margot whispered angrily, shutting the door with her free hand.

"Is this what you call presentable? Sweatpants—or whatever those are—and with *holes* in your clothes!" She shook her head in disgust.

"This is what I was wearing today, jeez. What's the difference?"

Margot ignored the question, and maintained her huffiness as she hissed, "Did you do this just to spite me?"

"What are you talking about? What's the big deal about how I look?" Lonnie was getting fairly huffy herself by now.

"Because I *asked* you—" Margot stopped, looked over her shoulder, and whispered even lower, "Forget it. Just take off that big, boxy coat, for pete's sake!" Shaking her head again, she muttered, "I've never seen her wear that coat before in her life, but she wears it tonight." Lonnie's mouth dropped open—her mother was behaving like a loon.

"Do you need any help out there, Mrs. Kelley?" An unfamiliar male voice sounded from the living room. *Who was that?*

"Uh . . . uh . . . N-no, I'm fine over here!" Margot called back, and wet her lips nervously. "Now, Lonnie—"

"Mom, what's going on?" Lonnie asked in a clipped, I'm-about-to-be-very-peeved-aren't-I tone of voice.

"Now, honey, just give this a chance—"

"Mom, what did you do?" Her voice rose, and she didn't care.

"Shh! Please, honey, you'll embarrass our guest," Margot urged.

"*What* guest?"

"Shh!"

"Mom, answer me!"

"Hello there."

Lonnie whipped her head around to see Thomas

Ellabee standing in the archway between the kitchen and the foyer. *Is it too late to be adopted?*

"Oh, hi, Thomas," Lonnie managed pleasantly. "H-How are you? I mean, how have you been since the last time I saw you?" *Not the time I saw you at the mall and hid because I didn't want to talk to you—the other time.*

"Fabulous," he beamed.

"Oh, well, that's nice to hear," she said politely.

"I'm doing absolutely fabulous," he repeated, with his default-contented smile in full effect. "And you?"

"Well . . .," she began, while Margot forcibly pulled the bulky parka off her, undoubtedly hoping whatever she had on underneath would be more attractive. For that moment, Lonnie was glad to be talking to Thomas, rather than catching her mother's face when she saw the pink-and-gray tie-dyed sweatshirt.

"I've been doing pretty well. Same old, same old—"

"Nonsense!" Margot yelped, too maniacally to be credible. "Lonnie, tell Thomas about all the exciting instructor positions you're applying for. But first, you two go into the dining room, and I'll put out dinner."

They moved into the dining room, per Margot's orders, and Lonnie tried her best to swallow her anger. For the moment. Her mother had gone too far this time. Ridiculously too far, but that was no reason to make Thomas feel unwelcome. He hadn't done anything wrong. It wasn't his fault that Lonnie didn't dig bouffants and already had someone in her life. A "boyfriend" in her life, to be exact.

Margot set down the salmon casserole giddily. It was the dish she was most proud of. . . . Too bad Lonnie hated salmon with a passion. Thomas certainly looked like he was enjoying it, though, which was obviously the goal of the entire meal. Lonnie's stomach growled as she picked at the crusty stuff on top and washed it down with some nice cold milk.

Thomas had requested it, springboarding a discussion with Margot about their shared "belief" in the importance of Vitamin D.

While Margot interviewed Thomas, Lonnie waited for the right moment to sneak into the kitchen and turn her glass of milk into a White Russian. She noticed her father's conspicuous absence at the table, and could only assume that he hadn't agreed with Margot's over-the-top meddling. Her mother had never done anything this extreme before—which told Lonnie that her mother was now panicking. It was as if she thought time was running out. It was as if she had no faith that Lonnie could attract a great guy on her own. It was damn insulting, is what it was!

"That's so interesting, Thomas! Lonnie, isn't that interesting?"

Considering that she'd been zoned out the whole time, it couldn't have been all that interesting, but Lonnie just nodded, smiling pleasantly. "Uh-huh."

"Lonnie, tell me about this instructor position," Thomas said conversationally, and pounded his third cup of milk.

"Oh. Well, so far it hasn't happened yet, but—"

"She's still making up her mind about exactly which college offers the most promise."

"Yeah, preferably one that acknowledges I sent a résumé," Lonnie said, and Margot gritted her teeth.

"What subject would you teach?" Thomas asked, as he started on the second helping of salmon casserole that Margot had automatically heaped onto his plate.

"I don't know. I think I could teach a few different subjects, depending on what a particular school is looking for," Lonnie replied. She ate a morsel of casserole crumb topping, and tried to make it last. "But my strongest area would have to be feminist theory."

"Well, I don't know if I'd use the term 'feminist,' honey," Margot interrupted. "Thomas, she earned a master's degree in sociology. With honors."

"And then I earned a master's in feminist theory."

"With honors," Margot added desperately.

"In fact," Lonnie continued, just to annoy her mother, "I'd consider myself a hardcore feminist."

"Really?" Thomas raised a wary eyebrow.

"I have a lot of rage."

"*Honey*," Margot chided.

"*Margot*," Lonnie mimicked, and knew it was shamelessly immature. Oh well.

"Well, that sounds nice," Thomas said, obviously eager to bring the table talk back to mind-numbingly dull subjects like vitamin D. Meanwhile, Margot glared at Lonnie with the you're-gonna-get-it-later look that only a mother can perfect.

"So, Lonnie, I haven't seen you in church in quite a while," Thomas stated placidly.

"Oh . . . I know, but . . . see . . . well . . ." Lonnie stumbled feebly. He'd hit a nerve. The truth was, she *did* sometimes feel guilty about her lapses as a good Catholic girl.

"With all the work Lonnie does at the *law* firm," Margot interjected quickly, "it's hard for her to have a regularly scheduled mass time. Honey"—she looked at Lonnie enthusiastically—"tell Thomas about the time you were Mary in the Christmas play!"

"You mean when I was nine?"

"Her Sunday school teacher asked her specially if she'd play Mary," Margot explained, ignoring Lonnie's question.

"Really?" Thomas replied.

"It was because I had the longest hair in the class," Lonnie said honestly.

"It was not," Margot corrected, and turned her attention back to Thomas. "The teacher thought she was the most perfect one for the part. Because she was so expressive and articulate."

Margot went on. "She's always been like that. Just

so expressive and creative and *bubbly*." Lonnie stared at her plate with a pained frown that could've come from sucking lemons.

"Like the time she dressed up as the Cookie Monster for her cousin's birthday party . . ."

Oh, no, *not* the Cookie Monster story! Lonnie had made the entire Kelley family take blood oaths that they'd never mention that again! She'd barely been thirteen; she'd been young and stupid. Aunt Christy told her the kids would get a kick out of it. How was Lonnie supposed to know years later she'd still be trying to live it down?

That was it. If Margot got out the snapshots of Lonnie in the big, hairy blue suit, with her permed mullet creeping out of the top, she was *out* of there!

". . . Well, the kids just loved it! And Lonnie went around passing out cookies and growling . . ." *Kill me. Kill me now.* What was next? The story of her first period? This was brutal.

"Mom, it's actually getting late. I've got to get going soon." Lonnie made sure to keep her tone polite and even, so her mother couldn't later claim she'd been rude. Or at least so her mother wouldn't have as much to act righteous about *when* she later claimed she'd been rude.

"Honey, wait, we haven't had dessert yet." The last time Margot encouraged Lonnie to have dessert was when she'd tried to convince her that canned pumpkin squash with a pinch of Sweet'N Low really wasn't all that different from pumpkin pie.

"I think I'll have to pass. I'm full." She pushed up from the table, cleared her place, and took her dishes into the kitchen. While she was dumping her uneaten casserole into the garbage disposal, she heard Thomas telling Margot that he had to be heading home himself. *Big surprise.* Couldn't her mother see that there were absolutely no sparks between them?

No, of course not. According to Margot, sparks

were "overrated." But all Lonnie had to do was think about the excitement she felt when she was near Dominick, and she knew her mother was wrong. Sure, she understood that the hot thrill of a relationship wasn't forever, and passion fizzled over time. Still, was there something wrong with wanting it, at least in the beginning? If she and Thomas went to bed tonight, they'd both fall asleep before they got their clothes off.

"Are you sure you won't take some leftovers?" Margot called out the door, as Thomas walked to his car. "Bye, bye! Thanks again for coming!" Lonnie leaned in the archway, watched her mother wave good-bye to her dream son-in-law . . . and primed herself for one hell of a confrontation.

"Well," Margot said calmly, "that's that, I guess." She moved briskly into the dining room to clear the rest of the dishes. Hmm . . . *Interesting*. If Margot wasn't angry that Lonnie had been withdrawn during dinner, that could only mean one thing: she knew Lonnie had a case to be furious, so she was avoiding opening up any kind of discussion. Undoubtedly, Jack had warned her against the whole idea, and now she didn't want Lonnie coming down on her, too. Unfortunately, that was just too damn bad!

She went into the dining room, where her mother was gathering up the casserole dish and serving spoon, and averting her eyes obviously. Finally, Lonnie sucked in a breath and said with stony fierceness, "Mom, what you pulled tonight was probably the most out-of-line thing you've ever done. You manipulated me, you embarrassed me, and you embarrassed Thomas. And you had no right."

Margot's eyes widened in tortured bafflement. Ever the martyr. "I was just trying to help. Don't start on me, all right? I've got a headache." She started to push past and go into the kitchen, but Lonnie blocked her.

"I'm not done yet."

"Wha—? Lonnie, I told you I have a headache and I don't want to fight."

"Mother, *shut up!*" Margot's eyes bugged out in horror, and Lonnie took advantage of her shock. "Do not *ever* interfere in my love life like that again, do you understand me? Yes, you gave birth to me, and yes, that gives you certain rights. But you do *not* have the right to control my life. And you do *not* have the right to make whatever hurtful, passive-aggressive comments you want! I'm a grown woman, and I think I've earned some respect by now. If you can't give me that, then I'm not going to visit you at all!"

Lonnie turned on her heel and stormed toward the front door. "Wait!" Margot called after her. "Wait!" she cried again, and captured her daughter's hand just as it was turning the knob on the front door.

Margot expelled a breath and said, "Honey, I just want you to find a nice man who will treat you well. What's wrong with that?" There was no way her mother was that obtuse. She just didn't have any arguments to cling to at the moment. Margot continued. "I just want you to find a nice boyfriend—"

"I have a nice boyfriend!"

"What? Oh, no—you're back together with Terry?" She looked queasy just thinking about Terry and the lack of husband potential he represented.

"No, I'm not with Terry," Lonnie said. "I have a new boyfriend. But he doesn't have anything to do with this." She let out a heavy, frustrated sigh. "This doesn't change anything that I just said. If Dominick dumps me tomorrow, that doesn't make your insane, lunatic meddling okay. Do you *get* that?"

"You never mentioned a Dominick before—"

"*Mom.*"

"What, you have a new boyfriend, and you don't even tell me?"

"Because I can't tell you! Because of *this*. This—what you did tonight! You just put all this pressure on things. You make it impossible to just feel safe—to just feel *good enough*. Why, Mom? Why do you have to do that?"

Margot stared silently for a moment, with her mouth agape, before she responded. "I—I don't make you feel good enough? You're my jewel. You're perfect, and you make me so proud."

Some of Lonnie's anger receded as she realized that her Machiavellian mother was just never going to get it. She said wearily, "Mom, just tell me you're not going to do anything like this ever again. Please."

"Okay. Yes. I promise." Margot paused, and then must have realized that Lonnie expected more in the way of an apology. "Really, honey, I'm sorry if I embarrassed you tonight. I honestly thought it would go better."

"It doesn't matter what your intentions were. That's the point," Lonnie stated firmly. "I don't want you interfering like that again. Ever."

"Okay, okay."

"Mom. *Ever?* " Lonnie wasn't letting her off the hook that easily.

Margot hesitated half a second, and then relented. "Yes, fine. Ever." Lonnie sighed, and her mother moved closer, opening her arms for a hug. "I won't do something like that again . . ."

Lonnie hugged her back. "Okay, Mom."

". . . without telling you."

"Oh, Lord."

"I'm sorry, honey. I just love you so much, and . . . I just love you so much."

Lonnie left half an hour later, after her mother finished grilling her about Dominick. On the way to her apartment, she engaged in some sappy, romantic fantasies. She called him just as they were turning X-rated.

" 'Lo," he answered.

"Hi."

"Hey! Are you home yet, or—"

"Get over here now."

"What—? Is everything okay?"

"Yes. I just want you here. Now."

"Um . . . okay."

"I want you. Now." She started burning up just thinking about it, and she could swear she heard him swallowing on the other end.

"Should I bring anything, like some wine, or—"

"Bring some condoms," she ordered.

"I'll be over in ten minutes."

"You live twenty minutes from me."

"I'll be over in ten minutes."

Lonnie jumped in the shower. Afterward, she only had time to throw on jeans and a sweater before she heard a knock at the door. She didn't give a thought to her appearance; she was too excited. The disastrous dinner with Thomas Ellabee had reinforced all her feelings for Dominick.

With wet hair, bare feet, no bra, and a racing heart, she went to answer the door.

Chapter Twenty

Dominick barely made it through the front door before Lonnie was kissing him and pushing off his coat. He made an unintelligible sound of surprise, which quickly turned into grunting. Wrapping one hand around her waist, he used the other to slam the door shut. She backed him against it and plunged her tongue into his mouth, running her hands under his navy sweater and up his bare back. His skin felt smooth and hot and wonderful as she moved her hands through his soft chest hair. He was kissing her hard, sucking her tongue, and rubbing her breasts.

Lonnie broke the kiss and lowered her head, sticking it half under Dominick's sweater to run her tongue on his chest aimlessly, wildly. He gripped her hair, willing her not to stop, and she ripped his pants zipper open. She was still kissing and licking his chest when she thrust her hand inside his boxers. She reached low to grip his testicles and heard Dominick's head *thunk* against the door. She lifted her head and saw him leaning back with his eyes closed and his mouth open. As soon as she started stroking his penis, he was breathing hard, and his eyes shut tighter.

His shaft was thicker than she'd anticipated. It

made her hotter. She held on to him tightly, moving her hand up and down, until Dominick's breath was coming in pants. "No . . . no more," he whispered. "We . . . need a bed." She couldn't agree more, pushing all her anxieties about sex—built up over four long years—out of her mind. Until she'd met Dominick, she hadn't thought about what she'd been missing, or how ready her body was for that kind of intimacy again.

Lonnie took her hand out of Dominick's boxers, nodding hazily, and pushed his sweater up. He pulled it over his head and whipped it off in less than a second. When she ran her eyes over his fully naked chest, she lost herself again, and started nuzzling his neck, then sliding down his body to nuzzle his stomach and the open vee of his fly. She sank to her knees and with both hands, pulled his pants and boxers down enough to fully free his erection. As she ran her tongue along his shaft once, he let out a strained groan and tangled his hands into her hair. Then she slicked her tongue over the tip, and he made gruff sounds like he was on the brink of control. Lonnie wondered where the hell her control had even gone at this point.

He clasped his hands around her upper arms, and brought her back up to look at him. He looked aroused and mindless, but his tone was teasing. "That wasn't exactly what I meant by 'no more.' " She laughed and hugged him. He wrapped both arms tightly around her, hitched her up until her feet rested on top of his, and started walking them over to her bed. Lonnie couldn't believe she wasn't protesting about being too heavy to carry, but for some reason, doing that with Dominick seemed needless and out of place.

The next thing she knew, she was on her back, arching and twisting, as Dominick snaked his tongue down her throat and over her breasts and worked both his hands beneath her panties. Her sweater had been lost somewhere on the walk to the bed, and her jeans had gotten tossed, too. He sucked on one of her breasts and slid a finger beneath her underwear and inside her. Instantly, she shuddered and arched up for more. He pushed his finger deeper, then slid in another, and she cried out. Both fingers moved inside her . . . deeper, deeper . . . until he pushed in a third, and she screamed, feeling unbelievably stretched, overheated, and desperate for him to go on and on.

"I can't wait," he breathed unevenly. "God, you're so wet. . . . You're so hot." Frantically, he hooked his thumbs in the strings of her bikinis and yanked them down. Lonnie couldn't even form any words, she was too hot and wanted this too much. She felt the bed tip, and realized Dominick was standing to shuck off his jeans and boxers completely. He climbed back onto the bed, crawling over her, with his tongue trailing up her body along the way, until he came to her face. Then he kissed her, and all she could do was moan and try to kiss him back with the same strength. She felt worn out and weak and they hadn't even done it yet. She also felt sweaty and frantic for more.

He broke the kiss to tear the foil of the condom wrapper with his teeth. She looked up at him with her eyes half closed. "Yes . . . yes," she whispered helplessly. He snapped it on and moved her legs so they straddled him, and he sucked on her neck while he pressed into her. Lonnie jolted at the unexpected pressure; only the head of his erection made it in easily. Dominick pushed himself harder into her, but didn't get very far.

Lonnie snapped out of her lusty haze when she realized what was happening. She was too tight for him; they weren't going to be able to make love after all. So much for going with the flow. So much for getting carried away with passion. Her cheeks burned with embarrassment as Dominick was grunting with each push but still not going anywhere.

He spoke first. Lonnie was dreading whatever he was about to say. Probably he'd try to lighten the mood with a joke about how it'd been a while for her. Damn it, she knew how long it had been, and the last thing she felt like doing was switching gears from passion to chitchat. She wanted this to be hot and thrilling. She wanted to make him feel good, not elicit his emotional support. "Oh, *God*, " he whispered. "You're so tight. I might come before I'm even inside you."

Perfect! He didn't think it was a lost cause, and he was still as turned on as she was. Now if she could just force her body to accept him. . . . She tried lifting her hips to drive him deeper, but it wasn't working; she was too tense. *Oh, God, this is a disaster!*

Just then she felt Dominick's lips brush against her ear, and his breath was hot and wonderful when he whispered, "Just relax." He wasn't moving his body anymore, but just holding her exactly where she was, as he trailed his mouth over her jaw. He paused at the spot just below her ear and kissed her softly. She muttered, "I'm defective," but her heart wasn't in it because he was making her too hot to think.

"Shh," he breathed into her skin, and licked a trail down the side of her neck. Half complying, she turned her head and sighed as he ran his tongue back up.

"You feel so good . . . ," he murmured directly into her ear. "God, you make me hot." She was becoming more and more mindless with each husky word. "Oh, Lonnie . . . oh, baby . . . I want you so much," he groaned, kissing her cheek and letting his lips linger there.

More mindless.

"Even if we don't get any farther tonight, you feel so good."

More mindless.

"Mmm . . . God, you make me crazy," and he slid his tongue in her ear.

Completely mindless.

She started writhing under him. Dominick slid his hand down and aroused her with a finger, even as his cock strained to be fully inside her. She cried out as he moved his finger in a circle and rocked his body into her. He was still whispering about how good she felt to him while he rocked harder. She gripped him and instinctively rolled her hips to bring him deeper. There was no pain, just incredible pressure, which now felt better than good.

Before she even realized it, Dominick was fully inside her and moving. At first he was slow and controlled, but when Lonnie's hands moved to his butt and pushed him even closer, he picked up speed. He whispered in her ear, "Harder?"

Breathlessly, she answered, "Yes . . . yes." He ran his hands under her knees and pulled her legs up to bring himself deeper. She gasped at the feel of him, and he thrust more fiercely into her. She broke into a sweat everywhere; she cried out, only vaguely aware of her own voice. He kept pounding—over and over—causing a friction that felt almost unbearably good. Losing control of her body, as it jumped wildly off the bed over and over, Lonnie urged Dominick on. "Oh, please . . . please don't stop. . . . *Don't stop.*"

Their bodies hammered into each other until the heat and friction were too much, and Lonnie came hard, screaming and not even caring. The second she was done, Dominick's hips jerked violently, bucking hard, and he pushed himself up on his hands. He let out a guttural cry, shuddered, and collapsed on top of her, panting.

* * *

Dominick was gently brushing his lips along the curve of Lonnie's neck as they lay in her bed with their arms wrapped around each other. She sighed and snuggled her body closer, and he tightened his hold on her. "I'm sure glad I came over tonight," he said in a low, teasing voice. She lifted her head to look into his eyes and smiled half dreamily. "Just to think that I could be home testing software right now"—he kissed her softly on her mouth—"instead of thinking about how I already want you again." He kissed her, this time more firmly, drawing her lower lip in and sucking it before he broke the kiss. Then he sighed and buried his head into the curve of her neck again. His rough stubble should've felt abrasive against her skin, but Lonnie found it as erotic and enticing as everything else about him.

She rested her fingers in his hair. "I'm glad you're here, too," she murmured. "I wanted to do this for a long time." He lifted his head and looked into her eyes, his sexy grin in place.

"Yeah? How long?" he asked, and brushed some of her hair back while his hand moved lightly back and forth on her cheek.

"Um . . . a while." She smiled mischievously at him. "What about you?"

"Since that first day we had lunch together three months ago," he answered without hesitation.

"Did you think it wasn't going to happen?" she asked, remembering how tight she'd been.

"No way," Dominick said.

"Why not?"

"I'd like to think I know what I'm doing," he said, grinning. "Besides, I knew if I didn't have you, I'd die. The anticipation was starting to kill me."

"Really?" Lonnie pulled back to look into his eyes. She searched his face hopefully, because she wanted so much for him to tell her that the reality was even better than the anticipation. She wanted him to say that it had been shattering and unbelievable, so she'd know it wasn't just her. They had both been passionate and out of control, but maybe sex was always like that for him.

"Lonnie," he murmured, and settled his hand on her breast, rubbing gently. "I still can't believe how it was."

His approving tone kicked up her confidence. "Satisfying?" she asked with saucy flirtatiousness she suddenly possessed.

"Hot as hell," he said. "When can we do it again?" He kissed her mouth, then down her neck, and ran his tongue along her collarbone.

She sighed, already hot for him again. "Don't you need some recovery time?"

He muttered something into her breasts about already having five minutes, which was plenty where she was concerned, and then he rolled on top of her. He rested most of his weight on his elbows, and she felt his erection thick and pulsing against her body. Not to compare or anything, but Jake had always fallen asleep after his orgasm and remained out cold till morning. Until now, she assumed that was the way it worked for all men. Obviously, she'd been wasting her time with the wrong guy!

Now, lying beneath Dominick—hard and ready, but still gentle and cuddly—Lonnie sighed happily. She looped her arms around his neck, and when their eyes locked, his expression turned more serious. "It's been a long time for you," he said quietly.

She could deal with that point of information better now that she was lying there blissful and sated. "Yeah," she answered simply, and started combing her hands through his hair.

"Christ, how come? You're so beautiful." He kissed her and let the kiss linger a moment or two. "And sexy," he added huskily.

"I don't know."

"You mentioned that you were dating someone that first day we had lunch, didn't you?" he asked.

"Oh . . . yeah. It didn't work out. It wasn't anything serious, anyway." She stopped short of telling him that *he* had been the most pressing reason why it hadn't worked out with Terry. Impulsively, though, she told him about Jake. How she didn't know why, but she'd lost the desire for sex after they broke up. And how she'd *thought* Jake had been the love of her life.

He asked, "What about Eric?" *Who?* "Remember?" *No.*

Oh, wait! Eric Yagher, Lonnie realized. She noticed that Dominick was suddenly using his a-little-too-casual tone. Then she understood: Dominick wasn't really asking her if Eric was a love of her life, but if she'd ever been with him. *In the biblical sense.* Hmm . . .

Obviously the answer was no, but Lonnie wasn't sure that he should be asking. There was something possessive about it, as if it mattered to him who'd been there before him, and Lonnie didn't know if she wanted to encourage that kind of thinking. Then again, there was something about Dominick that made her want to tell him every single thing about herself.

"I liked Eric, but that's all I did. Oh, except for when I stopped liking him." She leaned her head forward and pressed a warm, suctioning kiss to his lips.

"Good . . . He didn't deserve you," he muttered, before turning the kiss into something feral and blatantly sexual. Lonnie kissed him back while she reached her hand over to her nightstand, grappling to find the handle to the first drawer. She hastily yanked it open, felt around for a condom, and shoved it into Dominick's hand, as she rocked her body up and down suggestively.

It didn't take much suggesting. Anxiously, he tore the condom wrapper, and they both slipped back into the sweet oblivion of heat and sweat and sex.

Chapter Twenty-one

First thing Monday morning Lonnie sought out Macey. "Macey, can I speak with you?" Lonnie hoped she'd say yes, because she already decided not to take no for an answer. Lonnie was determined to corner Macey while she had the chance.

"Sure, Lonnie. What's up?" She pushed her glasses higher on the bridge of her nose. "Actually, I'm glad you stopped by, because I wanted to talk to you about something anyway." *Good start.* "Please, sit down."

She obeyed, but made sure to start speaking first, so they wouldn't get sidetracked. "Macey, I have to talk to you about something . . . well, ask you, really." Lonnie unfolded Twit's fax, which had been clutched in her hand since she'd taken it out of her bag that morning, and passed it to Macey.

"I wondered—between you and me—if you could tell me something about this."

Macey's face changed from random curiosity to pointed interest after she read the fax. "Where did you get this?" she asked softly.

Lonnie replied, "It's a long story." And all she needed was to start relaying it and then get interrupted by a phone call or a client before she made any headway with her inquiry. "What I need is to know what it means."

"What makes you think I would know?" Macey asked.

"I just—I don't know," Lonnie stammered. "I just hoped maybe you would. I mean, since Ann Lee used to work here, and . . . well, Sandra Neemas did too, didn't she?" She crossed her fingers under her lap and waited for some useful information.

Macey nodded, but said nothing. Obviously a more direct approach was needed.

"Did Lunther sexually harass Ann Lee?" Lonnie asked.

"What makes you say that?" Macey asked, furrowing her brows.

"I just . . . had a feeling. I remember that Ann Lee left abruptly, and Lunther was . . . I could be wrong, but—"

"You're not wrong," Macey said. She sat forward and clasped her hands together tightly. "Forgive me, Lonnie, but I am not clear on how this matter concerns you." It wasn't a challenge; it was an invitation to explain. Unfortunately, Lonnie couldn't quite do that because she'd promised Montgomery that she wouldn't tell anyone at Twit & Bell about his investigation. As far as they knew, Lunther's death was ruled a heart attack, case closed.

"Well . . ." *Think. Think.* What possible reason would she have to be inquiring about Lunther's history of sexual harassment? Suddenly, she thought of a good angle to use with Macey—one that wouldn't be *entirely* untrue, and might coax some information out of her.

"The truth is," Lonnie began, "I am just sickened by the thought that women today still have to deal with sexual harassment in the workplace." *Well, that part is definitely true.* "And I need to know because I need peace of mind." *Also, based in reality.* "I'm just

so worried that those women . . . on the list . . .
that they might not be okay. That they may have felt
traumatized, or . . ." *Felt like icing Lunther.* "So I was
hoping you could tell me what happened to them.
You know, so I could . . . sleep at night." *Utter
bullshit.*

A pregnant pause followed Lonnie's monologue.
Then Macey spoke.

"I understand," she said. She lifted her blue eyes
off of the piece of paper in her hands and settled
them on Lonnie's face. Her expression reflected a
kind of weary sadness that made Lonnie feel guilty
about deceiving her. She wished she could tell her
that she was really asking because she was an unofficial informant for the police, but then she'd have to
tell her that Lunther's death was murder, and *Oh, by
the way, Montgomery has it in his head that you're involved somehow.* Obviously that wasn't an option—
Montgomery would kill her if she did that. Or, at
least, make good on his regular threat to arrest her.

Macey continued. "You want to know because you
sympathize with them—with whatever might have
happened to them. You want to know if you can
help. If they *need* help. Is that it?"

Lonnie felt like a complete slug, but nodded. What
she'd said about sexual harassment sickening her—
not to mention making her mad as hell—was true.
But at the moment, that was the least of her concerns.
Right now she had to find out the connection between the women on the list and Lunther. More specifically, she needed to know if any of them had
enough motive to kill him.

"Did all these women work at Twit & Bell?" she
asked Macey.

"Yes. Although Mabel Wills and Courtney Adams
predate my employment here."

"What happened to them?"

"Like you said, sexual harassment interfered with their productivity—as it's designed to do."

"Well . . . were they fired because they wouldn't . . ." Her voice trailed off, waiting for Macey to fill in the blanks.

"No, they quit. Look, Lonnie, I don't know how well you observed Lunther around the office, but I can tell you right now: he was a self-obsessed bastard. Plain and simple. And he was never going to change. He wasn't capable of change. He was too stupid to change. These women moved on to other jobs that didn't force them to confront the same kind of abuse."

"How do you know they moved on?"

"You're not the only one who has a level of emotional commitment that few people understand." Lonnie guiltily contemplated hara-kiri with the nearest letter opener. "I checked up on Lunther's history as soon as I found out the kind of man he was. That's why he despised me. Well, among other reasons."

"What other reasons?" Lonnie pushed.

Macey looked at her squarely, appraisingly, and answered her even though she didn't have to. "I like you, Lonnie. You're sensitive to much of the unfairness that still exists. Obviously that's not much of a blessing. It's frustrating as hell." She stood up and walked over to look out the large plate-glass window behind her desk.

"To answer your question, Lunther hated me for knowing what he was *and* for using it against him." She turned around to meet Lonnie's eyes, which were unblinking and expectant. She sighed and started to explain. "I was planning to leave Twit & Bell—which thrilled Lunther, believe me. The last thing he needed was me around to remind him of his alter ego." *Alter ego?* "What didn't thrill him, however, was the threat of what I might do before I left.

"Lonnie, I'm no lightweight where retribution is concerned. I am not a person who blindly follows the learned 'ethics' that have been determined by a patriarchal society. If it were up to me, *Extremities* and *Death and the Maiden* would've had very different endings. I believe revenge is a dish best served *whenever*." She propped herself up on her windowsill, appearing more relaxed, as if just discussing this was alleviating some burden.

"After I found out about Lunther's *proclivities*, I told him that I planned to leave the firm and that I'd announce my resignation early this spring. What drove him crazy was that he was sure I was up to something—some scheme to 'screw him over.' How typical. After adversely affecting another woman's life, his only concern was the slight chance that he might be inconvenienced."

"Another woman . . . You mean, Ann Lee?"

Macey nodded. "I'd found out about his history of harassment a couple months ago, and that's when I'd confronted him. He assured me that he'd just been suffering personal problems, but that he'd gotten help. He assured me he had stopped. But then, when Ann left the firm so abruptly, I knew . . . he was still at it." Her face twisted into a taut expression of detestation.

"But how did you find out at all?" Lonnie asked.

"Sandy told me."

"Sandy?"

"She was my assistant. She left a year ago." *Sandra Neemas! The one who'd pressed charges a year ago . . . right after it happened to her.* "We stayed friends after she quit, but she told me the truth about why she'd left only a few months ago. She told me she'd pressed charges against Lunther, but she dropped them when she got her plum job in London. The point is: she moved on with her life, but that doesn't change what Lunther did.

"Anyway, after Ann Lee left, I confronted Lunther again and told him that he'd be sorry. You should've seen him squirm." She laughed humorlessly at the image and went on. "Of course, he assumed I would do something soap opera–esque, like blackmail him. Or tell all of Boston about his obsession." *Obsession?* "He never figured out that I'd undermine his power by simply inverting it."

Huh?

"I was taking his clients." She moved back to the desk and sat down again. "Remember that research project I gave you?" *The one that got me mugged? Vaguely.* "Those 'hypothetical' cases were Lunther's. Ann told me where he kept his legal notes, and how they were filed. You know the citations I needed you to look up for me?" Lonnie nodded. "Well, we all knew who Lunther's clients were, of course, and the overall scope of his cases. But what I needed to know were the exact kinds of legal strategies and loopholes he'd applied to them. So I copied those citations straight from his notes."

Lonnie still wasn't sure what Macey had hoped to gain from that, but she answered that question next. "You see, I was looking for the best angle I could find to convince his clients that their interests would be better served with me. I knew Lunther's legal maneuverings were hardly superior. It just took a little digging to uncover his ineptitudes."

So, Lunther hadn't known what was in the notebook specifically, but he'd known that Macey was up to *something*, and he'd been absolutely desperate to find out what it was. That was probably why he'd come up to Lonnie at the holiday party; he'd wanted to pump her for information.

"Anyway, it's all moot now. He's gone and I'm not about to mourn the loss to humanity."

Lonnie let a few moments pass, while she tried to digest all the information. That explained a lot, but she was still confused about the fax. Why had Twit hired a private investigator? What did the women on the list have to do with him?

"Macey, do you have an idea what this fax *means*? Why would Twit get this?"

"Oh, of course I have an idea! It's just a guess, but I'm sure a plausible one. Beauregard *loathed* Lunther. He was desperate to force him out of the company. The rumor was, he'd offered to buy him out repeatedly, but Lunther always refused. I'm sure Beauregard figured that if he did some good digging, he'd find some dirt—dirt that would finally give him *leverage*.

"And those women may not have pressed charges, but—as I learned from my own investigating—they're more than willing to discuss Lunther if asked." She rested her elbows on her desk in an uncharacteristically casual gesture. "Lonnie, Lunther Bell's days as a consequence-free harasser were coming to an end. How ironic that he died first."

"I see . . . So I guess his thing was, what, quid pro quo?" Lonnie asked. "You know, either put out or—"

"Oh, no! No, no, no. Oh, I'm sorry, I should've explained better." She leaned forward and said, "Lunther didn't want those women to sleep with him."

"What do you mean? W-what did he want?"

"He wanted them to baby-sit him. Literally." What kind of riddle was this?

"Macey, I'm sorry, I'm really not following you."

She nodded her head. "Of course you're not. I'm sorry. Lonnie?"—she paused—"have you ever heard of an 'adult baby'?"

Lonnie racked her brain, and all she could come up with was the memory of a *Jerry Springer* episode about grown men whose hobbies included wearing diapers and pretending to be newborns. But that couldn't possibly be what Macey was referring to, could it?

"Um . . . is that when grown men . . . dress up like babies?"

"For sexual excitement, yes. It's a type of role-playing fetish, which presumably rests on the tenets of domination and submission. Some would argue, however, that a man's desire to revert to infantilism has more to do with his inability to cope with the standards of masculinity."

"And Lunther was one of those—I mean, he pretended—?"

"Yes. He was an adult baby. And he was on the lookout for a woman to play the game with him. To act out the role of his 'caretaker.' He preyed on the women here who seemed the weakest because . . . Well, I have my own theories." She shook her head in more of the same disgust. Lonnie just waited for her to elaborate, so she did.

"I think Lunther preyed on women he worked with because it killed the proverbial two birds with one stone. To be crass: he got off on more than the role-playing. He literally *got off* on disabling a woman's power. If he could bully an assistant into doing what he wanted—for fear that otherwise she might lose her job—then he'd feel satisfied in his own ability to subordinate her. Economic subordination, in that case."

Lonnie sat back in the armchair, feeling drained and exhausted, even though she'd barely said anything throughout the conversation. She just couldn't believe all this corruption and debauchery had been going on under her nose the whole time she'd worked at Twit & Bell! Lunther Bell, an *adult baby*? It was all too much to imagine.

Macey's phone rang.

"Macey Green . . ." She talked to whoever was on the line for less than two minutes, but it was still enough time for Lonnie to try to come to terms with what she'd just learned. She knew Macey never particularly liked Lunther, but she'd never realized the intensity of her hatred. Suddenly, she had a thought. Was there any chance that . . .

Could Macey possibly have hated Lunther enough to put a stop to his harassment herself?

No, that seemed unfathomable.

"That was a friend of mine," Macey explained, setting the receiver back in its cradle. "Actually, she's the reason I wanted to speak with you today."

"What do you mean?"

"My friend Emma is the director of social research at Maine Bay College. I told her about you, and she requested that you send your résumé to her immediately."

Lonnie's mouth dropped. She couldn't believe Macey had done that for her. "Macey, I . . . I don't know what to say. That was so kind of you. . . ." She almost felt choked up, because it was just so unexpected, and she wasn't the type of person who inherently felt owed favors like that.

"Nonsense," Macey said gently. "You would be more than an asset there; it's just as much of a service to Emma as it is to you. And I can tell you right now, Emma is *very* interested."

Macey was all but promising her a job at Maine Bay College, and Lonnie knew it. Her stomach flip-flopped at the idea. It was the best lead she'd had yet, considering none of the schools she'd applied to had called her at all. She couldn't believe Macey had gone to that trouble for her. . . .

But then . . . now that she thought about it . . .

Why *had* Macey done it? Just to help her out? Or did she have another motive—like getting Lonnie out of the way?

Oh, God, I'm ridiculous.

All her snooping was taking its toll; it was making

her more suspicious every day. She had to get herself in check. Macey was her friend. Of course she only wanted to help her.

"What do you think?" Macey asked.

"I . . . Thank you so, so much. I . . . I'm just so honored that you helped me like that."

Just then the phone rang, and this time Macey stayed on the line. Lonnie took the hint and waved good-bye, quietly making her way to the door. This day was turning out to be one disorienting surprise after another. Lonnie didn't even realize that she was holding her breath until she got back to her desk . . . and it all came gushing out.

Chapter Twenty-two

"So am I gonna get any smutty details, or what? I mean, I am your sister. I think I have the right."

Lonnie laughed. "Hold on a second." She rested the phone receiver on her shoulder, rolled her chair over to the printer, and grabbed a copy of Twit's itinerary, which had the header: A LEADER'S DAY-AT-A-GLANCE. Per Twit's instructions, of course. She wheeled herself back to her desk and put the phone to her ear again.

"Okay, now where were we?" she asked Peach.

"You were dodging my probing questions about you and Dominick and the horizontal lambada."

"Ech—must you try to shock me with corny vulgarity?"

"Yes, I must," Peach replied. "Come on, seriously, how was it?" The only reason Lonnie hadn't been relentlessly grilled over the weekend was because she hadn't seen Peach since Saturday. She had gone to breakfast with Dominick on Sunday morning, and he'd convinced her to come back to his place so they could start making up for her four sexless years. She'd bought it willingly. And they'd had more sex

in eighteen hours than she'd known was possible.
Not that she was an expert, of course. All she did
know was that she'd been sore this morning in the
most fabulously primal way.

Just then, Lonnie's other line lit up. "Oh, Peach,
hold on. There's another call." She hit the button that
was flashing. "Beauregard Twit's line."

"Lonnie?" The bubbly male voice sounded
vaguely familiar.

"Yes?"

"What, you don't recognize my voice? It's Terry."

Jeez. Did this guy know anything about breaking
up? First his e-mails, now a phone call. She wanted
nothing to do with him, and last she'd heard, neither
did he. According to his insane tirade last week, she
"flared a temper" in him of volcanic proportions.

"Uh . . . hi," she muttered, feeling no motivation
to be friendly.

"Hey! How've you been?"

"Um . . . okay. Why are you calling me?" she
asked pointedly. She wasn't normally a rude person,
but this guy tore her apart over the phone only a
handful of days ago, and now he was acting chipper
and clueless. And she wasn't going to play along.

"Oh . . . well, I just wanted to say hi."

"Okay. Hi. But I'm on the phone with Peach, so—"

"Listen, about the last time we talked . . ."

Oh, this ought to be good. "Mmm-hmm."

"Well, I should tell you," he explained, "that I've
switched shrinks, and my new therapist made me
realize that I was really just projecting my own issues
onto you." *No kidding. I could've told you that for
free, buddy.*

"Oh, okay. Well, good to know. But I've really
gotta go—"

"Anyway," he went on, oblivious to her desperation to get off the phone. "Why don't we just forget

it? I wanted to come to Boston this weekend so we could hang out. How does that sound?" *Cruel and unusual!*

"Terry, I . . . No. No, I don't think that's a good idea. I've really gotta go, okay?"

"Well, okay, but—"

"Take care of yourself," she said. "Bye."

She clicked back to Peach. "Hey, are you still there?"

"Yeah, I'm here," Peach said.

"Sorry about that. You'll never guess who it was. Terry."

"What did *he* want?" Peach asked, obviously horrified.

"Nothing. I'll tell you later. It's not worth getting into. Now, what were you saying?"

"*You* were saying, remember? You, Dominick, The Double-Decker Loin Sandwich—"

"Ew, *enough.*"

Peach just giggled. "Well?"

"It was good." *Really, really good.* In truth, she hadn't known she could be so wild. She shut her eyes, embarrassed at the sudden memory of the way she'd yelled and screamed in Dominick's bed. Especially when he had his head between her legs. And when he had her pinned up against the wall. There was no way she was telling Peach that part.

"And?" Peach prodded.

"And that's it."

"Your narrative could use work."

"Okay, enough about me," Lonnie said. "I want to hear about your double date with Matt and Uncle Jean-Pierre."

"Jean-Paul."

"Right."

"Um . . ." Peach began slowly. "It was . . . hmm . . . what's the word I'm looking for?"

"What?"

"Revelatory."

"Huh? Can you speak normal?"

Peach giggled. "Okay, okay. Let's see. We went to Chez Noir in Newton, and Jean-Paul started telling us about his new car. In French. My first thought was that he was as big a jerk as Matt had implied. But, then, you'll never guess what happened."

"What?" Lonnie pressed the receiver closer.

"Cheryl started speaking back to him. *In French.* And I said, 'Cheryl, why didn't you tell me you knew French?' And you know what she said?"

"What?"

" 'You never asked.' " Lonnie held back a laugh. "Anyway," Peach continued, "she and Jean-Paul had a great time the rest of the night, just talking in French and cracking up at jokes no one else could get."

Lonnie asked, "Was that annoying at all?"

"No way—I was thrilled she had such a good time. Lonnie, you should've seen her. It was like for the first time, she was completely comfortable in her own skin. I think all the progress I've been making with her has just finally taken hold, you know?" Lonnie ignored her sister's immodesty, and agreed.

Peach continued "So, basically, Cheryl and I had a powwow in the bathroom. She told me that she really liked Jean-Paul, and I told her I didn't like Matt anymore—"

"Wait, what? When did that happen?"

"Oh, didn't I tell you? Yeah, I decided that he's too negative for me. I don't know if you ever noticed, but it's like every word out of his mouth is a put-down about someone else." Yep, that summed up Matt pretty accurately.

"I see what you mean," Lonnie said. "So what happened with Cheryl and Jean-Paul?"

Peach giggled. "She attacked him."

"What do you mean?"

"I mean, Jean-Paul drove Matt back to his apartment and me back to Iris's house, and then he and Cheryl went for 'a drive.'" Lonnie could picture Peach's handmade quotation marks. "She called me Sunday afternoon and told me they drove to the Cape, rented a cottage, and went for broke."

"What?"

"I know!" Peach enthused. "I guess you weren't the only one who had a fun weekend. I knew Cheryl was getting bolder, but I never expected a breakthrough like this."

"Tell me about it," Lonnie muttered, amused. Then she had a thought. "How does Cheryl feel today? She doesn't regret anything, does she?"

"Nope. She's going to Jean-Paul's house for dinner tonight. *Coq au vin.*"

Lonnie sighed. Life was so strange. One identical, unmemorable day followed the next, over and over. And then, out of nowhere, things got interesting.

"D?"

Dominick was vaguely aware of Harold's voice.

Harold walked closer and waved his hand across Dominick's line of vision. "Earth to D. Earth to D."

Does he have any idea how dumb that sounds? Dominick turned his head a fraction to make eye contact with his annoying protégé. "What is it?" he asked.

"D, I've been calling you for the past five minutes." It couldn't have been that long. "Didn't you hear me?"

"Sorry, I was just thinking." About the weekend he'd spent in bed with Lonnie. He moved his chair closer to the desk to conceal his burgeoning erection from Harold, who was on a need-to-know basis with all GraphNet matters. And a never-need-to-know basis with all personal matters. "What did you need?"

"D, quite frankly, we've got a problem." Harold's

face was grim and foreboding, but Dominick couldn't bring himself to feel anything more than utter contentment with life.

"What is it?"

"Well, I don't know how to tell you this, but I've found more errors in your work." That got his attention. "This code you gave me before—for the three D link—well, it's not viable." Harold tossed the printout down on the desk, and Dominick saw red ink all over it.

Not again! No, it wasn't possible. He'd been careful. He'd been precise. He'd double-checked his work. Then one of Harold's red-pen marks caught his eye. It was a circled word a quarter of the way down the page. It *couldn't* be. . . .

But it was. In the middle of his programming code, it read *lonnie*. What the hell was he thinking? Well, it was obvious what he was thinking, but how could he have made an error like that? Looking like an ass in front of Harold might be a more minor concern, but it was a concern nonetheless. He was the kid's boss, for chrissake! He was supposed to set an example.

"D, maybe you'd better have me go over your other files, too." Harold motioned to the shelf. "Want me to start with the pile back there?"

But Dominick didn't answer because the way Harold had said "back there" had sounded an awful lot like "black hair," and that made him think of Lonnie. Her long, shiny hair. Spread out on his pillow. Wet and hanging down her breasts in the shower. Falling on his lap as she ran her mouth all over his stomach, his cock, his testicles . . .

"Earth to D!"

"Will you stop saying that? Jesus, I hear you." *Now, what the hell had he said?*

Harold just shook his head, and walked out with a stack of Dominick's work. "Listen, whatever's preoccupying you, don't worry." He stopped at the door, turned, and flashed a high-wattage smile. "I got your back, D." *God, help me.*

"Hello?"

"Hi, may I speak with Ann?" Lonnie tapped her pen nervously on the coffee table, hoping this all didn't blow up in her face. On the way home, she'd thought about what Macey had told her, and after she'd arrived at her apartment, made a thoroughly depressing veggie burger, and popped open a can of diet Coke, she looked Ann Lee up in the phone book. She figured it couldn't hurt to feel her out and see if she might be a viable suspect in Lunther's murder.

Peach had left a note saying she'd gone crock-pot shopping with Cheryl, whose freelance catering was apparently taking off, so Lonnie figured now would be a good time to call.

"This is Ann," the voice on the other line said. "Can I help you?"

"Oh, yes," Lonnie said. "Ann, this is Lonnie Kelly, from Twit & Bell. I've been temping as Beauregard Twit's—"

"Lonnie, of course I remember you. I'm not that old yet! What can I do for you, hon?" She sounded positively perky and energized, not downtrodden and victimized. Then again, if she'd killed Lunther, she'd have a good reason to be upbeat since he was dead.

"Well, this is a little awkward, I guess, but I wanted to talk to you about Lunther Bell."

"Lunther? Why—oh, no. Don't tell me." She paused, and said, "What'd he say to you, honey?"

"Oh, no, no, nothing. Actually, I sort of . . . Well, I know what he was capable of. That's why I was calling."

"What do you mean?" Ann asked.

"I know this sounds weird, but I found out about

Lunther's—well, the way he harassed some of the women who worked for him. And I wanted to . . ." What could she say? She wanted to know if Ann killed him? Because, if so, she planned to run right to the detective in charge of the case and tell him? No, that wasn't going to get her anywhere. So she stuck with the same angle she'd used in Macey's office earlier. "I wanted to . . . offer my support."

"Honey, I'm not sure I follow you," Ann said gently. "What are you talking about, the adult-baby thing?"

"Yes, exactly," she replied. "You see, I've worked with women in crisis before and—oh, not that I'm suggesting that you're in crisis, or anything. But, I just meant . . . well . . . if Lunther had tried to coerce you into . . . inappropriate activities, I know how that can affect a woman."

"Oh." Ann said, sounding as if she were mulling over the question. "Lonnie, I don't really know how this all concerns you, sugarplum, but I remember you as a real sweetie, so I'm sure your heart's in the right place. So if it makes you feel any better," Ann went on, "I can tell you that Lunther surely did not coerce me into anything. He did mention to me that he liked to dress up like a baby, and he asked if I would play the little game with him. You know, be his English governess, or some such. Change his dirty diapers, feed him his formula, spank him, and some other things I can't remember offhand."

Lonnie felt nauseated by what Ann *had* remembered. Okay, this was hardly the point, but really: Lunther wore diapers *and* soiled them? Was it just her, or was something seriously wrong with the world? Just then, she recalled the afternoon that Lunther bent over in front of her, and the sight of his big, puffy rear end . . . Oh, *Lord*. Her stomach rolled at the possibilities.

"Of course, I flat-out refused," Ann explained.

"But he didn't threaten to fire me, or anything, if that's waht you mean by 'coerce.'"

"And he didn't coerce you by . . . force?"

"Oh, no, doll! He never got physical. Are you kidding? He enjoyed playing the infant far too much to play the bully. Lonnie, sugar, if you don't mind me asking, how'd you find out about all of this? I surely didn't tell anyone. Well, except for Macey, but she already knew most of it."

"I found out from Macey, too," Lonnie admitted. "I guess it sounds weird, but when she told me, I was . . . I don't know . . . I was just so worried."

"Worried about me? Lunther's not my boss any more. He can't hurt me now, honey. Although I think he was pretty harmless, anyway."

"Oh, don't you know?" Lonnie asked. "Lunther's dead."

"Dead?" Ann sounded shocked.

"Yeah, um, a heart attack."

"Oh, I had no idea!"

"But still," Lonnie pressed. "The harassment must make you angry." There was no doubt about it. She was fishing.

"Oh, hon, my instincts were right all along," Ann said. "You are a sweetie! You mean, you called me because you thought I had some pent-up rage, or some such?" She finished her question with a mirthful laugh, which made Lonnie feel somewhat foolish.

"Yes, I guess you could say that."

"Oh, hon," Ann said while chuckling, "that is really very nice, but you have nothing to worry about. Now, don't get me wrong. Lunther definitely told me more than I'd ever want to know about his personal life, but I never felt harassed. I really just felt sorry for the old guy."

"But you quit," Lonnie pointed out. "And so abruptly. Surely his requests made you uncomfortable enough that you wanted to leave the firm—"

"Yeah, well, I suppose you're right, sweetie. But a lot of it had to do with timing."

"Timing?"

"Sure. Oh, I'm not gonna lie to you, hon. I couldn't look at Lunther the same after he told me what he told me. I mean, one day he was my boss, a dignified attorney. And the next, he was an oversized newborn wannabe. Believe me, that made it pretty hard to take him seriously as an employer." She chuckled again and continued. "But, also, it happened that my fiancé's company had an opening for a program coordinator, which was a major step up for me. Lord knows, honey, Twit & Bell is no place for upward mobility. When they look at you as 'just a secretary,' no place is. So I left."

"But why was it such a secret where you went?"

"Sugarplum, I'm so embarrassed, but I didn't give my notice the way you're *technically* supposed to. I know it was so unprofessional of me, but the company wanted me to start right away, and it's not like I needed a reference, so . . . well, you know how it is." This was not how Lonnie pictured this conversation going at all. She'd assumed that Ann would have more unresolved feelings about what happened. But she wasn't even bitter!

Lonnie wished her luck with her new job and congratulated her on her impending marriage, and then got off the phone, mentally crossing one suspect off of her list. Ann Lee didn't have a motive to kill Lunther, but *someone* did, and Lonnie couldn't shake the feeling she was missing something. Something that was right under her nose.

Chapter Twenty-three

Lonnie was getting a sneaking suspicion that Twit's late arrivals to staff meetings were deliberate stabs at "making an entrance"—which was fine if "making an entrance" was supposed to elicit eye rolling and/or chortling. At the moment, the conference room was filled, and everyone was waiting for Beauregard to come in and "officiate."

Finally, the conference room door opened and he waddled in. But something was different. Twit looked irritated and less sure of his innate demigod status than he'd been in a while. At least, since Lunther had died.

"All right, people, let's make this a quick one," he said with a trace of weariness in his voice. "Ahem, let's see here . . ." He looked down at his papers, did the usual haphazard shuffling of them, and let out a sigh before he spoke again. "Okay, before we get into old business, let's cover new business. I have an announcement." *Oh good, this should only take most of the day to spit out.* "Lyn Tang's agreed to join the firm." *Or not.* Twit went on. "Under one condition, that is. She's being made"—his face tightened as he ground out the last word—"partner." His eye tic cha-

cha-cha'd and his jowls clenched and released, clenched and released.

Lonnie couldn't believe it. He'd been adamantly against replacing Lunther, but apparently his desperation to court Lyn Tang exceeded his stance on the partner issue. She looked around the conference table to gauge her coworkers' reactions, but their faces didn't give away anything more than approving surprise.

"Then I assume I need to run an ad for an assistant position," Bette said.

"Uh, no," Twit replied, shifting in his seat uncomfortably. "That won't be necessary. Lyn wants to bring her longtime assistant with her. But you can start processing the personnel paperwork for both of them."

"I think I know how to do my job," Bette commented. "I'll have my assistant get started right away."

Twit said, "Now, as for old business—"

"Wait!" Delia shouted, and then realized her abruptness and immediately tried to soften her demeanor, which was like turning steel into granite. "Um . . . before you go on, Beauregard, I just wondered what the insinuations are of this." Going for the twenty-cent vocabulary was a new, unfortunate twist. Matt hissed "implications" under his breath, and half the table laughed. Delia used a mango-colored acrylic nail to drag a clump of fried hair behind her ear, and continued. "Does this mean that Lyn Tang is going to be our boss, too?" She paused and smiled sheepishly. "I mean, is she going to be as powerful as you?" The contrast between Delia's rusty accent and her batting eyelashes made Lonnie cringe inwardly.

Twit blushed. *Yuck.* Would the man just get laid and get it over with? "Quite frankly, Delia, I suppose my answer would have to be . . . yes." He let out a nervous fake cough. "That is to say, technically, Lyn will hold a, shall we say, boss*like* position here, but"—he cleared his throat of absolutely zero congestion—"I assure you, I still call the shots."

His eye tic turned violent. "In a manner of speaking, anyway," he clarified, only confusing them more. "That is, to elaborate," he rattled on, shuffling his papers again, "she won't have *more* power than me, of course. That would be simply obscene. And she certainly won't be able to do anything without my approval."

Now it was becoming clear. Lyn Tang was coming onboard sharing nothing less than completely *equal* power with Beauregard. No wonder he looked so beleaguered; he'd started the firm and now he had to share it with a virtual stranger.

A miasma of awkward silence hovered over the conference table.

"Ow!" B. J. yelped in pain. "What'd you do that for?" he asked Delia sharply, and leaned down to rub his ankle.

"Sorry, my foot must've slipped," she said without feeling.

"B. J., please, let's stay on track," Beauregard scolded. "I want to make this meeting as quick as possible."

"But it's not my fault!" B. J. protested immaturely. "She kicked my leg under the table—"

"Oh, *Lord*, can we get on with it please?" Bette whined—equal parts disgust and labored patience. B. J. turned beet red, Matt snickered, and Delia put on her best wide-eyed-doe face of innocence. But with all that eye makeup, she looked more like Nosferatu. At least that was Lonnie's impartial opinion. One thing was clear: Delia was livid about something. Poor B. J. had just been the unfortunate recipient of her rage, it seemed.

Beauregard cleared his throat and addressed the

room again. "Now, for old business, how does February's budget look?" He turned his attention to the two accountants who'd come to the meeting. They spent the next several minutes reviewing the overall expense of the holiday party and explaining a change in policy regarding company reimbursements. Lonnie pretty much zoned out, though, since her temp status precluded her from getting reimbursed for anything, anyway.

"Very well," Twit said. "Does anyone have anything else to report?" Nobody spoke, so he continued. "Well, then, one final matter: we need to send back the company letterhead and envelopes we ordered from Paper Depot last month." That job went to Lonnie, so she perked up.

"We're going to have to place a new order," Twit went on. He paused, as if dreading his next words, and finished, "To go with our new company name."

"What?" a few people inquired at once.

Twit pushed himself off his chair, visibly gritted his teeth, and let out a strained sigh. "That's correct." He headed toward the glass door, and barely turned before finishing: "From this point on, the firm will be called Twit & Tang." He stalked out, and the room stared after him in silence.

It didn't last long. Within seconds, people were chatting and gossiping among themselves about Lyn Tang virtually usurping Twit's throne. The majority opinion regarded Tang with impressed awe. The minority opinion remained uncertain about what to think. And Nosferatu's opinion had an entirely unique feel to it. Once Twit was out of earshot, she muttered, "Motherfucking piece of shit, stupid-ass waste of my time," and stormed out of the conference room.

Okay.

Lonnie went back to her desk, wondering how Twit's bad mood was going to affect his long-term disposition. On the one hand, he should be happy;

Lyn Tang would bring her New England–wide prestige to the firm.

On the other hand, Twit's blissful autonomy following Lunther Bell's demise had abruptly come to an end.

The next night Lonnie and Dominick were entwined on her sofa, half watching *Goodfellas* and half making out. Takeout cartons were strewn about, and an open bottle of Pinot Noir rested on the coffee table.

"But, wait, I don't understand," Lonnie said, while Dominick slid his hand up to her breast. "Why'd he just kill that guy?"

"Who?" he mumbled against her skin.

"Joe Pesci."

"Killed who?" he muttered, and licked a trail from the nape of her neck to behind her ear. Lonnie shifted even closer.

"The waiter guy," she said breathlessly. Dominick lifted his head up and spared a glance at the television. His hair was ruffled and disheveled, and his eyes were borderline drowsy. "Oh. Because he wanted more respect. Also, he's psychotic."

"Great movie," she said sarcastically.

"It's a classic," he replied with a boyish grin, and went back to work on her neck. Her arms tightened around him just as her phone rang. "Damn," he murmured.

"That's okay," she whispered. "I'll let the machine get it."

After the third ring, the machine picked up, and played Peach's greeting. Then there was a beep. Then—

"Lonnie, it's Terry." She broke her kiss with Dominick and looked at the phone incredulously. "I really want to talk to you." *What for?* "Please gimme a call back as soon as you can. I miss you." She flew off the couch to shut off the machine before Dominick got the wrong idea from the utterly ridiculous message.

"By the way, I think I left my cupid briefs there—" She threw herself on top of the counter, hoping to smother the machine to death.

A few seconds passed before she slid off the counter and walked back to the sofa . . . where Dominick sat stiffly upright. "What the hell was that?" he asked, obviously a mix of annoyed, jealous, and it's-time-to-put-up-my-guarded-I-don't-give-a-damn-guy wall.

Lonnie swallowed and shook her head vigorously. "No, it's not the way it sounded." She sat down next to him. He remained staunchly rigid on the adjacent cushion. "Let me explain," she said calmly. He sat there silently, and expectantly, with an I-don't-care-all-that-much expression on his face that didn't fool her for a minute. "Terry is that guy I had been dating. The one I mentioned when we first went to lunch a few months ago," she said.

"But I thought it didn't work out. You made it sound like it was over."

"It is, believe me."

"So why is he calling you for his *briefs*?" he persisted.

"No, you don't understand. Terry and I dated casually, and only for a few months. He doesn't even live in Boston. As soon as I met you"—she touched his lower arm—"things with him started tapering off." Why get into details about all the insults he'd hurled at her over the phone? "Now it's completely over."

She slid her hand up and down on his arm lovingly.

"Well, obviously he thinks there's still something going on," Dominick said, avoiding her eyes. But she could tell his tone was softening up, and he was coming around.

"He's—" She looked around, struggling to explain it, herself. "I think he just doesn't have anyone in his life right now, so he's making more out of us than there was. Believe me, Dominick, my relationship with Terry was nothing. It was casual, not a big deal." She turned his face and cradled his jaw in her hand. "Nothing like us," she said softly. And kissed him.

His wall crumbled. He kissed her back gently, and ran his hands over her neck and back affectionately. "Forget about Terry," she whispered against his mouth.

"What about his underwear?" he asked, resting his forehead against hers.

"Forget that, too."

"Lonnie . . ."

"Well . . . the truth is . . ." She hesitated, but knew she had to tell him. "He visited me a few weeks ago." Dominick started pulling away, but she wasn't having it. She kept him locked to her, and explained, "It's not what you think. His visit had already been planned for a long time. Remember that day we spent at Borders?"

"How could I forget—it was the first time we kissed. And also, I got my face ripped open." Instinctively, she moved her hand to his temple and caressed the spot where he'd gotten a cut and a huge bruise trying to protect her.

"He came that night," she said. "That's part of the reason why I acted so weird after what happened between us. I just felt so guilty and confused, and believe me, the last thing I wanted to do was have a romantic weekend with Terry."

"So then he stayed over here?" he asked, irritated, and starting to pull away again.

"Yeah, but nothing happened. Peach was here, and everything was platonic. Really." He seemed to be mulling it over. "I'm crazy about you," she added on a whisper. "You're the only man in my life right now. And you're the only man I want."

He leaned in closer. "Well, not counting Twit," she teased, and his face broke into a grin. Hers followed, and soon there was a kind of warm haze that settled over them. Infatuation had become caring, and now it was out in the open.

The phone rang again.

Lonnie reluctantly let go of Dominick and went to answer it since she'd shut off the machine when she body slammed it. "Hello?"

"Lonnie? Hey!" Oh, *Christ.*

"What do you want?" she asked bluntly. "You just called."

"Oh—I know, but the machine cut off in the middle of my message. We need to talk—"

"No, I'm sorry, we don't," she said. "Please, Terry, I think it would be best if—"

"Just listen for a second, please!"

She relented because she thought maybe if he said his piece and got everything he had off his chest, he wouldn't bother her anymore. Meanwhile, Dominick came up behind her to hear what was going on.

Terry started rambling at some length about all the pressure he'd been under lately, how his bipolar mother was driving him crazy, how his car was impounded somewhere outside of Queens, and how he's struggled with low self-esteem since boyhood. This was worse than she'd thought it would be. He'd been yammering for almost ten minutes, and still hadn't mentioned their former relationship. Her feet were tired from standing there, and it was a little awkward having Dominick leaning against the mini-refrigerator, waiting to find out what the hell Terry wanted.

Finally, he broached the subject. "About us," Terry said. "All I want is a chance to explain all of this in person. I'm coming to Boston on Friday night."

"What—Friday? No, don't do that!"

"I have to come for a show anyway. Lonnie, please, I'm not taking no for an answer. I can't. I have too much to explain."

She surveyed her minikitchen with desperation. Why was he doing this? She didn't want to listen to his explanations about anything. He was the one who'd officially ended it, so why did she feel like he was the one who was desperately hanging on? "Terry, I—I can't. I have plans. Why don't I just give you a call sometime?"

"No, I'm coming into town on Friday anyway, and I need to see you. Please. Don't just blow me off after all the time we've spent together." Didn't he have it the other way around? Didn't he remember that lunatic phone call he'd placed to tell her that she didn't "stimulate" anything but his temper? "All I want is an opportunity to tell you what's been going on in my life lately. Please, Lonnie. Don't shut me out without letting me explain myself. We are *friends*, aren't we?"

Low blow, but effective.

Somehow he'd successfully made her feel guilty about trying to dodge him, which was truly ridiculous since he'd dumped her under no uncertain terms only a week before. Life was so *weird*. Nevertheless, she wasn't a heartless bitch, and if Terry was coming to town anyway, she figured it would only be decent of her to meet him for a cup of coffee and finalize things face-to-face. After all, she'd like to end on a nice note, rather than the bizarre, irate way they'd left things.

"Okay. We can meet Friday night—" Dominick stood upright, and his mouth dropped open. She held her hand up to calm him. "*But* just a cup of coffee, Terry, okay? I have plans Friday, so I can only grab a cup of coffee and talk for about twenty minutes."

"Fine! No problem!" Obviously Terry was excited. What Lonnie couldn't figure out was *why*. She told him to meet her at seven o'clock at the Starbucks on Boylston Street. She couldn't hang up fast enough. When she turned to face Dominick, he didn't look too thrilled.

"You're gonna meet this guy Friday night?" he asked as though it were the most ludicrous thing he'd ever heard. "I thought you said it was over!"

"It *is* over. Come on, you heard what I told him. I'm giving him twenty minutes, and then we can bring closure to this thing with Terry once and for all."

"Lonnie, wake up! He doesn't want closure; he wants *you*."

She shook her head. "No, you've got it all wrong. He didn't want us to keep seeing each other, either. I think all he wants now is a chance to apologize for being such an asshole about it. Believe me, there's no way he's trying to rekindle anything."

He didn't look very convinced, so she pressed on. "If you heard the things he said to me—well, let's just say he made it perfectly clear he wanted nothing to do with me romantically. Only he said it a lot more obnoxiously than that. I'm sure he just wants to apologize, that's all."

Dominick sighed heavily. "Okay, I mean . . . Look, I'm not trying to be possessive, or anything, but—"

"No, I understand," she said quickly. "I completely understand, but you have *nothing* to worry about." She sealed the space between them and encircled his waist with her arms. Hugging him tightly, she rested her head over his heart.

Reluctantly, he hugged her back. "But I still don't see why you have to go at all. Just blow the guy off. Tell him to drop dead."

"I can't do that! It sounds like he's having personal problems. That would be too mean." Her tone left little room for negotiation, and Dominick realized that. She hugged him tighter, pressing her cheek to his chest, and sealed the deal.

"I still don't understand why you're going," Peach said. She'd opted to spend her Friday night mixing paints on an oversize palette, while waiting for her cucumber face mask to crack. Matt would be so flattered.

"I already told you. I owe him that much—"

"You owe him shit," Peach said, and Lonnie rolled her eyes while she shrugged on her parka.

"Fine, fine. I don't 'owe' him. But . . . I don't know. We did date for six months."

"Not seriously."

"It's only decent that we end things face-to-face," she insisted, a little annoyed that no one seemed to grasp this concept but her. "Anyway, he begged me for twenty minutes of my time. What, I'm going to tell him that I can't spare that?"

"What about all those things he said on the phone?"

Lonnie shrugged and wrapped her black cashmere scarf around her neck. "Supposedly he'll explain all that."

"And you care about his explanation because . . . ?"

"I don't really care. But if he wants to apologize for acting like an ass, I'm not going to stop him," she said, and stooped down to double knot her fake Doc Martens.

"I think you just feel guilty because you were already with Dominick when Terry went psycho." Lonnie ignored her and grabbed her keys. Peach added, "Just don't let him charm you into giving him another chance."

"Okay, I won't. See you later."

"When will you be back?" Peach asked.

"Soon," Lonnie said. "This won't take long."

Chapter Twenty-four

❦

"Terry, I've been waiting here for thirty minutes!"
"I know, I'm sorry," he apologized through garbling static. "I got a late start, and there was a big detour near Waterbury."

"Oh . . . well, do you just want to forget it?" She tried to make the offer sound as nonchalant as possible—as if she weren't praying with all her might that he'd accept it. She'd been sitting at Starbucks, in a purple armchair, watching rain streak down the front glass in flickering lines that inverted streetlights and blurred Boylston traffic. She hadn't taken her cell phone, figuring this would be a quick cup of coffee. She should've known it wouldn't be that easy.

Finally, she'd braved the rain to use the pay phone on the sidewalk. And luckily, Terry had picked up his cell. Unluckily, it didn't sound as if he were right around the corner.

"No, I don't wanna forget it," he said, referring to her suggestive plea that they take the proverbial rain check. "Sorry I'm running late, but I definitely still wanna get together. Look, it's eight now. I'll be in the city within the hour." *An hour!* How did she get roped into these things? She was going to wait another hour just to meet him for a twenty-minute cup of coffee?

"We'll have dinner," he added.

Well, that answered that question. "Terry, I—no, I . . . can't do dinner," she lied. Technically she could, but she didn't want to. She wasn't hungry, and she didn't feel like killing an hour just so she could enjoy a strained dinner date with her ex-practically-semi boyfriend. Was it just her?

"Lon, I'm starving," he whined. "Come on, dinner, my treat. It's the least I can do for being so late."

"No . . . I—"

"Look, I gotta go, my battery's running down."

"Terry, wait!" she exclaimed. Honestly, she wasn't trying to be stubborn—she was simply trying to avoid being manipulated. "I never agreed to dinner," she stated firmly.

"What's the big deal?" he asked testily. "I can't believe this—I drive four hours to see you tonight and you won't have one quick dinner with me—*my treat*?" When he put it like that, it did sound pretty petty. Except . . . *Wait a minute!*

"What do you mean you drove four hours just to see me?" she challenged. "You told me you had to be in Boston tonight anyway!"

Static broke up the connection for a few defining moments.

"Lon? You there?"

"Yes . . . but . . ."

"Lon, listen, we'll go to that seafood place nearby."

"But—"

"I . . . I'll see you in an hour . . .," he croaked out before the line went dead.

Damn it! She slammed the phone onto its perch harder than she'd intended, and only then did she realize how drenched she was. The sleeves of her bulky white parka leaked steady, fat drops, and her hair—long, black, and soaked—was plastered to her face. Fortunately, she hadn't worn makeup, so at least she could avoid the goth effect. Yet, oddly, that provided little consolation at the moment.

Seeing the happy couples and packs of friends scurrying down Boylston, gathered under umbrellas, she felt jealous. Not for the umbrellas, but because they appeared to actually want to spend time with each other.

She dug into her pocket for change and placed another call. After three rings, Dominick's voice mail picked up. Great. She'd wanted to explain what was going on to *him*, not an automated answering service. He'd been at a conference all day, so she'd hoped they'd get to see each other later tonight. It was still a very good possibility, if Terry would just get here already. "Hi, it's me," she said after the beep. "I . . . Listen, I'm not sure what's going on for tonight. Terry hasn't even gotten here yet. I just spoke to him, and he's running late, and . . . well, now we're supposed to have dinner when he show's up . . . and his phone kept breaking up, so I couldn't get out of it. . . . Anyway, I'll call you when I get home, but I don't know when it will be. . . . Not that I think it'll be late or anything, but I just mean, I don't expect you to wait. Okay, your tape's gonna run out. I'll call you later. Bye."

She hung up, crossed the sidewalk, and went back into the warmth of Starbucks to get a decaf white-chocolate mocha to take the chill off. (Well, she didn't want to get a *cold*.)

Nearly an hour and a half later, Terry showed up. Unfortunately, Lonnie missed his entrance because she'd fallen asleep in her purple armchair. It must have been that third herbal tea that did her in. "Hey, Lon," he said, shaking her arm.

She jerked awake, and once she realized where she

was—and felt appropriately embarrassed by her public nap—she was overwhelmed by the painfully pressing need to pee.

Several minutes later, she emerged from the bathroom and actually caught Terry looking at his watch impatiently. She locked her jaw and decided to chalk it up to residual sleep delirium so she could get this night over with as civilly and *amicably* as possible. "Ready?" he asked.

They had no trouble getting seated at the restaurant since it was so late. Then Terry spent another half hour savoring his appetizer of fried calamari. Just as Lonnie was about to put her foot down and demand they speed up the meal, their waiter brought out a bottle of Dom Perignon. Terry must've ordered it when she was in the ladies' room earlier.

Immediately, she protested. "Terry, I don't want to drink this. It's too expensive and we're not celebrating anything."

"No way," he countered, shaking his head and sending a few light brown shaggy locks out of their loosely defined place. "Don't worry about it. My treat, remember?" And he smiled at her. His smile reminded her that he was only trying to be nice, and that made her feel guilty, because she still didn't want to be there.

She wasn't bored; she was *antsy*. It felt like eons had passed while Terry droned on about his career—how it was really starting to take off, how he was "this close" to getting a role in a commercial, how his agent saw big things ahead. Now, while he drank some more champagne, Lonnie tried to get a word in before he launched back into his self-aggrandizing treatise. "I can really only stay for one glass," she said. "Then I've got to get going, okay?" At this rate, she had no idea if he was ever planning to explain his tirade over the phone, and she really didn't care anymore.

"But my lobster tails haven't come yet," he protested, clearly irritated by her suggestion that she leave before he was fully sated. "And what about your flounder?" Oh, yeah, she'd forgotten all about her electrifying order of flounder broiled dry, with no butter or oil.

He smiled lightheartedly and asked, "What's the matter, you gotta hot date?"

She felt like shouting YES! but she really wasn't looking to hurt him, so she tried to move things right along. "Terry, didn't you want to talk about . . . you know . . . what happened?"

"What do you mean?" he asked, clearly baffled—or at least doing his best impression.

The waiter chose that moment to bring their meals. He set down the plates, and Terry started digging in. Between bites, he reached for the champagne bottle again, and only then did Lonnie realize that he'd already downed two glasses. Part of her wanted to drink more—enough to numb her annoyance—but a bigger part of her knew she had to keep her wits about her if she wanted to get out of there before sunrise.

This night was truly ridiculous. Was Terry actually going to sit blithely through the entire meal acting like nothing had happened? Never one to ignore food that was placed in front of her, she attempted to eat the blackened, bone-dry flounder. She gave up after two bites, and resigned herself to pushing it around with her fork.

What in the world must Dominick think by now?

By the time Terry finished his meal, it was 10:45. So far, all Terry had said was drivel. And he'd gotten even more insipidly chatty within the past few minutes . . . rambling, really . . .

Then she realized.

The Dom Perignon bottle was nearly empty, and she was still on her first glass.

"Didja ever wonder," he said jovially, while lifting his glass to clink hers, "why you park on the parkway and drive in a driveway . . . Wait . . . no, I got it wrong—"

"Listen, it's really getting late. "I'm going home. Unless there's anything else you want to say?"

"Like what?"

She struggled not to grab him by the collar and shake him. Opting instead for personal martyrdom, she kept calm, and said, "I thought you wanted to see me tonight because you wanted to . . . you know . . . explain what's been going on with you lately."

He looked utterly perplexed. "That's what I have been doing," he said cheerfully.

"Right, but—"

"Hey, that would be a great bit! Something about how once you buy a woman lobster, she loses interest real fast. You know, something about how you should talk to her first, *then* buy her lobster, so she'd have a reason to listen to you. D'ya know what I mean? What d'ya think?"

Something inside her *snapped*. Just like that, she traded martyrdom for confrontation.

Slamming her napkin on the table with an audible thump—her tight fist balling the pink linen up painfully—she ground out her words. "What do I think? Oh, a few things. First of all, I have been listening, but you've been babbling about *nothing*. Secondly, *you're* the one who got the lobster. And third, just because I've calmly listened to your bullshit for two hours, doesn't mean I'm unaware of what a manipulative ass you are!"

"What? All right, okay, just calm down—"

"I don't want to calm down!" Her temper was fully unleashed. "Terry, you lured me here tonight— you made me feel sorry for you, like you've just had a tough time of things lately, and you wanted to explain. But it was all bullshit, wasn't it? You just wanted to get me here. Athough, I can't for the life of me figure out *why!*"

"So I just wanted to spend an evening with my sweetie, is that so wrong?" he asked, leaning toward her and going for the boyish grin—but only succeeding in giving her access to his heavy champagne breath. Add that to his list of charms.

"I'm not your sweetie! What are you, nuts?"

"Shh—" he started, looking around the deserted restaurant.

"Terry, you dumped me! And on New Year's! You called me up and told me that you never wanted to see me again. *Is any of this ringing a bell?*"

He slumped back in his seat and looked at her with droopy eyes. "What, you mean you took that *seriously?*" he asked.

"Uh, yeah, the part about loathing me seems to resonate."

"Lon, come on, I told you I switched shrinks. Can't we just forget about that phone call? It was a mistake. C'mere"—he leaned forward again with his lips puckered—"gimme a little kiss," he begged and puckered harder.

He actually thought this was cute? The man—correction, *boy*—needed to grow up.

"Are you for real?" she demanded, recoiling in her seat.

"Come on, Lonnie Anderson," he crooned with drunkenness. "You know you still like me a little. Let's go back to your apartment and talk more about this." He grabbed her hand. Unlike Dominick's hands, Terry's were lukewarm and exceptionally smooth.

She snatched her hand away. "Why did you ask me to meet you tonight? I thought you wanted to apologize. I thought you wanted . . . *closure*. That wasn't what you wanted at all," she said, shaking her head because she'd been such a fool.

"I just want us to be the way we were," he replied. "I'm sorry if I was in a bad mood that day on the phone—"

"Bad mood? You went psycho on me!" He rolled his eyes as if she were being way too dramatic. "How can I put this?" she continued forcefully. "I think you're a complete jerk. I find you very *un*appealing. And now, if you'll excuse me, thank you for dinner, but I am going home, and I'd really appreciate it if you *never* called or e-mailed me again! *Ever!* "

She burst out of her chair and reached for her bulky parka. As she was shrugging it on, she saw something. . . . Oh, no . . . not that. *Anything* but that.

His chin was quivering, and his lower lip was trembling. He couldn't really be—

"Terry?"

He covered his eyes with his hand. Jesus Christmas, the boy was crying. And this wasn't Twit-crying—his shoulders weren't heaving; his eyes weren't dry. This was a silent flow of tear that rolled down his cheeks in spite of his hand.

Just *terrific*. Now look what she'd done! She tries to be a confrontational bitch—just this once—and it's a complete disaster!

She looked around the restaurant helplessly, unable to believe how this night had turned out. What had been scheduled as a quick cup of coffee had turned into a three-and-a-half-hour foray into the dark underworld of an obviously manic-depressive comedian with a drinking problem and Peter Pan issues. And now she'd made him cry.

"Terry, please . . ." She put her arm on his shoulder awkwardly. "Calm down . . . I . . . I'm sorry. I didn't mean to . . ." She fell down into the booth beside him. "Terry, please . . . I'm really sorry."

"It's n-not you," he stammered, and swiped his tears with the napkin she handed him. Now it was her turn to look around the restaurant to see who was watching. "It's . . . it's . . ."

"What?" she asked softly, and let her hand rest on his upper arm. She kept her face far from his, though, so he wouldn't misread her compassion for intimacy. If it weren't for his actual tears, she'd think she was still being manipulated.

"Don't get the wrong idea," he explained. "It's my anxiety medicine. I'm not supposed to mix it with alcohol—it makes me more emotional."

"Oh . . . okay," she replied, wondering if that meant she was off the hook and could continue her departure.

"I guess I just blow everything," he said with palpable dejection, and she realized she wasn't going anywhere yet.

"What are you talking about? You just told me all about how well your career's going." *Ad nauseam.* "Remember?"

"That's true. But I wish I hadn't blown it with you." He avoided her eyes, obviously self-conscious about his admission. Lord, he really was so immature.

"Well, what did you expect, Terry?" she asked gently.

"I don't know," he said. "I know I shouldn't have acted like such a jerk, but I still like you. I want you to be my girlfriend." Uh-oh.

"No, you don't," she said quickly. "We are not relationship material, and I think we both know that." *Please say you know that because I can't take much more of this!*

After a long pause, he said, "Maybe you're right. It's like, sometimes I want a girlfriend who'll be there for me, and then other times I just can't be bothered." He still couldn't make eye contact. "And I've just been so . . . confused. About my career. About everything."

She could relate to that. Who couldn't? Terry wasn't a bad guy—he just had his own issues, and she wasn't going to be the girl to make the difference. That was okay—that was *life*.

And she couldn't help thinking how grateful she was that Dominick Carter was in hers. He and Terry were so different. Dominick was fun without being inane, sensitive without being unstable, and sweet without being a basket case. Dominick *listened*, and gave as much as he took. She sighed and thought, *He's wonderful*.

"Confused about my future . . ." Terry was saying. "Confused about religion . . ."

"You're twenty-five," Lonnie interrupted. "It's fine to be confused, but don't you think you're making more out of us than there really was?"

He paused, then quirked his mouth a little, and shrugged. She knew him well enough to recognize that as agreement. Finally they'd gotten somewhere.

"Listen, Terry, I really do have to go," she said. "I'm exhausted, and it's been a draining week. But I'd like us to stay friends. Let's just keep it light, okay? Sometime drop me an e-mail and let me know how you are."

"Okay."

"But no forwards, *please*, " she said. He couldn't promise her that.

After Terry paid the check, they left the restaurant, and he hailed a taxi to take him to the nearest hotel. He paused before closing the door, and looked up at Lonnie who was standing on the curb. "Later, gator," he chirped, and added, "Thanks, you're beautiful!" as the cab peeled away.

Dominick was lying on his back with his hands crossed behind his head, watching his ceiling in the

semidarkness when his phone rang. He jolted a little
because the shrill broke his trance, and also because
he immediately figured it was probably Lonnie. The
latter thought made him wait to answer it. Two rings,
three, four—

"Hello," he said.

"Hi, it's me," she said. She was whispering so he
assumed she was trying not to wake up Peach. Assuming she was at her apartment by now. After all,
it was only past midnight, and she was supposed to
have met her ex-boyfriend for a "cup of coffee" at
seven-fucking-thirty.

"Hey." His tone was nonchalant.

"Hi," she said again. "You wouldn't believe the
night I had."

"Really?"

She must've picked up on his annoyance, because
she chimed, "Sorry it's so late." Then she went on
to explain how Terry had kept her waiting for two
hours, and conned her into some long, boring dinner,
but he'd finally gotten the picture that they were
through.

He believed her . . . he supposed . . . but he was
still jealous and pissed off anyway. And why did
Lonnie have to be so damn sweet—why couldn't she
stand Terry up? Or tell him to go to hell?

"Anyway," she said, obviously yawning while
speaking, "I'm going to sleep now; I'm exhausted."

"Do you want me to come over?" he asked. He
wouldn't ask her to come over in the middle of the
night because it wouldn't be safe, and she was obviously tired. But he still wanted her soft, cuddly body
that smelling like strawberry lying next to him. He
still wanted to see her.

"Oh . . ." she whispered. "Baby, I'm too tired
tonight."

"No, I didn't mean for sex. Jesus," he muttered.

"Oh. No, I know. I just mean I'm so tired I'll fall

asleep before you get here. This week has been so draining, and then tonight sealed it."

"Okay, whatever you want," he said flatly.

"You're not upset, are you?" she asked with predictable sweet concern.

"No."

"Because we're definitely doing something tomorrow night, right?" He could tell she was trying to be upbeat in spite of her exhaustion. That softened him up a little.

"Uh-huh," he said, half smiling into the semi-darkness.

"Good, I can't wait."

"All right, tomorrow. Good night," he said.

" 'Night, babydoll. Till tomorrow."

He hung up and settled back on his pillow, with both hands crossed behind his head. Well, she'd apologized for not calling sooner, explained what happened, and assured him that things were over with Terry. He should be satisfied. So why was he still pissed off and jealous?

Maybe it was because she didn't want him to come over. She'd said she was too tired, but still . . . he couldn't help but wonder . . .

No. She'd said Terry went to a hotel. He had no reason not to believe that. No reason to think he might be staying in her apartment with her. Lonnie wouldn't lie to him.

Of course, she hadn't even told him that Terry was still in the picture until she absolutely had to.

Forget it. He'd see her tomorrow, and he was sure by then all his doubt would fade.

Chapter Twenty-five

On the drive to Mabel Wills's house, Lonnie knew she was embarking on a long shot. She'd gotten her telephone number and address from the phone book. But when she'd tried to call, the number was perpetually busy. So, she'd borrowed her father's car, and decided to be impulsive. Now with a crinkled Mapquest printout, she was heading down the Mass Pike refusing to second guess herself.

She had no idea if Ann Lee's blasé attitude toward Lunther-the-Adult-Baby was typical or atypical, and she was at least going to talk to one other woman before she forgot about that list. Of course, there was always the possibility that Mabel wouldn't be home when Lonnie arrived. Or, even if she were home, she could refuse to speak to her.

Thirty minutes later, she found herself in the tiny town of Blueville, pulling into Mabel Wills's gravel driveway. She cut the engine on Jack's Oldsmobile, and walked up to the front porch, which was covered by a sturdy, wood-plank awning. After she rang the doorbell, she nervously fidgeted with her hair—pushing it behind her ears, then back in front, and then behind again. Finally an old woman opened the door.

"Yeah!" the old woman barked gruffly.

"Oh, hi. Are you Mabel?" Lonnie asked sheepishly.

"Yeah!" she barked again, and Lonnie quickly took in the image. Mabel Wills was a heavyset, seventyish woman with thick gray hair in a loose Martha-Washington upsweep and an unforgiving frown. She certainly didn't appear to be in the mood to entertain—much less confess to Murder One—but Lonnie hadn't driven all this way just to turn and run. As much as she wanted to at that moment.

"Uh, hi there," she began. "My name is Lonnie Kelley, and I'm currently working at Twi—"

"Sometime today!" Mabel commanded with impatience. "What the hell do you want already?"

Lonnie swallowed hard, and shifted her eyes, avoiding direct contact with Mabel's all-but-loathing stare. "Well, you see, I'm sure you've heard about Lunther Bell's"—*cold-blooded murder*—"passing."

"Who? Oh, right. The pervert. So, what about it?"

"Um, well, I don't mean to impose on you, Ms. Wills, but—"

"What's with the 'Ms.' crap? Everyone calls me M. W.—Maw for short—and you can do the same, or get the hell off my property." Lonnie nodded thoughtfully, as if that were more than reasonable.

Let's face it, Mabel made Delia seem genteel, but Lonnie was trying to go with the flow. "Oh, certainly, M-maw." *Jeez, that sounds dumb.* "Anyway, like I was saying, I was hoping I could ask you about Lunther Bell. Specifically, I wanted to know if—"

"What, already! Damn it, get to the point! I haven't got all year for you to spit it out. Jesus H. Christ. You're startin' to annoy the shit out of me!"

Annoying the shit out of someone hardly seemed like the precursor to a heart-to-heart, but Lonnie continued anyway, because she didn't know what else to do. She blurted: "Did you quit Twit & Bell because Lunther Bell had sexually harassed you?" Then she chastised herself. That hardly conveyed heartfelt concern. But was it her fault that *Maw*'s drill-sergeant bit had broken her concentration?

"Did he what? Try plain English, willya?" Well, she'd stopped shouting; that was good. "Do you mean, did he tell me about the baby shit? Is that what you mean?"

"Well . . . yes." She sighed in frustration. This was going horribly! Obviously Mabel was not traumatized by Lunther's antics. Unless he'd scarred her so much that she'd turned burly as a coping mechanism.

"You know what?" Lonnie backed away as she spoke, dying to make her escape. "I'm really sorry I bothered you, Ms.—uh, Maw," she said with as much sweetness as she could muster. It was all aspartame, of course, but as long as it got her out of there, she really didn't care.

Mabel only frowned more, until her mouth was contorted into a sneering, down-turned streak across her disgusted face.

"Um . . . best of luck with . . . you know . . . life." Lonnie gave a quick little wave. "Take care!" She scooted to her car as fast as she could, fiddled with the lock on the door—the whole time, casting nervous glances over her shoulder, while Mabel remained planted in the same spot, scowling and staring—and finally, slid into the front seat.

She reversed out of the gravel drive and peeled away, thinking, *never assume anything, and oh yeah, stop at J. P. Licks on the way home; you deserve a waffle cone.*

Hours later, Lonnie was with Dominick, in his bed. She was slowly moving up and down on his body, trying to get a steady rhythm going. But all she was getting was more frustrated because she was out of practice. When his body jerked up, hers would move up, too, and when she tried to press down hard, she couldn't get him as deep as she wanted. She had her legs straddled over his, and her hands propping herself up, as she desperately rocked her pelvis back and forth. Her moans were changing into strangled sighs of frustration.

One of Dominick's hands let go of Lonnie's naked butt and moved up into her hair, which was tangled and damp from perspiration. "Baby," he breathed, and gently pulled her down to him. He captured her mouth in a soft kiss, and then moved his mouth to her ear. "Will you let me help you?" he whispered. She could hear the shortness of his breath, and knew he was feeling just as frustrated and hot as she was.

She answered him by sighing, pressing her lips to his, and relaxing her whole body against him. He licked into her mouth, slid both his hands around her smooth back, and started to sit up.

Lonnie had a vague, arousing sense of Dominick's stomach muscles contracting and her legs moving out in front of her as he guided them both into a sitting position. He was still inside her, while he kissed down her throat and back up to her mouth. Then Dominick tugged on her legs, bringing himself deeper. She shuddered.

"Am I hurting you?" he asked suddenly.

"Oh, no . . . no," she murmured, and wrapped her arms around him tightly. Within seconds, she was on her back, with her head at the foot of the bed and Dominick was driving into her.

His steady thrusts quickened, and the friction overheated her in the most carnal and exciting way. "Wrap your legs around me," he urged.

Lonnie pressed down on the bed with her hands and brought her legs up to lock them around Dominick's back. *Oh, my God.* Her new angle had Dominick thrusting against a supersensitive place deep inside her she'd never even known existed. She clutched the comforter and cried out, and he bucked his hips harder and faster.

She barely realized that all the rocking had moved their bodies forward, and now her head was hanging over the edge of the bed. "I . . . Yes . . . *Ahh!* " she started breathlessly, then shut her eyes and gave herself up to the heat and lust and orgasm that she could feel coming with each thrust. As soon as she heard Dominick's choppy, hard breaths, she knew he was about to come, too, and it sent her over the edge. She climaxed, crying out mindlessly, and clinging to his sweat-slicked back.

He let out a strained cry; she looked up because she wanted to see his face when he came.

As soon as he was done, he buried his head in her neck and covered her entire body with his. Their sweat fused, and their breathing slowly returned to normal. Then he rolled onto his back, hugging her tightly, and rolling her with him. Her head ended up nestled in the crook of his neck, and she felt so content that she had to fight the urge to say "I love you." She knew it was just the mellowness and satisfaction and postorgasmic bliss that made her want to croon all sorts of romantic things to him, and she had to keep that in check.

"I love you," he whispered.

Her heart dropped. She felt a rush of euphoria, and suddenly her just-mellow-and-post-orgasmic theory seemed like a lot of crap. *I think I love you, too! You make me so happy!* But she couldn't say it. She hadn't uttered those words since Jake, and now she was afraid to say them out loud.

So, instead, she brought her hand to the center of his chest and placed it over his heart. She kissed his jaw and throat, and then replaced her hand with her mouth and kissed him there. Suddenly, she felt one tear drop from her eye, but she didn't know why, and before long, they both fell asleep. With her cheek pressed against Dominick's heart.

*   *   *

Lonnie rolled over onto her side, but couldn't make her heavy-lidded eyes open all the way. She snuggled closer to him and listened to his even breathing.

They'd made love twice that night. The first time had left a lingering burning sensation on her as she drifted off to sleep. A few hours later, he'd stirred in bed. She'd rolled a little closer, covered his thigh with her own, and things moved quickly from there. Instinctively, he stroked between her legs, and she climbed on top of him, having no problem finding her rhythm this time. Fortunately, one of them woke up enough to grab a condom from the nightstand, and they moved against each other—into each other—hard and fast. She sucked on his earlobe while he made sounds like she was fucking him into ecstasy. When he came, he held her to him, and there was something more possessive—more savage—between them than ever before.

The truth was, she was too happy to sleep. She was so elated to be here with Dominick rather than with Terry. Or Jake. Or any man in the world. Just then, he shifted onto his side, which she knew meant that he would wake up any minute. He always slept on his back.

He sat up slowly, rubbing his hand over his eyes, to coax them awake. Then he got up and walked to the bathroom, naked. She fully appreciated the view as the bathroom door closed. His body was the stuff of carnal fantasies, and that butt was about the most perfect peach she'd ever sunk her teeth into. Well, *not hard*. She heard the sink run, then stop; she sighed.

Dominick was one hundred and eighty pounds of gorgeous man, whom she pretty certainly *loved*, and she still had trouble believing all of it was real. He slid under the covers again.

"Hi," she said softly.

"Hi. You're awake," he said, and draped his arm

over her. She hugged him tightly and listened to his heart, which she loved to do, because it made her feel closer to him somehow. A silence fell over them for several minutes. She figured there was no need to fill the silence when they were so obviously in sync with each other in every way.

"So was it like this with Terry?" he asked. His tone was mild, as if the question *hadn't* just come out of nowhere. She lifted her head up.

"What are you talking about?" she asked, her eyes blinking in confusion.

"The sex," he said calmly. "Who's better in bed, me or him?"

"Well, if I had to guess, I would say you." Placing kisses on his chest, she repeated, "You, baby. There's no doubt in my mind."

"So then I'm better?" he asked again.

She assumed he was kidding, although she failed to see the humor. In fact, mentioning Terry at all seemed like a real buzz kill. But she wanted to keep things light, so she just grinned, and said, "Get real. Like I would know."

"Yeah, right," he said . . . kiddingly?

"What?" she asked, hoping she'd heard him wrong and that his tone hadn't been sarcastic. Suddenly, she noticed that although his arm was around her, there was no real grip. It was just lying limply across her side. "What are you talking about?" she asked again.

"Nothing. I'm just kidding," he said.

But she wasn't convinced. Why would he have said it at all? She pulled back from him. "You know I didn't sleep with Terry," she reminded him.

"Except for that night he came to visit."

"I told you that was completely platonic," she replied hotly.

"Okay, okay, relax. I'm only joking."

"You are?"

"Uh . . . yeah."

"You are not joking. You're being serious!"

"What are you getting so defensive about?" he asked. So now he was turning it around on her—where was this *coming* from?

"Dominick, you're implying that I lied to you about my relationship with Terry. Jeez, it wasn't *even* a relationship—it was nothing. Do you not believe that all of a sudden? Are you implying that I actually *did* sleep with Terry, when I told you I didn't?"

"Look, Lonnie . . ." He averted his gaze. "You're making a big deal out of nothing."

"So then, you know I'm telling you the truth?"

"Uh . . . yeah. Whatever you say."

"Don't patronize me! This isn't like you—what's going on? Why are you acting like this?"

"Like what?" he asked, and rolled onto his back, still not looking at her.

"Like an asshole."

After a beat of silence, he shrugged. "Fine. Let's just forget it." As much as she wanted to forget it, she couldn't let it drop yet. It wasn't just his so-called joke; it was the way he was now acting distant and clueless. One hardly needed a lifetime of dating experience to recognize that textbook-guy ploy a mile away. Something was up with him, and she needed to know what it was.

Meanwhile, he rolled over onto his side, as if he were simply tired and going to beddy bye. As if she didn't know that he always slept on his back!

She pulled on his shoulder until he faced her again. "Wait a minute. Don't turn away from me. I want to know why you made that comment about Terry."

"It was just a question. Jesus, you don't have to make a federal case out of it." She waited for more elaboration that never came.

"Is that all you have to say?" He shrugged and said nothing else. She sat upright in bed. "I don't understand this," she argued calmly. "You were being normal before."

It was true. Earlier, they'd ordered Chinese food and rented a movie. She'd given him a choice between *Portrait of Teresa* and *The Stepford Wives*, and they'd talked and laughed throughout the evening. He'd told her about his new idea for GraphNet's Web page, and she'd amused him with her tale of visiting Mabel Wills in Blueville. Everything had been fine between them. Better than fine.

Hadn't it?

What could've happened between then and now?

"Lonnie, I'm tired," he grumbled, as if *she* were tiring him to no end. "Can we just go to sleep?" he said, and rolled onto that damn side again.

"So you're not going to tell me what's bothering you all of a sudden?" she persisted.

"Jesus Christ, just let it go already. I'm tired."

For the next few seconds, she sat there, agape, disbelieving, and nauseous. Her cheeks were rage hot and fury pink. Could this really be happening? Could Dominick really have changed like this? *Well, to hell with him!* She wasn't going to play his mind games.

"Fine, I'll leave," she said, hurrying out of bed and into the bathroom, making sure to slam the door hard behind her.

Dominick let out a frustrated sigh. He knew he was being an asshole, and he knew why. But what did she expect? She went to meet her ex-boyfriend the night before, and he only knew about the guy because her answering machine had blasted his message. For all he knew, Lonnie never planned to tell him about her ex who was still trying to get in her life. For all he knew, the guy might not even really be an *ex*.

But that didn't sound right, even to him, as angry

and jealous as he was. Lonnie wouldn't lie to him . . .
not about something like that. Would she?

He'd thought he'd come to terms with last night—
with his doubts. He'd thought that he felt satisfied
with Lonnie's explanations. But tonight something in
him snapped.

It didn't take psychoanalysis for him to figure out
what it was, either.

He was in love with her. And, apparently, it was
one-sided.

Why else wouldn't she have said it back?

He wished she'd said it back. Which raised another
interesting point: when had he become so fucking
needy? He hated this. How jealous he was. How unsure he was that Lonnie was truly as innocent as she
said. And how possessively he felt toward her—as
though she were *his*, which was crazy. *Jesus*. Was
anything worth all this aggravation?

Inside the bathroom, Lonnie stared helplessly at her
reflection. How could this have happened? Just when
she was thinking life was nearly perfect, her *perfect* boyfriend had morphed into a perfect dick for no reason
at all. Here they'd had a wonderful day and night together, and now they were having a fight. Their first
fight. And after he'd told her he loved her.

Suddenly a chill ran through her.

Then she realized what had been so obvious the entire
time: it was just too good to be true. Why was she even
surprised? Her luck with men had always been awful,
and now, Dominick was just continuing the tradition.
Fine. If nothing else, at least her experience had taught
her not to draw out the agony. Better to end it quickly.

That still left the issue of facing him again. She
gritted her teeth, sucked in a deep breath, and got
ready to open the bathroom door. Then she heard a
knock. "Lonnie." His voice was a thick rasp. "You
don't have to leave," he said.

She whipped open the door and found him leaning

against the jamb with boxers on. "Oh, how generous of you," she scoffed, and pushed past him. As efficiently as she could, she stripped off his shirt, and shielded her bare breasts with her hands, as she circled the room looking for her bra. *Where was that damn thing again? Oh, to hell with it!* She snatched her caramel-colored sweater off the floor, and turned her back to the bed while she slipped it on.

"Lonnie, don't go," he said. She ignored him. "Come on. It's not safe." He plowed his hand through his hair. "Don't you think you're overreacting just a little?"

She stopped what she was doing to glare at him dead-on. Then she looked away, and jumped into her faded blue jeans.

"Look, let's just agree to disagree—"

"About *what*? I don't even know what you're talking about! I don't even know why you're acting like this," she said, trying to keep her voice from cracking, as tears stung her eyes. One spilled over her lower lid, and she immediately turned away from him, so he wouldn't see how upset she was. She snatched her keys from his dresser and her coat from his desk chair.

"Oh, Lonnie—" He came up behind her, his gut twisting in knots. "I'm sorry. Come here." He tried to turn her in his arms, but she resisted. He held on, though, and put his face in her hair. "I'm sorry, baby," he crooned softly. "I'm sorry."

She swiped the back of her hand across her cheek and turned to face him. He tightened his arms around her, pressed his forehead against hers, and said, "Really. I didn't mean it."

She slid her hands up his chest and whispered, "But why did you say that about Terry? What's *wrong*?"

He sighed. "Let's just forget it. I don't want to fight."

"But what are we fighting about? I explained what happened—"

"Look, it doesn't matter. Even if you slept with Terry, I don't want to talk about it. I just want to know that it's over now. That you're done with him."

She pushed him away, hard.

"Lonnie—" She grabbed her coat and bag, and stormed out of the bedroom. "Where are you going?" Dominick asked, following her to the front door. "Lonnie, wait!" He grabbed her arm as she was reaching for the doorknob. She yanked it away quickly. "Gimme a break. Why are you mad now?"

She held up her hand to silence him. "Don't make it any worse, Dominick."

"But—"

"In fact," she said, throwing on her coat, "I think it's over."

"*What?* That's ridiculous!"

"Why? It's obvious that this relationship isn't going to work, after all," she said curtly, struggling to keep some cool resolve. He made her cry once; she wasn't going to let him do it again. Not in front of him, anyway.

"What the hell are you saying?" he demanded.

"I just said what I had to say. Good night. I'm going home."

She clutched her bag fiercely and turned to leave before he could stop her. Using her cell phone, she called a cab and waited in the front vestibule of Dominick's apartment building for it to arrive. *So much for love*, she thought.

It was fun while it lasted.

Chapter Twenty-six

Lonnie made her way across the shaggy rug as quietly as she could, which was probably why she banged into the coffee table, accidentally dropped her keys, and then tripped over a book in the middle of the floor that she couldn't see because it was pitch-black. Suffice it to say, Peach woke up.

"Lonnie? Is that you?"

"Yeah, I'm sorry. I didn't mean to wake you up. Go back to sleep." She felt around for her bed and tried to climb onto it without having another clutzy incident. It was a nice idea, of course, but she'd forgotten that she'd left the phone there earlier, and she inadvertently sent it sliding onto the floor, banging hard right where the rug ended.

"I'm sorry!" she whispered sincerely. "Just go back to sleep."

"What time is it?" Peach's voice was thick with drowsiness, but Lonnie could already hear her shifting in bed.

"Late. I didn't mean to wake you; we can talk in the morning." She'd actually prefer that anyway, since she wanted to forget about the entire last hour, at least for the moment. She kicked off her shoes, shucked off her jeans and underwear, tossed her sweater God-knows-where, and climbed under her thick, cream comforter, uncharacteristically naked.

Peach's tiny book lamp switched on, and she said, "It's four o'clock. It *is* the morning. What happened, did you guys have a fight or something?"

Lonnie sighed. "Yeah. I don't want to talk about it. I think it's over."

"*What?*" Now Peach audibly shot upright. "What do you mean over? You guys are crazy about each other."

"I don't want to talk about it."

"All right, if that's how you feel," Peach said, and turned off her book lamp. Lonnie sighed to herself with exhaustion and gloom, and rolled over, ready to let sleep blur her mind for a while.

Silence filled the room for all of thirty seconds.

"Just give me a hint."

She sighed again and said, "I can't really. None of it makes much sense."

"Well, I need more to go on if I'm going to solve this."

Lonnie let out a laugh, in spite of her abject misery. "Peach, there are actually some things you can't solve. I'm tired; we'll talk in the morning."

"Did he make a crack about your body? Is that it?"

"Of course not. What are you saying? I'm getting fatter?"

"No, no, I'm just trying to think what he could've done that would make you want to end everything." There wasn't a hint of drowsiness left in Peach's voice; she was chatting away as if it were the middle of the day. *Oh well*, Lonnie thought. She sat up, looking in Peach's general direction, but only seeing the faded green glow of the tiny iridescent moons that hung above her sister's bed, and started to explain.

"I don't know what happened," she said. "One minute everything was great, and the next he was

accusing me of sleeping with Terry"—she sucked in
a breath—"and then I left. But really, it's fine. It's just
more of my bad luck with men. Whatever. I knew it
had to end sometime. Anyway, perennial spinster-
hood is not entirely without its benefits."

"Whoa, let's back up here," Peach said. "First of
all, define 'accuse.' "

"He asked me who was better in bed, and then
claimed he was kidding."

"Uh-*huh* . . ." Peach said, as if processing all the
necessary information.

Lonnie continued. "Then he started doing the
whole distant-guy routine."

"A-*ha* . . ." Peach said. "Let me ask you, would
you consider Dominick passive aggressive or more
obsessive compulsive?"

"Wha—I don't know. Neither."

"Mmm-*hmm* . . ."

"Stop doing that."

"Sorry."

"Well? What do you think?" Lonnie asked.

Peach shrugged. "Did he apologize?"

"Yeah, he tried, but there was no point."

"Why not?"

"Because he was still acting like he didn't believe
me. It's like, out of nowhere, he's gotten it in his
head that there was more to the Terry situation than
what I told him."

"So how did you leave things?"

"I told him it was over," Lonnie replied simply.

"You didn't," Peach groaned.

"What, you're on his side?"

"No, of course not! I just . . . Lon, I just don't want
you to . . ."

"What?"

"Overreact."

Lonnie balled her fists at her side, and squeezed

her eyes shut in frustration. "Peach, did you not hear a word I said? He thinks I slept with Terry when I told him that I didn't!"

"No, he's irrationally afraid you might have, and it's eating his guts out. There's a difference," she said calmly.

"I fail to see the distinction."

"What I'm trying to say is, yes, Dominick acted like an ass. But if you give up on the whole relationship now, you're never gonna get to see him grovel and beg for your forgiveness, which—believe me— he will."

"He should grovel!" Lonnie said indignantly.

"He will."

Lonnie propped her head with her hand. "But you know what the weird thing is? I don't even think he really believes that I lied about Terry. Part of me thinks he said it just to pick a fight with me. Does that make any sense?"

"Of course," Peach said. "Maybe he was trying to push you away because he doesn't believe he deserves happiness."

"I don't think that's it."

"Or he could always be mad for some other reason."

"I guess," she said, searching her brain and still not knowing what'd been bothering him.

"Don't you think you should find out what it is before you junk the whole relationship?" Peach argued. "You should at least explain to Dominick, in detail, why his behavior was totally unacceptable, so he won't do it again."

"Why should I have to explain it?" she snapped. Then she expelled a breath and continued. "If he doesn't understand on his own—"

"Please. He's just a dumb guy."

"Oh, that makes me so mad! I hate that 'just a dumb guy' excuse. It's a complete cop-out! And it's

degrading. I mean, how would men feel if they knew
how many times women just automatically con-
cluded that they're simply 'too dumb' to be responsi-
ble for anything they say?''

"Are you kidding? They'd love it; they're the ones
who came up with it. Lets them off the hook for
everything." Peach softened her tone. "Look, I'm on
your side here, believe me. But I just don't want you
to—''

"What?"

"Use this as an excuse to sabotage your love life.
You sort of have a history with that."

"I do not," Lonnie said . . . not completely convinced. She had to admit that she didn't have the
best track record when it came to men. Until Jake,
she'd pretty much avoided relationships by finding
fault with any guy who'd taken an interest in her.
After Jake, she'd used his asshole status as an excuse
to shun sex . . . not to mention love, by taking up
with Terry, a clown she'd never take seriously. Then
her relationship with Dominick had suffered several
awkward stops and starts that were pretty much all
her doing. Now she was poised to run again.

But still . . . it was different this time.

"It was a fight," Peach went on. "That doesn't
mean everything has to be over."

Lonnie plopped backward onto her pillow. "I don't
want to talk about it anymore," she mumbled, and
rolled over. "Good night."

This time Peach took the hint and settled back into
bed. " 'Night."

The dark silence lasted this time, and kept Lonnie
awake for a while. Dominick had acted like a jerk,
and as far as she was concerned, that was his problem. *His loss*. Period.

So why, over an hour later—as she watched the
sun break the vaguest hint of light into her apartment—did she still feel a painful pit in her stomach,

a vacuous hole in her heart, and the hot wetness of
the spot on her pillow where her stupid tears had
fallen?

Mondays were bad enough, but this one was dragging on miserably. Every time the phone rang, Lonnie hoped it was Dominick. But it wasn't. Not once.
Less than two days had passed since they'd last spoken, and she missed him terribly.

Too bad there was no way in hell she was going
to call first.

This wasn't a question of maturity. *Really*. It was
a matter of principle. He was the one who'd offended
her, and he should be the one to call. If he didn't
grasp that, well, then she was better off without him.

Then again . . .

In the heat of battle, she *had* sort of declared the
end of their entire relationship. Please, did he actually take that literally?

To top things off, Twit informed her that Delia was
going to sit at her desk while she was out of the
office Tuesday and Wednesday. A bundle of nerves,
Lonnie was planning to drive to Maine Bay College
the following morning to meet Macey's friend Emma
and go through a few interviews before heading back
to Boston on Wednesday afternoon. That was stress-
ful enough, but now with the Grand Master B sitting
at her desk, Lonnie would have to worry about lock-
ing her drawers.

BRRINNG!

She answered her phone, trying to remember the
new greeting Twit had taught her earlier. "Beauregard Twit's central headquarters for financial litigating prowess. Whom shall I tell Mr. Twit, Esquire,
is calling?"

"Hey, kid. You got a minute?"

"Oh, hi, Detective," she said, hearing the usual ruffling of papers, and phones ringing in the background. "What's up?"

"Remember how we were supposed to talk about B. J. Flynn?"

"Oh, right. You never called me back; I thought you weren't that interested."

"Well, I am now. What did you want to tell me?" Montgomery asked.

"Why? What's going on?"

"I ask the questions," he said, and she could just picture the cocky expression on his face.

She told him about what Matt had said about B. J.'s job insecurity, and her conversation with Bette, who'd confirmed that Lunther had planned to fire the poor guy.

"Why?" she asked again. "Is B. J. a suspect now?"

"Everyone's a suspect." He paused, as if deciding how much to say. "But Flynn got arrested this past weekend."

"*What?*" she exclaimed. "Are you sure? I just saw him this morning."

"Yeah, Stopperton ended up letting him go with a warning."

"But what did he do?" B. J. was a lawyer, for pete's sake!

"He got into a fight with a homeless guy near Faneuil Hall. Apparently, the guy asked him if he could spare a dime, and Flynn snapped."

Lonnie's eyes widened. "Define snapped," she said.

"Well, according to one witness, Flynn started screaming about how he's had to work for every dime he has, and then he grabbed the guy's tin cup and threw it. It almost clocked a couple coming out of Houlihan's."

"B. J. did that?" This was too much to believe. She'd never known he had such a bad temper.

"It gets better," Montgomery said. "Or worse, depending on your perspective. He slugged the homeless guy. Just missed his nose. That's when a squad car showed up, and Flynn ran. You know the steps outside of City Hall?"

"Yeah."

He chuckled. "Well, apparently, Flynn took 'em three at a time, and it was quite a sight." She could only imagine. "Anyway," he went on, "Stopperton caught up with him in Copy Cop, trying to hide behind a color printer."

"I can't believe this," she said, shaking her head. "But how come they let him go?"

Montgomery snorted. "The homeless guy dropped the charges after B. J. gave him a fifty."

"How ironic."

"Yeah. Anyway, I need you to do something for me. Two things, actually."

"What?"

"I need you to keep an eye on B. J. I mean, really keep close tabs on him. Without being an obvious, nosy pest, that is."

"Don't try to change me, Detective." He laughed. "What's the second thing?" she asked.

"Try to stop dreaming about me. I'm too old for you." She laughed.

After she hung up with him, she glanced at the clock. 5:28 P.M. Well, she'd had about all she could take of the office. Sighing, she shut down her PC and tried to mentally will the phone to ring. Very predictably, it didn't work.

She coiled her scarf around her neck, gathered up her coat and bag, and headed toward the elevators . . . determined to coast right past twenty.

Tuesday morning Dominick had barely finished half of his first coffee before he gave in and called Lonnie. He'd thought about her a thousand times

since their argument, but he still hadn't been sure if
he should call her. He couldn't help wondering if it
was worth it—if he really wanted to be so involved
at this point in his life. In theory, he did. But theory
hadn't prepared him for the intensity of their relationship, and he didn't know if he liked it. Honestly,
he was used to feeling more in control.

Looking at it logically, he was planning to start his
own company within a year. Did he really need the
extra burden of a serious relationship? For chrissake,
Lonnie was probably moving to Maine, anyway! Did
he really want to be involved when he had no idea
what the future even held for them, if *anything*?

And he'd decided: yes, that was exactly what he
wanted. He wanted *her*.

After she'd stormed out of his apartment, he'd let
his anger consume him for the rest of the night. But
in the morning he'd awoken with a dull ache in his
stomach. He knew that she hadn't lied to him, and
as soon as he recalled those big, guileless eyes blinking in confusion, the ache got sharper. For that reason alone, he'd wanted to call her. He'd wanted to
apologize for acting like a jackass. But he couldn't.
Not until he was sure of what to say.

Now it had been three days, and he'd already
growled at his sweet little landlady and absently put
on different colored socks more than once. Fortunately, he'd successfully run the status meeting earlier, though, proving to himself that he still had a
head for his job. He had to admit it filled him with a
twisted sense of pride to have Harold's respect again.

So he was on top of work again. That was good.
Very good. But still . . .

He was determined to get that affectionate, black-
haired cutie back in his life no matter what amount
of groveling it took.

Of course, she'd have to pick up the phone first.

Finally on the fourth ring, there was a click, and

then a female voice: "Beauregard Twit's central head-quarters for financial litigating prowess. Whom shall I tell Mr. Twit, Esquire, is calling?" Except it wasn't Lonnie. He'd know his girlfriend's mellifluous, honeyed voice anywhere, and this raspy Boston-accented one wasn't it.

"Hi, I was looking for Lonnie," he said, and could've sworn he heard the woman snort before she answered.

"Uh . . . Lonnie stepped away. Can I take a message and have her call you back?"

"Oh, sure. Could you have her call Dominick when she gets a chance?"

"Dominick. Got it. Any other message?"

He thought for a second and added, "Yeah. Tell her . . . it's important."

After he hung up, he picked up his coffee mug and headed to the kitchen to reheat it. Until he heard back from her, he was determined to stay focused on his work.

On Thursday morning, the elevator dinged on twenty-three, and Lonnie got off absently, still engrossed in thought about her interviews at Maine Bay College. Overall, she thought it had gone well. Late Tuesday afternoon, she met Macey's friend Emma who was the director of social research, and they'd talked for two hours about Lonnie's background and goals. Then on Wednesday morning, she'd met with the dean of liberal arts and the chair of social studies for a breakfast interview that seemed to go smoothly. Of course, there had been a few loaded moments, like when the chair asked her if she "espoused more of a postmodern or poststructuralist pedagogical methodology." She'd bluffed her way through it by claiming she preferred a combination of both, but not really either, and that seem to mystify him enough that he dropped the subject with a knowing nod.

Now she shucked off her ice-blue coat, tossed it onto her chair, and looked at her phone, expecting to see a flashing red light indicating voice mail messages. There was no flashing light. Then she remembered that Delia had covered her desk the past two days, so if someone had called—*oh, just a generic "someone," not anyone in particular*—it would be probably be written down somewhere. She plopped down in her chair, on top of her coat, and searched for phone messages. She looked across her desktop, under folders, behind her monitor, inside book jackets. Everywhere, anywhere.

She couldn't believe it. Dominick hadn't called her at all! She'd felt sure that she'd return to the office—after two days' absence, and after four days without speaking to him—and find a message. But he hadn't even called once. How could that be? Didn't he miss her the way she missed him? Namely: painfully, desperately, hopelessly. Obviously not. Apparently, he was just going to give up on her, on them, on all of it.

Well, *fine*.

It took all of three seconds before she was in full sulk mode, complete with targetless rage and futile bitterness. She decided she needed some caffeine to nurse her self-pity, so she headed to the kitchen, hoping there would be a pot of coffee ready and waiting. She was half right.

Delia was wiping the counter of some errant coffee grounds as the pot finished percolating and a heavenly aroma filled the lime green–tiled room. But as soon as she saw Lonnie, she brought a hand up to stop her from getting any closer to Mr. Coffee.

"This isn't for you," she declared unapologetically. "Beauregard's meeting with clients at nine thirty, and this pot's for them."

"Oh, okay." Lonnie felt devastated—which she recognized as slightly irrational—but she'd be damned if she'd give Delia the satisfaction of seeing how badly she wanted the coffee. Now that she thought about it, she didn't know when or why Delia had become her mortal enemy, but at this point, she was just running with it. She turned to go back to her desk, but stopped midpivot to ask, "By the way, did anyone call for me Tuesday or Wednesday?"

Delia looked at her dead-on, got that Nosferatu thing going with her eyes, and replied simply, "Nope." She turned her attention back to the countertop, and Lonnie tried to hide her disappointment as she made her way down the hall to her desk. She found Matt waiting there for her.

"Hey," she said.

"What's up with your sister?" he asked sharply.

"What do you mean?" *Don't tell me Peach didn't end things with you. Don't tell me I'm going to have to do it.*

"I left three messages on her cell phone"—*Cell phone! Of course. Dominick must've left a message on my cell phone*—"and she never called me back. Also, she hasn't e-mailed me. What's the deal?" He sounded unusually testy, but then why was she not surprised that Peach—sassy, adorable, and heartbreaking—was able to penetrate Matt's otherwise pathological apathy? Well, if Peach thought Lonnie was going to do her dirty work and dump him for her, she could think again.

"Gee, I have no idea," she said, and put her hand to her head as if contemplating something. "Although, come to think of it, she did mention she was having a really busy week at work."

That seemed to relax him a little. "Oh, really?" He paused and shrugged casually. "Okay, well, if you talk to her," he said, "tell her to give me a call."

"Sure, uh-huh, no problem!" She was nodding a

bit too hard to conceal her overcompensation. Oh well. Matt was a big boy; surely he'd figure out on his own that Peach had lost interest. They made small talk for a few minutes, during which Lonnie surreptitiously reached into her coat pocket, switched on her cell phone, and glanced down to read the display screen. NO MESSAGES. So much for that comforting-but-fleeting notion.

Less than a minute after Matt disappeared around the corner, Twit did the duck's two-step toward her desk. This time he brought with him an overbearing and pungent odor. *Good Lord, what is that stench?* It smelled like a cross of incense and dead lilacs and musk. Perhaps it was an unusual cologne that could've been halfway decent if it had been applied with any subtlety. She glanced up at Twit's face and noticed that his eyes were closed as he approached, as if he were in deep thought—or orgasmic bliss— and the minute he opened them, he jerked his head back, startled to see her.

"Oh! LaDonna . . . er . . . what are you doing here? I—I was under the impression you weren't coming back till tomorrow." He tensely shifted the weight on his legs, and *ahemed* to fill the silence.

"No, I took Tuesday and Wednesday off for my interviews. But that's it."

"Ah . . . yes, well . . . I see." He made a show of clearing his throat again, and it hit her. He'd saturated himself in cologne and sashayed over, thinking Delia was still sitting there. This was too much! She wanted to burst out laughing at what a tool he was. She wanted to ask if he had any spare nose plugs. She wanted to thank him for inadvertently lightening her black mood. Before she could do any of the above, B. J. barreled over. And her senses sharpened, because she immediately remembered his arrest and that Montgomery had asked her to keep a close eye on him.

"Beauregard!" he bellowed. "Did you catch the Celtics game last night?" His manic cheeseball grin was back, and his best-buddies-with-the-boss histrionics had him all but salivating.

Before Twit could comment on the Celtics game, however, B. J.'s face contorted into a revolted grimace, and he exclaimed, "Whoa! Lonnie, I think you OD'd on the perfume!" He shot a sideways look to make sure Twit had heard his hilarious remark, and went on. "Is there some new guy working here we don't know about?"

He kept darting his eyeball over to Twit while he teased her. "Lonnie, if you're trying to get someone's attention . . ." but his voice trailed off, as he undoubtedly realized that Twit was far from laughing. Instead, Twit shifted his leg weight again, and his face apocalypsed into red dawn.

"Actually," B. J. backpedaled, "it smells sort of good, now that I think about it. Really classy." A futile attempt to save his own ass—not to mention Twit's pride—but then, backpedaling usually was futile.

An awkward silence fell, during which more nausea settled in the pit of Lonnie's stomach. She figured she'd better expedite this little tête-à-tête if she wanted to get rid of Twit and sneak off to Starbucks to get a much-needed and deserved caffeine jolt. "Is there something you need, Beauregard?" she asked.

At first, he appeared flummoxed; then he shook his head. "No, not at the moment. I'll speak with you in a bit. Fare thee well," he finished, and turned on his heel. In Twit-speak, "Fare thee well" was interchangeable with "Best" as a closer. Lonnie had learned not to question these things.

"Well," she said to B. J., who was still standing in front of her desk, "I'm actually going to run and get a coffee." She rose from her chair, grabbed her nowsmushed coat out from under her, and headed toward the glass doors.

"I just can't seem to get anything right," B.J. said, and only the pathetic self-loathing in his voice stopped her. She turned and saw her diminutive, dejected coworker shaking his head, as if to say: *why me?* Of course the gesture was inappropriate, considering the fact that B. J.'s sycophantic blunders were, indeed, his own fault, but it was a heart-wrenching scene, all the same.

B. J. didn't *seem* like a bad person, but she couldn't disregard what Montgomery had told her about his arrest over the weekend. If he'd really attacked that homeless man, then he had to have a considerable temper hiding in that little body. Lonnie couldn't help wondering how far that violence would extend. Would B. J. be capable of *murder*?

She moved toward him, about to offer some consoling words—okay, and to size up his character a little more—but he turned around before she got the chance. He darted down the hall and out of sight.

She pushed purposefully on the glass doors and boarded the elevator, never so grateful for odorless air in her life. The ride down to the lobby was quick, although when the display screen flashed FLOOR 20, some lovelorn angst clutched her chest without warning. Then she got angry. *Toughen up*, she thought. *It's over with Dominick. Get used to it.*

Chapter Twenty-seven

Twenty minutes later, Lonnie came back up the same elevator with two skim cappuccinos in her hands, and she felt a lot better. Nothing like some artificial stimulation to create an natural good mood. She headed down the hall to Macey's office.

"Macey?"

"Lon? Is that you?" Macey was normally too formal for nicknames. But then, she'd already seen the way good spirits could transform Macey into a bubbly creature who says "natch."

"Yes," Lonnie said, and gently nudged the ajar door all the way open. "Hi. I thought you might like a cappuccino."

"Oh, thank you!" Macey's voice sang across the office, and she flashed a wide, enthused smile before adding, "Lon, you are so precious. *You*, I'm going to miss." She shot across the room and swept the cappuccino out of Lonnie's hand. She took a long, luxurious sip, and smiled again. "Thanks. This is fab!"

Lonnie let a laugh slip out because Macey's giddiness was a little contagious, and she made her feel so appreciated that it put a refreshing, uplifting spin on her day. "Sure, no problem." Then she noticed what Macey had been doing before she'd interrupted. She'd been packing.

There were large cardboard boxes lined along her back shelf, and half her bookcase was empty. Her minifridge was wide open, defrosted and bereft of Snapples, and the sight was not only jarring; it was deflating. *Macey's leaving.*

"What's going on?" Lonnie asked, even though she knew.

"Oh." Macey followed Lonnie's eyes to the boxes behind her, and said, "I'm leaving earlier than I'd expected. It was unplanned, but I just got the most terrif call from Sandy. Her firm is looking for a new legal advisor. I'm moving to London! Yay!" She did a little dance in place, and completed the behavioral anomaly by clapping her hands together excitedly. "Yay me!" she squealed, and captured Lonnie in a hug.

Lonnie hugged her back ambivalently. Eighty percent of her felt saddened by the news that Macey was leaving the firm, while twenty percent of her didn't want to be suspicious but was. It just seemed so sudden. And leaving the *country*? Lonnie scolded herself for being too paranoid, but still wasn't completely convinced that she was.

"Lon, I'm sorry to leave with no warning, but you don't need me here anyway." *Yes, I do.* "You're strong and smart and you've got what it takes." *To do what?* "I talked to Emma this morning, and she said Maine Bay loved you."

"They did?"

"They were very impressed."

"Really?"

"They thought you were bright, articulate, and innovative." *Me?* "You're in, Lon!" Macey continued cheerfully. "Of course, I shouldn't be telling you this, but Emma told me they're going to offer you a two-year instructor position."

"Really?" Excitement of her own started pooling in Lonnie's chest.

"That's not all," Macey said, took a breath, and then blurted in spite of her conscious attempt at composure, "There's a possibility for free doctoral courses. You could earn your Ph.D. while you're working there!"

"Oh, wow." Lonnie let out a held breath and realized she was temporarily speechless. She'd thought the interviews had gone well, but she couldn't believe they'd gone that well. What incredible news, and so fast! Unfortunately, saying good-bye to Macey was taking some luster off the moment. Her mentor was leaving, going across the Atlantic Ocean, and she'd probably never see her again. Why did good things always have to happen in sync with bad ones?

They talked for twenty more minutes, and then finally, Lonnie realized Twit would be missing her, so she turned to go. Right before she left, however, she told Macey about Ann Lee and Mabel Wills. She didn't know why, but she wanted to get Macey's feedback. Of course, what Lonnie couldn't reveal was that she'd only talked to them because she'd been investigating Lunther's death

"I don't get it," Lonnie said. "Those women didn't seem the least bit affected by the way Lunther had propositioned them. They didn't even think it was a big deal."

Macey nodded and patted Lonnie's arm affectionately. "I know you wanted to help them."

"But they didn't need my help—"

"No, maybe not individually. Those women are tough, they're strong, and they do their best to control their own destiny."

"But—"

"*They're* not the problem. The problem is people like Lunther." She looked around, as if searching to find the right words, and said, "Quite simply, he was a lemon tree."

"Oh . . . wait . . . what?"

"How can I explain this?" She took Lonnie's hand in her own. "I'm saying that just because women take lemons and make lemonade, doesn't mean the lemon tree is off the hook. The fact that so many lemons get dropped into women's work lives is a problem. It is *the* problem. Do you understand?"

"I—I think so," Lonnie said.

"See, the problem is, working women have become so proficient at developing coping strategies for all the unjust predicaments they face that people barely notice how unfair it is to *have to* cope with those predicaments."

"Oh. I understand exactly what you mean," Lonnie said, because she did.

"Just remember, I'm only an e-mail address away, if you ever need anything."

"You've done enough for me already!"

"Or if I ever need anything."

"Oh, of course. Of co—"

"That's how it works."

Lonnie smiled at Macey—as sincerely as Macey was smiling at her—and said, "I've got it now." They hugged one last time before Lonnie walked back to her desk, feeling a disturbing, but strangely life-affirming swirl of emotions. As soon as she sat down, her phone rang.

"Beauregard Twit's central headquarters for financial litigating prowess. Whom shall I tell Mr. Twit, Esquire, is calling?"

"Oh, please. That's the most ridiculous greeting I've ever heard in my life. He's actually making you say that?"

"Hey, Peach," Lonnie said, pleased to hear her sister's voice. "Yep. It's a miracle I even remember it half the time. What's up?"

"Nada. I'm just waiting for Iris's second coat to dry, and then I put on clear."

"Huh?"

"Her toenails."

Lonnie cringed and clicked on her e-mail icon, hoping Dominick had sent her a message. Preferably one confessing his sincerest apologies for their misunderstanding and declaring his undying love. But she'd settle for a lunch invitation. . . .

"So now you're giving Iris pedicures? Peach, what kind of job *is* this?" No lunch invitation. No message from him, period.

"I don't mind. It's easy. Although I could've done without sanding her calluses first thing in the morning, but—"

"Yuck, I don't want to hear any more."

"Okay, okay."

"You're an artist," Lonnie said. "I think you should be looking into having your hands insured, not . . . not . . ."

Peach giggled. "You're acting like it's manual labor."

"Well, it's twisted. At least concede that point." Lonnie closed her empty inbox with palpable disappointment. She was beginning to detest e-mail.

"Okay, okay," Peach said, and giggled some more. "By the way, what's up with Cheryl and Jean-Paul?"

"Still going strong."

"Really?"

"Yep. Although Cheryl mentioned that at first J-P felt a little self-conscious about his age, because he's fifteen years older than her."

"Oh, wait," Lonnie interrupted, just realizing. "This isn't one of those father-figure things, is it?"

"No, I don't think so. I think it's a maturity thing. J-P's past the age of playing games, and Cheryl can't be with someone who plays games, because she's been *out* of the game so long she wouldn't know how to win if he were to play them. Get it?"

"Yeah." *Vaguely.*

"Speaking of being out of the game, have you talked to Dominick?"

"Have you talked to Matt?"

"Nice dodge. Answer the question."

Lonnie sighed, "No. But it's not like he's talked to me, either."

"Meaning?"

"Meaning: if he really cared, he'd—"

"Call," Peach finished irritably. "I know. I know."

"So you agree."

"No, I just know how your mind works," she said. "Lon, you're a total sexist. No offense."

"What are you talking about?"

"You just assume that Dominick is sitting back smugly, knowing full well he can call anytime. How do you know he's not just as unsure as you are?"

"Right," Lonnie scoffed.

"He's probably just as desperate to talk to you."

"Right."

"Right, that's why you're a sexist."

"Peach—"

"Just call him, for chrissake. You know that's what you're dying to do anyway."

"I am not. And even if I were, it's too weird now."

"Why?"

"Because it's Thursday. It's been almost a week; it seems weird now."

"Call him," Peach commanded, as if Lonnie were Cheryl, just waiting for the next directive. *I don't think so. . . . Well, maybe one call wouldn't hurt.* "I gotta go," Peach said. "I'm being summoned."

"To apply the third coat?"

"No, to change the channel. The batteries on the remote died. Oh, that reminds me! I've gotta pick up some double As at lunch. All right, I'll see ya at home." After they hung up, Lonnie thought about Peach's advice for another minute before yanking the phone off its cradle and punching Dominick's number so hard her fingertips hurt. *You're pathetic*, she thought, and then mentally implored, *Please answer. Please answer.*

Dominick's voice mail picked up, and she set the phone back down before she could leave an embarrassing message. She checked her e-mail once more before resigning herself to all work and no play, and dove into the latest stack of papers Twit had left in her inbox.

Her stomach growled ferociously at exactly 1:35. She felt like throwing Twit's notes across the room. He'd left her about a hundred different letters to type—all of them needed "A-SAP," of course. Meanwhile, he'd taken the rest of the staff out to lunch, as one last hurrah before Lyn Tang started to work at the firm. Lonnie sensed a divide-and-conquer thing going on with Twit, who was obviously already anticipating a power struggle with Tang. Not only was Lonnie left out, she had a feeling she'd be filling out Diners Club reimbursement forms into the following week. Oh, joy.

She pushed away from her desk and headed for the kitchen, which—all too often in her life—seemed like the right thing to do. She opened the refrigerator to get the orange muffin she'd bought from the Atrium that morning. Only it wasn't there. Lonnie looked behind every expired creamer and tin-foiled blob that was labeled with a DO NOT TOUCH Post-it. Still no muffin. Disappointed, she shut the refrigerator door and turned to leave. That's when she saw her muffin in the trash basket. It was just sitting on top of a soiled-napkin heap, still wrapped in its decorative Atrium cellophane.

Her stomach knotted. This was just plain cruel! It

hadn't even been eaten—just tossed out, unopened. Only one person at Twit & Tang would be capable of sadism this early in the day. And Lonnie just wished she had it in her to give it back to that lycra-clad, acrylic-clawed bitch!

But she didn't.

In general, she wasn't really into revenge. She'd admit it was often deserved, but she just didn't have the patience or aptitude for devising retaliatory schemes. Basically, she subscribed to that "living well" theory out of sheer laziness. Nevertheless, it was more than that this time. Quite simply, she was too heartsick over Dominick to go ballistic over a damn muffin.

As she headed back to her desk, she thought about Matt. She hadn't seen him since he'd grilled her about Peach that morning. He was probably at lunch with everyone else, but she'd swing by his office anyway, in case he'd stayed back. Now seemed like just as good a time as any to pump him for more information on B. J.

On her way to Matt's office, she heard a drawer slamming and another being yanked open. Then there was a manic rustling of papers, and she realized it was all coming from Bette's office, which was right next door. Bette didn't go to lunch? That didn't seem right; missing company events wasn't her style. She wanted to steal a peek inside, but the door was closed.

Suddenly she heard chattering in the distance—the staff was back from lunch.

The sounds from inside Bette's office got louder and more frantic. And a familiar croon coming from down the hall got closer and closer: "Juliet! Darling, I'm losing you—are you on the boat?" Well that settled that—obviously Bette *wasn't* in her office, going through her own drawers like mad. But she was headed right this way.

Lonnie rounded the corner of the nearest cubicle so she'd be inconspicuous but still at a good vantage point to watch Bette's door.

"Oh, Juliet dear, the reception from the yacht is just dreadful. I can barely make out what you're saying. I'll ring you later to check on my little gorgeous angels. Give them kisses for me!"

The door swung open. Lonnie hunched down lower and peered over the partition wall as B. J. bolted out of Bette's office clutching a blue folder in hand and looking panicked. He cut a quick right, and avoided Bette, who cluelessly strolled into her office several seconds later. And while B. J. escaped down the hall with brisk strides, Lonnie was left wondering what on earth it all meant.

Chapter Twenty-eight

"New shirt, D?"
    "No."
  "New tie?"
  "Nope."
  "Something's different."
You annoying the shit out of me sure isn't it. Dominick finished stirring sugar into his coffee and tried to escape the kitchen without making any more small talk. Or dodging small talk, if one wanted to be technical. Harold followed. But then again, his cubicle was adjacent to Dominick's office, so neither had much choice in the matter.

  "Hi, Dominick."
  There was no mistaking the feminine—and refreshingly *un*Harold—lilt in the voice. "Hey, Mo. How're you doing?" He half grinned at her, and continued into his office. When he heard Harold say hello, and the drop in enthusiasm in Mo's voice, Dominick almost chuckled. *Almost.* But at the moment he was too damn irritable to crack more than half a smile.

  "Dominick, are you going to happy hour tonight?" Looking up from his monitor, he saw Mo standing in the doorway, smiling openly, invitingly.

"Ah, no, I don't think so." What would be the point? Happy hour just reminded him of Lonnie, and he had too much work to do anyway. Not just for GraphNet, either; he was scouting out locations for his software business.

He just had to tell himself to forget Lonnie—a girl who was certifiably *psychotic* if she was dumping him just because they'd had one stupid fight. Well, there was no "if" about it; she'd never returned his call, sending a clear signal that she wanted nothing to do with him anymore. Fine. Obviously he couldn't *make* her call him back. He couldn't make her see how great they were together. It was that unnamable something between two people—that inexplicable pull. They shared great laughs, great talks, great sex. Make that very hot sex. The kind that had nothing to do with experience or kinkiness or gymnastic ability, and everything to do with chemistry and trust and love.

Women. Fine, that was it. As far as he was concerned, the fairer sex mess had messed with his head enough for a while. Fairer, *my ass.*

"Why not? You've gotta come," Mo encouraged sweetly—cooingly. Not that he minded. It was nice to have a girl actually *appreciate* him. Unlike old What's-Her-Name . . .

Lonnie Gwendolyn Kelley.

"Nah, I don't think so," he said.

"I might go, M," Harold said, suddenly appearing next to Mo. "If we can get the new links finished in time." She flashed him a brief look and said, "Oh, that's nice," with what sounded a little like forced sweetness.

"D, I'm telling you, there's something different about you today," Harold said.

"He didn't shave," Mo offered immediately.

Dominick ran a hand over his jaw, just realizing himself that he hadn't shaved. Come to think of it, had he combed his hair before he left? In a split-second of alarm, he grabbed on his pant legs to check his socks. Both navy blue. Okay, he wasn't completely going to hell yet.

"Well, have a drink for me," he said, and turned back to his monitor, knowing it was an idiotic thing to say, but at the moment he couldn't worry about the staleness of his repartee. He didn't want to talk about happy hour; he just wanted to be left alone.

"D, the CD-ROM I sent to E-Bizz accidentally got returned. Do you want—"

"I'll deal with it later," he replied in a clipped tone.

"But shouldn't we—"

"*Later.*"

"Okay, D. I just—"

"I'll take care of it," Dominick growled.

"All right, no problem," Harold said. "By the way, was that girl I saw in your office last week your girlfriend?"

"Harold, just get the hell out of here!"

His so-called protégé scurried away—terrified of his so-called mentor—and Dominick experienced a fleeting pang of guilt. Then he checked his voice mail, his e-mail, his regular mail. Nothing. The word summed up everything all too well.

The next morning marked the first Saturday of Lonnie's "Weekend Exercise Regimen," which she'd outlined the night before, after an even-Medusa-is-hotter-than-me tantrum.

It also marked the last.

She returned from her "run" having walked two-thirds of it, and then finding herself helplessly drawn to Au Bon Pain on the way home. She opened the front door, carrying an Asiago bagel and slurping a diet Coke, having cheated on the first day of her new exercise plan and not overly caring. Her decent mood had everything to do with her new job. Emma had called the day before and offered her a two-year position, just as Macey had said she would. Lonnie told Emma she'd get back to her on Monday, but inside, she knew her answer already. She was heading to Maine in the fall to begin her future.

She walked into the apartment, and right away spotted Peach dabbing some sea-green paint onto the far left corner of *BosYork*.

"Hey."

"Hey! Thank God you're home!" Peach exclaimed. Then she qualified, "I mean, I just didn't know where you'd gone."

"You were asleep when I left. I went for a run. Well, sort of."

"You never run."

"I said sort of." Lonnie chucked her keys God knows where, and set her breakfast on the coffee table. "Do we have any paper towels? Wait, what's that smell? What, you're cooking?" She followed the scent of baking chocolate that came from their minialcove-of-a-kitchen. "What's this?"

"Yeah, I'm helping Cheryl," Peach said, and followed Lonnie over toward the oven. "Three dozen Godiva fudge brownies. She needs them for a high tea she's catering today."

"High tea?"

"I know. I know. Iris's friends may be pretentious, but hey, they provide a lot of good catering opportunities."

"That's nice," Lonnie said absently, and went back to the sofa.

She glanced up at her sister, who appeared to be painting, but . . . something was off. Peach seemed fidgety. She kept looking over her shoulder, and she was moving her paintbrush against the wall with tiny, artificial strokes. *What's she up to?*

Suddenly, there was a knock at the door.

"I wonder who that is," Lonnie said, and rose from the sofa with a hunk of bagel sticking out of her mouth.

"Wait!" Peach blurted. Lonnie turned, looked at her questioningly, and she said, "Take that bagel out of your mouth. Here, let me get another paper towel and you can wipe yourself off—"

"What are you talking about?" Lonnie interrupted, ripping the bagel out and swallowing the portion that was already in her mouth. "Why are you being so weird today?"

"Weird? No reason," she said too innocently, and tried an accompanying too-innocent shrug. "I mean, I'm not." There was another light knock on the door, and Lonnie moved to answer it. She looked through the peephole first, and her stomach dropped.

Dominick!

After a couple of deep breaths, she opened the door, with knots in every major organ and a profound hope that she didn't have Asiago breath. "Dominick," she said, deliberately neutral. "Hi."

He looked genuinely surprised to see her. *What the hell?* What did he expect? Obviously he'd come to see her, to talk to her, to make amends, to reconnect—

"Is Peach here?" he asked.

"What?"

He swallowed uncomfortably—*good, serves him right!*—and repeated his question. "Is Peach here? She asked if I'd stop by and take a look at her laptop." He barely even made eye contact while he spoke. *The nerve!* Here he'd shown up at *her* apartment after not calling her for a week, looking gorgeously rumpled and unshaven, and then asked to see her sister! Boy, did she know how to pick them, or what? Fine, then. All men were awful, wretched beasts, and no, damn it, she was not a sexist.

"Excuse me?" She tried to keep the woman-scorned wrath out of her voice, but failed. "You're here to see Peach?"

"Hi, Dominick!" Peach said, hurrying over to the door. "Come in."

"What's going on?" Lonnie planted her hands on her hips and waited for an explanation from one of them.

Dominick avoided her eyes again—appearing terribly bored by her mere existence—and replied, "I told you. Peach asked me to fix her laptop." His face was hard and impervious, and his normally hot-lava eyes were now cold black stones. From what she could tell, that is, since he was barely sparing her a glance.

"It's *my* laptop," she corrected angrily.

"Right this way, Dominick," Peach said, pulling him by the sleeve into their apartment, and Lonnie's blood boiled.

"*Peach!*"

"Lon, I told you, the D drive isn't working. You know we can't afford to get it fixed ourselves, and Dominick will probably figure out the problem right away."

"You know what?" he interrupted. "Why don't we just forget it? I've got other ways to spend my time." He started toward the door, shaking his head angrily.

"Dominick, wait! You said you'd help me!" Peach declared in an overly dramatic, woe-is-me appeal. Her sister, the con artist.

"You said she wouldn't be here," he stated bluntly, still not looking at Lonnie.

He'd said *she* as if she were a particularly revolting mutant alien life form. A *deaf* mutant alien life form. "Could you not talk about me like I'm not even here?" she asked in a huff.

"Whatever. Do you want your damn computer fixed or not?"

"Peach," Lonnie said, ignoring Dominick and giving him a taste of his own medicine, "I told you I'd fix it."

"Lon, you know less than nothing about computers. No offense."

"But—"

"You know it's true," Peach went on. "You thought a zip disk was a floppy that's blank."

Dominick snorted, and Lonnie shot him an icy glare.

"Lon, it's true," Peach said.

"Gimme a break—"

"Look, you want me to stay or go? Just tell me now," Dominick demanded, looking pissed and unyielding and gorgeous and perfect. And she loved him more than ever. *Damn him.* He hadn't called or e-mailed, he'd blown off their whole relationship over some stupid fight, and now he'd shown up at her apartment, giving her obnoxious attitude, and she still wanted him. She wanted to throw her arms around him and never let go. She wanted . . . oh, Lord, so many things. Him. Them. Forever.

"Fine. Fix it. But I'm going out—" The phone rang, interrupting her, and Lonnie grabbed the receiver. "Hello?"

"Hi, it's Cheryl. Is Peach there?"

"Oh, sure, hang on," Lonnie said, and turned to give the phone to Peach . . . who was looking suspiciously expectant.

"Hi," Peach said, clearly knowing exactly who it was already. She stole a few glances at Lonnie and Dominick, while she went on melodramatically. "Oh, *really*? Well, that certainly *does* sound like an emergency! My, yes, certainly I'll help you out. After all, what other choice do I have?" The last part came out theatrical enough to make Lonnie worry. *What now?*

"Okay, I'll be there right away!" She hung up the phone and announced, "Well, Cheryl needs me to help her with something right away." She grabbed her red-gold-and-black patchwork jacket out of the closet. "Oh, no!" She threw her hand to her forehead in a faux I-just-thought-of-something gesture. "I can't just leave the brownies unattended! They're still cooking. Lon, will you stay and keep an eye on them till I get back?'' While Lonnie grappled for words, Peach took advantage of the silence. ''Thanks a lot! Well, I'll see you guys in a little while—''

''Freeze!'' Lonnie commanded.

''Shit,'' Dominick said, patting his coat pockets. ''I just realized, I left my backup disk in my car. I'll be right back.'' After he was gone, Peach tried to make her own escape, but Lonnie stopped her.

''You're not going anywhere. I want to speak with you right now.''

''Gee, wish I had the time—''

''*Now.*''

Glancing to make sure Dominick was nowhere in sight, Lonnie shut the front door most of the way, and said, ''I can't believe you!''

''What—''

''First you call Dominick behind my back—''

''The computer—''

''Stuff it.''

''I didn't even think you'd be home!'' Peach protested innocently.

''Nice try. You were all panicky that I *wasn't* home. If this isn't the most obvious setup in the whole world—''

''Like you're so original. 'If he really liked me, he'd call.' That's the oldest refrain in the universe.''

''Yeah . . . well . . . tried but true.''

''Oh, I was afraid there wouldn't be a trite platitude we could use to help us illuminate things.''

''I'm furious with you right now,'' Lonnie whispered, in case Dominick was on his way up the stairs.

''That's just what you think now,'' Peach declared, and started buttoning her jacket. ''And fine; if it makes you feel better, you're right. This is a setup. So, big deal. You're my sister, and you're fucking up. Whose job is it, if not mine, to clean up your messes?''

''You're a menace.''

"Thanks," Peach said, pleased with herself.

"What do you not understand about *little sister*? I'm supposed to butt into *your* life. And . . . I don't know . . . call you 'squirt,' not take any crap . . ."

Peach scoffed, "Let's not waste our time with fantasies." She finished the last button, sighed as if terribly put out by Lonnie's denseness, and said, "Dominick's a winner. Just look at the latest evidence. What guy agrees to fix the laptop of a girl who hasn't called him in a week?"

"So this is all to save my love life?" Lonnie asked.

Peach replied, "Well, I can't deny that there's a slightly selfish motivation, too. Honestly? You're becoming a nightmare to live with. No offense."

"What are you talking about?"

"You snapped at me three times yesterday. And last night I heard you singing 'Every Rose Has Its Thorn' in the shower. Come on, how much am I expected to put up with?"

Lonnie grinned in spite of herself, in spite of Peach, in spite of the sullen man getting his backup disk, in spite of everything. "Dominick's probably left anyway. He probably got in his car and drove away."

"Right. Just like he probably came over so he could fix your laptop."

"What?"

"Good luck," Peach said, smiling, and headed out the door, passing Dominick on her way. "Later, Dominick. Thanks again!" The door thudded closed, and left Lonnie standing in silence with the object of every emotion coursing through her.

"Well, my laptop's over there," she said, motioning toward the small table by the front window. Dominick just nodded and moved past her.

"Mind if I take off my coat?" he asked.

"No, of course not." They were acting like strangers. *This sucks.* She bit hard on her lower lip to keep from crying. Or screaming at him.

Lonnie went over to her bed, climbed on it, and sat cross-legged, feeling awkward. Suddenly she had a memory of Dominick holding her in that very spot, beneath the puffy comforter, pressing their bare bodies together and kissing her cheek softly as they drifted closer and closer to sleep. Great, now her bed—happily celibate right along with her, for years—held only memories of sex with Dominick.

She'd just have to buy a new bed; it was that simple.

"You got anything to drink?" Dominick called over his shoulder. "That is, if it's no trouble. I forgot to bring my own tap water with me."

Smart-ass. "Really, I think I can get you a drink without too much drama," she said coolly, and went to the kitchen sink. "Are you sure you just want water?" she called out, and stuck her head in the half fridge. "We have diet Cherry Coke, too. Um . . . and, what's this? Oh yeah, some V8. It looks sort of old, though, and Peach put it in a pitcher. I'm not sure why."

"Water's fine," he said, suddenly right next to her. She almost jumped, not expecting his low, purring voice so close, and not expecting his beautiful body so close, either. *Relax. Relax*, she told herself, and closed the refrigerator door. She avoided his eyes—black, potent, and dangerously magnetic—and turned to take a glass out of the cupboard. Her heart was racing, and she was determined not to let it show.

She stood at the sink, filling a wine goblet with water, when she felt Dominick's arms slide around her, encircling her waist. He tightened them and pressed his chest against her back. "I'm sorry," he whispered in her ear, and hugged her closer.

She struggled for the breath she'd need to formulate an appropriate response. After all, it wasn't as if she was just going to fall right into his arms again.

She was still angry with him. Wasn't she? She wasn't so sure when she almost immediately sagged limply against him and let her head drop back so his lips were grazing her neck. He nudged her hair aside with his nose, and kissed her slowly, sweetly, applying just enough wet suction to provoke an instant hot flash.

She shut her eyes and let a moan escape, while he worked her neck and grew hard against her. Instinctively, she rubbed herself against his groin, and her breath came up shorter. "Dominick," she whispered, as his tongue trailed down her neck, and his lips sucked her skin. "I . . . I'm sorry, too."

She pushed hard against his erection—which grew even bigger—and he let out a strained groan, right before pressing them both toward the sink. Desperately aroused, as his palms found her breasts, Lonnie used every ounce of restraint she had to turn in his arms and pull back from him. "Wait a minute," she said, trying to get her voice back. "We can't just start making out like nothing's happened." *Although, why we can't, I have no idea,* she thought, as she looked up at his rugged five o'clock shadow and heavy-lidded, jet-black eyes. *Okay, get it together.*

He plowed his fingers through his hair and sighed. "Lonnie . . . I'm sorry I was such an asshole. Hell, when I say something stupid, call me on it, yell at me, but don't let it be the end of everything."

"But . . . I . . ." He reached for her again, and she kept him at bay with her arms. "Wait. We need to clear everything up. About Terry—"

"Forget Terry," he interrupted. "I know there was nothing between you. I mean, I know what you told me, and I believe you."

She hadn't been prepared for that. "But you said—"

"I didn't mean it. I'm sorry. I was jealous. I don't have a better excuse than that." She started mulling it over, and he added, "I don't want to lose you after I just found you. Can't we move on from here? Can't we start over?"

She smiled slowly. "Well, which one do you want? To move forward, or to go back?"

"Both, as long as you're mine again."

The oven timer dinged, and Lonnie moved past him to check on Peach's brownies. He moved toward her, but she opened the oven door so that it served as a barrier between them. She glanced down at the brownies. They were still gooey-liquid-brown, so she shut the oven door again. There went her barrier. Then she noticed that Peach had the oven set at 200 degrees, when brownies cooked at around 375. At that rate, they'd be done by sunup the next day. God, when she got her hands on that little con artist . . .

"Look, Lonnie," Dominick said, "if you want to forget all about us because of that one fight, then maybe it's for the best anyway, because I'm not perfect. I say a lot of stupid things. So if that's the way—"

"No, it isn't that!" she said, and sealed the space between them. "I want to be with you, but only if you trust me."

"I know I shouldn't have acted so possessive," he said sincerely. "I swear, it's not even like me. I don't know what's happened to me since I met you."

"I know, the same thing happened to me! I don't even know how, but it did. That's why every time I see the red-haired girl from your office on the elevator, I just want to shake her skinny, gorgeous bones. I want to tell her to stay away, *you're mine*."

"Who, Mo?" he asked, grinning.

"So then you admit she's skinny and gorgeous?" Lonne said, pointing at him accusatorily, but with a smile behind her eyes.

"It was the red-haired part," he said calmly, and smiling confidently, he moved a few inches closer.

She held up her hand to stop him from getting too

close. "My point is, the possessive thing is only okay if you trust the other person—"

"I do." He moved closer in spite of her hand.

"I mean it, Dominick. You have to trust me."

"I swear to you I do. You're the sweetest girl I've ever met. I trust you."

"And respect me."

He cocked his head to the side. "C'mon, Lonnie, you *know* I do."

"Uh . . . yeah," she said, and when he looked bothered by her doubt, she gloated. "See, how do you like it?"

He pulled her into his arms, and she rested her cheek on his chest and added on a sigh, "I don't know how this is all going to work out but—"

"We'll figure it out somehow," Dominick said quietly, not willing to break the moment by thinking about the future. Not now. He grinned. "And, just so we're clear, this reverses your breaking up with me the other night?"

"Well, that was sort of an accident anyway." She giggled, and hugged him tighter. "But then when I never heard from you—"

"I called you Tuesday, but you never called me back."

"What?" She lifted her head to look at him.

"Yeah, I talked to some woman and left a message."

She thought for a second. "Oh, damn. I was out of the office Tuesday and Wednesday."

"You were?"

"Yeah, for my interviews, remember? I told you that."

"Oh, I forgot, I've been such a mess."

She smiled. "Anyway, I never got the message because my mortal enemy was covering my desk."

"How do *you* have a mortal enemy?" he asked, smiling.

"I don't know. It just sort of happened."

"I'm crazy about you," he said. "Promise you'll never accidentally break up with me again."

She slid her hands up his chest, clutched his shirt, kissed him so deeply she lost herself, and when she finally came up for air, she felt only half lucid in the most liberating and extraordinary way. "We should probably stop this now, before Peach comes home."

He grinned, caught her lower lip in his mouth, kissed her again, and said, "I have a feeling your sister's not coming back for a while." Their mouths moved on each other passionately, deliberately, with arousing suction and wet heat. Finally, Dominick pulled his head back and looked dazed when he spoke. "Listen—not that it makes any difference—but I had no idea about this whole setup. I swear."

"I believe you."

"Did you think I did?"

"No. I doubted it, but I was hoping maybe . . ."

"If it helps any, I only agreed to fix her laptop because I thought it would make you feel guilty about not calling me."

"It's *my* laptop," she teased and leaned into him again, loving the feel of his solid, strong body. Suddenly, he hitched her up. She locked her legs around him, and he walked them over to her bed, kissing and nuzzling her throat on the way.

When he set her down on the puffy comforter, she looked into his eyes, and he decided to try again. "I love you," he said softly.

She didn't hesitate for one second. "I love *you*," she whispered. "I love you so much." Within seconds they were lying together, exchanging soft words about their future, and melding their bodies into one beautiful tangle of lust, love, bliss, and life.

Chapter Twenty-nine

At 12:30, as B. J. stepped onto the elevator, Lonnie pushed away from her desk and headed down the hall. She'd decided to wait until he went to lunch before she ransacked his office. She just hoped that the folder he'd stolen from Bette was still around so she could figure out what he'd been after.

She looked around to make sure nobody was watching as she opened his door, and walked into his office. Shutting the door behind her, she thought, *Make this fast.*

She riffled through the papers and notebooks on his desk, careful not to make a mess, and uncovered nothing of particular interest. Then she looked in a big desk drawer that was unlocked, and found only discarded pink phone slips and a mountain of protein bars. In his top desk drawer was the usual top-drawer fare: pens, pencils, and assorted crap.

Hmm. She looked around the room, surveying her options, and spotted what could very well be the mother lode: the gray filing cabinet by the window. Scurrying from his desk to the window, she pulled on one of the filing drawers. All she got was frustrating resistance. It was locked, which, in all honesty, she could've predicted. She yanked more violently for another two seconds, and then came up with a different strategy.

Darting back over to B. J.'s desk, she opened that top drawer again. She frantically pushed aside pencils, pens, floppy disks, and boxes of staples, until she came across a set of tiny keys. Thank God people were predictable.

The third key she tried opened the filing cabinet.

And she got lucky. The second drawer—which appeared to be on eye level for both her and B. J.—contained the blue folder. It must have been crumpled just enough to fit, because it sprang forward a little when the drawer opened. She pulled it out and read the tab. P-FLYNN. Bette regularly referred to her "p-files"—or personnel files—so this had to be B. J.'s.

She had to hurry, because for all she knew B. J. would pick up something for lunch and come right back. Racing against the clock, Lonnie opened the folder and scanned the contents. Since B. J. had only been with the firm for a year, there wasn't much there. Two performance evaluation reports, and a salary increase evaluation. She focused her attention on B. J.'s performance reports. One report was dated June 30th of that year, and the other was dated December 31st.

December 31st! That was just a couple of weeks ago. Lonnie glanced at the bottom of each page; both reports were signed by Twit. Should she risk taking the time to read the comments on B. J.'s evaluation? If she took the folder, B. J. would realize it was missing, and that might send him into a panic. At this point, she didn't know what he was capable of, and she'd rather not find out.

She was about to stuff his p-file back in the drawer, when something on the June 30th report caught her eye. In the margin, there was a handwritten notation that read "PNH." It wasn't Twit's handwriting, either. She checked the December report. "PNH" was written on that one, too, and preceded by two asterisks.

PNH. What did that mean?

She heard someone in the hallway. Lonnie stuck the reports back inside the folder, and crammed the whole file into the open drawer. Kneeing it shut, she headed for the door.

It opened before she got to it. She froze.

"What are you doing in my office?"

She flinched at the sight before her. B. J. was standing in the doorway with his hands balled into furious fists, and his face was a cross of shock and fury. Lonnie's own face went from creamy peach to beet red, as she struggled to explain herself out of this awkward situation. "Oh, B. J., I . . . I was just . . . looking for you." She gulped and reminded herself not to tip her hand. There was no reason that B. J. had to know she suspected him of a lot more than a Napoleon complex. "I was just wondering if you had a three-hole punch," she said weakly.

"Stay *out* of my stuff," he growled, squinting his eyes menacingly.

"Okay, well," she began, walking to the door backward, "like I said, I just needed a stapler—I mean, a three-hole punch. Well, both, actually. Okay, so . . . see ya later!" She completed the frenetic departure with a coy little wave that was hopelessly out of place, but she didn't care. She just wanted to get out of there.

It wasn't until she got back to her desk and fell into her chair with palpable relief, that she wondered how bizarre life must be if she was this scared of B. J.

"So, how's the Twit?"

Lonnie switched the phone to her other ear, before she stated the obvious. "Annoying, neurotic, afflicted by a profound God complex, the usual," she said. "This morning he told me to measure his office when I get a 'free moment.' I mean, a *moment*? He's crazy."

"Why do you have to measure his office?" Peach asked.

"Because he's decided to get new wallpaper. According to the fax he just sent out, he's settled on Regal Platinum."

"The man needs serious therapy."

"I can't help but wonder if it's just a coincidence that today is also Lyn Tang's first day," Lonnie commented.

"Ah."

"Actually," Lonnie went on, "Lyn seems cool. I like her. She's no Macey, or anything, but I think she has potential."

"You and your deep-seated psychological need for an on-call role model," Peach remarked.

"Please, don't start with the diagnoses right now, okay? I'm in a good mood, and I want to stay that way." Lonnie felt all right now that B. J. had left for the day, and soon, she was going to take off herself. She wanted to tell Peach about breaking into B. J.'s office and what'd happened after, but she couldn't take the chance that someone would overhear her.

Less than an hour after she'd escaped B. J.'s office, she'd e-mailed Bette, claiming she had a friend who was interested in pursuing a career in human resources. She'd asked her a couple generic questions about hiring policies and interviews—to pass along to her "friend"—before asking Bette about the HR term "PNH." After all, odds were good that Bette had written that notation in B.J.'s file.

Lonnie was praying she'd take the bait, but so far, she hadn't replied to the e-mail.

"Why are you in a good mood?" Peach asked her now.

She shrugged to the air and said, "I don't know. Life's short; play hard."

Peach groaned.

"Wait, *don't* even say it!" Lonnie protested. "Slogans are not the same as trite platitudes," she explained, grinning and waiting for her sister to challenge her. But she didn't. She just giggled and said, "I love you, Lon."

After Lonnie hung up, she checked the clock: 5:29. Out of the corner of her eye, she saw Lyn and Bette approaching her desk. Perfect! Now she'd get a chance to ask Bette in person.

"But I don't know. I've just always enjoyed Hilton Head in the spring and Lake Wanda in the fall," Bette was saying to Lyn. "Of course, nothing tops November skiing in Vermont."

Lyn nodded. "True. I do love skiing. I assume you've been to the Ridgemont?" She looked away from Bette to smile at Lonnie before handing her a set of documents for Twit.

"Uh . . . let me think now," Bette began, leaning against Lonnie's desk, as Lyn was. "Hmm . . . the Ridgemont, the Ridgemont . . ."

"It's a luxury condo community right in the mountains. I'm surprised you're not familiar with it."

"Oh, well," Bette said, waving her hand as if to brush away the inconsequential information. "A condo association, that explains it. You see, Reggie and I have our own mansion right there on the mountain."

"Mansion?" Lyn raised an eyebrow quizzically.

"Lodge," Bette corrected. "I meant, we have our own lodge-mansion sort of place that we go to—stay at. That is, we own it, so we stay at it."

Was it just Lonnie or did that sound a little fishy? True, Lonnie didn't ski, had never been to Vermont, and knew nothing about architecture, so perhaps a "lodge-mansion" was a real thing. But from Lyn's expression, it didn't appear as though she was completely convinced, either.

Bette blushed. Her face—which was normally characterized by layers of age-defying, consciously earth-toned foundation—took on an unnaturally pink hue. Lonnie's first instinct was to try to alleviate her embarrassment somehow. But as soon as Bette shot her a snide sideways look, as if she were a nosy peon eavesdropping on a private conversation, Lonnie went with her second instinct. Namely, not giving a rat's ass one way or the other.

"A lodge-mansion," Lyn repeated, too evenly to be anything other than skeptical. "How nice. Where did you say it was located?"

"The mountains," Bette answered.

"No, I mean, where *specifically*? Perhaps we've skied the same slopes." Lyn's tone was mild, but there wasn't much mistaking the challenge that underlay it. Lonnie couldn't believe she lucked out with front-row seats, so to speak, as someone knocked Bette Linsey's pretentiousness down a peg. Fabulous.

"Specifically? Well, it's around the area—"

"What's the address?"

Apparently, she was really going to push this. Bette might as well have been on the witness stand by the way Lyn fully expected her to provide clear, truthful answers. This bordered on the ridiculous, of course, but it really wasn't any more ridiculous than the usual office happenings.

Just then Bette was saved by the ring of Lonnie's phone, which was getting predictable in its bad timing. "Beauregard Twit's central headquarters . . ."

She recited the rest of Twit's id-versus-superego greeting, while focusing 99 percent of her attention on the two women in front of her desk. The caller mentioned something about wallpaper swatches, but Lonnie didn't really catch it. She was too busy watching Bette to make sure she didn't slip away before she got some information out of her.

She hung up just as Lyn was heading out the main glass doors and Bette was turning on her heel to walk away. "Wait, Bette!" Lonnie said. Bette turned around and raised a sculpted brow. "I . . . um, did you get my e-mail?"

Bette was still blushing—obviously being mortified by Lyn didn't agree with her. So in standard corporate form, she opted to take it out on the temp. "Right, that e-mail about your *friend* who's thinking of pursuing a career in human resources." Her voice was thick with condescension. "Well, you tell your *friend* that one doesn't just jump into human resources. One must possess skills."

With that, she offered a brief smile good-bye, and walked off. "But, wait . . . PNH!" Lonnie called after her, but it was futile because Bette had already disappeared down the hall.

Lonnie's phone rang. "Hello," she said absently.

"Kid."

"Oh, Detective! I'm so glad you called me!" she said. She filled him in on B. J.'s personal evaluation reports.

"You read my mind," Montgomery said, sounding anxious.

"What do you mean?" she asked.

"Shit! We just got a call. I gotta go. But I gotta tell you something."

"What is it?" she demanded.

"All right, I'm coming! Just stay away from Flynn," he ordered, putting a stern emphasis on each word. "I can't explain it to you now; just *stay away from him*. You got it?"

"Well, he saw me in his office before—"

"*What?*" he barked angrily.

She swallowed. "How else could I get the file?" she argued.

"Jesus Christ!" he yelled. "What'd I tell you about being inconspicuous?" She struggled to remember his *exact* words. "Great, so now he knows you're onto him."

"Not necessarily—"

"I'm coming! I really gotta go," he said quickly. "Do me a favor: get the hell out of there! D'ya understand? Just go home, lay low, and I'll explain everything to you later."

"O-okay, but—"

"Just do it! Oh, wait, kid? Have you seen Matt Fetchug around?"

"Uh, yeah, I saw him just a little while ago."

He sighed. "Okay, good. He's all right." *Damn it, what is Montgomery saying? And why does he always have to go when I want to talk to him?* "I'll call you later."

A click and he was gone.

Chapter Thirty

"So I see the D drive's still not working."
"Oh . . . yeah," Lonnie agreed, and shut the front door behind her. "Sorry, but every time Dominick starts to fix it, he . . . gets distracted." She tossed the mail on the sunshine-yellow table, and kicked the front door closed with her burgundy heel. After she took off her coat, she made her way over to the sofa. "How was your day?" she asked Peach as she sank into the cushions.

"Okay," Peach said over her shoulder as she typed away on Lonnie's laptop. She was sitting at the oak table in the corner of the room facing the window, with her back to the rest of the apartment.

"What are you working on?"

"Hold on a second . . . okay," she said as she clicked the mouse, and swung her chair around to face her. "Sorry. I was just IM-ing Iris," she explained. Ordinarily, Lonnie would've been tempted to tell Peach how disturbingly *odd* that was, but at the moment, she had much graver things on her mind.

"So, how was your day?" Peach asked. She looked incurably sweet, sparkling, and streaky gold, and Lonnie felt a pang of sentimentality, realizing how much she'd miss living with her sister when she moved to Maine.

"Very strange . . . and scary." She explained what'd happened at the office, and how she hadn't gotten any information from Bette because of the bad timing. Then she described her disturbing conversation with Montgomery, and his unnerving inquiry about Matt's well-being. "I just don't know what to do about this," Lonnie said. "I know Detective Montgomery wants me to lie low, but how can I do nothing when there's a chance that . . . I don't know . . . Matt could be in danger?"

"I'm sure if he's in danger, the police are taking care of business," Peach assured her. Lonnie wasn't that easily convinced. Not because the police wouldn't take care of business, but because they might not do it quickly enough.

"I guess," she mumbled half-heartedly. "I just wish I'd gotten to ask Bette what the PNH notation meant in B. J.'s personnel file."

"What makes you think what was in B. J.'s file is important?"

"I don't know. Maybe it would tell me something more about him. Like maybe he has a medical condition that affects his mental state. Or maybe he has a history of a certain type of violence. It might give us some clue what he's gonna do next."

"Maybe he has a prison record," Peach said, and after a two-second pause, slapped her hands on her knees. "All right, let's go."

"Where are we going?"

"Bette's house," she said simply, and retrieved her coat. "Is it snowing out?"

"Wait, Peach, we can't do that."

"Why not?" Before Lonnie could answer, Peach said, "What's the problem? We swing by her house and ask her about B. J.'s file."

Lonnie's face scrunched up in disbelief—that settled it, her sister was certifiable. "That is so . . . awk-ward! She's gonna think I'm stalking her, or something!" Peach scoffed and rolled her eyes. "And how am I gonna explain my obsessive interest in this? No, I'm sorry, this is too ridiculous."

"Lon, we'll plan the specifics in the car. Now, let's go." She started pulling her sister by the arm and up off the sofa.

"You want me to drive all the way to Bette's house, at night—"

"It's barely seven thirty. Where does she live anyway?"

"I don't know. Newton."

"*Newton?* That's only a fifteen-minute drive from here, and you know it!"

"But I don't even know her address."

"Oh, well, why didn't you just say so?" Peach went back to the laptop. "I'm still online; just tell me how to spell her last name, and I'll do a Google search."

"You're not gonna find anything—"

"Google is god; now hit it." It was her nonnegotiable voice; there was no point fighting.

"Okay, it's: L-i-n-s-e-y."

It took less than two seconds for Peach to begin gloating. "Forty-four Glassgow Boulevard. You can thank me later. Come on, put your coat on," she said, and tossed the furry, ice-blue heap at her sister.

"Wait—"

Peach pulled her hair up into two side-buns. "Lon, seize the day. Besides, there's nothing good on TV tonight. Let's move. We can go get Dad's car." Begrudgingly, Lonnie rose to her feet, and followed orders. "Nothing ventured, nothing gained," Peach added with a lopsided grin. "Come on, I'm speaking your language, how can you resist that?"

"Oh, all right," Lonnie acquiesced, and grabbed her cell phone and her keys.

"Wait! Let's call Dominick, too," Peach said. "It wouldn't hurt to have a man there for protection. You know, just in case."

"Just in case what?" Lonnie asked, suddenly nervous. Maybe this was a bad idea after all.

"You know . . . just in case B. J. beats us there."

Lonnie swallowed. Then she reasoned, "I think we can handle it ourselves, Peach," she said. "Do we really need a man to protect us?"

"We're the brains; he's the brawn. What's the problem?"

Well, when she put it like that, it didn't seem so bad. "Okay, let's go," Lonnie said, being uncharacteristically impulsive . . . and liking it.

They called Dominick from her cell phone, and he agreed to come. The conversation had been cut short, though, because Lonnie had forgotten to recharge her battery. But neither she nor Peach realized how bad the traffic would be, and an hour later, they were just approaching Dominick's building. And Peach was yawning.

"Lon, don't get mad, but after you get Dominick, could you guys drop me home?"

"What? You're the one who convinced me to go—"

"I know, but this is turning out to be really boring. No offense."

"Well, what did you expect? A car chase? We haven't even gotten to Bette's house yet—you know, the so-called interesting part of the evening."

"Yeah, I know, but I'm just not feeling it anymore. Do you mind?" she asked, yawning again.

"Oh, fine," Lonnie said, but she lost all irritation the second she saw Dominick approaching the car. He got in the backseat and didn't even sulk about not riding shotgun. *I'm lucky*, Lonnie thought, and smiled at him. "Hey."

"Hey, baby," he said, and leaned forward to kiss her cheek. "Hi, Peach. So what's the plan again? We got cut off before."

"Well, now the plan is to drop Peach off at home"—

"Sorry, guys."

—"and then drive by Bette's house, and hopefully get a simple answer to a simple question."

He nodded, leaned back in his seat casually, and said, "I'm on board with that." After they dropped Peach at home, several minutes went by before Dominick said, "We should talk about Maine."

Lonnie focused her attention on the road. She'd been trying to avoid talking about Maine. She didn't want to think about what was going to happen when she moved. Undoubtedly, they'd try a long-distance relationship, and it would most likely fall apart within a matter of months. She didn't want to think about it, talk about it, or worry about it. She just wanted to enjoy the time she and Dominick had with each other now.

"Let's not talk about Maine," she said, and cast a sincere look at him. "I don't want to think about saying good-bye. Not yet."

"I don't want to think about saying good-bye, either. That's the whole point." He paused. "How would you feel if I came with you?"

"You mean . . . what, help me move in?" She had a feeling that wasn't what he meant, but she had trouble believing he would really want to pick up and move to Maine. That seemed too extreme. Didn't it?

"No, I meant . . . what if I came, too? Wait, before you say anything, just think about it. I'm starting my own business, anyway. I can start it wherever I want. I just have to pick what office space I'm going to rent. Besides, Maine is ripe for the software industry right now." He'd obviously already put a lot of thought into the idea, and that alone sent shivers through her.

"But, Dominick . . . don't get me wrong. I'd love to have you with me." She took one hand off the steering wheel to rest on his leg. "Of course I'd love that—so much. But still . . . I think it's way too soon for us to think about living together."

"Living together? Oh, *no*, that's not what I want!"

"Sound more horrified at the idea, that was nice," she muttered, and he laughed.

"No, no, that's not what I meant," Dominick said. "I just meant that I agree. It is too soon to move in together. And the last thing I want to do is have to adjust to a new career *and* a new roommate."

"Well, me either," she agreed, a little defensively, and turned onto Glassgow Boulevard.

"I know. That's why if I went to Maine, I'd get my own place. Look, I've given this a lot of thought, and I want to do it."

"But what if we broke up, and then you'd be stuck out in Maine—"

"I wouldn't be stuck anywhere. It's not like I'm married to Boston. I'm not even from here, like you are. I only came here for GraphNet, but I'm moving on now, and Maine's just as good a place as any."

Lonnie started to panic. This was all happening too fast. What if Dominick set up his business in Maine and then hated it there? He'd end up resenting her, and then their relationship would end even sooner. She couldn't let that happen.

"I'm sorry, Dominick."

"What do you mean?"

"I can't say yes." She slotted Jack's car to the right, and put it in park.

"What do you mean you can't say yes?"

Ignoring him, she motioned to the gorgeous stucco

mansion, numbered 44, across the street. "This is it," she said, and cut the engine.

THE LINSEYS was inscribed on the mailbox in gold calligraphy, and the streetlamps were bright enough for Lonnie to make out a silver BMW with a personalized license plate that read: REGINALD parked in the driveway. "Do you want to come with me, or wait here?" she asked. He shot her a look like she was nuts, and then opened his door.

It took only a few steps forward before Lonnie realized that the only lights were streetlights; Bette's house was completely dark. "Maybe nobody's home," she whispered. They got to the door, and Lonnie sucked in a nervous breath. So what if she looked like a raving fool to her coworker? She was just a temp, after all. Dominick rang the doorbell. They waited a couple minutes before they rang it again. Still no answer.

Typical. "Oh well. Let's go," she said, with resignation.

They were halfway across the cobblestone path that bisected the lawn when a square of light hit the property. They turned around, and saw that it had come from an upstairs window. "Maybe she is home," Lonnie said.

"You want to ring the doorbell again?" he asked, sliding his arm beneath her neck and rubbing gently.

"Um . . . I don't know. I really do want to talk to her."

He mulled it over for a second, then suggested, "Let's just see if any other lights are on around the house. At least see what the deal is, before we go back to the city."

"Okay." They rounded the corner and moved to the side of the stucco mansion, where things were still completely dark. Just then, a large rectangular window on the side of the house lit up.

Instantly, they crouched down, as an image of Bette crossed in front of them. Her hair was wet; she must have been in the shower when they'd rung the doorbell. She was wearing a plain white robe, holding a box of cheap Zinfandel in one hand and a red plastic cup in the other. And she was standing alone . . . in the middle of a completely empty room.

"Is that her?" Dominick whispered.

"Yeah. But, wait . . . I don't get it. The house looks totally empty on the inside. Where's the furniture? Where's . . . I don't know, anything?"

"Where's the people? Didn't you say that Bette is married with kids?"

"Yeah. She has two daughters. Although, it is after nine—they could be in bed. But where's Reginald? His car was parked outside."

They watched as Bette plopped down on the bare floor, sitting cross-legged, and violently ripped at the tab on her box of wine. She filled the red plastic cup to the rim and set it down on the floor. She got up again and went into another room, out of sight.

"Talk about depressing," Dominick muttered, and Lonnie agreed, before turning her attention back to the window.

"Look," she said, pointing. They both watched as Bette came back into the empty room, carrying a large mirror. She sat down on the floor. She held the mirror in front of her so she was looking directly at herself. Then she smirked and brought her cup of wine up to tap its reflection, creating an illusion of two cups clinking each other in a "cheers" motion. Lonnie thought, *What the hell*, just as Bette burst into tears.

"What the hell?" Dominick muttered. Lonnie was temporarily speechless. "What do you think?" he whispered.

"I . . . I don't know," she whispered back, shaking her head, confused. "Maybe . . . Hmm. Maybe Reginald left her," she offered.

"Yeah, and took all the furniture, it looks like," he said. Lonnie leaned forward to get a better look, and dropped her cell phone. It landed right on a rock, making a loud, crashing thud, and Bette jerked her head around. Lonnie jumped onto her stomach, to get out of view, but she didn't know if she'd done it quickly enough. Dominick started to come out of the bushes to help her, but she commanded him not to. "No!" she whispered. "No, stay hidden. I think she might've seen me!"

"What do you want to do?" he whispered through the bushes. "Do you want to just get out of here?"

"Yeah, okay, but look through the window. What's Bette doing right now?" *Please say she's back to bawling in isolation and doing fake toasts with lousy wine.* Suddenly that never seemed more innocuous. Here Lonnie had been worried how awkward it would be to show up at Bette's door . . . imagine peering through her window like a psycho!

"Uh . . . well, from what I can see . . . she's . . . staring right at me," Dominick said.

"What are you talking about?" Lonnie asked, panicked. "She can see you?"

"No, I don't think so. But she's looking out the window, right in my direction. I doubt she can see through the bush, but let's get the hell out of here before—oh, *shit!*"

"What? What?" Lonnie was still lying facedown on the ground right below the windowsill, hoping Bette wouldn't walk over and look out her window.

She started belly crawling backward to make her way to the bushes for cover, and she heard Dominick say again, "Shit."

"What?" she asked, poised midcrawl, halfway between the windowsill and the bushes, with an undoubtedly savage mud trail on her clothes.

"Lonnie, just stay down, whatever you do," he warned in a steely voice.

"Will you please tell me what's going on?" she demanded.

"She has a gun."

"*What?* What the hell are you—*a gun*? Where did it come from?"

"She grabbed it from somewhere. I have no idea. But she's gripping it and looking right at the window."

"Omigod, omigod."

"Baby, we gotta get out of here," he ordered.

"I know," she said, doing the fastest backward belly crawl of her life. (At least, so far.) He crept behind the bushes, meeting her midway, and took her hand.

"She must've heard the noise, and thinks there are prowlers," he offered, while he pulled her along the side of the house, toward the front.

"Oh, God, let's go before she shoots us."

"C'mon, she's not going to shoot us," he said. "If she thinks we're prowlers, she'll call the police."

"Oh please, don't you watch Lifetime?"

Just as they got to the front yard, the heavy oak door swung open, and the porch light went on full blast. "Who's there?" Bette yelled into the semidarkness. "I see you," Bette called, her voice trembling. Lonnie knew the porch light was bright enough to illuminate figures on the front lawn. She'd tried to hide behind a tall, skinny shrub, but since Lonnie was neither tall nor skinny herself, it didn't provide much cover.

"I said *who's* there? Who *is* it?" Bette cried out.

Lonnie gripped Dominick's arm. "What should we do?"

"We can't run now; she might shoot at us. That would be ridiculous, but still."

"All right, I'll just have to tell her it's me, and deal with the awkwardness later," Lonnie said, reminding herself that she was just a temp, and that even if she got fired from Twit & Bell, she could easily get another job that was just as exploitative and degrading. "How do I get myself into these things?" Lonnie muttered to herself before she came clean. "Bette, wait!" she called. "Please don't shoot! It's me, Lonnie!"

"*Lonnie?*" Bette repeated, confused, and put the gun down at her side.

"Um, yeah, Lonnie Kelley. Please, I didn't mean to startle you."

"Well, what the fuck are *you* doing here? And who's that with you?"

Lonnie and Dominick took tentative steps forward. "I'm so sorry, Bette," Lonnie said. "I didn't mean any harm. This is my boyfriend, Dominick."

"Oh, right, from the holiday party," Bette said, as they came into clear view.

"Bette, please allow me to explain," Lonnie started, wondering just how she was going to do that without looking like a weirdo, even to herself. "Remember those HR questions I asked you at the office today? Well, you were right. I was asking for myself, not a friend."

Bette smiled patronizingly.

"Anyway," Lonnie went on, "you know how I was out of the office last week for interviews?"

"No. I hadn't noticed."

"Yeah, well, at one of the interviews, someone mentioned the abbreviation 'PNH,' and I had no idea what they were talking about. Um."—she darted a look at Dominick for support, and he tightened his hand around hers—"I just need to know what it means. Maybe it sounds obsessive, but I can't stop thinking about that . . . interview."

"Oh. I see. Well, I'm sorry it didn't work out for you, dear," Bette said. "Generally, PNH stands for possible new hire."

"Possible new hire," Lonnie repeated.

"Yes. I make a note of it when an employee's performance is inadequate enough to raise questions about whether or not he should be replaced."

Lonnie thought for a second. It made sense, of course, that B. J.'s performance report would have a PNH notation back in June, considering Lunther's intention to fire him. What seemed strange was that the notation was also made on the report dated December 31st, after Lunther had died. That meant that B. J.'s job status was just as precarious before the murder as it was after. And he had to *know* that, or he wouldn't have been so desperate to get his hands on the file.

And *that* made her wonder. Was it possible that B. J. had much less of a motive to kill Lunther than she'd assumed?

"Let's go inside and I'll explain more," Bette suggested. "It's cold out here."

"Okay," Lonnie agreed, and pulled Dominick by the hand inside the lovely albeit absolutely empty stucco mansion. Bette shut and locked the front door behind them.

"You like my place?" she asked sarcastically.

"Oh . . . yes, yes," Lonnie managed politely.

"It's great," Dominick added.

"A lot of light," Lonnie said stupidly. "Um . . . I love the hardwood floors." *Great going. Remind her of how the floors go on forever, with no rugs or furniture. Next, tell her you like the pristine white walls, and remind her how devoid they are of art and photographs.*

Wait! Why *were* Bette's walls devoid of photographs? Lord knows, she was proud of her family. They shamelessly graced the surface of her desk at work. Surely, even if Reginald had left her, she'd still keep pictures of Burberry and Skylar-Blaise in the house.

"Take a good look," Bette sneered. "It's the last image you're gonna see."

And then she cocked her gun.

Chapter Thirty-one

"**B**-Bette?" Lonnie swallowed hard, and felt her heart thudding against her chest. Dominick tightened his hand on hers fiercely. It was the only thing that steadied her, and she never wanted to let it go.

"What's going on?" he asked Bette, trying for an even tone of voice.

"Oh, shut up," she snapped. "The last thing I'm in the mood to see is *young love*." She said the words with disgusted acrimony, and then pointed her gun even closer at them. "In fact, let go of your hands. Let them go!"

Lonnie jumped, dropped Dominick's hand, and only then did she realize how sweaty her own was. Sweaty with fear and anxiety and impending doom; obviously, being a pessimist didn't make this situation any easier. "Bette," she said gently, "I-I don't understand. I said I was sorry for trespassing. If you'll just let me explain—"

"Explain what? How you're not gonna tell anyone the truth? How it'll be 'our little secret'? Spare me. I didn't buy it from Lunther, and I'm sure as hell not buying it from some temp."

Lunther? *Oh, God, no.* Surely Bette didn't mean—

"So now you know. It's all crap. It always was. And if I let you and him go, then pretty soon everyone will find out about my real life." Was all this just because Bette didn't want anyone to find out that her husband had left her? Was she *that* obsessed with image?

"Bette, it's none of my business, and I certainly don't intend to tell anyone," Lonnie said.

"Yeah," Dominick agreed automatically. "We won't say a word. We swear."

"Right!" she scoffed. "How could you possibly resist? Who could pass up telling this story?" *Well, that seems a bit over the top.* "The story of a woman so desperate to be in the upper class of society that she'd actually invent a husband and two children."

Or not. "That story will get you more than a few friends at the old water cooler, eh, Lonnie?"

Lonnie stood there, stunned, almost not believing what she was hearing. Reginald Linsey wasn't real? Bette had made him up? But that was crazy! What about Burberry and Skylar-Blaise . . .? They were fictitious, too? She could only assume that the Linsey dog, Ellis, and cat, Josephine, weren't any more legitimate. This had to be the most bizarre thing she'd ever heard in her life.

And now Bette was telling her that her life had come to an end.

Oh, God! Please, no!

No, this couldn't happen. *Not now.* She couldn't let it happen. She looked over at Dominick plaintively, desperately, wishing more than anything she could hold his hand again. His black eyes were soft and molten and told her he was almost as scared as she was. Bette commanded them to move farther into the house and away from the front door.

"Oh, sorry I can't offer you a seat," she said sarcastically. "But just trying to hold down the mortgage on this place—and wear enough expensive clothes

to fit my image—preclude me from such *luxuries* as
furniture. Oh, and let's not forget all the payments
on *Reggie's* beamer." She glanced into the adjoining
room, and then back to Lonnie and Dominick. "Obviously, expensive wine and glassware don't fit into
my budget, either, as I'm sure you saw for yourself.

"Sit down," she commanded harshly, waving her
gun. "It'll be less of a mess that way." She let out a
quick, bitter laugh, and added, "Not that I'm an expert on murder. I've only killed one person, but hey,
I got away with it, didn't I?"

"You killed Lunther," Lonnie whispered, more to
herself than to Bette.

"You catch on fast," she said with the intellectual
superiority that could only be reserved for the ever-
disdained temps, but Lonnie didn't think now would
be the time to point out the irony of Bette's snobbery.

"Look, I'm not a monster, okay? And I'm not
crazy. Do you understand?" She thrust her gun forward again. "I'm not crazy!" She sucked in a shaky
breath. "All I did was slip some shit into his drink
as the night was winding down, and then try to leave
before it took effect. Unfortunately," she went on,
"he staggered into the coatroom just as I was getting
my coat. The idiot actually spent five minutes com-
plaining to me that he felt sick! I almost laughed in
his face!" She plowed chipped French-manicured
nails through her less-than-sleek-at-the-moment crop
cut. "He started backing up, leaning against the wall
for support, and I thought I heard footsteps approaching, so I covered him up with some coats, and
got the hell out of there. It was all so *perfect*."

Lonnie and Dominick were sitting on the floor, a
foot apart, just listening to Bette's almost-manic con-
fession. Well, they didn't exactly have much choice
in the matter. Half of the time Bette was talking, she
was looking off into the distance, as if she were only
vaguely aware of their presence in the room.

"Lunther should've minded his own business," Bette said, shaking her head in weary frustration. "But he had to go and have me investigated. Greedy slob."

"Was he blackmailing you or something?" Lonnie asked quickly. "Because, if so, I think that is just so awful and I can certainly understand why you'd need to kill him."

"Oh, can it."

"Okay," she said overeagerly, with a fake smile plastered on her face, and Dominick shot her a warning look to tone it down.

"I'm assuming you must know something or you wouldn't have come here," Bette said. "I've seen how tight you are with Macey. What does she know?"

"Nothing! I mean . . . I don't even know anything. Not really."

"It's ironic that Macey doesn't know more," Bette remarked. "Because if she knew I killed Lunther, she'd probably thank me. They hated each other, but then, I guess I don't need to tell you that."

Lonnie and Dominick kept silent, and Bette kept talking. "That's what made Lunther investigate me. He was obsessed with the idea that Macey was going to convince Sandy Neemas to refile sexual harassment charges against him. So he wanted me to fudge negative performance evaluation reports—you know, falsely document complaints about Sandy during her employment with the firm. He figured that would be his defensive strike if they tried to claim she had to leave because of any kind of harassment."

"But Lunther liked to keep the gun loaded, if you know what I mean. He wanted to come to me with his request only after he knew he had me under his thumb. So he had me investigated. Undoubtedly, he just expected to get a little dirt to hold over my head. He never dreamed that my whole life—the whole image I'd created for myself—was completely made up. That's why he had to die."

"Mmm . . . that does make sense," Lonnie said as agreeably as she could.

"You should've seen the way he gloated when he told me he knew," Bette said, ignoring Lonnie and talking more to the air. "I was so distraught, I started cleaning out my desk, packing up my pictures and personal effects, and got ready to run. But then I realized: where would I go?"

"The pictures," Lonnie echoed almost inaudibly, suddenly remembering the day of the party, when she'd noticed that Bette's desk was missing her family photographs.

"Those damned pictures," Bette went on. "Hired actors. And wouldn't you know the fucking cat was the most expensive one!"

"But if you knew about his sexual harassment," Dominick injected, trying to pacify Bette—or just keep her talking; Lonnie wasn't sure which— "couldn't you use that to blackmail him back? And, you know, keep him quiet about you?" he asked.

"No, you don't *get* it!" Bette yelled, full of rage again. "He *knew*. No one can know, or it's not real! So what if I knew about what a bastard Lunther was—I even knew about him missing a critical court date because he was carrying on with Delia, but how would that help *me*?"

She buried her forehead in one hand and kept the gun held out in the other. "You just don't get it," she scolded bitterly. "I've worked so hard to create my image. I've practiced the act so much—everything, from my mannerisms to my signature, and there was no way I could work side by side with someone who knew it was all bullshit! There was no way . . ." Her voice trailed off, shaky now, and suddenly, tears sprang to her eyes.

"Bette—" Lonnie began soothingly.

"Don't patronize me!" she snarled, as her tears fell onto the hardwood floor below. "All I've ever wanted was to be rich. But it wasn't for the money itself. It was for the whole package. The perfect husband, the perfect children, the au pair, the trips to Hilton Head and Cabo; all of it. But I couldn't get any of it on my own, and I thought even if I invented it, my life could be full just living out the fantasy. Just having people treat me the way they would if I really were everything I pretended to be. But the reality is—" Her voice broke off again, as she bawled some more and blew her nose into the sleeve of her robe. "The reality is . . . my life stinks! It's so empty. The worst part is, all I've got is bullshit, and I can't even afford to lose that. I can't lose the one thing I've got—total and utter bullshit!" She leaped to her feet and walked over until she was just inches away from them.

"What are you going to do?" Lonnie asked, terrified.

"What does it look like?" Bette retorted, wiping her face with the back of her free hand and shoving the gun against Lonnie's temple with the other. In that moment, Lonnie became her pounding heart; nothing else existed. She felt like she'd stopped breathing.

"No, please," Dominick pleaded, his face pale and horrified. "Please, don't do this!"

"Don't worry," Bette said. "You're next." She put her finger on the trigger . . . and her doorbell rang. "Oh, who could that be?"

Please, God. Please, God. Please, God.

"Who is it?" Bette called out, still holding her gun to Lonnie's head.

"Ma'am? It's Detective Montgomery. Could you open the door?" the gruff voice called back, and Lonnie almost burst into tears. *Thank you, God. Thank you, God. Thank you, God.*

"Oh, shit!" Bette uttered savagely. "Uh . . . Detective, I can't talk now! Please come back another day!"

"Uh, ma'am, I'm afraid I can't do that. Please open the door." His tone wasn't threatening, but it was firm, telling Lonnie that Montgomery had no idea the extent of what was going on inside Bette's house, but he knew enough to push the issue.

"Please, Detective! Please, I-I'll go down to the station first thing in the morning—"

"Open the door, *now!*" he demanded, and when she didn't do it, he busted the heavy oak door open. "Ms. Linsey!" Montgomery called out as he made his way through the empty, dark house. Bette froze in place, nervously, unsure what to do next, when Montgomery appeared in the archway.

"Freeze!"

Instinctively, Bette jammed the gun hard into Lonnie's temple, wordlessly warning Montgomery not to come any closer. "Ms. Linsey," he said slowly, carefully. "Please . . . don't do anything crazy—"

"I'm NOT crazy!" Bette shrieked, shoving the mouth of her gun even harder against Lonnie's head, as two more tears streaked down Lonnie's cheeks.

"Okay, okay," Montgomery said, holding his hands up in surrender. But he was still holding his revolver, and Lonnie knew Bette would have to be beyond distraught not to notice.

"Give it to me," Bette snapped, and extended her free hand out as far as she could, reaching for Montgomery's gun. "Now!" Montgomery leaned forward, with his weapon in hand, and Bette must have finally realized how precarious the exchange would be. "Stop!" she yelled suddenly. "I-I mean, just drop the gun on the floor. Then kick it over to me." Montgomery froze for a moment longer, and then followed her order.

Bette didn't dare bend down to pick up Montgomery's gun; she'd lose any advantage that way. But at the same time, she was leaving a loaded revolver on the floor only two feet away from Dominick. She didn't seem to notice that.

"I don't know how I'm going to get out of this," Bette said bitterly. "I just need to think. I need to think." She brought her hand up to her forehead and scrunched thin folds of skin with her fingers. "Think, think, think!" she commanded herself. Meanwhile, Lonnie wished she could do something more productive than stay frozen on her knees with tears streaming down endlessly and her heart beating painfully hard.

Just then, Officer Stopperton ran into the room, gun in hand and blue uniform hanging loosely on his skinny frame. "Oh, no!" Bette yelled, looking beside herself. "Can I ever get a fucking break?"

"There are more cops outside, Mrs. Linsey. You'll never get out of here."

"Stop lying! There's just the two of you."

Montgomery held up his hands again and looked completely sincere when he said, "I'm not lying, ma'am. If you don't believe me, check for yourself."

Bette backed up only less than a foot to try to catch a glimpse of her front stoop through the opening crack of her curtains. But it was enough. Without premeditation, Dominick took advantage of the situation. He flew onto Montgomery's discarded revolver, grabbed it, and pointed it at Bette. She was so stunned that Montgomery was able to snatch her gun out of her hand.

The second he did, Lonnie sank back on her heels and let out a breath so deep that for a second she thought her lungs had collapsed. She was shaking, still trembling inside out with fear. Dominick lurched across the hardwood floor to gather her up in his arms. Both of their foreheads were dotted with perspiration, and Lonnie had tears running down her cheeks. "Omigod, omigod," she kept mumbling as Dominick hugged her, and his body felt more than a little unsteady, too.

"No!" Bette screamed. *"No! No!"* The scream turned into a wail, and she burst into hysterical sobbing. She knew what they did: it was all over.

After Bette had been arrested and taken away by two of the police officers, Montgomery offered to take Lonnie for a cup of Irish coffee to calm her nerves. She said no, but thanked him with all her heart—about a hundred times—for saving their lives.

"How on earth did you know I was here?" Lonnie asked him.

"I called to make sure you were staying home—*like I told you*—and your sister informed me what you were up to. I knew you wouldn't do what you were told."

"But how did you know about *Bette*?"

He sighed. "It's a long story." She shot him a cross look that said, *I think I have the time*, and he explained. "We discovered that there was no Reginald Linsey living in this house within the first week of our investigation. So I had Bette come in to finish making her statement, and I mentioned it to her. She explained that her husband had left her, and that she was still devastated and humiliated, and she didn't want anybody to know—"

"I can't believe this!" Lonnie interrupted. "You *knew*? How could you not tell *me*?" she asked, annoyed, and filled with an admittedly inappropriate sense of betrayal.

"Hey, I couldn't take the chance you'd say something to her at work. She might've figured out you were working with the police, and then word would've gotten around the office."

"I wouldn't have said anything!" she protested.

"Maybe not. But you probably would've done some

of your oh-so-suave sleuthing, and that's just as good."
Considering Montgomery had just saved their asses,
Lonnie decided to concede the argument for the moment. "Anyway, she begged us not to say anything,
and we really couldn't see any harm in it. It certainly
didn't seem related to Lunther Bell's murder.

"Then tonight we had a major break in the case.
Apparently Bette had left her sunglasses at the station. They were real expensive, I guess, because the
department secretary took 'em home with her. That's
where Stopperton comes in."

The lanky uniformed cop stepped forward and
added, "A few days ago, I overheard her complain-
ing that the sunglass case had this powdery residue
in it, and she'd thought she'd gotten something really
nice, but she hadn't." He smiled crookedly. "Our secretary's sort of a kleptomaniac. Anyway, I was only
interested because I'd heard her say she took it from
a suspect."

"He pressed her on it," Montgomery jumped in,
"and found out they were Bette Linsey's. On a long
shot, he had the lab run a test on it. The results were
in tonight, and that's when he told me what he'd
been up to." Lonnie waited expectantly, and he finished, "Potassium chloride."

"Officer Stopperton," she said with some awe,
"you mean you did that all that on your own? You
went to all that trouble *just in case* there was something there?"

He shrugged, and his hat slipped a little more.
"I'm trying to get promoted."

Montgomery said, "It wasn't enough to charge
Bette with murder, but it was enough for me to
worry like hell when Peach told me you'd gone to
confront her about something."

Lonnie asked, "But how come you told me to stay
away from B J.?"

"Yeah," Dominick piped in. "How come you thought Matt might be in danger?"

Montgomery explained what Stopperton had learned from B. J.'s former roommate at Dinkle College, Stanley Turner. Apparently, B. J. had been so paranoid that he would fail one of their prelaw classes, he'd cheated on a midterm and then threatened to kill Stanley if he ever breathed a word of it. The threats had been credible enough for Stanley to take him seriously, and move out. According to his story, B. J. was particularly competitive with him because they were the same year, and while B. J. struggled desperately, Stanley got straight As.

"So, B. J. had threatened this guy, but he never actually made good on it?"

"Right. But we still had to find out if there'd been any incidents like that since, and make sure Matt Fetchug wasn't in danger, since he and Flynn joined the firm at the same time, and Fetchug was doing great, while Flynn was just barely hanging on to his job."

Lonnie nodded. "So, basically, B. J. is a thoroughly messed-up freak, but at this point, not a criminal?"

"Right," he agreed. "Well, not counting the Faneuil Hall episode."

Dominick looked questioningly at her, and she said, "I'll tell you about that one later," and leaned into him. "Detective, there's just one thing I don't understand."

"Yeah?"

"How come you and Officer Stopperton are working together? You're not partners, are you?" They couldn't be; one was a homicide detective and one was a uniformed cop.

Montgomery shrugged. "He's my protégé."

Lonnie laughed. If life got any more bizarre, she didn't know if she could bear it.

They talked for a couple more minutes, and then, as she turned to go, Montgomery touched her arm. "Hey, kid," he said. She looked at him, waiting for whatever it was he was going to say, and her eyes were swirls of green and pink from all her crying. "My heart almost stopped tonight when I saw Bette's gun on you." He paused awkwardly, then said, "You're all right. That's all I'm trying to say."

She smiled, and tears started to fall again, despite her best intentions. "Thank you for saving our lives," she said quietly. "In case I haven't mentioned it." And she pulled him into a hug before he could see it coming.

Dominick took her home and stayed with her. After they explained what happened to Peach, they went to bed. And once Lonnie was warm in her hearts-and-stars pajamas, with Dominick's arms wrapped around her, she slept deeply.

Every dream was a reminder that she was lucky and blessed and still very much alive.

Epilogue

The next week, Lonnie sat in Dominick's Nissan, trying to talk some sense into the man. They were parked in Margot and Jack's driveway, about to go inside for dinner, when Dominick brought up the subject of Maine. Despite Lonnie's reasoning, he seemed unwilling to consider any other option than moving, and being with her. *The man has nerve.*

"You might be bored there," Lonnie said, probably for the fifth time.

"You'd be there," Dominick replied.

"But it's not as exciting as Boston."

"I hate excitement. Present company excepted."

"There's probably not as much to do there."

"You'd be there."

"But if we broke up—"

"Don't even talk about us breaking up, because it's not gonna happen."

"How can you know that?" she challenged. "Things change, relationships change. Look at me and Jake—"

"Jake's a shit." *Valid.* "And I'll be damned if I don't get to marry you someday." Her mouth dropped open, and he said, "Sorry to break it to you, baby, but it's gonna happen at some point. It has to."

"Why?" she asked in a near whisper, suddenly floored by the whole conversation, and by how elated and alive it made her feel.

"Because . . ." He brought his hands to her rosy cheeks, and looked magnetically through her green—honey-brown eyes. "You're the one," he said, as if the answer was so obvious.

She felt tears sting the backs of her eyes. She threw her arms around Dominick and hugged him so fiercely she wondered if he could breathe. He didn't voice one complaint, though, and only held her to him, murmuring sweet words into her ear.

"You're the one," he said. "And don't try to get out of it."

She smiled into his neck. "I won't," she said softly, and turned her head to kiss him. "Wait!" she said, breaking their kiss. "What about your family?"

"What about them?"

"They haven't even met me. I mean, they're gonna wonder about some girl who's dragging you to Maine."

"No way. They'll love you. We'll drive to Connecticut and introduce you to the family next weekend, if you want."

"Okay," she said, beaming.

"Oh, just so you know, my parents are really traditional," he said, gently brushing silky strands of her hair away from her face. "They might ask you if you're pro—breast-feeding, but just ignore them."

"*What?*"

"Skip it. Skip it," he said, waving his hand. "So that covers my family. Now, as for your parents, any tips before I go inside?"

"Nope," she replied, taking his hand in her own. "Just act very respectful of me, be your usual charming, wonderful self," she said. "And—oh yeah—if possible, throw in something about your earning potential before dessert." He quirked his mouth into a disbelieving grin. Lonnie just smiled and said, "What can I say? My parents are just as sexist as yours."

He grinned wider—making her stomach knot, her heart race, and her blood heat—and he said, "I'm on board with that." Hands locked, they headed for the front door.

Over dinner, the whole family laughed, overate, and maybe overdrank a little, while they congratulated Peach for winning the art contest. Her logo had been chosen, and the timing couldn't have been more perfect. With the five thousand dollars in prize money, she'd be able to keep Lonnie's studio apartment for herself. For a while anyway, and when she started to run out of money, she'd just come up with another harebrained scheme. That was Peach. Cheryl and Jean-Paul came to dinner, too, and they really did seem very happy together. When they didn't think anyone was looking, Lonnie noticed, they'd murmur things to each other in French and laugh quietly.

Margot and Jack made their approval of Dominick evident by the way they kept offering him more of everything—food, wine, and elbowroom at the table. Lonnie reasoned that they wouldn't want to keep him well fed, satiated, and pampered if they didn't want to keep him around.

Now, everyone made their way into the cozy family room, with espresso and biscotti. "So, Peach," Jean-Paul said, "what are you going to do now that you're a rich woman?"

"Hmm . . . I don't know. I *just* don't know," Peach said dramatically. "Maybe buy a couple new paintbrushes, save money to go visit my sister who's abandoning me." She shot Lonnie an affected *how-could-you?* look of despair, and added, "And basically just continue touching the lives of all those who come in contact with me." She batted her eyelashes, and Lonnie made a retching gesture.

"You got greedy," she said to her little sister.

"You're right," Peach admitted, smiling and pleased with herself.

"Dominick!" Margot interjected. "Have you seen pictures of Lonnie when she was younger?" Lonnie tried to muster up her usual irritation, but couldn't seem to. She didn't really mind if Dominick saw all her nerdy eighties photos. "Peach, where are the Cookie Monster ones?" *Not even those. Okay, still those.* Luckily Peach read her mind.

"I burned them," Peach said. "Sorry, Mom." She winked at Lonnie, who just looked at her, thinking, *I love you.*

When everyone was engrossed in conversation— even Jack, who'd set his latest book aside—Dominick pressed a quick kiss to Lonnie's mouth. The kiss was all sweetness and romance and love, and this time she had no doubt she was looking directly at her future.

She looked around the room, and then back at him, thinking, *I love you all so much.* She sighed and smiled and suddenly she knew. Life was a bowl of . . . plums.

"**O**kay, I'll call you tomorrow. Bye." After Reese hung up, she tossed her pink-and-silver cell into the backseat, and cranked the volume up on George Michael's *Last Christmas*.

Speeding down Route 46 was giving her the same nostalgic feeling it always did. The same stores, the same restaurants, the same construction projects that still weren't finished. It seemed like nothing changed in or around Goldwood, and as far as she was concerned, that was a good thing.

Thinking about what her sister Angela had said about bridesmaids' dresses, Reese found herself squirming a little in the worn upholstery. She'd put on a few pounds during finals week, and even before that, she was a snug size 8. And not one of those streamlined, statuesque snug-8s, but a five-foot-three snug-8, which was a whole different kind of thing.

At least the dress itself wasn't bad. It was a sleeveless, backless, hunter-green sheath, with a medium slit up the side. They got to wear long gloves, too, which, for some reason, felt like a real coup. As the maids of honor (Angela refused to be called *matron*), Angela and Reese were also supposed to wear floral wreaths in their hair. She hadn't seen it yet, but she assumed it would be fine.

Despite her worries about the upcoming fitting, Reese found herself, five minutes later, sliding into the parking lot of a familiar Burger King. As she wound her car into the drive-through line, she fast-forwarded her tape to the Sinead O'Connor track, and started chewing on her lower lip.

She couldn't believe Ally's wedding was only a few

weeks away. It would be strange to see her little sister get married. Granted, she was only a year younger than Reese, and granted she was keeping her name. But still—it seemed like an enormous change.

The ceremony itself also promised to be fairly weird. Their mother had invited half the town because she'd "felt bad," and now was freaking out because Ally and Ben were so disorganized. She'd made it clear that she expected Reese to mingle with all of the guests, so no one would feel uncomfortable.

On top of that, Ben's best man was Brian Doren.

Brian Doren!

Reese was catapulted into a flashback of the one night she'd spent with Brian two years earlier.

Ally and Ben had dragged her to a New Year's party, and that was where she'd met him. Reese had been almost immediately attracted. Tall, dark, handsome—she couldn't figure out why Brian didn't have girls all over him. Oh, wait, *she'd* been all over him. But that didn't really count because he'd been so adorable and sweet, and also, she hadn't kissed a man since Pete.

And as far as kissing went, he was *incredible.* Especially compared to every other man she'd kissed in her life, who were all from the same school of hard mouths, whipping tongues, and jagged teeth. Not that she'd kissed all that many people, but still, it was what she'd come to *expect.* But Brian was different; he'd raised the bar. Well, briefly, anyway. The only person she'd kissed since was Kenneth, who'd dropped the bar. Hell, he'd *buried* the bar.

Absently, Reese ran her fingers across her mouth now, remembering the way Brian had moved his lips softly on hers, just gently coaxing them open. And when he'd slid his tongue inside her mouth, it was slow and scorching. It had felt so unbelievably good, that she'd lost control. Much like the boys who's kissed her all too aggressively in the past, Reese had been too excited to slow down.

Feverishly, she'd grabbed Brian by his navy cable-knit sweater, pulling him down lower, while she stood on tiptoes, and crushed her open mouth against his. Crushed *him,* body to body, against the wall, wildly French-kissing in the deserted hallway of an uptown apartment, at an otherwise overrated New Year's Eve party.

In fact, it was only after the post-ball-dropping, forced excitement quieted, that they pulled apart, lips wet, but still vaguely connected by lingering saliva and longing. (Okay, so maybe the night wasn't such a distant memory for her after all.)

Anyway, the encounter never got the chance to become awkward because Reese heard Ally's voice from the other room asking if anyone had seen her sister. That was when she'd moved off Brian's body, feeling his hard, enticing groin before they parted, and wishing he hadn't waited until the end of the party to make his move.

Reese had never told anyone about that kiss. She felt too stupid to. That night, she'd joined the ranks of people who randomly made out at parties for empty thrills, and that hardly seemed worth a broadcast. And it wasn't as if Brian had said anything to Ben, or Ally would've found out, and then Reese *definitely* would've heard about it.

Anyway, Brian had never pursued her after that night so Reese had simply buried it—remembering it as a helluva kiss, and a moment of weakness on her part. End of story.

She inched up in her car, now smelling the heavenly aroma of fatty grease and fried, processed meat. She figured she might as well have one more really great meal before she got to her mother's house. That was when junk food would cease being fun. It wasn't her that her mother *meant* to be annoying—she just couldn't help herself. She had this maddening habit of interrogating the family about their diets, always wanting to know what they were eating and *why*. Reese had already exhausted every conceivable answer, even: "Crap. Because I'm using food for love." Still, her mother never got the hint.

Basically, Joanna Brock was a slave to her own high culinary standards. She had French food on the brain 24-7 even though the entire family was Irish (with just a splash of Italian). But lately, Joanna had expanded her obsessions. According to Ally, their mom was now completely addicted to *The Wedding Story*, a TV-show on the cable station TLC. What had apparently started as a reference for planning Ally's wedding had turned into an extensive, annotated VHS collection with back episodes.

*   *   *

Reese turned her car into the comfortingly familiar driveway of the stone-and-brick house she'd grown up in. It was high up from the street, with lush evergreens enclosing it, as well as densely planted rhododendrons that would've been blooming gorgeous deep-pink if it weren't December.

After she set the car in park, she cut the engine, and sighed. She *loved* this place. It was both cozy but secluded, like the other homes on the street, but special.

"Hello?" Reese called out, shutting the heavy oak door behind her. The two duffel bags she'd taken out of her trunk were weighing her down, so she dropped them by the door. "Anyone home?"

"Oh, hi!" her mother called. "In here, sweetheart!" Reese followed Joanna's voice to the family room, and found her curled up in a ball on the sofa, under a patchwork quilt, with a fire flickering in the fireplace, and some repetitive *Wedding Story* piano music echoing off the TV.

"Hi, Mommy!" She leaned down to kiss her mother on the cheek.

Joanna angled herself to press "Stop" with the VCR remote, and reached up to hug Reese tightly. "Sweetheart, I'm so glad you're home! Have you finished your toast for Ally's wedding?"

"Mom, I don't even have my coat off."

"Oh, well I was just interested," Joanna said innocently. Reese gave her another kiss on the cheek, and then pulled back to shrug off her hooded fleece jacket. "Is that all you wore for a coat?" Joanna asked "Reese, it's December! Don't you have a winter coat?"

"Yeah, but—"

"We're gonna buy you a winter coat while you're home."

"I have one, but—"

"Sit, sit. How was your ride? Let me hear all about it."

"There's really not much to tell." *Unless you count my fast food run, which I won't.* "Where is everybody?"

"Ally's out with Ben, and your father's in his study. By the way, there's left over *poulet a la crème* in the fridge."

"No, thanks. I had something on the way over." *Whoops!* Joanna's head shot up. "You did? What?" she pried. "Not fast food, right?"

"It was just a cheeseburger, jeez," Reese replied, a little embarrassed.

Joanna groaned and fell back against the sofa cushions in martyrdom.

"What were you watching?" Reese asked, deflecting the conversation.

"Oh I was bored, so I took out a tape of *Wedding Story*. Tape 14, Episode 2b. Rodney and Claire."

"Ah. Well put it on. I'll watch, too."

Joanna nodded, and pressed "Play" on the VCR remote. Reese watched as Rodney and Claire's story unfolded. It was one of those nauseating "the minute I set eyes on her, I knew" stories. *Yuck.* Reese wasn't cynical about love—in fact, deep down, she was a romantic. But she just hated hearing people claim they "knew" the moment they looked at someone, because real life didn't work like that. If it did, she would still be with her ex-boyfriend, Pete, instead of getting an occasional postcard from him in South America where he'd bolted three years ago to do humanitarian work.

She'd looked at him, and she'd only *thought* she knew. That was the point.

"Isn't that *nice*?" Joanna crooned, clearly taken in by the sappy, televised emotions playing before her. "He said he just *looked* at her, and fell completely in love."

"Uh-huh."

"He's so sweet. You can just tell he's one of those steady, dependable, teddy-bear types. That's what you need."

"Mom, please don't start."

"What, am I allowed to talk?" she asked the room. "Am I allowed to have an opinion, anymore?" Reese rolled her eyes as her mother continued, "All I'm saying is that would be good for you. A real easygoing, engineer type."

"Mom, what does being an engineer have to do with anything?" Reese said, exasperated. "You're obsessed with engineers."

Joanna scoffed (clearly in denial). "Oh, don't be ridiculous!"

"It's true, you're so fixated on how engineers are supposedly easygoing. Where do you *get* that?" Reese demanded.

"I'm just going by all my life experience. Remmi's husband is so handy, he painted their whole summer house last year by himself. Don't you see, sweetheart, that's how those engineer types *are*. They like doing stuff like that, you know, repairing things, putting things together—"

Reese scrunched her face. "So, why is that relevant to *me*?"

"Reese, I don't think you realize how important it is to have a husband who's *handy*. And, all I'm saying is that you want an easygoing personality. You know, someone who's just going to love you so much, he'll go along with all your quirks."

"Mom, please—can we just drop it?"

"But you got to *get out there,* honey." *Mom's version of dropping it.* "You're not gonna meet anyone ringing up books at Roland & Fisk."

Reese took a sip of scalding tea in order to keep herself quiet. The most annoying part about this was that her mother *knew* she was sort of dating Kenneth, yet she was acting like he didn't exist.

It really angered her—it was as if Joanna automatically assumed the relationship weren't going anywhere. How dare she? She didn't know anything about it. So maybe Kenneth wasn't overly demonstrative, and maybe they weren't an official item, but that didn't mean they couldn't *become* official. He was interesting, articulate . . . okay, nerdy as hell, but in an intriguing way. In fact, Reese had a recurring fantasy that involved messing him up, driving him crazy, and turning him into her personal boy-toy from that point forward.

Reese fixed her eyes on Rodney and Claire, who were now smashing wedding cake all over each other's faces, getting icing clogged up each other's noses, and laughing like it was hilarious.

"Mom, I'm gonna go up," she said, dragging herself off the sofa. She realized she was tired after all, and brushed a kiss across her mother's cheek. " 'Night. Don't stay up too late."

"I won't," she replied, and returned her attention to the next story dying to be told. Lila and Ralph.

The last thing Reese heard as she picked up her bags in the front hall, and began climbing the stairs, was: "The minute I laid eyes on Ralph, I just *knew*."